... For nothing is less under our control than the heart—having no power to command it we are forced to obey.

—Héloïse, in a letter to Abelard

Falcon's Fire

by

Patricia Ryan

A TOPAZ BOOK

TOPAZ
Published by the Penguin Group
Penguin Books USA Inc., 375 Hudson Street,
New York, New York 10014, U.S.A.
Penguin Books Ltd, 27 Wrights Lane,
London W8 5TZ, England
Penguin Books Australia Ltd, Ringwood,
Victoria, Australia
Penguin Books Canada Ltd, 10 Alcorn Avenue,
Toronto, Ontario, Canada M4V 3B2
Penguin Books (N.Z.) Ltd, 182–190 Wairau Road,
Auckland 10, New Zealand

Penguin Books Ltd, Registered Offices:
Harmondsworth, Middlesex, England

First published by Topaz, an imprint of Dutton Signet,
a division of Penguin Books USA Inc.

First Printing, December, 1995
10 9 8 7 6 5 4 3 2 1

 REGISTERED TRADEMARK—MARCA REGISTRADA

Printed in the United States of America

To my sister, Pamela Burford Loeser,
with love and gratitude
for helping to give birth to this story

A Dream Come True

Thorne kissed her forehead, her temple. He laced the fingers of one hand through her hair while the other kneaded her back, smooth and wet, pressing her to him.

Her hair covered her like a mantle. Where its cool strands parted, he could feel her breasts, warm and soft, against his bare chest. A small, civilized voice told him to pull back. *I will,* he thought. *Just let me hold her, just for a moment.* Her eyes were closed, her lips so ripe and inviting. No, he wouldn't kiss her mouth. Then he would truly be lost. *I won't kiss her,* he thought, lowering his mouth to hers. *Just a touch* ... He brushed his lips against hers and heard her sigh.

These are Martine's lips touching mine, he thought dizzily. His tongue parted her lips, seeking her heat, the sweet, intoxicating taste of her. *I have to touch her. Now* ...

"A powerful debut historical novel by an exciting new talent, *Falcon's Fire* will ignite your imagination and passion for medieval romances." —Kathe Robin, *Romantic Times*

"An exceptionally good and beautifully told story. If you enjoy a book with an excellent romance, which also includes characters you love to hate, this one is definitely for you." —*Rendezvous*

Chapter 1

Martine of Rouen watched the seagull soar out of the dawn sky from across the Channel. It flew over the vessels in the Fécamp harbor for some time, as if trying to pick out one from the rest. Finally, its choice made, it descended in a graceful spiral to alight next to her on the railing of the *Lady's Slipper* as thirty oarsmen propelled the merchant longship smoothly out of her dock.

" 'Tis a good omen, milady," the ship's pilot said, and smiled. "A blessing on your marriage to Baron Godfrey's son." He was a massive Englishman, nearly toothless. His face formed a landscape of boils; his French was spoken with an unpleasant, guttural accent.

Martine had not believed in omens since the age of ten, particularly good ones. Why fool oneself into expecting the best, when logic foretold the worst? This journey to England, a place she had never been, to marry Edmond of Harford, a man she had never met, filled her with a dread that no omen could erase.

Sensing her brother's comforting presence behind her, she turned to look up at him.

Rainulf met her eyes with a reassuring look, then returned the Englishman's smile. "A good omen? And why would that be?"

The pilot pointed to their small visitor on the railing beside Martine. "That gull be an English herring gull, Father—er, milord." He frowned, his mouth agape. Martine knew he pondered the correct form of address for someone who was not only a priest and the son of a Norman baron, but a relation of Queen Eleanor herself.

" 'Father' is fine," Rainulf said. "My fealty to my God

supersedes even that to my cousin." He nodded toward the bird. "So you think our little friend here has flown all the way from England just for us?"

"Aye, milord. *Father.* 'Tis a lucky sign for milady." He grinned at Martine. "That wee creature flew a great distance and come straight to you, milady, to escort you across the Channel to young Edmond of Harford. If you feed him crumbs, he'll most likely stay with us till we dock at Bulverhythe Harbor tomorrow. And then it's certain your marriage will be a union of love, and your sons many."

A union of love? Martine shuddered at the thought. As a child, she had watched her mother's union of love claim her will, her reason, and finally her life. In a choice between marriage and the convent, Martine had consented to marry, but she hadn't consented to love. Nor would she ever, omen or no omen.

The pilot stared at her, waiting for some sort of response. *Do all Englishmen share your primitive ideas?* she wanted to say. *If Sir Edmond does, I'll hardly need a gull to predict how miserable my marriage will be.* That's what she *wanted* to say, because fear unleashed in her a reckless temper. But this Englishman, despite his coarseness and his childish superstitions, clearly meant no harm. For that reason, and because Rainulf constantly begged her to be civil, she held her tongue. She even tried to smile, but couldn't quite manage that. Excusing herself to her brother, she descended the narrow stairway to the main deck and ducked into the cabin. The heat in the tiny compartment assaulted her even before she closed the door.

The *Lady's Slipper* had but one enclosed cabin, tucked into the stern beneath the quarterdeck. It was a dim, airless little chamber, crowded with Martine's and Rainulf's baggage, but it was private, reserved exclusively for their use during the crossing.

Martine ducked her head to avoid the low ceiling and unpinned the gold brooch that secured her hooded black mantle, tossing both into a corner. On her head she wore a saffron-dyed linen veil, intricately draped and tucked so as to reveal only her face, from eyes to chin. When she removed the veil, her hair spilled to her hips in a flaxen sheet.

There could be no mistaking that Rainulf and Martine were related. Both were tall, silver-blond, and fine-boned, as were the Northmen from whom they were descended. They bore a striking resemblance to their father, the late Baron Jourdain of Rouen, and although they had different mothers, both women had been fair and blond.

Through the cabin's single tiny porthole, Martine watched the rugged Normandy coastline gradually shrink into the distance. She felt something stir against her legs and flinched, but when she looked down, she saw it was just her cat, a sleek black tom with white boots.

"Don't worry, Loki." Abandoning the cool facade with which she distanced herself from men like that Englishman—from all men except Rainulf, in fact—she sank to the floor and gathered the cat in her arms.

"They say England is . . ." *Cold and wet.* Shivering, she buried her face in his fur. "Perhaps there are lots of mice there. I'm sure *you'll* be happy."

The oak planks that formed the cabin's ceiling and the floor of the quarterdeck groaned as Rainulf and the pilot crossed to stand directly above her.

When the Englishman spoke, she could hear his words clearly through the porthole. "The young lady, your sister—she's not much for friendly conversation, is she, Father?"

Rainulf answered him with a long sigh.

"You'll pardon my asking, Father, but has the baron's son had the honor of being introduced to milady as yet?"

A pause; then, "Not as yet."

The pilot chuckled in a knowing way. "Aye, but I'd pay a month's wages to be witness to *that* meeting."

Why doesn't she just ask me where it is? thought Rainulf. He sat cross-legged on the cabin floor, fanning himself with his black skullcap as he watched his half-sister rummage through his traveling bags. Reaching within his robe, he withdrew a folded sheet of parchment.

He chuckled. "Gyrth thinks your Edmond will be in for a nasty surprise when he discovers how cold and haughty you are, and that what you need is the firm hand of a real man to crack your ice."

Martine paused in the act of unlocking a small wooden trunk. "Who's Gyrth?"

"Our pilot. The man whom you so contemptuously ignored this morning."

Dumping the trunk's contents on the swaying floor, she got on her hands and knees to sort through its contents. "How did you know his name? You always seem to know everyone's name."

"I ask."

After a moment of silence, she met his gaze and smiled to acknowledge the implied criticism, gentle though it might be. Her deep blue eyes, ignited by the shaft of noon sunlight from the porthole, widened when she saw the parchment in his hand.

"Is that it?" she asked. "The Saxon's letter?"

"The Saxon has a name."

She groaned and rolled her eyes, holding out her hand for the letter. "Rainulf, please. You know I can't remem—"

He held the letter away from her. "You can't remember the name of my closest friend?"

"Your closest friend? You haven't seen him for ten years—not since the Crusade."

"He's my closest friend, and he has a name. Everybody has a name, Martine, even Saxons. And since this particular Saxon has gone to all the trouble to find you a husband—the son of his overlord, no less—the least you can do is try to remember his—"

"Brother, I think you vex me just for sport. 'Tis unbecoming in a priest." She reached for the letter, and he edged away from her. Grinning like a cat, she suddenly lunged, throwing him to the floor. His head hit the edge of the trunk and he yelped in pain, but she paid him no heed, snatching the letter with a gleeful laugh.

Rubbing his head and looking around for his skullcap, Rainulf said, "Did the nuns not tell you 'tis a sin to do violence to a man of the cloth?"

Martine unfolded the letter. "The nuns told me many things. I retained what seemed useful and discarded what didn't."

He found the cap, replaced it, and sat up. For a convent-bred eighteen-year-old, Martine was remarkably irreligious. Despite his best efforts to strengthen her faith, it remained weak, and there were times that he feared for her immortal soul. Perhaps his failure to properly guide her stemmed from his inability to guide himself, for had not his sin of pride undermined his own faith? If the truth be told, he worshiped his own intellect more zealously than he worshiped his God. What of *his* immortal soul?

" 'Tis hot as blazes in here," he said, rising to his feet. "I'm going above deck. I can't breathe."

He took the six steps to the quarterdeck in three long-legged strides. As he paused at the railing to breathe in the warm sea air, Martine called to him from the porthole.

"Thorne Falconer!" she exclaimed triumphantly. "The Saxon's name is Thorne Falconer!"

First came the seagull. Then came the storm.

Martine reread Thorne Falconer's letter—the letter that described her future husband—many times, until she could barely see the ink on the parchment. When she finally looked up, she saw that it had become dark, although it was still early afternoon. The sky through the porthole was no longer blue, but a leaden gray.

From the baskets in the corner came the yapping of the puppies and the incessant squeaking of the young falcon. The black cat paced furiously, and when Martine tried to pick him up, he drew his lips back and hissed.

"Loki!"

Martine heard sharp cries above deck, the raised voices of sailors calling to one another, and the pounding of feet. She opened the cabin door, but no sooner had she set foot on deck than her hair, still loose, flew in all directions, whipped by wind and sea spray. She twisted it in a knot and held it firmly while she went in search of Rainulf.

The main deck bustled with noise and activity. Martine picked her way carefully, maneuvering around the barrels, crates, rowboats, baggage, and tackle crammed into the gangway. The few other passengers, who sat huddled in the middle near the big drinking cask, stared at her openly as she made her way through the mayhem.

The single sail, a giant, blue-and-yellow-striped square, snapped angrily as four men struggled to lower it, yelling

at the top of their lungs to be heard above the wind and
sea. On either side of the ship, men pulled in their oars
and shuttered oar holes against the violent waves. Some
tied down cargo, while others tugged at the cords that
stretched a linen awning across struts hastily erected along
the main deck. Martine stepped carefully, both to avoid
getting in their way and because the vessel had begun
to pitch in rhythm with the churning sea.

Just as the boat listed violently, slamming her painfully
into one of the struts, she saw her brother, Gyrth, and
two sailors—one enormous, the other small and slender.
They stood on the little raised deck at the prow with
their backs to her, looking up. "The wind has changed
direction," Gyrth observed.

"What does that mean?" Rainulf asked.

Gyrth pointed to the sky, where dark clouds boiled.
"A storm."

"A bad one?" Rainulf looked down at the pilot, who,
by way of an answer, grimly crossed himself. After a
moment, Rainulf and the sailors did the same. Martine
didn't bother with the gesture; it was one she reserved
for when she was being watched.

"A storm coming out of the blue like this, catching
seasoned sailors unawares," Gyrth said. " 'Tis a bad
omen, for sure. If the lady had fed the gull as she was
asked, we would still be sailing under clear skies. But he
flew off, and then the clouds rolled in, and now—"

His next words died in his throat as blue light flared
within the clouds, spawning two rivers of quicksilver.
They snaked toward the horizon, writhing and sprouting
fiery rivulets, then dissolved into a dark silence.

No one spoke. The wind suddenly ceased, and Martine
gripped the railing with both hands, waiting. But the
thunder, when it came, was merely a distant, gentle rumble, an ominous whisper.

Gyrth turned to Rainulf and shook his head. "We're
in for it. And all for the lack of a few crumbs of bread
for a wee—"

"Stop it," said Martine, the words quivering in her
throat. Gyrth, Rainulf, and the sailors all turned toward her.

Rainulf, his eyes dark with warning, closed a hand
over her shoulder. "Martine ..."

She jerked away from him and turned to face the pilot squarely. If silence branded her as haughty, she may as well speak her peace. "You've no right to say these things." She pointed to the two sailors, their eyes wide in the unnatural darkness. "They think it's *I* who brought this thunder and lightning on their heads."

"But milady—the omens—"

"No more of your *omens*!" Her voice rose of its own accord, and she had no power to stop it. "I'm sick of hearing how I bring visitations of seagulls and summon storm clouds from the heavens!" She shook with frustration. "Believe me, if I had such powers, I would use them to silence your tongue forever, so you should never speak of omens again!"

Forked lightning illuminated the sky, and a discharge of thunder cracked open the heavens. Rain burst forth in a stinging sheet, driven by a wind so violent, Martine and Rainulf had to cling to each other simply to remain standing.

They stumbled down to the main deck and through the teeming gangway to their cabin, slamming the door behind them. The little room was dark and reeked of damp wool. Rainulf shuttered the porthole, but the wind sought out every chink in the cabin walls, and Martine found herself shivering in the very place that had so recently seemed like an oven. She grabbed Loki and hugged the frightened animal, wrapping her heavy mantle about the two of them, then curled up next to Rainulf on the floor, bracing herself against the violent pitching of the boat. An occasional flash of lightning illuminated the cabin with its cold, wavering light. Otherwise, it was as dark as night.

Rainulf never moved, except to pat his sister's hand when she clutched at him. She tried to control her trembling and the pounding of her heart, but in truth she dreaded that the boat would split open and sink. Of all the ways to die, drowning—struggling for air, waiting for your lungs to fill with water—was surely the most horrible. Death by water was her special nightmare, the one that would not go away. She felt a cold sweat trickle down her sides, and she squeezed Loki harder, causing him to spring from her with a growl of indignation.

The sailors shouted constantly to one another, and the

puppies whined pitifully, but these sounds were nearly swallowed up by the din of thunder, waves, and rain. From time to time she heard sounds that made her stomach tighten and her throat constrict—the sickening snap of wood shearing, the crash of something falling, the rumble of a loose barrel rolling and bouncing across the deck.

Finally, toward late afternoon, the rain lessened, the boat settled into a gentle roll, and a hazy half-light filled the cabin. Rainulf stretched, rose, and, bowing deeply so as not to hit his head, gazed through the porthole. Martine studied his aristocratic profile as he calmly examined the sea that had come close to swallowing them up.

At four and thirty years of age, he was uncommonly handsome, with his short flaxen hair and gentle hazel eyes, and Martine knew that women were drawn to him despite, or even because of, his vocation. She knew that he had enjoyed the company of many women before taking up the cross for God and Louis a dozen years before. Upon returning from Crusade, he took his vows, and, to her knowledge, he had been celibate ever since, although he must have been tempted. He was chaste, he was wise, and he was compassionate. Everyone thought him the perfect man of God. Only Martine knew how heavy the burden of his priesthood had become.

Still staring through the porthole, he said, " 'Twas most unwise to threaten to silence Gyrth's tongue. I've seen a simpleminded old woman whipped unmercifully for cursing her neighbor's crops."

"So you've told me many times. If I take a solemn oath never to curse anyone's crops, will you stop lecturing me?"

He turned his serious eyes on her and straightened until his head touched the low ceiling. "There are many ways to make people hate you, Martine, not all of them self-evident. There are punishments more horrible than you can imagine for 'crimes' you would never think of as crimes. Take Master Abelard, for example. The greatest man I've ever known. For the 'crime' of loving Héloïse, he was punished with castration. Then, years later, when he returned to teaching, there was the 'crime' of applying logic to the study of theology—a crime which, incidentally, I practice myself, but with discretion. For that crime, he was not only excommunicated, but sentenced to perpetual silence at Cluny. The most brilliant man in the known world not permitted to speak! Indiscretion is dangerous, Martine. You must learn to watch what you say."

"Yet, if I keep silent, I'm seen as aloof and haughty."

"It's . . . the *way* you keep silent, Martine. You're so . . . so . . ."

"Would you have me meekly hold my tongue, with downcast eyes and a blush upon my cheek? 'Twas my mother's way. 'Twill never be mine."

He began to say something, then merely shook his head and abandoned the attempt at reprimand. With a glance at her drab tunic, he said, "Sir Edmond will probably be there to greet us when we dock tomorrow. Mayhaps you would want to wear something more . . ." He shrugged.

Her stomach burned with apprehension at the thought of meeting her betrothed. Nerves frayed, she snapped, "Why should I care about pleasing a man I've never met? I didn't choose Sir Edmond. You did, you and Thorne Falconer. And I didn't choose to get married. You chose it for me. Make no mistake, the only reason I agreed to this marriage was because you want to be free of me."

He crouched next to her, compelling her with his eyes to look at him. "It's not what I want, little sister, it's what I need. I need to regain my faith, and I can't do it in Paris, surrounded by students who hang on my every word as if it were Holy Scripture. I need this pilgrimage. My soul needs it."

She took a calming breath and rested a hand on his shoulder. "They say you're the best-loved teacher Paris has seen since Abelard. They're begging for you at Oxford. Do you think God wants you to waste your gifts by leaving your students and prostrating yourself at every shrine between Compostela and Jerusalem?"

"Yes." The intensity of his gaze took her aback. "I think God wants me to humble myself. I think that's exactly what He wants."

She sighed. How pointless to try to talk him out of it at this late date. "And you'll only be gone a year?"

He covered her hand with his. "Perhaps two."

"Two years?"

"And when I come back, I'll be teaching at Oxford, not Paris, so we'll see each other quite—"

"Rainulf, I need you! You can't leave me for two years!"

"You'll have a husband to care for you. You won't be alone." He patted her hand and said carefully, "You know, it's not impossible that you might even grow to love—"

She clapped her hands over her ears and turned from him.

"Martine, for God's sake." He reached for her, but she pulled away and wrapped her arms around her up-drawn legs.

He shook his head. "You act as if love were some dreadful curse."

With her back still turned, she said, "Isn't it? Look what it did to my mother. It made her weak, it destroyed her. She worshiped Jourdain. *Worshiped* him! She thought he'd marry her when your mother died, and he let her believe it. But barons don't marry their mistresses, do they?"

Quietly he said, "No. They don't."

"She didn't know that. She trusted in love. She was a fool." Martine turned to face her brother. "I'm not. Marriage might be inevitable, but love is a trap I'll never fall into."

"It doesn't have to be a trap, Sister. Love can free the soul, it can liberate—"

She laughed harshly. "Free the soul? Jourdain *owned* my mother's soul. When he married his thirteen-year-old heiress and abandoned Mama, he took her soul with him. Mama had nothing left after Jourdain was through with her. He'd used her up. She was empty."

Her throat tightened, and she trembled. She closed her eyes and rubbed them, and an image came unbidden, as it often did, both awake and in her dreams: a luxurious gown of apple green silk, shot through with gold threads and adorned with thousands of tiny beads, floating on the breeze-riffled surface of a lake. The gown her mama had sewn for the wedding that never came, the gown in which she had finally surrendered, in despair, to a watery death. The pain this vision brought had gained strength with the passage of time, until it felt worse than desolation, worse than grief; it had become a live thing, a dark and heavy thing that rose from her belly to her throat, squeezing her from within.

When she opened her eyes, she found her brother staring at her, his expression sad and a little helpless. She took a deep, shaky breath and swept the image from her thoughts. Struggling to smile, she said, "I've heard tell there's no summer in England, and it must be true, because the closer I get, the colder—" Her voice caught, and she bit her lip, willing herself not to cry.

Rainulf moved closer, put his arm around her, and patted her gently. Did he really know her? Did he have any idea how much she feared this marriage, how much courage it took to go through with it for his sake? He whispered something, and she turned toward him so she could hear.

"I know. I know, Martine. I do."

A fanfare of trumpets from the quarterdeck announced that they were docking. Martine rose to peer out of the porthole and Rainulf followed her. The rain, which had fallen steadily since the storm, had almost let up. She could make out a multitude of other vessels jostling one another in the dreary mist enveloping Bulverhythe Harbor, the harbor for Hastings.

"Remember, Martine," Rainulf cautioned. "If anyone at Harford Castle questions you about your family or your parents or your relation to the queen—"

"I'm to keep my counsel," she impatiently recited. It was to hide her illegitimacy that Rainulf had sought her a husband so far from the place of her birth. Godfrey of Harford had been so excited at the prospect of uniting his second son with a relation of the queen that he hadn't bothered to ask questions. No one at Harford knew that she was but a bastard cousin to Eleanor of Aquitaine, who was formerly queen of France, and now, having divorced Louis and married Henry Plantagenet, was queen of England. Even Sir Thorne, who had arranged the betrothal contract, knew only that she was the half-sister of his old friend and fellow Crusade veteran; Rainulf had never volunteered the circumstances of her birth.

"Mind that you do keep your counsel," Rainulf said. "So far I haven't had to lie outright, because it's simply assumed you're legitimate. We've been lucky. So far. But if Lord Godfrey were to find out the truth, there would be no question of a marriage. Your reputation would be ruined, as would mine, and quite possibly Thorne's—"

"Don't worry," she snapped. "I know what's at stake."

She returned her attention to the harbor. They were gliding toward an empty dock with one small figure on the pier, a boy. She heard him call out "Sir! The *Lady's Slipper*! She's here! Sir!" and watched as he ran away from them up the pier, disappearing into the fog.

Presently a larger figure emerged—a man wearing a black cloak, its hood raised against the rain—and walked toward the end of the pier.

She could feel her heart drum in her chest. All she knew about Edmond was what Sir Thorne had chosen to communicate—that he was the younger of two sons and had been knighted by his father several months before, that he would be coming into his manor upon his marriage, that he was comely, and that he hunted. Sir Thorne had gone on for some length about the hunting, but had mentioned no sports or other pastimes of Edmond's.

"People don't just *hunt*," she said.

Rainulf stared intently at the hooded man. "Hmm?"

"He's got to do something else. Doesn't he?"

"I suppose so," he replied distractedly.

The cloaked man stopped a few yards from the end of the pier and stood waiting in the somber drizzle while men scrambled down from the boat to tie her up. He was tall, nearly a head taller than the sailors bustling around him. She couldn't make out his features because of the hood, but she could see that he was clean-shaven. The black cloak fell straight from his square shoulders, and his chausses and shoes were also black.

"Is that him?" Martine asked, feeling foolish even as she uttered the words, since Rainulf had no more idea than she what Edmond looked like.

"That's him," Rainulf said. Martine took a deep breath.

From behind them, someone cleared his throat. They turned to see Gyrth, scratching his boils and looking at the floor. "Begging your pardon, Father, but ... I was wondering, if you've got the payment handy ...?"

"Of course. Eighteen shillings, wasn't it?" Rainulf withdrew his purse, and Gyrth stared at it greedily, actually running his tongue over his lips in anticipation of the coins within.

Martine pinned her mantle over her head, picked up her brass lockbox and Loki's basket, then followed the men out of the cabin. The rain had stopped at last, but a cold, gray mist still enveloped the harbor. While Rainulf paid Gyrth, Martine stood half-hidden behind a strut to steal a glimpse of Sir Edmond.

He was looking up, at the clouds. As she watched him, a strange thing happened. His face became gradually suffused with golden light, until it shone like a beacon in the mist. Transfixed, she followed his gaze upward to find that the clouds had parted, framing the sun in a circle of dazzling blue. It was the sun's warm rays that had transformed him so magically. There was always a logical explanation, she reminded herself. And yet the temptation to believe in good omens was strong upon her in that moment.

He pushed back his hood as he lowered his head. His hair fell to his shoulders, and looked to be the color of brandy—brown with some gold in it, as if he spent a great deal of time outdoors. To her alarm, he looked directly at her, and she saw that his eyes had stolen the radiant blue of the widening patch of sky above him.

His face had been carved of such noble planes that it might have been that of some young emperor on an ancient coin. It seemed clear from his expression of recognition and pleasure that he knew who she was. Rainulf had undoubtedly written an accurate description.

He seemed to look not just at her, but into her, his bright, penetrating eyes locking with hers and peering deep inside, to where her most secret hopes and fears lay curled up, waiting. It was as if she were transparent, her very soul lying naked for his inspection. She felt she should look away, that it was impudent to hold the gaze of a stranger in this manner. But then, this man was not a stranger in the true sense. He was her betrothed. In less than two months, he would be holding her in his arms. What harm could there be in merely looking at the man she would spend the rest of her life with? For the first time ever, she felt not fear at the prospect of marriage, but anticipation.

It is this man who will speak vows with me, this man who will bring me to his bed, this man who will sire my babes.

Now he smiled at her, a welcoming smile that lit his eyes and etched deeply creased dimples. Without willing it so, she returned the smile, then dropped her gaze and looked away. The flirtatiousness of the gesture embarrassed her, yet her actions seemed beyond her power to dictate.

When she returned her gaze to him, he was looking elsewhere, at something over her shoulder, something that made him grin in delight. She turned to find Rainulf behind her, cupping his hands to his mouth.

"Thorne! Is it always this blasted cold on this miserable island, or only in August?"

Thorne? Thorne Falconer? Dear God. She wheeled in openmouthed astonishment toward the man on the pier as Rainulf swept past her and leaped onto the gangplank. A burning heat crawled up her throat and consumed her face as she watched her brother embrace the man with eyes of sky.

It was Sir Thorne! Not her betrothed! When she had asked Rainulf if that was him, her brother had, naturally, been thinking of the friend he hadn't seen in a decade, not of the boy Martine was to marry. And Edmond was a boy, being merely nineteen. The man now greeting Rainulf with such warmth, hugging him and slapping him on the back, was at least ten years older than that.

"Martine!" Rainulf called to her. "Come meet Sir Thorne!"

Releasing a shuddering breath, she willed calm upon herself and followed her brother onto the dock. When Rainulf introduced her to his friend, she found herself unable to look him in the eye, and wished desperately that her face were not as red as she knew it must be.

" 'Twill warm up presently," Sir Thorne said. His voice sounded deep and resonant, his French flavored with just a trace of an accent to betray his Saxon origins.

Coming from him, the accent was, although a bit harsh, not unpleasant.

He nodded to Martine. "My lady has brought the Normandy sun with her, I think." There was that smile again.

He was right about it warming up. The chill receded and the sky brightened even as they spoke. Bulverhythe Harbor was changing from a place of darkness and cold to one of light and shadow, of blues and greens and golds, of the singing of sparrows ... and the mocking laughter of gulls. Martine looked up and squinted at the sun, ashamed for having considered its appearance a good sign.

There were no such things as omens, particularly good ones.

Chapter 2

It was turning into an afternoon of surprises. Thorne Falconer had never liked surprises.

The first one had been the late arrival of the *Lady's Slipper,* delayed as she was by the storm. Since Harford Castle was half a day's ride north of Hastings, they would have to set out immediately if they expected to get there before nightfall.

He motioned to his page, standing a respectful distance away on the pier. "Fane, go get Albin and bring the horses."

"Yes, sir. Shall I fetch your men as well? I know which alehouse they're in."

"Aye." The boy sprinted away, Thorne and his guests following at a more leisurely pace.

"Your men?" Rainulf said. "You must have gotten more important than I'd realized."

Rainulf had been another surprise, in his black robes and skullcap! Though Thorne knew that his old friend had long ago taken his vows, whenever he thought of Rainulf, he saw him as he had been in the Levant—unshaven and unwashed, in rags filthy and shredded from battle and long months of captivity.

Thorne smiled. "Fane misspeaks himself, but I tire of correcting him. They're Lord Godfrey's men, of course. Sir Guy and Sir Peter. Knights, like myself."

"And Albin?"

"My squire. He and my falconry assistant are the only men I can rightly call mine. And, of course, Fane and the boys who run errands for me."

Fane and Albin came into view with their mounts, packhorses, and litters. Thorne had brought two litters from Harford. One was an elegant curtained couch suspended between two dappled grays, for Lady Martine.

The other was a utilitarian wooden box, into which some dockhands began loading baggage. Lady Martine was staring at the curtained litter and frowning.

Rainulf's sister had been yet another surprise, in her saffron veil and homely gray tunic, like some humble postulant. Thorne had expected silk brocade, fur trim, and glittering jewels. After all, she was the daughter of a Norman baron and a cousin of the queen, however distant.

Despite her attire, he had recognized her immediately. Rainulf had written that she resembled him, and from what little he could see of her, she seemed to. Like her brother, she was tall. He wondered if she shared his fair hair, but from her dark eyebrows and lashes, he suspected not. Too bad; such hair would be stunning on a woman. She did have his smoothly sculpted, aristocratic features, but on her the effect struck him as slightly off-kilter. Hers was a face of highly polished imperfection, as if some eccentric sculptor had actually *wanted* the cheekbones a bit too pronounced, the mouth too wide. She should have been plain, even homely, but there was a spark in her eyes, a crackle of intelligence, that he couldn't help but find attractive.

Rainulf was watching his sister regard the litter with grim distaste. "Thorne . . . I neglected to tell you. Martine hates riding in litters. You don't have a spare horse, by any chance?"

Hates riding in litters? "Just one. For you."

Thorne turned to the lady to discuss the matter with her, but she pointedly walked away. It pleased him to see her approach the curtained litter, but his pleasure was short-lived, for she merely deposited upon its brocade seat the brass box and basket she had been carrying, then closed the curtains around them as if to make it plain that she would not be riding there. He sighed and looked toward Rainulf, who smiled and shrugged.

For his part, Thorne found the Lady Martine somewhat less than amusing. First her abrupt change in attitude, and now this demand for a horse, when he had gone to the trouble of bringing a litter all the way from Harford for her.

At first, her coldness had taken him aback, considering her shy smile from the deck of the *Lady's Slipper*. Upon reflection, he had to admit that this kind of treatment, warmth followed by haughty withdrawal, was exactly what he would expect from a Norman gentlewoman. The sad truth was that, although she didn't dress like a child of privilege, Lady Martine acted like one.

Albin spoke up. "She can have Solomon, Sir Thorne!" The dark-haired young squire smiled shyly at Martine and patted his enormous chestnut stallion on the flank. "I know you'd prefer a mare, my lady, but if you think you can handle him, you're welcome to him."

She didn't thank him, merely took the reins he offered.

"What will you ride, then, Albin?" Thorne asked.

"One of the packhorses. I don't mind."

Fane came running up, followed by Guy and Peter. Albin and Fane usually accompanied Thorne on his errands to Hastings, but this time he had thought it best to bring his men along as well, considering the recent trouble in Weald Forest, through which they were obliged to ride. Also, it was a diversion for them. They welcomed any excuse to leave Harford and ride down to Hastings when there was no local war or tournament to occupy them.

Rainulf said, "I thought Edmond would be with them."

"Ah ... I'm afraid he was delayed away from the castle. I know he would have wanted to greet you personally—especially my lady."

He nodded in Martine's direction. She held his gaze for a moment that seemed to stretch beyond time. Her eyes, blue as midnight, searched his, just fleetingly, as if seeking something precious that she'd lost. Thorne stood transfixed, remembering his first glimpse of her just a short while ago, and feeling the same connection, the same uncanny sense that she knew things about him, and he about her, that they couldn't possibly know.

He blinked, she looked away, and the moment ended. By the time he'd taken a steadying breath, she had already mounted Solomon, brushing off Albin's awkward efforts to assist her. The rest of the party mounted up as well, and they set off. Thorne's surprise, Martine handled the assertive stallion with easy assurance, as if he were the tamest mare.

Thorne steered the group away from the disreputable lanes that surrounded the harbor, in deference to the lady's sensibilities, but smiled inwardly at his own misguided chivalry. It was quite absurd that he should want to protect her from the sight of taverns and brothels, since she had doubtless seen many such establishments in Paris, and she didn't strike him as the squeamish sort.

The streets were congested with people that afternoon, even though it was not a market day. The rain had forced them indoors all morning, and now that it was clearing up, they swarmed out of the overhanging shops and town houses to attend to postponed business. The roads were narrow seas of mud. The stench of excrement mingled with that of woodsmoke, roasting meat, and boiling fish. Pigs wandered idly among the pedestrians, snuffling through the filth in the sewage channels and scattering with panicked squeals before the party on horseback. Thorne could not imagine why anyone who had a choice would live in a town.

He swiftly guided the group north, out of Hastings and into dense and tangled Weald Forest, where they rode double-file along the narrow, well-used traveler's path. Although the sky had cleared and the sun shone, little of its warmth and light filtered through the leaves. That which did fell in dappled patches of gold on the meandering dirt track, like a handful of scattered coins.

It was August, and the woods were ripe with growth. Ferns and mosses competed with gnarled vines, wild mint, and colonies of tiny blue violets. Thorne opened his ears to the breeze-riffled leaves and the trill of myriad birds and insects. He breathed deeply of the scent of loamy earth and the sweet, musky fragrance of plants about to go to seed.

Ahead of him, the lady Martine and her brother rode side by side. From time to time, Rainulf would lean over and touch his sister's hand, sometimes speaking softly to her, as if comforting a frightened child. Most curious, since she struck Thorne as exceedingly self-composed, if enigmatic.

When they were several hundred yards into the forest, he quietly unsheathed his sword. Albin, riding next to him, and Guy, bringing up the rear, promptly followed suit. Peter, up in front, cocked his head at the sharp whisper of steel against leather, then withdrew his own weapon. Thorne saw the lady Martine direct a questioning glance toward her brother.

Rainulf peered into the dense foliage on either side of the path, then looked back over his shoulder at Thorne. "Expecting trouble?"

Thorne glanced at Lady Martine's back and hesitated, not wanting her to feel unsafe. "Not really. Just standard precautions in a dark forest."

Still staring straight ahead, Martine said coolly, "Sir Thorne, since you've placed me in a dangerous situation, kindly do me the favor of telling me what that danger is so that I may be prepared in case it comes. Don't compound the problem by pretending it doesn't exist."

Peter stifled a chuckle, and Rainulf turned and grinned at his friend. Thorne suddenly felt the fool for having taken the trouble to spare the lady's feelings, since she clearly had total command over them.

"So," he said, "my lady has a tongue, after all."

Martine's back stiffened. Good; he had raised the vixen's hackles. Now, as a gesture of civility, he would smooth them. "In truth, the danger's not so great as my lady fears. There was an incident in this forest not long ago involving bandits, but it's unlikely such men would attack a party of this size."

That should satisfy her, he thought, but only momentarily, for she said, "Of what nature was this incident? Who were the victims?"

"A baron and baroness from northwest of here. The young Lord Anseau and his wife, Aiglentine."

"They were robbed?"

Persistent wench. "Aye." Thorne wondered what it would take to melt her frost, and decided to try to find out. "And their throats were cut."

Rainulf crossed himself and Martine nodded, still without turning to look at him.

"The barons are outraged, of course," Thorne said. "And Olivier, our lord earl, has vowed to find the men responsible and inflict the worst tortures you can imagine before giving them to the hangman."

The lady made no response to this.

"And find them, he will," the Saxon continued. "He'll

have to. Not only to serve justice, but to satisfy the king's chancellor."

"Thomas Becket?" Rainulf said. "What's his interest in this?"

"The lady Aiglentine was the daughter of a close friend of his, and he was quite fond of her. Becket wants these bandits caught and an example made of them. Olivier has organized every man, woman, and child in Sussex, and beyond, to look for them. They will most assuredly be caught, and God have mercy on them when they are."

"Yes, God have mercy," Rainulf murmured thoughtfully.

Thorne said, "The men who were Anseau's vassals are up in arms, as well. He was a respected overlord, strong but compassionate, and everyone loved the lady Aiglentine. At the time of her murder, she was heavy with child. The baby died as well, of course, so in fact, there weren't two victims, but three."

Martine half turned toward him, as if she had wanted to say something, then thought better of it. She wore a grim expression, and when she briefly sought out Thorne's eyes before turning away, he saw such abject sadness in them as to take his breath away.

She bewildered him, this humbly clad baron's daughter. She was aloof and ill humored, yet her eyes—those dark and fathomless eyes—drew him in.

He mentally shook himself. He could ill afford to be too curious about Martine of Rouen. She existed merely as a thing of value, a commodity to be exchanged for . . . for his very future. As such, he needed her desperately. Or rather, he needed desperately for her to marry Edmond of Harford.

Then would come his reward, his land. Land for which he had clawed and struggled for ten long years, land which he had deserved long before this . . . land which would, God willing, finally be his.

As they left the forest, Martine saw the knight in front of her sheathe his sword, and Sir Thorne and the others followed suit. She realized that she had been holding herself rigid in her saddle for some time.

"You can relax now. The danger's past," her brother

assured her. She smiled at him, and in the act of smiling, the tension that had gripped her melted away, and she actually did relax.

It had been cool in the forest, but now that the sun warmed her, her woolen mantle was stifling. She unpinned it and draped it across her arm.

They rode westward through rolling pastures and occasional small woods, finally coming to a dirt road leading north, which they followed. The riders now had room to regroup and spread out, Sir Thorne and his squire riding well ahead of Martine and Rainulf, and the others well behind.

Seizing the opportunity for a private conversation with her brother, Martine said, "Do you think he can read? Sir Edmond?"

"Nay," Rainulf said. "Otherwise Thorne would have mentioned it in his letter." He smiled indulgently at her groan. "You've spent the past year in the company of Paris scholars and seven years before that at St. Teresa's, so you take reading for granted. But the fact is, most men can't."

"Sir Thorne can. And he's a Saxon!"

" 'Tis because I taught him."

"*You* taught him? When? During the Crusade?"

He nodded. "We spent a year shackled in leg irons next to each other in a hot, stinking little underground cell. We had to do *something* to keep busy." He spoke in too light a tone; in his eyes, Martine saw a glint of something dark and unforgiving.

"You never speak of those times," she said.

He stared into the distance. "I'm ashamed."

"Ashamed of having been captured?"

"Nay. That couldn't be helped. I'm ashamed of the things I did before I was captured. The men I killed."

"But they were the enemy. Infidels."

"They were men," he said quickly. "Men like myself, men who believed as fervently as I did that they were fighting for a true and just cause."

"But you were!" she insisted. "You were fighting for Christ."

He laughed shortly. "That's what I thought. But I was gullible. We all were. In fact, what we unwittingly fought for—and died by the thousands for—was power and riches, the protection of lucrative trade routes to the East. The only good the experience did me was meeting Thorne when I was taken prisoner by the Turks."

"Was it just the two of you, then, being held?"

"God, no. There were dozens of us—in the beginning, that is." He paused, and Martine sensed that he was considering whether to tell her more, to speak of those things that he would rather forget.

Finally he said, "They were French peasants, most of them, but there were some Germans. Thorne was the only Englishman. This wasn't really England's Crusade, and only the most zealous among the English joined us. He was young—seventeen, I believe—but the most accomplished bowman I'd ever seen. His size helped. It takes a big man to handle a longbow. He spoke very little French, and I didn't understand a word of English, but we became friends anyway. 'Twas good to have a friend in that hole, I can tell you. Especially one who managed to stay alive. The others kept dying off. Once a week they were removed, along with the other refuse."

"My God," she whispered. She began to understand his reluctance to speak of these things.

His voice became a low monotone. " 'Twas hell on earth. Those who didn't die were all driven mad eventually. They'd howl and weep.... Some would even laugh hysterically, hour after hour. 'Twas their minds seeking to escape what their bodies could not."

"But you didn't go mad. Did you?"

"Nay. Nor Thorne. We kept our sanity by occupying our minds. We taught each other our native languages. I learned that he was a Saxon freeman, the son of a woodsman. He'd followed Louis out of idealism but soon became just as disillusioned as I. Thorne asked me to teach him what I'd learned at Cluny and Paris. I introduced him to the fundamentals of logic, the ideas of the Greek philosophers, geometry, arithmetic, and, of course, theology. I taught him to read French and Latin by scratching letters into the sandy floor with my crucifix."

"How did you get away from there? Did you escape?"

His eyes were grim. "Death was the only way to escape that place. Nay, 'twas Eleanor. She managed to locate me and paid a ransom for my release. I demanded

that the others be let go as well, and our captors must
have been bored with us, because they obliged with very
little fuss. I brought Thorne back with me to Paris and
introduced him to Eleanor. He adapted remarkably well
to court life, although he didn't like it very much. He
admired Eleanor, but he had complete contempt for the
silly romantic intrigues of her lords and ladies. And as
a Saxon, he was an oddity. He told me he felt like Charlemagne's elephant—an exotic, primitive beast on display for the curious to gawk at."

Martine studied the big Saxon's distant form and
imagined him towering over a gaggle of wide-eyed, over-
dressed courtiers.

"Also," Rainulf continued, "he missed his family in
Sussex and was anxious to return to them. I asked Eleanor to write him a letter of introduction to Baron Godfrey, whom I'd met in Paris years before, and it must
have been a good one. Godfrey knighted him six months
after his arrival at Harford Castle, and made him his
master falconer soon after that. They say he's the finest
falconer in southern England—perhaps in all of
England."

Up ahead, Sir Thorne pointed out something in the
countryside to the young man next to him. On either
side of the road stretched rows of narrow cultivated
fields planted with wheat and rye and separated by turf
banks. The stooped peasants toiling in the fields stood
up as the party rode past, shielding their eyes to get a
better look at the travelers.

Martine recalled how the Saxon had looked standing
on the pier in the gray mist, his face glowing with mysterious light, his sky-blue eyes smiling at her. She took a
deep breath. "I was wondering something. Sir Thorne is
such a good friend of yours, and he *is* a knight, after all,
so he's a nobleman, even if he isn't of noble blood. I
mean, I was just wondering—"

"Why I didn't betroth you to Thorne?"

Martine blinked, suddenly self-conscious. "Not that I
would have wanted you to, I just—"

"He's landless. There are others like him in England,
bachelor knights who live in their overlord's household
because they've yet to earn a manor of their own. They
can't marry, because they've no home to bring a wife

to, and nothing to offer the family of a noble girl in the way of a bride price."

"Do you mean that even if he wanted to marry, he couldn't? How awful for him."

"I suppose so," Rainulf allowed. "But my primary concern has to be for you, not him. I had to betroth you to someone with property. 'Twould be different if you had holdings of your own. Then I suppose you could marry whomever you wanted. But I gave all my lands to the Church when I took my vows, and I've none left to settle on you."

"Ah."

One of the field laborers, a hunchbacked old man, cupped his hands to his mouth and shouted, "Sir Falconer!"

The Saxon waved, calling out something in that guttural language that sounded so odd to her ears. She had heard men speak Danish, and also German. English sounded very much like these tongues, but it had a different cadence to it, and the words, when put together, had a different sound. Not as musical as Danish, nor as gruff as German.

"To be perfectly frank," Rainulf said, "I doubt Thorne would have agreed to marry you even if I'd proposed it. You're quite a marriage prize, but your value as a bride is largely a matter of status."

"My supposedly legitimate relationship to the queen."

"Exactly. For a man who already has property, you're very much the catch. But Thorne has nothing. And even if he someday earns a manor and is free to marry, he'll want to increase his holdings. He intends to find a woman with property of her own to marry. He's told me as much in his letters."

"I see," she said, her voice gone hard. Far up the path, Thorne and Albin laughed at something. She did see. She saw it all too clearly now. "He's an ambitious man, your friend," she said quietly.

Rainulf glowered at her. "Martine, you know perfectly well that noblemen marry for property, not love."

"I should," she snapped. " 'Tis a lesson I learned in a cruel way at a tender age."

"Thorne is not Jourdain," he said. "Just a man trying to make the best of his life."

"At my expense."

"What?"

"Why do you suppose he was so eager to marry me to the son of his overlord? Merely to accommodate you?"

"Aye. Why else?"

She sighed irritably. "You said yourself I have great value as a bride. Sir Thorne's arrangement of this marriage will undoubtedly put him in good stead with Edmond's father. And that, in turn, will put him one step closer to earning a manor, which he then intends to supplement with some young girl's inheritance. The idea of being *used* like that, just to further someone else's ambition, makes me feel—"

"Thorne is a man of high ideals. He'd never use a sister of mine to such ends."

"You've both used me to suit your own ends, and I daresay my betrothal has worked out rather nicely for both of you. We'll know how it worked out for *me* when we get to Harford and I meet Edmond."

Chapter 3

They rode in silence until the late afternoon sun formed a low orange ball in a sky of unearthly blue. Martine couldn't remember ever having seen a sky quite that extraordinarily blue in France. If there were skies such as this in England, perhaps she could be happy here, after all. The setting sun gilded the ripening grain with its fire and sliced long shadows into it. A warm breeze scented with hay drifted over the fields, which the villeins were beginning to abandon for home and supper.

Presently the sun winked out on the horizon, staining the sky the color of peaches—a beautiful color, but Martine missed that special, English blue. The breeze that had been warm before sundown now chilled her, and she decided to put her mantle back on. She slowed Solomon to a walk and shook out the long cape. But as she did so, the breeze caught it and sent it sailing ahead of her. Martine cursed inwardly and braced herself for the possibility that the stallion would shy.

Indeed, as the mantle sailed past his eyes, Solomon's head flew up, his eyes rolling white. Martine instinctively wanted to grab both reins and hold on tight, but instead she seized the inside rein and pulled the startled animal in the same direction he had shied, forcing him to dance in a frenzied circle. She caught a glimpse of Thorne's restraining arm before his squire. Sensible of him; Albin would only have gotten in the way.

Solomon executed one last complete circle, snorting in frustration, before she could rein him in. Sighing in relief, she leaned over and patted his neck. Thorne nodded respectfully in her direction. Albin looked sheepish.

Her mantle had landed in a heap on the road. She began to dismount, but settled back into the saddle when she saw Albin jump down from his humble mount. He picked up the mantle, handling it as if it were the shroud of Christ. After gingerly dusting off a few spots, he carried it toward Martine, only to have it snatched from his hands by Sir Thorne as he rode past.

"Thank you, Albin," said Thorne.

The squire replied with a resigned "Sir" and remounted his packhorse. Thorne gave the garment a few good shakes, then brought his steed close to Martine's. Ignoring her outstretched hand, he draped the mantle carefully over her head and shoulders, smoothing down and adjusting the cloth as he did so. His movements were economical, his touch firm but gentle. Martine, nonplussed, looked down at her hands on the reins. She rarely blushed, but this Saxon had made her blush twice in one day!

Men rarely touched her. The code of chivalry frowned upon physical contact with a lady. Although Sir Thorne disregarded the code, he did so without apparent disrespect to her. It surprised her that he would want to make this thoughtful gesture after their testy exchange in Weald Forest. He had a bit of trouble securing the mantle with the brooch, his long fingers fumbling a bit as he patiently worked the pin through the black wool. His hand as it brushed her throat was warm, his scent earthy but clean, like the forest after a rainfall.

When he had finished, she knew she should thank him, but feared that her voice would catch in her throat. At any rate, he didn't seem to expect it of her. He merely nudged his horse and continued ahead of her down the road.

Not long afterward, as the sky deepened from peach to violet, she spotted Harford Castle in the distance, crowning the top of the only hill for miles around. Its size impressed her, dwarfing the humble structures on its south side. She could make out about a dozen cottages and the steeple of a church, which Thorne identified as the barony chapel.

As they neared it, however, she felt a pang of disappointment at the simplicity of its construction. Even in silhouette against the evening sky, she could see that the keep was but an enormous stone box with a rectangular turret at each corner, surrounded by massive curtain walls. There were no fancy towers, no ornamentation, no interesting bits of architectural detail at all.

The road led them past the cottages and church, curving west around the hill on which the castle stood, a river curving to the east. The party followed Thorne along a side path up the hill, past a palisade of sharpened poles, and over the drawbridge leading to the gateway. A small door in one of the metal-faced oaken gates, just big enough for one person on horseback, stood open, and they rode through it into the outer bailey.

It was too dark now to make out more than an expanse of flat lawn and the shadows of structures built up against the insides of the curtain walls, some of which were dimly lit from within. People milled about; she could hear their voices and sense their watchful eyes. The air smelled of cooking, but also of the farmyard; animals, manure, and hay.

Martine regretted not being able to see everything right away. She had an enormous curiosity about castles, having read about them in books and heard about them in the tales of jongleurs. If she were to tell Sir Thorne that she had never set foot in one before, he would find it hard to believe. He must assume that she had been brought up amid such luxury. Well, she would have almost two months within it, for she and Rainulf were to remain at Harford Castle as guests until the wedding on the first of October.

They crossed a second drawbridge to the inner bailey. Aside from the keep, the only building Martine could see appeared to be a thatched stone shed set against the south wall, from which she heard strangled screams.

"What on earth?"

The knight named Peter said, "Surely you know the scream of a falcon, my lady." Peter had a Nordic look to him, even more so than Rainulf. He was clean-shaven, and his eyebrows and eyelashes were the same pale color as his long, kinky hair—the longest hair she had ever seen on a man, falling halfway to his waist.

Falcons. "Oh, of course."

" 'Tis Sir Thorne's hawk house."

Thorne corrected him. "Lord Godfrey's hawk house."

"Aye," Peter conceded. "and Sir Thorne's birds—that

is, my lord's birds—have missed their master, and sense his return."

The group dismounted on the flagstone court in front of the keep, handing their reins to the waiting stable hands. A young red-haired man emerged from the hawk house and ran to Thorne.

"Sir! Azura's broken a tail feather, the new merlin is sneezing, and Madness won't eat!"

Thorne said, "These problems can wait until morning, Kipp. There's a young gyrfalcon in that basket over there. Take her into the hawk house and see that she's made comfortable. She needs complete darkness. Light no candles or lanterns and speak gently to her. Wrap the perch with linen."

"Shall I fit her with jesses and bells?"

"Nay. Handle her as little as possible. I'll be waking her tonight, and I'll take care of that myself."

"Yes, sir."

Thorne turned to his squire. "Albin, go up and tell Lord Godfrey and Edmond that our guests are here."

"Yes, sir!" Albin ran up the front steps of the keep, disappearing in the dark, looming stone box.

Martine's stomach felt tight, her mouth dry. What would Edmond be like? Was he anything like Sir Thorne? Where was Loki? Loki would be afraid in this new place. Loki would need her.

A hand closed over her shoulder. When she turned around, Rainulf gently placed the cat in her arms. "I thought he looked a bit nervous," he said, and smiled.

"He is," Martine agreed. "A bit."

A wavering light appeared in the entrance to the keep. Albin stood there, holding a torch in one hand while his other arm supported a heavy, unsteady old man carrying a tankard. Martine heard Thorne hiss some angry English words under his breath. Albin caught his eye and shrugged helplessly.

The man looked old, indeed, at least sixty. Martine knew immediately from the fur trim on his green overtunic that he must be a man of noble blood, obviously Lord Godfrey. He was a large man, thickly built, but with a belly that swelled beneath his tunic out of proportion to the rest of his frame. His chin-length hair and forked beard shone like polished silver in the light of Albin's torch, and a network of broken veins reddened his nose and cheeks. He clutched at Albin and howled with glee when he saw Rainulf.

"My little friend is a priest!" he bellowed as he lumbered down the stairs, assisted by Albin. His voice was slurred from drink. "When I saw you in Paris, you were but . . . twenty?"

"Seventeen, my lord," Rainulf corrected.

"Well, you looked older. Acted older. Come here!" Rainulf and Godfrey embraced, exchanging kisses on both cheeks.

Rainulf led the older man to Martine and made introductions. The baron swayed slightly despite Rainulf's and Albin's efforts to hold him upright, and his eyes seemed to have trouble focusing. He squinted at Loki, bringing his face precariously close to the tense animal in order to get a better look.

"A *cat*? Is it yours?" he asked Martine.

"Aye, my lord."

"Hunh. Well . . . perhaps it'll provide some sport for the dogs." Now he peered as closely at Martine as he had at Loki. He had a stale, beery smell, as if he had been sweating some dank brew for years. "So this is the Lady Martine. You look just like the Mother of God herself."

Sir Thorne met Martine's eyes briefly. She sensed rueful amusement, and something else, harder to define. To the baron he said, "Where is Edmond this evening, sire?"

"Hunting with Bernard and his men." Martine knew that Bernard was Edmond's older brother.

"Still?"

Godfrey shrugged. "They often go for a week at a time. You know them."

"The betrothal will be formalized the day after tomorrow," Thorne said.

"I'm sure they'll be back by then. In the meantime, I'm still master of Harford, and I know how to treat my guests. You must be hungry."

With some help from Albin and Rainulf, he turned and led his guests and knights into the keep and up the circular stairs within a corner turret. The stairwell was a narrow, winding passage of carefully worked masonry, lit by torches that filled the spiraling passage with their resinous fumes. Godfrey exited on the second level, and Martine and the rest followed.

She heard it even before she stepped out of the stairwell: low, menacing growls that caused Loki to hiss and unsheathe his claws. Martine tightened her grip on the cat and backed up, taking in the great hall and its inhabitants, human and canine.

It was a cavernous room, larger even than Rainulf's lecture hall at the university, but with less majesty, an enormous stone box, tall and long and wide. The few windows were small, barrel-vaulted openings in walls as thick as the height of three men, and the only furniture consisted of rows of long tables littered with the remains of a just-eaten supper, which a crew of servants busily cleared away.

At the opposite end of the room a low fire crackled in a pit against the wall. There was a hood over the pit, but most of the smoke escaped it, rising to linger below the soot-blackened ceiling as an acrid cloud of haze. On the wall over the fire pit hung an enormous battle-ax flanked by boar tusks, and at intervals along the walls were torches and the stuffed heads of stags with racks as big as trees.

A gallery—the castle's third level—ran all around the room about halfway between ceiling and floor. In one of its arched openings stood a woman looking down at Martine as if she were examining a small and peculiar animal. She looked quite peculiar herself, Martine thought, a spectacular little bird of bright plumage trapped in a henhouse.

She appeared about thirty, very thin and quite pretty, but in a strained way. Her skin seemed too pale, her coloring a bit too vivid, probably from face paint. She was heavily bejeweled and wore a tunic of purple silk, very snug through the bodice and hips. Martine knew that it must be laced tightly up the back in the new style just catching on in Paris. She was probably married, since her hair was covered. In apparent imitation of Eleanor of Aquitaine, she wore with her fillet and veil one of those chin straps that they called a barbette. A plain-faced young woman stood behind her, similarly attired, but in pink, and without the veil.

The growling came from near the fire pit. A thin, balding priest stood at one of the tables cutting fist-sized chunks off a half-eaten haunch of venison and tossing them to a pack of dogs at his heels. They were hunting dogs—wolfhounds, spaniels, and a mastiff—and although the mastiff still greedily snapped meat out of the air, the dogs had obviously caught Loki's scent. They stood staring at the cat with hackles raised, quivering.

Lord Godfrey grinned and said, "Here it comes." As if at his command, all the dogs, the mastiff included, came bounding with fierce howls across the enormous room, leaping benches and tables. They knocked one tabletop clean off its trestle, dumping a tureen of soup into the rushes covering the floor. The servants tackled three or four before they had gone very far, but one—a huge wolfhound—eluded capture and raced toward Martine fangs bared.

Thorne immediately grabbed Martine and shoved her back against the wall, shielding her with his body. The wolfhound leaped onto him, but he sent it flying with a well-placed kick. He looked back over his shoulder as the rest of dogs were subdued, but didn't back away from Martine or loosen his iron grip on her arms.

Being as tall as most men, Martine didn't often feel physically dominated by one, but Sir Thorne's sheer size overwhelmed her. He was long of limb and powerfully built, his shoulders massive, his chest hard as rock beneath his tunics. As he pressed her to the wall, she could feel the solid muscles of his thighs flex against hers, causing a peculiar, shivery warmth to course through her. She had the most disconcerting instinct to put her arms around him, and she knew with appalling certainty that were she not holding Loki against her chest, she might have done just that.

She squirmed, trying to make space between them. He looked down at her for a moment, and then smiled slightly and slowly eased himself away, his big hands sliding down her arms before he released her. She quickly stepped away from him. The dogs, she saw, had all been rounded up. Lord Godfrey lay sprawled in the rushes, laughing unroariously at the spectacle.

The woman in purple had descended to the main floor of the hall and now strolled toward Martine, an odd

silver-handled wooden stick swinging from her wrist by
a leather loop. She was short, Martine now saw, and
indeed skinny, but had about her the presence of a
larger person.

Most of the dogs congregated near the fire pit, where
they sat watching Martine and Loki with frustrated intensity. One of the wolfhounds stood just several yards
away, however, right in this woman's path. She regarded
him with a wary revulsion, carrying the stick in a threat-
ening posture as she passed. He responded with a snarl
that made her jump and shake the stick menacingly over
her head. He calmly turned and trotted away.

"Lady Martine," Thorne said, "may I present Lady
Estrude of Flanders, soon to be your sister by marriage.
She's the wife of Bernard, the brother of your
betrothed."

"My lady," Martine said, as Estrude inspected her
with unconcealed amusement.

Finally Estrude turned and announced to the assembled company, "She can't very well be Edmond's bride.
From all appearances, she's already the bride of Christ!"
Lord Godfrey, the priest, and the young woman in pink
all got a good chuckle from this, but Sir Thorne
looked grim.

Estrude pouted. "What a sour face, Sir Thorne! Don't
worry. Didn't I promise I'd be nice to her? I'll treat her
just like a real sister." She extended her spindly arms,
smiled with her too-pink mouth, and said, "Welcome to
Harford Castle, Sister Martine!"

"Let their limbs be stretched till they pop from their
sockets!" Godfrey bellowed down the length of the dinner table, his voice thick with drink. Thorne wondered
how he could still be conscious. "Let their eyes be
gouged from their heads!"

Shortly before their arrival at the castle, a messenger
had stopped by with important news: The three bandits
who had murdered Anseau and Aiglentine had been
caught that morning, sleeping in an abandoned mill.
They were now being held in a cell at the castle of Olivier, Godfrey's earl and overlord. They would hang, of
course, but not before preparatory torture to extract
confessions and uncover accomplices.

"Let them be dunked in boiling water! Let their flesh be torn with red-hot pincers! Let their feet be soaked in salt water and goats lick them down to the bone!" Thorne had never heard that last one before. From the puzzled look Rainulf exchanged with him, neither had he.

Thorne watched Martine, who was directly across the table, staring at the slabs of meat on her trencher—untouched except for the bits she had sliced off for her cat. The animal that had spawned so much mayhem just a short time ago now lay curled contentedly on his mistress's lap, licking his paws and wiping his greasy face with them. The dogs sat gathered around Martine's bench, watching this feline ritual with rapt fascination.

The spilled food and drink had been quickly cleared away. All but one trestle table, perpendicular to the rest and located next to the fire pit, had been disassembled and removed, and a second supper laid for the latecomers. Godfrey, Estrude, and the baron's parish chaplain, Father Simon, had already eaten, but remained to keep their guests and knights company at table. The other members of the household either hunted with Bernard or had retired early.

"Let hot pitch be—"

"Sire," Thorne interrupted, nodding toward Martine. "Perhaps the lady would prefer a different subject of—"

"The Franks have the most ingenious methods," said Godfrey. "Father Simon here traveled throughout France till just two years ago. He was describing some of the damnedest things in fascinating detail last night. Simon, tell them what you saw them do in Autun, with the leather boots and the molten lead."

The priest pressed his thin lips together. "Sire, surely what I saw in Toulouse was more interesting." Godfrey frowned. "Those two heretics who were tied to stakes and burned alive? And then there was Arnold of Brescia four years ago. I saw *him* burned—"

"Alive?" Estrude exclaimed.

Father Simon shrugged. "They were guilty of heresy. The flames of the pyre were naught to what they'll feel for eternity."

The baron waved his tankard, spilling ale into the

rushes. "Aye, but the stake is a form of execution, not torture."

"That's arguable," Rainulf mumbled.

"Rainulf!" Godfrey exclaimed. "You've just come from Paris. Have you come across any new methods of . . . coaxing confessions?"

Rainulf took a slow sip of wine. "My lord, I'm afraid I've little interest in such things, except inasmuch as they may be eliminated." Ignoring Simon's smirk, he continued directing his comments toward the baron. "I agree with the first Pope Nicholas that a confession must be voluntary and not forced."

"Father Rainulf is a very learned man," Simon said, "renowned in Paris, Tours, and Laon for the breadth of his knowledge of logic and theology. 'Tis an honor to sit at the same table as him." He half bowed toward Rainulf. "But isn't it true that in the three hundred years since Pope Nicholas wrote those words, the Church herself has come to accept and encourage such righteous torture in her own ecclesiastical courts?"

"The Church's ways aren't always what God would wish," Rainulf said, reaching for his goblet.

Father Simon pounced eagerly. "It would seem a university education is all it takes to make one privy to the wishes of God."

"Nay, but it does make one less susceptible to the baser wishes of man, such as the wish to inflict pain."

Lacking a retort, Simon faked a yawn, and Thorne noticed Martine smile as she stroked her cat. Hers wasn't such an awkward face after all, he decided. The features he had at first thought out of balance did, upon reflection, have a certain undeniable charm, a charm all the more compelling when she smiled. It seemed to give her pleasure to listen to her brother engage in this supper-table debate. She must have heard many such exchanges during the year she spent with him in Paris.

Rainulf was a proponent of the controversial new movement called *disputatio,* in which argument between teacher and student replaced the traditional, dryly authoritative *lectio.* From his letters, Thorne knew that he had spent the past year tutoring Martine in this manner—just as he had once tutored Thorne—and Thorne speculated that perhaps this had been the origin of Martine's contentious nature.

In general, he admired people who liked to argue. Contentiousness he viewed as a sign of intellect and an unwillingness to accept things as they were, which was often all for the good. And it was the opposite of meekness, which he despised in either sex as a badge of servitude.

This was the first time he had seen her smile since she had smiled timidly at him from the deck of the *Lady's Slipper*. That was before she had withdrawn so inexplicably. Was it merely arrogant teasing on her part, or was there more to it? He couldn't recall having said anything to offend her, but women of her class tended to be thin-skinned.

That saffron veil enhanced her air of mystery. Unmarried women usually wore them only to hide some unattractive feature. Perhaps she had thin, patchy hair. More likely she had been afflicted with some form of pox as a child, and now hid the marks on her forehead with it. It was a common enough disfigurement. When Thorne undressed a woman for the first time, the question was not whether she would have pockmarks, but where and how many.

Aye. It must have been the pox. What a shame for such a face to be so scarred. Perhaps Edmond would find the flaw so objectionable that he would want to call off the betrothal. He felt a fleeting pleasure at the thought, and frowned in self-reproach. Was he mad? That should be the last thing he wanted.

Apparently Lady Estrude, seated to his left, had noticed the frown. As Father Simon launched into a description of the burning of the two heretics, she leaned toward him and said, just loudly enough for his ears alone, "Why so melancholy, Sir Thorne?"

Thorne realized she must have been watching him gaze across the table at Martine, lost in thought. He tore a crust off his trencher and dipped it in his ale. "Do I appear so, my lady?"

"Indeed. Or else under a spell of some sort." She took a sip of wine, glancing at Martine and then back at Thorne. "Is that it? Are you bewitched?" She chuckled.

"Curious. I thought your taste ran more to little Saxon goosegirls and Hastings whores."

Insufferable woman. Thorne calmly ate the ale-soaked bread.

"I suggest you take care," she murmured. From the corner of his eye, Thorne saw her painted lips curve into a sly smile. "That peach has been promised to Edmond. He might not take kindly to your tasting it before he's had the chance."

Thorne automatically glanced across the table toward Lady Martine, only to find her looking directly at him. Her eyes widened slightly as he met her gaze, then she abruptly looked away, two spots of pink blossoming on her cheeks.

Estrude smiled knowingly as she studied Martine's discomfort. " 'Twould appear the lady is also under some spell of enchantment. Fascinating." Leaning close to Thorne, she whispered, "Don't you think so, Sir Thorne?"

He did, indeed, but it wouldn't do to let her know that. Feigning disinterest, he took his eating knife to the stag. One of the spaniels saw him lifting the piece of meat to his mouth with his fingers and dashed around the table, eager for a handout. They were stupid creatures, but still one would think they would have grown wary of Estrude's dog stick by now. The spaniel jumped onto the bench and squeezed between them, panting in anticipation and slapping her with its tail. She raised the stick, but before she could lower it, Thorne grabbed the animal by the scruff of its neck and tossed it away from the table.

Estrude looked disappointed. So did the spaniel, until Thorne issued a short whistle from between his teeth. The dog's ears perked up and its mouth flew open, ready to catch the piece of meat the knight threw his way.

Estrude glowered at him. "I didn't know you cared for Bernard's dogs. Or is that spaniel one of yours?"

"I keep mine kenneled, where they belong," Thorne answered. "As for Bernard's, I'd like to feed them to the falcons. But I'd like to feed that stick of yours to the fire."

Estrude pushed her trencher back and folded her arms on the table, leaning toward Martine. "My lady, I can't help asking just where in the name of God you got that cat."

Martine's aloof expression revealed no hint of irritation at Estrude's tone. Thorne admired her composure. "In the convent where I was brought up. Cats were the only pets the nuns were allowed to keep."

"Ah, yes," Estrude said. "I forgot you'd gone to a convent school. St. Teresa's, wasn't it?" Martine nodded. "I myself didn't go to school." She nodded toward the girl in pink. "Like Clare here, I spent several years in the household of a neighboring baron, serving the lady of the house. My parents wisely felt that such an education would serve me best when I became a baroness myself."

Thorne said, "Perhaps my lady Estrude will someday have a chance to test that theory, when her father-in-law's time on earth is done and she actually becomes a baroness." Martine smiled at his subtle rebuke, which he found absurdly pleasing. "My lord Godfrey is a man of great health and vigor. God willing, that time won't come for many more years."

From the corner of his eye, he saw Estrude look grimly down the table toward Godfrey, asleep with his face on the tablecloth, his mouth open, snoring loudly.

Returning her attention to Martine, she asked, "How long were you at Saint Teresa's?"

Martine hesitated. "For seven years, my lady. From the age of ten until I joined my brother in Paris last year."

"Did you see much of your family during those years?"

She glanced warily toward her brother. What was this?

Rainulf, looking uncomfortable himself, said, "Nay, my lady, she did not. 'Twas too great a distance for easy travel."

Estrude's eyes widened, and she made a show of gazing in astonishment around the table. "You mean to say she had no contact with her family for seven years? Didn't she miss them?"

Smoothly Rainulf said, "Much as I'm sure my lady Estrude misses here own family in Flanders. How long has it been since you came to England to live, my lady? Ten or fifteen years? It must be very hard on you being away from them like this."

No wonder Martine relied so on her brother. He was her rescuer, her protector. But why had he felt she needed protection from Estrude's harmless prying? Perhaps his enigmatic sister was hiding more than pockmarks.

Thorne sighed. He had never liked surprises, but they could be especially troublesome when one had a great deal at stake. And his stake in Lady Martine's marriage to Edmond was great indeed, considering the land it would likely earn him. If the lady had secrets, he had best unearth them himself, before others had the chance, and soon, before the betrothal ceremony. Perhaps tomorrow he could contrive to get her alone for a while. Without Rainulf to protect her, she might be coaxed into revealing whatever it was the two of them seemed so intent on hiding.

He rose and went to the head of the table. "I'm going to help his lordship to bed," he said, hauling the inebriated baron to his feet and guiding him in the direction of his chamber at the far end of the great hall.

Estrude rose as well. "I'll go with you."

He was not in the mood for this. "Don't trouble yourself, my lady. I'm fully capable of handling—"

"I didn't mean I'd help you put him to bed. You've had enough practice at that, God knows. I only meant I'd light the way." She lifted a candelabra from the table and came to stand very close to him, out of earshot of the rest of the diners. Gazing up with half-closed eyes, she purred, "I would dearly love to show you the way, Sir Thorne. I wish you'd let me."

Her face looked unnaturally white in the flickering candlelight, her lips dark as plums. Her large brown eyes, encircled by black powder, glittered seductively. She had applied her paint with a heavier hand than usual this evening—for him?—yet he could still make out, on her left jaw and cheek, the faint shadows of bruises almost healed, testament to her husband's most recent rage.

Was it to spite Bernard that she had embarked on her recent campaign to seduce him? Thorne knew better than to think she had suddenly taken a fancy to him after all these years of mutual animosity. Nay, she wanted something from him. He didn't know what, nor did he care to find out. Let her play out her tiresome little intrigue on a more gullible victim.

"If I wanted someone to show me the way," he said slowly, his voice barely above a whisper, "I'd use a little Saxon goosegirl or Hastings whore, wouldn't I?" Now it was her turn to blush, a mottled pink stain creeping up her throat and disappearing beneath her pale face powder. To underscore his refusal, he allowed his dismissive gaze to sweep over her boyishly thin form before settling on her eyes, which were narrowed in anger and humiliation.

"As I said," he added, turning away, "don't trouble yourself."

Martine watched the tall Saxon surreptitiously as he emerged from Lord Godfrey's chamber and strode toward them across the great hall with his graceful, long-legged gait. He wore an unadorned knee-length tunic of a deep, warm red. The longer undertunic was black, like his chausses and shoes. Despite the simplicity of his garments and his humble origins, he was the noblest-looking man Martine had ever seen.

As Thorne took his seat across from her, Rainulf rose, saying, "Excuse me. I want to check on our baggage, and those puppies."

"Puppies?" said Lady Estrude.

"Aye. One of Lady Martine's betrothal gifts to Sir Edmond is a litter of fine bloodhound pups."

Estrude daintily lifted a cheese-filled wafer to her mouth. "More dogs. How thoughtful."

She took a tiny bite and chewed it slowly as she watched Rainulf walk away and then said, "Tell me, Lady Martine, will your family be here for the wedding? I don't suppose they'd want to make the crossing just for the betrothal ceremony, but surely they'll want to see you married."

Martine looked toward the doorway in the corner, but Rainulf was gone. Summoning a casual tone, she replied, "I'm afraid not, my lady."

"Nay?" Estrude seemed perplexed.

From the corner of her eye, Martine saw Sir Thorne watching her closely as he reached for his tankard.

"I know your father is dead," Estrude said, "but your mother is still alive, is she not?"

"My—my mother?"

"I understood there was a baroness," Estrude persisted. "Lord Jourdain's second wife. Isn't she your mother?"

Martine looked again toward the corner doorway. When she turned back, she saw the eyes of every person at the table fixed on her, waiting for her answer.

Chapter 4

Thorne rose and walked around the table toward her. "My lady," he said, straddling the bench next to her, in the spot vacated by Rainulf, "I've been wondering. Does your cat have a name?" Loki hissed, and Estrude looked as if she wanted to.

"Loki."

"Loki!" He grinned in delight. "That's perfect. Loki that trickster, the sly one, the shape-changer."

"You know the legends of the North?"

"My mother used to tell them to me." He allowed Loki to sniff the back of his hand. To Martine's surprise, the cat began licking him.

She said, "My mother did, too." Thorne seemed to make no effort to keep his distance from her. His left knee pressed her thigh, and when he leaned toward Loki and his arm brushed hers, she flinched at the feel of hard muscle beneath the soft woolen sleeve.

"We're cousins, then, you and I—both descended from the Northmen. They call me a Saxon, but there are none of pure blood left in England or North France." His gaze traveled from her eyes to her lips, and then he leaned toward her. Martine gasped, thinking, *My God, he's going to kiss me!*

He paused, his face very close to hers. "What scent is that?"

Martine realized she had stopped breathing. Swallowing hard, she said, " 'Tis a perfume I make from sweet woodruff and oil of lavender."

"It's different," he murmured, backing away slowly. "Lovely."

"I'm surprised you think so," Estrude said. "I've always found those herbal concoctions a bit too tiresomely subtle. Rose oil is my scent of choice. No other flower is quite so sweet.''

"Nor quite so cloying," Thorne observed, "especially once it's a bit past its prime."

Estrude stiffened, her face a mask of indignation. Thorne merely nodded toward Loki, who was still purposefully licking his fingers. "Is this animal's tongue supposed to feel this way?"

" 'Tis rather rough, I'll grant you."

He grinned. "Lord Olivier could put Loki and some salt water to good use."

Gradually, so as not to alarm the cat, he moved his hand, trailing his fingers around to the animal's back. Loki tensed as this stranger began gently stroking him, then settled happily into Martine's lap, purring and nesting with his paws. Thorne caressed him firmly from head to tail. His purr deepened; his eyes closed. Martine could feel every caress through the cat's warm, vibrating body. It felt exactly as if Thorne were caressing her.

His hands were large, but well shaped, not the coarse, meaty hands of the villein. He wore a ring on his right hand, a cabochon ruby surrounded on all sides by golden talons that gripped it as a falcon grips its prey.

" 'Tis a handsome ring," Martine said.

"I'm fond of it. Lord Godfrey gave it to me when he made me his master falconer. 'Tis the thing I prize most in the world. Or it was until tonight." He looked at Martin, and his blue eyes took her breath away. "A white gyrfalcon is an extraordinary gift, and a valuable one. Your brother is very good to his friends."

He held her gaze for a brief, searching moment, and then, almost shyly, looked back down at Loki. "I'll need a name for my bird. Can you think of any goddess from the North who might like to be a falcon?"

That was easy. "Freya."

"Of course!" His warm smile relaxed Martine. "Freya!"

"She had that magic falcon skin, remember? So she could fly to the underworld and see the future."

"That's right. Loki used to borrow it, in fact."

"She was the goddess of beauty and love," Martine said.

"And of death," said Thorne. "Beauty, love, and death. Quite like a falcon."

Martine said, "I heard you say you were going to 'wake' Freya tonight. What does that mean?"

" 'Tis how you get a new bird used to you. You stay awake with her all night, until she thinks of you as almost a part of her."

"I've never tried to stay awake that long," Martine said. "Isn't it difficult?"

Estrude interrupted. "Our Thorne is reputed to be a man of unusual endurance. 'Tis well known he prides himself on his self-control." She leveled a peculiar, knowing look at him. "How nice for young Lady Martine to have made a friend so quickly. Edmond will be sure to appreciate your kindness."

Thorne bit back the urge to answer Estrude's sly innuendo with some clever barb. 'Twas best to let the matter lie, for, as usual, she had paired insolence with keen perception. In truth, he did find the lady Martine desirable, although he shouldn't. She was ill humored and aristocratic, both characteristics he normally abhorred in women. She was also obliged by contract—a contract that Thorne himself had arranged, and upon which his future depended—to marry young Edmond.

Then why was he so drawn to her? Why did he ache to touch her? Why did her scent stir him as it did? The answer, of course, was that it had been weeks since he had shared his bed, and his body craved the touch of a woman, any woman, without regard for good judgment or common sense. Chastity might be all right for men like Rainulf, men of the spirit, but it made him restless; worse, it made him susceptible to the charms of the wrong women.

When Rainulf reentered the hall, Thorne quickly rose and returned his friend's place to him. The serving girls came back with dessert, and Thorne smiled at the plump redheaded woman in charge. "How goes it, Felda?"

"Same as always, Sir Thorne." She set before him a bowl of fragrant candied orange peel and one of sugar. "How was Hastings?"

"Same as always."

Guy said, "Felda! What's the new girl's name?"

Thorne followed the gaze of the others to a beautiful

woman moving down the table, replacing pitchers of wine and ale with new ones of brandy and spiced beer. Felda grinned at Guy while the new girl acted as if she hadn't heard.

"Her name's Zelma," Felda said. "But she only speaks English, so save your breath."

"I don't need words to tell her how I feel," said Guy. "Zelma!" When the wench glanced in his direction, he blew her a kiss, whereupon she wheeled around and sauntered away from him, looking vaguely bored. She had dark, heavy-lidded eyes and arched black eyebrows, but her most striking feature was her great mass of thick, blue-black hair, which she wore in a linen snood. The loose hair that spilled from it in unruly tendrils gave her a disheveled air, enhanced by the fact that the cord lacing up the front of her low-cut brown kirtle had come loose. Her generous bosom swelled precariously above the gaping fabric. Should she stretch just so or lean over too far, her breasts would surely be revealed in their entirety.

Thorne watched her discreetly over the top of his tankard as he took a drink, grinning to himself when he noticed Rainulf doing the same. Albin, Peter, and Guy, on the other hand, gaped at her much as the dogs gaped at Loki.

Lady Martine looked from Zelma to Thorne and back again, then dropped her gaze to her lap and proceeded to pet her cat with studied—and almost certainly pretended—indifference. Could it be that she was jealous? Perhaps Estrude had been right when she hinted that Martine seemed to be under some spell of enchantment.

It was a spell, then, that had been cast upon them both. Luckily, however, it was a spell with a simple cure, at least as it affected him. If abstinence made him lust unwisely, then all he really needed to set him straight was a friendly tumble—but not, God knew, with Estrude of Flanders. Her kind demanded tedious affairs, for which Thorne had little patience. Complicating matters in this case would be Estrude's husband, Bernard, quite possibly the most dangerous man Thorne knew.

Father Simon broke Thorne's reverie by rising and delivering a stream of long-winded good-byes. A group of adolescent boys in the corner watched in silence as he exited the hall. The moment he disappeared, they brought out their dice, kicked aside the rushes, and squatted down, commencing animated play.

Estrude said, "Lady Martine, have you no one to serve you? No lady's maid traveling with you?"

"Nay, my lady. I had no such person in Paris."

"We shall have to find one for you." She turned to her maid. "Clare, do you known of anyone? One of your sisters, perhaps? The fat one. She's got nothing better to do."

"She has fits, my lady," Clare said.

"Yes, but in between the fits, she'd be fine, I'm sure." She nodded happily. "I'll send word to your father tomorrow that we'd like her to—"

Thorne said, "Perhaps Lady Martine would prefer to choose a maid herself from among the house servants."

"The house servants?" Estrude said in disbelief. "But surely the daughter of a baron would prefer a girl of breeding to one of these—"

"Why don't we let Lady Martine decide?" Thorne turned to Martine. "My recommendation, if it's of any interest to my lady, would be Felda." Estrude gasped. "I've known her for many years. She's reliable, has a good heart, and will serve you as well as any girl of noble birth."

Felda displayed as much astonishment at this referral as Estrude. Martine looked at Rainulf as if for guidance, but he smiled and spread his hands as if to say, *This is up to you.*

"Felda," she said, "would you be at all interested in this position?"

"In being a lady's maid?" Felda said, grinning. "I should think so!"

Estrude shook her head. "This is preposterous."

Martine said, "Then it would please me greatly to have you."

Felda yelped with delight. Then she leaned over, took Thorne's face between her fleshy hands, and kissed him on the lips.

Thorne grinned. "Don't make me sorry for suggesting you."

"Nay! I'll be wonderful. Oh, milady, thank you. Can I start now?"

Martine shrugged. "I suppose so."

Felda called to the boys playing dice in the corner.
"Pitt! Sully! Brad! You and them others go heat up
some kettles of water and bring them upstairs to milady's chamber, then fetch the big tub. Hurry, now!"
Groaning, they pocketed their dice and left the room.

"A bath!" said Lady Martine. "I haven't had one
since leaving Paris. 'Twill be heaven."

Felda grabbed two of the serving girls. "Beda, you
come help me unpack milady's things. Carol, go out to
the cookhouse and bring back one of them fresh squire's
loaves and a hunk of that ripe Brie. Milady didn't touch
her supper. Also some of that buttermilk, and some
brandy. Put them next to her bed."

As the guests rose from the table, dozens of house
servants settled down in the rushes and prepared to
sleep. The torches were extinguished one by one. Soon
there would be only candlelight, and then the candles
would be blown out, and darkness would consume the
great hall.

Thorne bid the assembled company a collective good
night, then turned to stare after the new serving girl as
she entered the stairwell, carrying two pitchers. Just before she disappeared from view, she turned and caught
Thorne's eye, holding his gaze for a brief but meaning-
ful moment.

Smiling to himself, Thorne jogged after her.

"Zelma!"

The kitchen girl paused on the stairs just below the
landing, a pitcher in each hand, and looked up at him.
When she saw who it was, she smiled, turned, and leaned
back against the curved stone wall.

"You're coming undone," he said in English, and
began smoothing stray hairs off her face and tucking
them into her snood. She watched him calmly. Even
when his hands lowered to her breasts, she didn't move.

Two wolfhounds trotted down the stairs, but otherwise
Thorne and Zelma were still alone. He lifted the two
ends of the cord that had come unlaced and tugged hard,
pulling the kirtle once more snugly around her chest.
With slow deliberation, he tied the cords into a bow.

"You're the Saxon knight," she said. "The falconer."

He liked her raspy voice. It reminded him of the cat's tongue.

He tied the ends of the cord and arranged the bow just so, then rested his fingertips on her breasts, gauging her reaction out of the corner of his eye. There was none except perhaps a lowering of her eyelids and a slight smile.

He allowed his fingers to move slowly, tracing feathery patterns over the taut brown wool. He heard her sigh, felt the warmth of her breasts beneath his trailing fingertips. Soon his aching need would be satisfied. Lust was but a demand of the body, like thirst. He had a raw thirst that needed quenching, and it didn't matter whose cup he drank from. Tonight it would be Zelma's.

He encircled her with his arms. "Come outside with me."

"I'm married," she said.

All the better. Married women tended to be realistic, not expecting his heart to worship them as his body did. "Where's your husband?"

"Hastings."

Thorne smiled, then leaned down and closed his mouth over hers. She yielded to the kiss, allowing him to explore the warmth of her lips and tongue with his own. He closed his eyes and Zelma's face transformed into another, pale and mysterious, shrouded in saffron veils. The veils shifted, and he found himself gazing into the deep blue eyes of Martine of Rouen. His heart drummed in his chest; desire overwhelmed him. When he took her full lower lip between his teeth, a moan rose in her throat.

Voices from below made him open his eyes. Three of the boys who had been playing dice were coming up the stairwell, each carrying two huge buckets of steaming water. Thorne broke the kiss, but they had seen and heard enough. They snickered as they passed, the first one mumbling, "Sir."

"Boys."

Zelma said, "You're taking a chance, kissing me like that. My husband's Ulf Stonecutter. Do you know him?"

"Nay."

"Well, he's quite a big man."

He lowered his hands to her hips and pulled her

against him so she could feel his desire—desire for another, but desire nonetheless. "How do you know I'm not bigger?"

She smiled, but not, he sensed, in amusement at his reply. She looked like someone who had an idea she wanted to test. Nodding toward her pitchers of spiced beer, she said, "Would you hold these for me?"

He took one in each hand, finding them full and quite heavy. She must be a strong woman. Then, as casually as she might lift a tablecloth, she pulled up his tunics, loosened the waist-cord of his chausses, and reached into them with both hands. Thorne gasped as they closed around his erection, feeling him with liberal familiarity.

"Bless me," she said. "So you are."

"Zelma!" With the two heavy pitchers and no place to put them, he might as well have had his hands tied. His only option would be to drop them and let them crash on the stairs, spilling their contents in a waterfall all the way into the bailey. It did not seem like a good plan.

Thorne heard voices on landing above—Peter and Guy. Zelma must have heard them as well, but made no move to let him go. Thorne shook his head, amused at her audacity despite his embarrassment.

The men found his predicament hilarious, laughing as they squeezed past with their full tankards. Guy said, "Careful, now. A fall down these stairs would be a nasty thing."

Zelma stroked him with tantalizing expertise. "You're a regular stallion, that's what you are. I daresay you could do me some damage with *this*."

The serving girl named Carol came running down the stairs on her way to the cookhouse, calling out as she passed, "That one's married, Sir Falconer. Her husband's enormous!"

"Your Ulf is quite a legend," Thorne said.

"He's a wonderful man, and I love him very much. It's just that I've got a real weakness for big, tall Saxons. 'Tis quite a burden, really. I *try* to be strong."

"Of course you do."

More footsteps from above. With a sigh of irritation, Thorne looked up . . . and beheld the lady Martine, gazing down on him from the landing.

Shock kept him rooted to the spot, robbed his tongue of the power of speech. At first she frowned slightly in obvious puzzlement. Then, with a strange and horrible detachment, Thorne saw her gaze travel slowly from his face to Zelma's, and finally to Zelma's hands where they disappeared beneath the hem of his tunic. Her eyes widened, and she took a step back.

With her nunlike dress and her hands clasped primly before her, she looked like a saint who had just stumbled upon some sinners and didn't quite know what to make of them. Despite her coolness and her intellect, she was, he reminded himself, a convent girl, unused to the ways of the world. He would have understood if she had gasped in horror, had turned and fled. But she merely returned her gaze to his, and he lacked the power to look away. His eyes were riveted on hers as the kitchen wench, oblivious to everything but her little game, continued to fondle him.

To look upon Martine's face as those skilled hands worked their magic both aroused and disturbed him. He wondered what Martine was thinking. Did she know that he had imagined her in Zelma's place, had seen her eyes behind the shifting veils, felt the warmth of her lips on his? Did she know?

He saw something in her eyes . . . a secret knowledge, an understanding.

His heart pounded; he could barely breathe. He closed his eyes, willing Martine gone. She mustn't be here. She mustn't know.

"Are you all right?" Zelma asked, her hands stilling.

He opened his eyes. The landing was empty.

Zelma said, "You looked dizzy for a moment."

A moment. Yes, a moment. It had just been a moment. Martine had appeared and left in the space of two heartbeats, but it had seemed much, much longer.

He took a deep breath and banished all thoughts of Martine from his mind. "I'm fine. Come outside with me." Zelma's teasing had driven him perilously close to the edge. He would not let her finish him here in this stairwell, like some randy youth who had to take what he could get. He had to get her to the hawk house.

She shook her head. "I don't think so."

"You won't get pregnant. I'll finish outside of you."

"I'm barren as a stone. Doesn't matter."

He wouldn't have to pull out! He had to have her. Perhaps she feared that he would hurt her. She had commented on his size, something about him doing her damage.

"I'd be so gentle," he said. "You'd never even know I was in there."

"Ah. Well." Abruptly she let go of him, pulled her hands out of his chausses, tightened the cord, and adjusted his tunics. "There's hardly any point to *that,* now, is there?"

"What?"

"If I wanted to fall asleep in the middle of it, I'd spread my legs for that Sir Guy or one of them other fine Norman ladies. A real Saxon stallion should be able to make a woman scream."

"Zelma—"

She turned and descended the stairs, saying, "Try again when you're not in such a gentle mood."

He watched her disappear and stood staring after her, still holding the pitchers. The throbbing ache in his groin was suddenly matched by a headache of blinding intensity. He turned, closed his yes, and pressed his forehead against the cool stone wall. It had been a trying day.

More voices came from below—Peter and Guy on their way back up from wherever they had gone—but still Thorne didn't move. Their conversation trailed off as they came up behind him. For a moment they regarded him in silence, and then Peter put a hand on his shoulder, saying softly, "Thorne?"

"Aye?"

He tapped his empty tankard against one of the pitchers. "Mind giving me a refill?"

Martine sat down in the hot, scented water and leaned back against the smooth wood of the tub. She closed her eyes and sighed. All the woes of the world were expelled from her in that sigh, replaced by a delicious, consuming warmth. She slid down until only her head and knees were above water, her hair hanging over the side of the tub and spilling onto the rush-covered floor.

Felda pulled up a stool, draped the hair across her lap, and spent a wonderfully long time brushing it. The feel of the stiff boar bristles against her scalp intoxicated her. Such sensual luxuries were foreign to Martine. She wondered what it would feel like to be caressed by a lover, and her mind instantly conjured up a picture of Sir Thorne and the black-haired kitchen wench. She saw them locked together, doing that which she had heard described, but which she had never been able to fathom anyone wanting to do—and then imagined herself in the wench's place.

The longing, the pulsing void deep within her belly, came as a shock. She wanted him to enter her, to consume that void. Never in her life had she felt so empty.

"The bath smells heavenly," Felda said. "What was that you put in the water?"

"Lovage and oil of rosemary," Martine murmured.

"I seen all them oils and powders when I unpacked your bags. Beda said you had enough to set up a stall on market day."

Martine opened her eyes. Her chamber, barely illuminated by the light from a single oil lamp, was but a cell within the thickness of the keep's massive stone wall. It was so small that there was barely room in it for a small chest, the stool, and a narrow, curtained rope bed, upon which Loki now slept. The bathtub took up nearly all the remaining space.

She took the bar of lavender-scented soap that Felda handed her and began washing up. "Some of my herbs are from the garden at the convent, some from the Paris physicians who taught at the university. I used to sneak into their lectures. One of them even let me assist him with his patients."

"Sit up now, dear. Let me do your hair." Felda poured steaming water over Martine's head, then lathered her hair with the lavender soap. "Stand up now."

Martine stood, and Felda poured a bucket of hot water over her to rinse her off, then began drying her with a large linen cloth. No one had ever done such things for her before, but self-consciousness soon gave way to the novel pleasure of being pampered.

Felda tossed the damp linen into an empty bucket and helped Martine on with her wrapper. "Sir Edmond's going to be one happy young stag when he gets your gown off on your wedding night and sees what he's got

himself. He'll have mounted you twice before you can
make it to the bed.''

"Felda, really." Martine regretted the reproach the
moment she uttered it, but Felda's comment had summoned afresh those disturbing mental pictures of Sir
Thorne and the kitchen wench.

"Oh, I'm sorry, milady. My big mouth is always getting away from me. Here I promised Sir Thorne I'd be
such a good lady's maid and I go prattling on about such
things, and you a convent girl."

The boys who had poured Martine's bath were now
playing dice on the other side of the chamber's leather
curtain. Felda called them in to empty and remove the
tub, then took a fresh linen and toweled Martine's hair
with it. "You must be hungry." She handed her mistress
a piece of bread and a cup of buttermilk, sat her down
on the stool, and began combing her damp hair. " 'Twill
be a warm night. You hair should be dry by morning."

The bread tasted fresh, the buttermilk smooth and
tangy. Felda seemed like a good sort. Like someone
Martine could talk to, someone she could ask questions
of and expect candid answers. Attempting a nonchalant
tone, she asked, "What is he like, by the way? Sir
Edmond?"

"He likes to hunt, milady," Felda said, handing Martine a slice of cheese.

"Yes, but what else? Doesn't he do anything else?"

Felda combed in silence for a while, then said, "You
see, it's the way he was raised. After his mum died. The
Lady Beatrix, God rest her soul." She stopped combing
for a moment, and Martine knew she was crossing herself. "Eleven years ago Easter."

She sighed and continued. "The whole household
went downhill after that. Lord Godfrey never has gotten
over it, but that's another story. Your Edmond was only
eight years old, and suddenly no mum. I mean, it's not
like he'd had much of one before, her being so sick all
them years. But all of a sudden she was gone, and his
lordship ... well, he wasn't much use to the boy, in his
state. 'Twas Bernard raised that boy. Bernard and his
men."

"His men?"

"His knights. There are four here at the castle, besides

him and Thorne. And Edmond, now that he's been
dubbed. Two are his and two are Thorne's."

"But surely they're all Lord Godfrey's."

"I'm not telling you how it should be, milady, but how
it is. If you'd rather not know—"

"No, please." She turned and looked into the other
woman's kind green eyes. "You know I want to know.
Everything. You must always tell me everything."

"Yes, milady." She poured Martine a generous brandy
and handed it to her. "Bernard's got his men, and
Thorne's got his. We call them the dogs and the hawks,
'cause Bernard hunts with his dogs, and Thorne with his
hawks. Not that that's the only difference between them,
God knows."

"What else? Tell me about Edmond."

"Like I said, Bernard and his men raised little Edmond. Bernard's much older, you know. He's a good
six and thirty by now. Him and his men took the boy
everywhere they went: hunting, whor—uh, on trips to
Hastings ... everywhere. Godfrey'd wanted to send him
to a monastery school, or perhaps to serve one of Lord
Olivier's knights, but Bernard wouldn't have it. He said
the boy needed him, and he wasn't going anywhere. In
truth, I think 'twas him what needed the boy."

"How's that?" The brandy warmed her stomach and
made her drowsy. How delicious to drink brandy while
having one's hair combed.

"Edmond adored Bernard. Looked up to him like he
was the Lord God himself. Always copying him and trying to please him. I think Bernard needed that. I think
it made him feel ..."

"Hmm?" Martine's could barely keep her eyes open.

"Never mind. You're half asleep, and I've said too
much, as usual. Let's get you into bed."

Felda took Martine's wrapper and tried to put a shift
on her, but Martine hated nightclothes and refused. The
linen sheets felt cool against her bare skin, the feather
mattress soft.

Felda tucked her in snugly, then moved about the
chamber tidying things up and hanging clothes on hooks.
Martine watched her with heavy eyes, enjoying her comforting presence, the freckles spattered over her plump
arms and face, the coppery glow of her hair in the lamp-

light. As she worked, Felda hummed a peaceful, haunting melody; it was a familiar tune, a popular love canso that comprised part of every jongleur's repertoire.

Martine closed her eyes, and the melody danced slow, measured circles around her, like a bird ... like a seagull seeking her out, coming to escort her to her beloved. As the gull spun and twirled in the blue sky of England, it grasped the sun in its claws and pulled it, trailing a glowing thread of light ... a golden ribbon.

It was the ribbon of omens ... of good and bad fortunes ... of fate. Around and around her it spun, in rhythm with the song of true love, until she was wrapped in a glowing cocoon ... unmoving, unseeing, sinking, drifting, floating ... bound by the ribbon of fate.

Chapter 5

There it was again, that sound. Like a little gasp.
Martine opened her eyes. She had the sense of
having slept for some time, and the faint aura of dawn
glowed through the thin white curtains enclosing her
bed. Where was Loki?

Soft footsteps. Someone was in her room.

Martine listened carefully. "Felda?"

The movement stopped, replaced by silence. Martine
sat up, holding the sheet to her chest. From the other
side of the curtain, Loki mewed, and then came a
sharp "Shh!"

It had not been a man's voice, more like a young
woman or a child. Tentatively Martine parted the curtains and peeked through, then smiled.

In the middle of the room stood a little girl, no more
than five or six, holding Loki in her arms and staring,
wide-eyed, at Martine. She was a dirty, unkempt little
thing, barefoot and wearing a stained tan kirtle backward. Despite her tangled brown hair and the film of
grime on her face, she was a pretty child, with large,
dark eyes now wide with fear. Perhaps she was the
daughter of one of the house servants, who had wandered upstairs to find the strange pet master Edmond's
betrothed had brought.

"Good morning," Martine said. The child just stared.
Martine wished Rainulf were there. What would *he* say
to her? Of course! "What's your name?"

Still no response. Perhaps she didn't understand
French. It seemed that many Saxons spoke little of their
rulers' tongue. Martine had heard Albin speak a kind of
anglicized French to the stable hands. Martine tried to
remember some of the Anglo-Saxon words she had

heard Thorne speak to the peasants they had passed on their way to Harford yesterday.

"Good afternoon," she said in English. The girl looked bewildered.

Martine rose and approached her, which caused her to shriek and back into a corner. Loki sprang out of her arms, and she crouched, hiding her face in her filthy hands.

The leather curtain parted and Felda entered, bearing a tray of wine and bread. At first she didn't see the child. "Good morning, milady. I forgot to ask you last night whether you broke your fast in the morning or preferred to wait till noon."

"I can wait," Martine said, and pointed to the corner.

"Lady Ailith!" Felda said. "What in heaven's name are you up to?"

Lady Ailith? The girl mumbled something into her hands.

Felda leaned over her. "What's that, dear?"

"She's naked!"

Felda glanced at Martine and grinned. "Well, milady, when you sneak into someone's bedchamber uninvited, you pretty much have to take what you find, don't you?"

A pause, and then the little head nodded.

Martine donned her wrapper and said, "You can look now. I'm covered up." Ailith peeked between her fingers, then sighed with relief and stood up. Felda introduced the little girl as Edmond and Bernard's niece, the only child of their sister, Geneva, wife of the Earl of Kirkley. Geneva and Ailith had been guests at Harford Castle for some time.

Martine said, "I see my lady knows how to dress herself!" Ailith looked down at her backward kirtle and patted it, grinning with pride. "Do you bathe yourself as well?"

Ailith screwed up her face, and Felda said, "Her little ladyship don't care for baths."

"I can see that," Martine said. "One would think her mother would insist."

Ailith said, "Mama has a headache."

Martine looked to Felda, who said, "The countess has had a headache for some time now, milady. She pretty much keeps to her chamber."

"I see," said Martine. "But one can't go without baths forever. Fetch the tub, will you, Felda?"

Felda said, "Oh, she won't let you bathe her, milady. I've tried."

"I'm not asking her permission," Martine said, grabbing the child as she tried to dart out of the room. Ailith shrieked, clawed, and kicked, but Martine held tight.

"Fetch the tub," she calmly repeated. To her astonishment, the child bit her right hand, hard. Martine clamped an arm around Ailith's forehead, immobilizing her in a headlock. It was a skill she had perfected at St. Teresa's, helping with the younger girls. "And do hurry."

By the time the sun had fully risen, her little ladyship had gotten as clean as she would ever be.

"I don't *want* to come out," Ailith wailed, sliding deeper into the now cool water and gripping the sides of the tub with stubborn determination.

"Please, milady," Felda said, standing over her, linen at the ready. "Come out for Auntie Felda. Please?"

Martine pushed up the sleeves of her wrapper, plunged her arms into the water, and hauled out the wet, flailing child.

"*You* dry me off!" Ailith demanded.

Martine said, "Is that the way you ask for something?" Ailith looked perplexed. "Please."

"Please what?"

Martine shook her head. She took the linen from Felda, wrapped the child up, and lifted her in her arms, hugging her tight.

"Hold me like a baby," Ailith said. Martine shifted her in her arms, carrying her as she would a swaddled newborn. "Now make believe I'm *your* baby, and I've just been born, and you love me more than anything. Say, 'Oh, my precious babe ... I think I'll name you ... *Robert*!'"

"But that's a boy's name."

"I'm a boy baby. Say it!"

"I'd rather you were a girl."

"A *girl*? Do you want your husband to cast you aside? Call me Robert." She kicked her legs. "*Say* it!"

Martine looked at Felda, who nodded sadly. So that's why Ailith and her mother were living at Harford Castle.

The Earl of Kirkley had repudiated the marriage—cast Geneva aside—for her failure to bear a son.

Martine sat on the edge of the bed, squeezing Ailith in her arms. "If you were my little girl, I wouldn't trade you for all the sons in Christendom. And I'm sure your mama feels the same."

Ailith dug her face into Martine's shoulder and mumbled, "No, she doesn't."

Felda came up with a clean lavender kirtle for Ailith, and Martine painstakingly combed the tangles out of her damp hair. Then she tied a purple fillet around the child's head, saying, "This is how my mama used to fix *my* hair."

"Look how pretty you are," Felda said, holding Martine's little looking glass while Ailith inspected the results.

"Will Thorne think I'm pretty?" she asked.

Felda winked at Martine in response to her look of surprise, saying, "Lady Ailith plans on marrying Sir Thorne when she grows up."

"He should have his land by then," Ailith explained.

Felda rolled her eyes. "Don't turn down any good offers while you're waiting for *that,* milady."

"What do you mean?" Martine asked.

"What I mean is, if Lord Godfrey intended to grant Thorne a manor, he would have granted it by now. Thorne's getting impatient, he is. He's been in Godfrey's service for close to ten years now, and proved his worth many times over. The way he figures it, the baron don't want to lose him as master falconer, and that's why he won't deed him a holding."

Martine said, "You seem to know an awful lot about Sir Thorne."

"Everyone needs someone they can talk to, even a man like Thorne. He tells me things he would never tell anyone else."

"Are you and he . . . Is he your . . ."

Felda hooted, waving her hand in dismissal of the idea. "My Lord, no! We're chums, is all. Known each other for ages. Nay, my sweetheart is Fitch, the village ironmonger. Whenever he can sneak away from his wife, that is."

"He's married?"

"You should see her, milady. Arms like hams, and legs like haunches of venison. Once in a while he likes to tup a wench he ain't scared to death of."

"If I can't marry Sir Thorne," Ailith mused, oblivious to the conversation going on over her head, "then perhaps I'll marry you, Auntie Felda."

"Thank you for thinking of me," Felda said.

"Now that I'm pretty, I can get married," Ailith said. "If you're not pretty, no one wants to marry you, and you have to become a nun."

Martine said, "Then you'd better help make *me* pretty. Your uncle Edmond comes home today." She pictured Edmond riding up to Harford Castle on a white steed, such as the one her father used to ride—such as the one Sir Thorne rode. "Pick out something nice for me to wear. Something that won't make me look like a nun."

Ailith scanned the garments hanging on the wall. They were all drab and plain, with one exception, to which she immediately gravitated. It was a tunic made of polished Egyptian cotton crinkled into tiny pleats, and the color was extraordinary—a rich, vivid blue with a hint of violet.

"Wear this! This one! It's *beautiful*! Dark blue is my favorite color. Is it yours?"

"Aye," Martine replied distractedly.

" 'Tis the same color as your eyes, milady," Felda pointed out.

That's what Rainulf had said when he gave the tunic to Martine as a birthday gift—that he had chosen the fabric for its color, the product of a remarkable new dye from the East called indigo, because it was the precise blue of her eyes.

"I thought I'd save that tunic for the betrothal ceremony," Martine said.

Felda said, "Lady Estrude's having outfits made for the betrothal *and* the wedding, as gifts."

Martine fingered the unusual blue fabric, remembering Estrude's comments about her the night before. She wouldn't look like a nun in *this*. "I'll wear it."

The silk stockings, garters, and soft kid slippers had been dyed to match the tunic. Ailith brought each item to her, supervising as Martine put them on, and com-

menting approvingly on the results. The kirtle was white
with long sleeves lightly embroidered in gold and teal.

When Martine finally pulled the tunic down over her
head, Ailith clapped her hands in delight, and Felda just
stared. Although the garment was cut full, with no lacing
in back to draw it in, the fine pleating had given the
fabric a certain amount of stretch. It clung just enough
to highlight the elegance of Martine's statuesque frame,
without revealing too much. The sleeves were tight until
they reached the forearms, where they flared dramatically, falling in rippled folds to the floor.

Felda tied a golden, tasseled girdle over Martine's slim
hips, and then opened her mistress's small jewelry box.
"There's not much here, milady, if you don't mind my
saying so. These are quite nice, though." Martine took
the dangling pearl earrings Felda offered and put them
on, then reached in for a handful of little gold rings,
which she slid onto her fingers and thumbs.

Martine sat on the stool and let Felda brush her hair
into a glossy spill of silvery gold. Ailith sat on the floor
and stared, transfixed. Then, armed with a mouthful of
pins and using both strong arms as if she were wringing
laundry, Felda twisted the thick hair into a massive coil
at the nape of Martine's long neck. Martine added a
narrow circlet of hammered brass.

Felda nodded, smiling. "He'll grow faint when he
sees you."

"Who?" Martine demanded, before she could stop
herself.

"Sir Edmond, of course! Who else?"

Turning away, Martine shrugged as casually as she
could. Leaving Felda to tidy up, she took Ailith in one
hand and the brass box that contained her rarest herbs
in the other, and left in search of the cookhouse. She
had some rare new spices from the East that she wanted
to give Lord Godfrey, but the cooks would have to be
shown what to do with them.

Heads turned when she left her chamber. She paused
in one of the gallery's arched openings to glance down
into the great hall, and every person there looked up
and fastened his gaze upon her. The servants tried to be
discreet, half turning their heads and sliding their eyes
to look. Guy and Peter, playing chess, nodded toward

her and smiled at each other. Estrude stood stock-still and looked her up and down with the narrowed eyes of someone who suspects she has been swindled. Albin dropped something, which shattered. Martine quickly pulled Ailith into the stairwell. Once outside, the child skipped behind Martine, holding one of her long sleeves in each hand, flapping them like the wings of a butterfly.

In the daylight, the inner bailey looked to be nothing more than a flat lawn of cropped grass surrounded by the huge stone walls. The hawk house, nestled against the south wall, was the only structure in the bailey besides the keep. They passed it at a distance on their way to the outer bailey, and Martine saw two boys—one in each of the two doors—sweeping straw from the hawk house onto the grass. Bundles of fresh straw leaned against the small building's stone wall. In one window stood a tall figure in white, with a white bird on his fist— Thorne holding Freya.

He stared fixedly in her direction.

Martine turned toward the inner drawbridge and quickened her pace, suddenly very conscious of what he saw as he gazed upon her. He would see the distant figure of a tall young woman with a child bouncing behind her, waving the sleeves of her indigo gown back and forth, back and forth. He would see the knot of silver-blond hair like white fire in the morning sunshine ... the glint of gold and brass, sparks that winked as she walked.

She had almost gotten to the drawbridge when she heard his voice, fairly close behind her. "I barely recognized you. You look quite fetching today, my lady."

She smiled, wondering how to answer him. But as she turned, she saw Ailith running toward him, squealing, "Thank you!" He had followed after them, and was now several yards away, squatting down to greet the young girl. She tried to throw herself into his arms, but he held her back, saying something about Freya, who still clung to the gauntlet on his left hand. He had been addressing the compliment to Ailith, of course. Martine commanded herself not to blush as she joined them.

Ailith said, "Your hair's wet, just like mine!" His damp hair was combed back off his face. He wore a shirt of bleached linen over dark braies, and woolen hose bound by crisscrossed strips of linen. On his feet were short, worn leather boots. This was a workingman's costume, unlike the fine tunics and chausses he had worn the day before.

"I've had a bath," he answered. "Just as you have, it seems."

"Sir Thorne bathes in the river," Ailith told Martine. "He knows how to swim! He learned in Lisbon." Martine had never known anyone other than herself who could swim. "When I grow up, I'm going to bathe in the river, too."

"Perhaps in the summer, my lady," said Thorne. "In the winter, you'll prefer a nice warm bathtub, as I do." He stroked Ailith's hair, the honey-gold beauty of which became more and more evident as it dried.

He said, "What a good girl you were to have let Auntie Felda bathe you and fix your hair so nicely."

" 'Twasn't Felda," Ailith protested. " 'Twas Auntie Martine."

"Auntie Martine?" Thorne looked directly at Martine for the first time since she had joined them, his gaze lingering curiously, for some reason, on her forehead.

Ailith stroked her hair proudly. "Do you like it?"

He nodded, smiling warmly at her. "Very much."

" 'Tis how her mama used to fix *her* hair. You know what?"

"What?"

"Auntie Martine doesn't eat breakfast. And she knows English. At least 'good afternoon.' And she knows all about herbs. She keeps them in that box. And she wouldn't trade me for all the sons in Christendom. And she doesn't cry when she's bitten!" Thorne scowled and looked inquiringly toward Martine, who smiled and held up her hand, displaying the purpling teeth marks. "She doesn't even scold me!"

Thorne sighed. "Then I don't suppose it's my place to scold you for her. You seem to have learned a great deal about her in a short time." With a glance in Martine's direction, he added, "The rest of us heaven't been so fortunate."

"Want to know what her favorite color is?" Ailith asked.

"If you'd like to tell me."

"Dark blue, like her tunic. 'Tis the same color as her eyes."

"No wonder it's her favorite, then."

"Know what she calls her cat?"

Thorne smiled. "Loki. The shape-shifter. The changer." His gaze traveled over Martine's gown and hair. "Like his mistress."

Ailith thrust out her lower lip and scowled. "You knew!" Suddenly she grinned. "Bet you don't know what she wears to bed!"

Martine grabbed her hand and began pulling her toward the drawbridge. "Ailith . . ."

"Nothing!" Ailith squealed, struggling against Martine as she led her away. "She sleeps *naked*!" Two porters leaning against the turrets of the inner gatehouse looked from the child to the woman to each other, grinning.

Thorne didn't grin, Martine saw as she turned to lift Ailith in her arms, deciding to carry her rather than wrestle with her. He wore just the hint of a smile as he stared after her. He stood very slowly, taking care, it seemed, not to disturb Freya.

Martine hurried through the gatehouse and across the drawbridge with Ailith screaming "Naked! She sleeps naked!" and didn't stop until she was well within the outer bailey.

Martine left Ailith in the cookhouse playing with one of the cook's daughters, who had a collection of baked clay animals. In the daylight, the outer bailey resembled a small walled village of thatched stone and wood. People, dogs, chickens, and pigs crossed paths in the packed mud, all there to serve their baron's various needs. The only truly idle creatures she could see were children Ailith's age or younger, who gathered with balls and bats or small wooden soldiers, which they marched purposefully through the mud.

As she recrossed the inner drawbridge, she noticed a putrid odor rising from the ditch below. Looking down, she saw several inches of stagnant, scum-covered water in the bottom of the long trench. A pinpoint of fire on the back of her hand caused her to wince. She slapped at it, crushing the tiny insect, a mosquito. The rainwater in the bottom of the ditch must be an excellent breeding ground for such pests.

There were other indications that Harford was not a well-kept castle. The rushes in the great hall smelled of mold and were littered with bones and other debris. Those dogs ran wild, like unruly children who had never been taught discipline. The servants varied in their dedication to their work, but there was no one with a firm hand to oversee them and make sure castle business was properly attended to.

This firm hand would normally have been that of the mistress of the house, but Beatrix, baroness of Harford, had died eleven years before. Lord Godfrey had evidently never felt the need to remarry, having two sons and a daughter as heirs. And he did not seem to be equal himself to the task of looking after his home, preoccupied as he was with drinking and hawking. According to Felda, he was incapable of controlling his own knights, who had split their loyalties between Thorne and Bernard.

As she thought of Thorne, she heard him say her name. She stopped short just inside the inner bailey, frowning in puzzlement.

"Lady Martine," he repeated. She turned around. He stood leaning against a gatehouse turret, a different bird on his fist. Had he come back to wait for her? Why?

"Sir Thorne."

He approached her and nodded at the bird, a small brown falcon with a white throat. "This merlin has a cold. I was wondering if you might have any stavesacre for her in that box of yours."

"Stavesacre? Yes, I do."

As she opened the brass box and reached into it, he said, "You haven't got any cardamom as well, have you? 'Tis good for their stomachs."

"I believe I do," she answered, fumbling among the various packets and jars.

He lifted the box right out of her hands and strode with it toward the hawk house. "You can set this down on my worktable."

Chapter 6

Martine followed Sir Thorne, reflecting that she hadn't much choice; he had taken her most valuable possession right out of her hands. Those herbs and spices had come from every obscure corner of the known world, and some were as rare as the most precious gems. She had no intention of letting them out of her sight, as he surely must know.

The boys who had been changing the straw were gone. He led her through the door to the right, ducking as he entered. She ducked, too, although the doorway was tall enough for her. They were in a little living chamber. She saw the narrow bed and realized this must be where he slept, although it apparently served as a workshop as well. There was a table against one wall, on which were arranged various tools, jars, flasks, and boxes, as well as tangled piles of leashes and a row of little leather hoods with feather plumes, each on its own wooden stand.

Thorne set the brass box on the table, then ducked through a leather-curtained doorway and disappeared into the other side of the hawk house. Martine took the opportunity to inspect the chamber further. A brazier, not in use at present, took up one corner, and above it hung a collection of leather gauntlets on hooks. In the opposite corner stood a beautifully carved armchair, and next to it a small table on which sat a book and a little bowl containing what looked like strips of raw meat. On top of the book lay a white feather.

She lifted the feather, but a sudden piercing scream startled her into dropping it. It was Freya, tethered to a perch nearby, and evidently displeased at having Martine so close. Sir Thorne emerged through the leather curtain, took up the feather, and trailed it gently over the young falcon's wings, speaking softly to her in English.

"Why English?" Martine asked.

"They respond better to it than to French. 'Tis a language simple and direct, much like themselves."

Although Martine couldn't understand a word he said, his voice was so deep and sonorous, his tone so soothing, that she began to relax right along with Freya. The bird turned her head and stared at her master fixedly with one fierce, unnerving eye as he reached into the small bowl and brought forth a strip of meat. Martine expected him to hold it up to her beak, but instead, he drew it across her feet, whispering gently to her all the while. After several moments of this, she pecked at the tidbit, then grabbed it in her beak and flung it into the straw covering the floor.

Thorne smiled as if at a mischievous child and repeated the gesture with a second piece of meat, then a third and a fourth, each time with the same result. Martine wondered at his patience. Finally Freya deigned to hold a piece of meat in her beak. When she swallowed it, Thorne rewarded her with animated words of praise, then fed two more slivers directly into her mouth.

He retrieved the bits she had tossed about the room, returned them to the bowl, and crossed to the worktable. Martine followed him and began rummaging through her box in search of the herbs he wanted. She spread packets and jars over the table as she did so, and many of these Thorne opened and squinted into, sometimes tasting the contents. But when he uncorked the little blue glass vial and began to insert a finger, she immediately grabbed his wrist. "Hemlock."

"Hemlock!"

Her slender fingers could not meet around his wrist. It felt as hard as oak to the touch, but warm. She released it abruptly, almost pushing him away, then took the vial, closed it, and returned it to the box, aware the whole time of him watching her, his gaze strangely intent.

She cleared her throat. " 'Tis an ingredient in a surgical sleeping draft I know of. In a very tiny amount. More could kill you." She handed him the little bag of stavesacre. "Take what you need. I'm curious to see how you use it."

He put a pinch in a stone mortar, then added three

peppercorns from his own supplies and ground them quickly to dust. He poured something from a jug into the mortar—Martine smelled vinegar—and said, "I'll let it sit for a while till it's ready. Then I'll put some on the merlin's nostrils and palate. That and some warm hen flesh should cure her cold."

He took some extra stavesacre and a few cardamom seeds, storing them in little jars, then said, "Have you ever held a falcon?"

"Nay."

"Never?" Of course her truthful answer would surprise him, she realized. Women who had grown up in noble households were used to handling birds of prey, if only the smaller varieties, like that merlin. Had he asked the question in a deliberate attempt to trip her up? Was he beginning to suspect, after Estrude's interrogation regarding her family, that she was hiding something?

He took a small gauntlet from a hook above the brazier and handed it to her. "Follow me." He held the leather curtain aside for her. She hesitated, then stepped into the other room.

Several of the birds cried out and flapped their wings as Martine and Thorne entered, but he calmed them with a few soothing words. There were about a dozen, of different species, on perches atop iron rods set into the stone floor. It was dim and cool in the room, the only light coming from between the slats of the window shutters, although several unlit brass and horn lanterns hung on chains near the ceiling. The scent of fresh straw perfumed the atmosphere. It also smelled of the birds, but not offensively so.

She attempted to put the gauntlet on her right hand, but he took it from her and pulled it onto her left, then placed a hand on her back. She tensed at the touch, at the heat from his palm that penetrated the thin fabric of her costume. But once he had guided her to an enormous gray gyrfalcon and removed his hand, the spot where it had been felt cold, and she wished he had left it there.

"This is Azure," he said. "Lord Godfrey's favorite." He threaded a leash through the little swivel on one of

Azura's jesses and wrapped it loosely around Martine's gloved fingers.

"This one?" Martine said. "But she's so big!"

"She's the tamest of them all. Here." He took her gloved left hand in both of his and pressed it into a fist, then guided it toward the bird's feet. "She's well trained. She knows what to do. Don't let her know that you don't."

Martine gasped as the huge bird stepped onto her fist, clinging tightly with her powerful claws.

Thorne said, "If you're nervous, she'll be nervous. A nervous falcon is a dangerous thing to be that close to."

"You have a talent for placing me in dangerous situations, Sir Thorne."

"You seem to handle yourself fairly well, my lady." He met her eyes. Quickly she returned her attention to the bird.

"What's the matter with her tail?" she asked, pointing to a spot that looked damaged.

"One of the feathers is broken. I had wanted to imp it today, because the baron is eager to fly her soon, but my assistant's not here to help me."

"Imp?"

"Sew a new one on."

"You can do that?"

"Certainly." A pause, as if weighing something. "Would you like to see?"

"But you said you couldn't do it because your assistant's—"

"You can help me," he said, holding the curtain aside again and motioning her into his living chamber. He dragged the armchair close to, and facing, the bed.

"What do I have to do?" The bird weighed her arm down so heavily that she had to use her right hand to support her left. She realized how strong Thorne must be to be able to hold them for hours while he and Godfrey hunted.

He collected some items from the worktable and tossed them and his gauntlet on the bed. "Just sit in that chair." She did. He draped a clean linen cloth across her lap and then gently took hold of Azura and placed her on the cloth with her back up and her tail toward the bed. Next, he laid a square of dark wool over her head—

to keep her calm, he explained. Taking a strip of leather from his worktable, he tied his hair back, then sat on the bed opposite Martine, one long leg on either side of her chair.

She could not get used to this physical closeness that he seemed to take for granted. Although they were not touching, she felt surrounded by him, penned between his thighs in a most intimate way. She could feel the heat from his body, smell the Castile soap with which he had bathed that morning. Azura flinched, and she realized she had been gripping the bird too hard.

"Just hold her lightly," he said. "So she knows you're there." First he took a small sheet of parchment and slid it under the damaged feather. Then he reached into a little wooden box and withdrew a gray feather the exact color of Azura's tail.

"I save them when they molt," he said. Using a small knife, he clipped the new feather to the proper length and trimmed the end of the old one. From another box he took a tiny needle, which he threaded with silk. Then he began sewing the feathers together.

Martine had never seen a man sew. Needlework was the domain of women, and the sole creative pursuit of most noble ladies, although Martine had absolutely no patience for it herself. He hunched over the bird, frowning in concentration as he worked the little needle in and out of the feather's shaft with his long fingers. His big hands were surprisingly precise in their movements; his stitches were small and neat.

Martine said, "How did you come to learn about falcons?"

"How did you come not to?" he answered, still intent upon his work. "I've never known a lady of your rank to be so unfamiliar with them."

She stared at the top of his head. His questions were becoming more direct. With this bird on her lap, she couldn't just get up and leave, much as she would have liked to. Had he planned it this way?

The silence grew heavy. Thorne paused to look up at Martine, his expression thoughtful.

As he resumed sewing, he said, "I've kept birds of prey since I was a child. One afternoon when I was shooting small game, my arrow accidentally brought down a sparrow hawk. So I climbed the tree where she'd been nesting and took her young and raised them. After that, I trained other sparrow hawks, then goshawks and kestrels. 'Twasn't till I entered Lord Godfrey's service that I was able to work with falcons.''

"They say you're an accomplished bowman. Is that because you grew up hunting?" If she asked the questions, she wouldn't be the one obliged to answer them.

He said, "If you do something often enough, you get good at it. When I was young, I hunted and chopped wood, and little else. We were poor, and I was the only surviving son." He glanced at her, smiling. "I chop wood very skillfully as well, but it impresses no one."

She couldn't help smiling back. "Were there any sisters?"

He took two stitches before answering. "One. Louise."

"Do you ever see her anymore?"

Two more stitches. "Every time I look at Ailith." Leaning over, he bit the silk thread and tied it off, his warm hands brushing hers.

"No, I mean—"

"There." He pulled on his gauntlet, lifted Azura, and took her on his fist. Pointing at the bruised teeth marks on Martine's hand, he said, "I should lend you that gauntlet the next time you propose to give her little ladyship a bath." His changing the subject, as if she had been asking things that were none of her business, rankled in light of his own prying questions.

"She won't bite me next time," Martine said.

As he walked Azura through the leather-curtained doorway, he said, "Where did an only child like yourself learn to handle children so well?"

An only child? That was surely no slip of the tongue. She waited until he had reappeared, and said, "I have two brothers."

Thorne hung the gauntlet back on its hook. "But they're much older, are they not? And you spent seven years in a convent. It must have been rather like being an only child."

She removed her gauntlet and handed it to him. With icy restraint she said, "You know I have two brothers. You know perfectly well I'm not an only child."

He looked at her searchingly, and took his time answering. When he did, his words were measured, as if he were choosing them carefully. "My lady, I know almost nothing about you. Only that Rainulf calls you his half-sister, and that you panic when questioned about your family. 'Twas I who recommended you to the baron as a suitable bride for his son. Your betrothal will be finalized tomorrow. Do you blame me for trying to find out before then whether I've misled him somehow?"

He *had* been laying a trap for her. Prying into her secrets under the guise of pleasant conversation. Why, if he intended to unearth the truth about her, had he saved her last night from Estrude's nosy interrogation? The answer came to her in his own words. It was he who had recommended her as a suitable bride for Edmond, presumably for his own advancement. It would serve him ill for her to be found out by everybody before he had the chance to do so himself. He could then, of course, decide whether to expose her or keep her secret, and he would undoubtedly do whatever best served his purposes.

Suddenly she mistrusted him intensely. If she was not as she seemed, neither was he.

Walking toward the door, she said, "Rainulf thinks you've arranged my marriage out of friendship. I told him it was out of ambition, but he doesn't believe me. He likes to think that everyone is as good as he is."

"I don't deny or apologize for my ambition. I'll do whatever it takes to rise above the circumstances of my birth. If I should someday have children, I don't ever want them to suffer the cruelties of poverty that your kind thinks nothing of imposing on mine. Your marriage does serve my ambition, but it also serves my friendship with your brother, which means more to me than you'll ever know."

" 'Tis a very touching speech," Martine said, standing in the doorway. "You've obviously given a great deal of thought to how my marriage serves your purposes. I don't suppose it's ever occurred to you to consider whether it serves mine."

She slammed the door and walked back to the keep.

Sausage pie and peas with bacon water constituted the midday meal. Lord Godfrey, Sir Thorne, and Albin were absent from the table. They were flying the falcons, and had taken their dinner with them to eat as they hunted. Lady Geneva, Ailith's mother, chose not to dine with them, either, but no one offered an explanation for this.

Martine passed the afternoon exploring the lower levels of the keep with Ailith.

The first floor was the guardroom, nearly as large as the great hall, but with arrow slits instead of windows, and no place for a fire. There had been no attempt to make this room comfortable or attractive. The wooden floor was bare of rushes, and the walls displayed not hunting trophies, but a dizzying array of weaponry: gleaming broadswords and axes on one wall, and on another, rows of slender spears, javelins, and lances. There were dozens of graceful longbows and even a few of the outlawed crossbows, as well as thousands of arrows and bolts bound into bundles like kindling. To Martine's way of thinking, the most menacing objects there were the brutally simple maces and throwing clubs, whose destructive power depended on mass and weight rather than finesse.

She and Ailith descended with a brass lantern to the cellar, a cold, fetid cavern with walls of weeping rock and a floor of beaten earth, in the middle of which had been dug a well. Piled up around the perimeter were pyramids of barrels and stacks of crates.

Ailith looked around excitedly. "Auntie Felda says there's a secret passageway down here! If I'm good, she'll show me where it is someday!" She ran to a barred iron door streaked with rust.

"This is where the bad people stay. If I can't stop bothering Mama, she's going to have me locked in here."

Martine followed her to the door and jimmied aside the plate covering the little peephole, which stuck halfway.

"Lift me so I can look!" Ailith begged. Martine held her up, and they pressed their heads together to peer into the dark compartment. The lantern didn't help much, but Martine could make out the wet granite walls. The cell was no larger than a privy chamber, and just as rank, stinking of stale urine and rotten straw. She heard a faint rustling as something scrabbled beneath the straw. There would be a horrible little room much like this one in Lord Olivier's keep. The bandits who murdered Anseau and Aiglentine would be there, waiting for the noose between sessions of unspeakable tortures.

An occasional drip of water rang through the silence; otherwise the cellar was as quiet as a crypt.

Shivering, Martine carried the child to the stairwell. "Let's get out of here. We'll go find my brother. Then perhaps you can take us up to your mama's chamber and introduce us to her. The more I hear about her, the more eager I am to meet her."

"Leave me be," groaned Ailith's mother. "I don't want any more headache powders."

Rainulf took the little cup from his sister, thinking that it was often those most in need of help who resisted it most strenuously. " 'Tis not a headache powder, my lady," he said, tilting the cup so that she could see the amber liquid within.

Martine said, " 'Tis a tonic for melancholia. An infusion of valerian, skullcap, and mistletoe. Quite effective."

Geneva, Countess of Kirkley, took the cup, tipped it over, and poured its contents into the rushes. Then she handed the empty cup back to Rainulf, pulled her woolen blanket up to her chest, and turned her dark, listless eyes upon Martine.

She reclined in bed amid a mountain of feather pillows, wearing a soiled sleeping shift. Streaks of gray dulled her lank black hair, and her face had the color and texture of candle wax. Rainulf knew that Martine did not consider Lady Geneva to be ill at all, just lazy. His sister understood incapacity of the body, but not of the soul.

"Melancholia?" Geneva said. She pointed a finger at her daughter, half-hidden behind Martine's skirt. "Ailith! Did you say anything about melancholia to—"

"Nay! I said you had a headache! I did, I—"

"I surmised it," Martine said, reaching behind to pat Ailith comfortingly. "They say you never leave your chamber, and I know that you've been . . . that you no longer—"

"That I've been cast aside? I think melancholy is a

perfectly natural response when one has been tossed away like kitchen scraps to the dogs, don't you? I hardly think it requires a tonic, since it's what any rational person would feel under the circumstances.''

From down in the bailey Rainulf heard Thorne and Lord Godfrey returning from their afternoon of hunting, and he waved to them from the window as they entered the keep. Martine stiffened at the sound of Thorne's voice. For a woman of such intellect and perception, she could be exasperatingly wrong about people.

"You should have taken the tonic," Martine told Geneva. "You should get out of bed and get dressed and get on with things."

Rainulf shook his head. "Martine . . ."

Of course she barreled on, ignoring him. "Your melancholy may be natural, but 'tis nonetheless ruinous. Not only for you, but for your daughter. She needs you. Not just your horrid threats about locking her downstairs in that cell, but *you*. A proper mother. And if you really knew what was best for you, you'd realize that you need Ailith, too."

"Need *Ailith*?" Geneva sat forward, quivering with indignation. "Why do you think I'm *here*?" She balled her hands into fists and screamed, *"She ruined my life!"*

Ailith cowered behind Martine. Rainulf went to her, picked her up, and left the room, only to find Lady Estrude and Clare listening in the gallery, their hands over their mouths to stifle their giggles. Geneva screamed louder than ever. Ailith clapped her hands over her ears and pressed her face into his shoulder.

"If she'd been a son, like she was supposed to be, I'd still be mistress of Kirkley, instead of that harlot my husband's taken to his bed! Need Ailith? I wish to God she'd never been born!"

A hunting horn sounded in the distance. Estrude and her maid stopped giggling. Clare bit her lip and looked toward the sound with her sad, shining little eyes, but her mistress bore an expression of weary resignation. Geneva ceased her screaming. Martine stepped into the hallway and looked toward Rainulf as the horn sounded again.

"Oh, good," Estrude drawled, her voice hard. "The boys are home."

Soon came the distant yowling of the dogs and the whoops and halloos of the hunters. Martine wondered which voice was that of her betrothed. For the third time since arriving in England, she felt her stomach tighten in anticipation of seeing him.

Felda appeared and took Ailith from Rainulf. "You've met the hawks, Father," she said. "Now come the dogs."

Martine followed Rainulf down the winding staircase from the third level to the first. Even through the thick stone walls of the keep, they could hear the party approach, like rolling thunder barreling closer and closer. By the time they reached the guardroom, the men were already there. To Martine's astonishment, they were still on horseback, having ridden their mounts right up the stairs and into the keep. Not only that, but it seemed the hunt had yet to conclude.

They had run a wounded deer into the keep ahead of them, a magnificent stag with a spread of branched antlers to rival those on display in the great hall.

Martine, at the foot of the stairs next to her brother, stood paralyzed with disbelief at the pandemonium before her: six or eight mounted men, a dozen or more deerhounds, and the stag, all galloping, leaping, howling, and screaming in a nightmarish whirlwind. The hunters mainly kept to the perimeter of the guardroom, where they rode in overlapping circles around the dogs and their terrified prey.

The animal ran wild, crazed with panic and pain. Five arrows protruded from its shoulders, haunches, and neck, but apparently these had not been mortal wounds. Martine wondered how a party of experienced hunters could fail to bring down a deer in so many shots, and then realized, with a wave of revulsion, that they weren't trying to kill it at all. They were tormenting it for sport, much as they might bait a tethered bear.

The cry of a baby rose above the din, quite perplexing until Martine realized it was the stag, bleating in terror. Blood ran from its wounds and foaming spittle flew from its mouth as it thrashed to and fro, struggling to remain upright. Martine looked into its eyes, which were swollen in agony.

"Stop this!" she screamed, but her words were swal-

lowed up in the cacophony that filled the guardroom.
Something had to be done. This had to stop. She looked
toward Rainulf, thinking he would know what to do. He
met her eyes and shook his head, grim-faced, as if to
say the situation was out of their control. Rainulf was a
man of no small wisdom. He knew all about this compul-
sion to inflict pain; he knew when it could be stopped
and when it couldn't. It horrified Martine to feel so helpless in the face of such cruelty.

Which one was Edmond? Was he part of this? The
horsemen were a blur of whirling capes and drumming
hooves; she couldn't hope to make out one from the rest.

No, that was wrong. There was one. One who sat mo-
tionless on a flaxen-maned sorrel stallion before a wall
radiant with row after row of steel broadswords. The
one to whom the others looked from time to time, the
one who pointed out directions and spoke commands.

He wasn't Edmond. He was too old, in his mid-thirties
at least. He had straight hair, black as ink, and a gray-
flecked beard trimmed close. His tunic was the color of
amethyst, his cloak of black lambskin. Around his neck,
on a silken cord, hung an ivory hunting horn chased with
gold and onyx. His eyes, small and dark, glinted as he
watched the stag careen and snort and stamp its hooves.
He was smiling, but it was a dead smile, a smile of the
lips but not of the eyes. Alone amid the turmoil, he
seemed eerily calm.

This was Bernard. As she realized this, she saw him
notice her for the first time, standing in the stairwell
watching him. He nodded, still smiling that lifeless smile.
When Martine did not respond, the smile left, and his
eyes, hard and black as a reptile's, studied her slowly
from head to toe. Then the smile returned, but it was
different now, more of a smirk. He returned his attention to the deer, and so did Martine.

Much of the animal's fur had become soaked with
blood. At one point its legs buckled and it gored one of
the deerhounds in the hindquarters with the tines of its
antlers. The dog collapsed, yelping, then rose unsteadily
and began limping away. Bernard dismounted, and his
men slowed their horses so as not to trample him underfoot. He grabbed a mace and kicked the dog to the floor.
Then, with a single downward blow, he crushed its skull.

Tossing the weapon aside, he lifted the lifeless animal by a hind leg and flung it out the door.

The stag still blundered about convulsively, crashing into the rack of crossbows. As if this had given Bernard an idea, he pointed to the rack and called out, "Boyce! Over here!" One of his men—big and burly with a long, wiry red beard—dismounted and tossed him a crossbow and bolt. The crossbow was an instrument of ungodly power that could speed a bolt clear through the finest armor. For that reason the Church had forbidden its use against Christians, but not, it seemed, against deer.

The men reined in their mounts to watch Bernard load and cock the weapon. His target now lurched uncontrollably, its hooves skidding on its own blood and feces.

"Shoot it in the nose!" someone hollered.

"Aye! The nose!"

Boyce said, "Meaning no disrespect, Bernard, but I wouldn't waste the effort. 'Tis a moving target. Thorne Falconer's the only man I know who could make that shot."

"I think too much is made of the woodsman's talent with the bow," Bernard said. "When was the last time he deigned to favor us with a display of it? Perhaps he's lost his touch from letting his birds do the work his arrows once did. I, on the other hand, have stayed in practice."

He took careful aim and released the bolt, but it missed the stag completely and grazed Boyce's upper arm before embedding in the wall, between two blocks of stone. The men burst out laughing as Boyce's eyes rolled up, his face twisting into a grimace of pain.

"Damned if you weren't right, Boyce," Bernard called out over the guffaws. "I shouldn't have wasted the effort!"

Boyce looked down at his wounded arm and then up at Bernard. Presently he began to chuckle and then roar with laughter, his face reddening and eyes tearing with the effort of it.

"Damned *right* I was right," he choked out, slapping his thighs. It astounded Martine that he could even speak, after having been shot by a crossbow. "Never try and show off with a moving target. Look." He pointed with his good arm toward the stag, still upright on its wobbly legs, its head flailing back and forth., "It's *still* moving. Damn thing just won't give up."

Martine heard footsteps on the stairs behind her, and then a pair of strong hands took her by the shoulders and moved her aside so he could pass. It was Thorne.

Bernard lost his smile as soon as the Saxon stepped into the guardroom. "Ah. The falconer. Just in time to join the merriment."

"*Now* we'll see some shooting," said Boyce.

Bernard said, "Boyce thinks you can hit this stag in the nose. I say your reputation exceeds your skill." He and Thorne regarded each other with ill-suppressed hostility. Presently Bernard's humorless smile returned. "Care to prove me wrong, woodsman?"

Thorne said, "Someone give me a shortbow."

"Dear God," said Martine, stepping into the room. She looked on in dismay as Thorne caught the weapon that someone tossed him, and the arrow that followed. To her surprise, Rainulf seemed unperturbed by his friend's participation in this nightmare. Could he really be that forgiving?

Well, she wasn't. As Thorne began to draw the bow, she reached out and grabbed the arrow from him, then struck it as hard as she could against the stone wall, snapping it in two.

"You disgust me!" she said.

The guardroom was frozen in silence for a brief moment, the only movement the thrashing of the deer. Then came the low whistles and disbelieving chuckles of Bernard's men. She faced Thorne squarely, ready to tell him exactly what she thought of this cruel sport, and of him for accepting Bernard's challenge. The way he looked at her disarmed her, though. Instead of the anger she had expected, she could swear she saw the briefest flicker of amusement, and something else—admiration?—in his eyes.

Nevertheless, when he turned back to the guardroom, he said, "Another arrow." As soon as he caught it, Martine reached for it, but this time he grabbed her wrist in a powerful grip, then looked to Rainulf for assistance. Her brother took her firmly by the arm and led her back toward the stairwell.

The stag bolted in various directions, tottering on its

legs like a jointed toy soldier. Thorne drew the bow, watching, waiting for the right moment.

Bernard said, "Well, woodsman? Can you hit it in the nose?"

As the animal swung around to face him, Thorne swiftly dropped to one knee, aimed, and took his shot. The stag's head flew up and it lost its footing, crashing to the floor in a clatter of antlers. Its eyes rolled up and it emitted a ragged wheeze. Then it settled into the stillness of death, Thorne's arrow protruding not from its nose, but from its breast.

Thorne rose, his expression neutral in response to Bernard's sullen glare. "Probably."

The arrow had clearly pierced the stag's heart. It dawned on Martine as Rainulf released her arm that mercy for the tormented beast had been Thorne's intent all along. Rainulf had realized this from the first, assumed it. Why had it not occurred to Martine? Her cheeks burned with shame for having presumed the worst, and she felt silently grateful to Thorne for not looking in her direction.

Bernard eyed Thorne with cold antipathy. Boyce choked with laughter at what he evidently considered a fine joke, but the rest of Bernard's men groaned in disappointment and muttered invectives under their breath.

"I think the falconer disapproves of our little sport," Bernard said tightly. "Spirits tend to run high toward the end of a long hunt, and the men welcome such diversions. But you wouldn't know about that, would you, woodsman? You take your lap birds out and come home a few hours alter with your pathetic catch of small game that wouldn't fill the belly of one of these dogs. I honestly don't know how you can hold your head up. My little brother was bringing down boar before he had hair on his—" he glanced toward Martine, smirking, "chin." His men snickered.

Thorne scanned the room. "Did Edmond return with you from the hunt?" His eyes rested on Boyce, sitting against the wall with blood running down his arm. "Or did you accidentally shoot him, too?" Only Boyce laughed, although some of the others appeared to be biting their lips.

"My brother has, indeed, returned safely. He'll be in shortly, with a gift for his bride." Bernard turned his hard eyes on Martine. "This *is* the lady Martine, is it not?"

Thorne said, "Martine of Rouen and her brother, Father Rainulf . . . Bernard of Harford."

"So I gathered," said Martine, her voice flat.

A low murmuring arose from Bernard's men. Martine heard whispers of "*She's* a cold one" and "The boy'll have his hands full."

The whispering abruptly ceased, and Martine followed the gazes of the others to the doorway. A young man stood there, looking upon her with grave interest. She knew immediately that this was Edmond.

Chapter 7

Her betrothed was comely, as had been promised, with dark eyes and skin brown from the sun. His lips were full, his neck ropy with muscle. Unlike his brother, he was plainly dressed, his hair stuffed into a threadbare blue woolen cap. He stood with his weight on one hip, both hands clutching a gray blanket tied around something enormous that rested on the floor beside him. She caught a whiff of gaminess and wondered about the contents of the blanket.

Bernard stepped around the dead stag and plucked Edmond's cap off his head. Black, curly hair, matted from its recent confinement, sprang forth. It was long, falling past his shoulders. With his swarthy features, that hair, and his layers of drab garments, he looked like a barbarian—or an infidel.

"My dear Lady Martine," Bernard said, "may I have the honor of introducing your betrothed . . . my brother, Sir Edmond of Harford."

The couple continued to stare at each other. Neither said a word, nor did they move. The tension proved too much for Bernard's men, who soon commenced their whispering and snickering.

Thorne said, "Edmond, your brother tells us you've brought a gift for Lady Martine."

Bernard nudged his brother forward. Edmond approached Martine, dragging the bundle with him. The blanket, she now saw, was spotted with dark patches. It was blood, she realized—blood that had soaked through from the inside. The closer he got, the more sickening became the stench that rose from the bundle, causing her nostrils to flare and bile to rise in her throat. She watched his hands as he untied the blanket. They were dark brown, but not from the sun; they were too dark for that. Dirt? No, more like something liquid that had dried. Blood. His hands were covered with dried blood.

He flung the blanket open, releasing a wave of unspeakable foulness to which he seemed oblivious. "For our dinner tomorrow," he said, straightening up. "Our betrothal dinner."

It was a boar. The huge, black-bristled creature lay limp and dead on the bloodstained blanket. From its gaping mouth, flanked by blood-spattered tusks, protruded a grotesque purple tongue swarming with insects. These same insects crawled over its open eyes and busied themselves among its many glistening wounds.

Martine took a step back and felt the first stair step at her heels. Edmond nervously clenched and unclenched his blood-brown hands as he glanced from her to his brother and back, as if waiting for some response from her.

The others still stared at her. Stared and stared, expecting ... what? What should she say? *Oh, thank you. Thank you for this dead boar. That dead stag. The dead dog. Dead dead dead.*

His hands were covered with blood—covered with it!—and everyone was staring, staring, staring—

She turned and ran up the stairs, her heart beating out a warning that her logical mind could not accept: that the bloodstained hands of her betrothed were an omen. An omen of evil. An omen of death.

"He'd been *hunting,*" Rainulf repeated. "That's why there was blood on his hands. Pull yourself together." He wished she would stop this incessant pacing. Back and forth, back and forth, as half a roast duckling grew cold on its trencher. She had insisted on taking her supper alone in her chamber, and now refused to join the others downstairs.

"He's had a bath," Rainulf offered, sitting on the edge of her bed.

"It's too late. I've seen him in his natural state. He can't fool me."

"Martine, I wouldn't have betrothed you to just anyone. Thorne watched Edmond grow up, and he assures me there's never been any sign of bad character, or—"

She stopped pacing and turned to face him. "He'd say

anything he had to if it would get me to agree to this wedding. He as much as told me that he arranged this marriage to further his ambitions."

"He told me the same before supper. He was afraid I'd hate him for it, as you do."

Loki writhed against her legs, and she lifted him and held him to her chest. "Don't you?"

"Nay! He's never claimed to be a saint, Martine—merely a man trying to make the best of his life. Thorne grew up with nothing. He's seen the tragic consequences of poverty. 'Tis no sin for him to want to better himself. In fact, I believe 'tis a noble goal in God's eyes."

"He told me he would do whatever it takes to achieve that goal. Those were his words. Whatever it takes. Suppose it takes some act of sin—stealing, or killing, or—"

Rainulf laughed. " 'Twould have been a worthy subject for disputation with my students. Does a noble goal justify a sinful—"

"Stop it, Rainulf." Her quiet reproach stung more than if she had screamed invectives at him. Even the cat seemed to glare accusingly at him before leaping from her arms. "Don't make light of my doubts and fears. You never have before. You've always understood. I've never even had to speak of the things that scared me. You always knew what they were."

She was right. He was failing her. He should soothe her fears, not mock them. Perhaps, as his faith waned, so did his ability to lend comfort to those in need, even to his beloved sister.

Martine opened the window shutters and breathed deeply of the warm night air, then stared down into the bailey, her gaze fixed on something he couldn't see.

"Martine." She turned away from the window. Her eyes were large and sad. "You don't have to marry Edmond. We can leave here tomorrow morning, before the betrothal ceremony. I'll pay Godfrey a small—"

"I'll marry him," she said flatly.

"Aye, but I know you have misgivings. I . . . I'll put off my pilgrimage until you're settled."

" 'Settled.' That means marriage or the convent. We both know I wouldn't make a very agreeable nun. I mean, they do still expect you to *believe* all that primitive, superstitious—"

"Martine!" But he couldn't help smiling.

"So that leaves marriage. And since you went to a great deal of trouble to find Sir Edmond for me, I may as well marry him as anyone else. If I'm lucky, he'll find me as unpleasant as most men do, and then I'm sure it won't be long before he takes a mistress and leaves me in peace."

Rainulf stared at the grim young woman before him. "You won't even give him a chance to earn your—"

"I'll give him *nothing*!" she snapped. "If I were to give him anything at all, any part of myself, he'd keep on taking and taking and taking, and leave me empty." She crossed her arms and looked away.

"Martine, look at me." She did. "You're very strong. You're not Adela, as you're fond of pointing out."

At the mention of her mother's name, Martine returned to the window. "She was destroyed by love," she said, her back to Rainulf, her gaze fixed as before. "She gave her heart completely to Jourdain, and he took it as if it were his due and gave nothing in return but grief." She always referred to their father by his Christian name, Rainulf realized, as if trying to deny the very fact that he had sired her. Her hatred for him ran deep and strong, years after his death. "He used her. He consumed her as fire consumes straw."

Rainulf rose and joined his sister at the window, wondering what had so commanded her attention. He could see nothing of interest. The bailey was deserted and moonlit, the only bright spots the candlelit windows of the hawk house.

"My lady?" came a woman's voice from beyond the chamber's leather curtain. Martine groaned inwardly. *Estrude.* What did *she* want?

Rainulf met her gaze with an amused expression and mouthed, *Behave yourself,* then waited for Martine's grudging nod before pulling back the curtain. "Good evening, my lady."

Estrude swept into the room in a purple silk wrapper, her hair unbound and loose. It was wet, a riot of auburn curls. Although she had evidently just taken a bath, for some reason she had reapplied her face paint. Martine wondered why someone would go to such trouble before retiring for the night. "Father ... Lady Martine. Am I interrupting? I could come back later."

"Actually—" Martine began.

"Actually, we're delighted to see you," Rainulf finished, with a carefully polite smile for Estrude and a swift censorious glance for Martine. "We've had so little time to get to know you."

"You're very kind," Estrude replied. "In truth, I only stopped by to ask a favor of your sister." She turned to Martine. "I confess that I've been most curious about that perfume of yours, the one made from lavender and ... sweet cicely, was it?"

"Sweet woodruff," Martine corrected.

"Thorne certainly seemed taken with it," Rainulf said.

Estrude's face went blank, and she turned away from them to glance curiously around the chamber. "Did he? I didn't notice."

Liar, thought Martine, suddenly on guard. *You noticed, all right. Nothing slips by women like you.* "Is that so?"

Estrude met her gaze unblinkingly. "Yes, my dear, it is. And, as I say, I've been most curious about it ever since last night. Do you suppose you might consent to let me try some on?"

"You want to wear my perfume?" The notion appalled Martine. It was a fragrance she had created, and which was hers and hers alone. For this awful woman to wear it—to smell like her—made Martine cringe.

"Just tonight," Estrude said. "To see what it's like."

Martine started to shake her head, but Rainulf stabbed her with a glare of warning and walked over to the little chest on which her toiletries were set out. " 'Tis something of a compliment, is it not, sister?" He located the little vial of perfume and handed it to Lady Estrude. "If you like it, I'm sure Martine will be happy to share the recipe with you."

Estrude chuckled as she pulled out the stopper. "I'm not very clever with herbs, but thank you for the offer." She sniffed the vial and frowned. "It *is* different." Shrugging, she proceeded to apply liberal splashes of the scent to her throat and arms.

"That's ... rather a lot," Martine said. "It's stronger than it seems."

"I like my scent strong," said Estrude, closing the vial and handing it back to Rainulf, who replaced it on the chest. She lifted her wrist to her nose and inhaled. Martine noticed the silver-handled dog stick looped around her wrist; apparently she never left her chamber without it. "I'm afraid this isn't quite to my taste after all. But," she added dryly, "I'm ever so moved by your generosity in sharing it with me."

After Estrude had bid them good night and left, Martine turned to her brother. "What do you suppose *that* was all about?"

Rainulf's brows drew together. "She simply wanted to—"

"Nothing about that woman is simple."

Rainulf shook his head. "Your nerves are affecting your temper—as usual. You must learn to be civil even when you're distraught."

Martine groaned and covered her ears with her hands. "No more lectures tonight, Rainulf—please."

He nodded. "You're right. This is a difficult time for you, and I'm not helping."

"Nothing can help," she replied sullenly.

"Sleep can help," he said. "You're still fatigued from the journey, and you need to be rested for the betrothal ceremony tomorrow. I'll leave you now, but you must promise to go to bed right away. No staying awake and fretting. And no dreams of floating gowns or lakes filled with blood. If the nightmare comes back, come and wake me up and we'll talk—"

"It comes almost every night lately. I can't wake you every night."

"Yes, you can."

She smiled gently, grateful for his offer, although she had no intention of accepting it. She burdened her brother enough without ruining his sleep. He would be gracious about it, as about everything, and attempt to ease her mind with soothing words, but it really wasn't fair to him. Besides, in truth his mild words eased only her mildest woes. At times like this, when her heart ached and she shivered with nameless dread, she needed comforting arms, not comforting words.

"Sleep well, Martine," he said, and left her chamber. She crossed to the window and opened the shutters.

The hawk house still glowed from within with warm yellow candlelight.

He touched her. Casually, comfortably, as if he had every right in the world.

A dark form passed across one of the hawk house windows. How would *he* soothe her fears, if it were his place to do so? He was no saint, as her brother had pointed out, nor did he pretend to be.

The dark form appeared again and paused, framed within the little golden square of light. She could make him out clearly now. He wore no shirt, and Freya clung to his fist. As he looked toward the keep, she quickly reached out and pulled the shutters closed.

Thorne twitched in his sleep as the candle's flame leaped and danced in the breeze. A despairing moan rose within him when the flame fluttered toward the straw thatch hanging down from the ceiling of the dismal little hovel. Closer, closer . . .

No . . .

The thatch ignited, bursting into flame, generating a firestorm that swept through the village in a matter of minutes.

Above the roar and crackle of the blaze rose a little girl's scream: *"Thorne! Help me! Please, Thorne!"*

Louise. He panted as he ran through the narrow streets, searching in vain for his sister while flames engulfed everything in sight. "Where are you?" he gasped. "Where are you?"

"Here I am," came the whispered reply—but not from Louise.

Cool fingertips stroked his sweat-dampened brow. He stopped thrashing and lay still, breathing in a subtle and mysterious scent. . . .

Sweet woodruff and lavender.

"I'm here," she whispered, and gradually she materialized in the moonlit semidarkness of the hawk house. He saw her leaning over him in his narrow bed, saw her midnight eyes, her cascade of silver-blond hair. "You were having a bad dream," she murmured.

Oh, God. Martine. She'd come to him. She was here.

He tried to reach for her, but his arms were curiously heavy and wouldn't move. He struggled, but she took his face between her hands and whispered, "Shh. Just lie still."

Her mouth, warm and sweet, closed over his. He wanted to kiss her in return, but he couldn't. He inhaled her intoxicating fragrance, his breath coming faster and faster, his heart thundering in his chest.

She untangled the sheet from around him and stripped it off. He felt the cool night air on his unclothed body and saw that she, too, wore nothing. Arousal consumed him with an urgency he'd never felt before.

Her hand closed over him, and he moaned. *Oh, God. Martine . . . Martine.* He tried to move, to respond to the rhythm of her caress, but his body, although rampant with need, felt leaden, immobile. He felt his fingers curl into fists, and realized he had grasped handfuls of linen sheeting.

She straddled him. He held his breath as she guided him into her, groaned as she lowered herself onto his rigid shaft. He heard her gasp. She stilled for a moment, and then she began to move, drawing herself up his full length and down again, and again and again, until he thought his heart would explode from pleasure.

"Martine," he whispered as she rode him, driving him swiftly toward completion. He cried out as his climax neared, and heard a falcon scream in reply. Freya. He'd disturbed Freya.

Martine stilled, and fumbled for something on the bed . . . a silver-handled stick, Estrude's dog stick.

He blinked, and came fully awake. Estrude—not Martine, but Estrude—raised the stick high over her head and looked around, panic in her eyes.

He released his fistfuls of sheeting, grabbed the stick, and tore it out of her hand. "What the hell—"

"Where is it?" she demanded. "Where's the damn bird?"

His mind reeling, he nodded toward the corner, where the white gyrfalcon sat tethered to her linen-wrapped perch.

Estrude relaxed when she saw that the creature was secured and couldn't hurt her. Birds of prey were even worse than dogs. Dogs went for the throat, but birds went for the eyes.

"Get off," Thorne growled, dropping the dog stick on

the bed and seizing her around the waist. He tried to lift her off of him, but she had anticipated this and writhed out of his grip.

She began moving with wanton enthusiasm, as she did whenever she wanted to finish Bernard quickly, and soon his struggles ceased. Indeed, he grabbed her hips and thrust so hard that she felt as if she were being stabbed by a lance. Suddenly he stopped, grimacing, and tried to life her off again.

"I want to pull out," he said hoarsely.

"No, you don't," she said, continuing as before.

"Get off!" But it was too late. He shuddered, digging his fingers into her flesh. She felt the hot rush of his seed within her, and smiled to herself. The Saxon muttered some unintelligible oath in his primitive tongue, then closed his eyes and lay still for a few moments.

Estrude looked down at him in the silvery moonlight. His face and body glistened with perspiration; his hair was damp with it. With his eyes closed like that, he looked as if he were asleep. She took the opportunity to inspect him shamelessly. His shoulders were very wide, his smooth chest and long arms well muscled. It perplexed her at first that his left arm was so much larger than his right. Then she remembered that he held those huge birds of his on his left hand all day. His wide torso sloped down to narrow hips and those almost unreasonably long legs. She thought he must be the most beautiful man she had ever seen. That was very far from her reason for wanting to bed him, but it couldn't be denied.

Perhaps now that it was over, he wouldn't be able to find it in his heart to be angry with her for tricking him. After all, she was an attractive woman, and now that he knew what an eager lover she was, he would certainly want her again. Perhaps he would even initiate the next tryst himself. There might have to be several.

But when he opened his eyes, she saw no affection in them. "What's the matter with you? Do you *want* to get pregnant?"

"Would you mind?" she asked. "You must have dozens of bastards scattered between here and Byzantium."

"None that I know of. And I don't want any from you."

"Rest easy, then. I've been married for fourteen years.

If I could bear children, don't you think I would already have done so?

He seemed to be mulling that over. At any rate, she felt him relax under her.

"That's better," she said with a reassuring smile. "You just like to be the one in control, but you'll soon get used to my ways. Perhaps next time you won't be so—"

"Next time? Are you mad?" He sat up, pulled her off of him, and tossed her roughly aside. Rising from the bed, he grabbed her wrapper from the floor and flung it at her. "Leave."

Ignoring the wrapper, she watched him yank his chausses from a hook and pull them on. "You'll see. You'll come to me." She smiled coyly. "Some evening when you're thinking of her ... wanting her and knowing you can't have her—"

Tying his chausses, he said, "That's what brothels are for."

"Ah, yes. Your Hastings whores. I believe I proved myself an enthusiastic bed partner. What can they offer you that I can't?"

"A man has to be able to respect a woman he takes to bed. You've got a whore's enthusiasm without a whore's character."

"What?"

He turned his back on her to lift the ewer from the chest at the foot of the bed. "Whores tend to be honest. You've got the scruples of a snake." He began to drink.

"You ... *bastard*!" She shook with anger. "I'm a *lady*! Almost a baroness! You're nothing but a crude Saxon pig. You belong in the barnyard, rutting with the other animals. You have no idea how to treat a lady in bed."

He paused in his drinking. "I never invited you to my bed."

"Any man of noble birth would have welcomed my attentions, regardless of what tricks I had used. He wouldn't have just—just taken his pleasure and pushed me aside, I can tell you that. He'd have seen to my pleasure first. That's what a gentleman does."

He set the ewer back down on the chest. "There's always your dog stick."

It took a moment. When she understood, she began to burn with rage. It inflamed her, fueled by the humiliation of rejection. She looked at the stick, then at Thorne, his back still to her, running his hands through his damp hair.

She closed both fists around the silver handle and jumped down from the bed. The power of hate buzzed in her arms. She raised the stick high as he turned to face her, then slammed it down on his head in a blinding arc. The impact jolted her.

He doubled over. She saw blood.

From the corner came screeching and the beating of wings. Thorne knelt on the floor, gripping the bed with one hand while the other covered his forehead. Dark spots appeared in the straw beneath him. Estrude looked at the blood on the stick and felt the room twirl slowly.

He rose to his feet, his eyes grim, blood trailing down his face from the gash on his forehead. She took a step back.

He grabbed the stick and whipped it out of her hands in a blur. Estrude stumbled back against the bed, her mind racing in fear. *This will hurt.*

He braced one foot against the bed and raised the stick.

"No!" She collapsed in the straw, curled into a ball, wrapped her arms around her head. She heard the crack of splitting wood and yelped.

The moment passed. She was unhurt.

She looked up, still shielding her head. Thorne held half of the dog stick in each hand, having snapped it over his leg. She watched as he hurled the pieces into the empty brazier, where they clattered harmlessly. When he turned back and looked down at her, his eyes no longer held anger. To her dismay, he now looked upon her with pity.

He lifted her cloak from the bed and offered her his hand—an unexpectedly chivalrous gesture. She didn't take it, but helped herself to her feet and snatched the cloak from him. She preferred his anger to his pity.

As she fastened the cloak, he took the rag from the washbowl and began wiping his bloody face with it. Confident now that she wouldn't be beaten, Estrude said, "You deserved that."

"Let's say I did, and leave it at that. Just go. Don't

come back here again, and never speak of this to anyone, including me. Pretend it never happened."

She crossed to the door, her eyes on his back. Still
holding the rag to his head, he dipped his cupped hand
in the washbowl, walked over to the still-agitated falcon,
and sprinkled her gently with water, which seemed to
calm her. Estrude tried to think of one final remark,
some scathing statement that would put him in his place
and give her the last word.

Without turning to look at her, he said, "Leave."

She did, closing the door behind her, and walked a
few paces. Then, pausing long enough to pull her cloak
closed, she broke into a run and didn't stop until she
was inside the keep.

Chapter 8

" A nd I will take you for my husband," Martine
said, her right hand resting on a small gold cas-
ket encrusted with emeralds, which held a finger bone
of Saint Boniface. Sir Edmond then handed her a single
white glove, symbolizing the bride price—some of his
father's most valuable holdings—that he would be obligated under the betrothal contract to pay her in six
weeks, when they became man and wife. Finally the couple clasped hands while reciting the pledges that formalized their agreement to wed.

Martine had never understood the appeal of ritual.
Her betrothal ceremony, held in the barony chapel and
officiated by Father Simon, had been a meaningless reci-
tation of prayers and vows. Thank God it was now over.
Several times she had thought she might swoon, if not
from boredom, then from her confining costume. She
had been obliged to wear the outfit that Estrude had
given her especially for the ceremony, and she thought
she would suffocate in it.

The kirtle was of rose-colored silk lined with red wool
and edged at the hem, throat, and wrists with red-dyed
marten. Over this went a pearl-gray silken tunic woven
through with silver threads and trimmed around the
neck and trailing sleeves with heavy bands of silver
braid. It laced tightly up the back, and felt so stiff and
snug that Martine felt breathless and could scarcely
bend over.

In fact, it so confined her that she had immediately
resolved to wear something else instead. She reached
behind to unlace it, but couldn't manage, thus contorted,
to loosen the knot that Estrude had so carefully tied.
Felda refused to help her until she consented to look at

herself in the mirror, and then she wasn't so sure that she wanted to change, after all.

Granted, the costume was uncomfortable, almost unbearably so. But even Martine had to admit that it was beautiful. Or rather, that she was beautiful in it. She had thought that the gown would make her look as compressed as she felt, but it actually exaggerated rather than minimized her curves. She looked like a statue cast in a silver: a statue of a regal, straight-backed young woman with high breasts, a narrow waist, and slender, rounded hips.

Estrude then produced a long sash of braided silver cords strung with pearls, which she looped around Martine's waist and tied low in front, followed by a mantle of silver brocade. The vision was now complete, and Martine couldn't bear to destroy it. She would put up with the discomfort for one day. For one day she would look like a gleaming goddess—a Valkyrie.

Estrude tried to get her to wear a barbette, but this Martine refused. Instead, she had Felda plait her hair into two long, heavy braids, over which she wore a sheer veil topped by a circlet of silver filigree. Martine could tell that her stubbornness angered Estrude. So be it. Although Estrude's gifts were generous, Martine bristled at the woman's condescension. She had dressed Martine as she would have a child, or a doll. Martine knew that Estrude cared for her not in the least; Martine existed as something to adorn for Estrude's own amusement, and then ignore. Already Martine had learned that men alone commanded Estrude's full attention. Other women were, like herself, ornamental vessels for men to fill or leave empty, as they chose.

From the chapel, the betrothal party proceeded on foot to the riverbank east of the castle, where they would celebrate with a midday feast and some hawking. Godfrey, Olivier, Thorne, Guy, and Peter all carried hooded birds of prey on their fists, even during the service. Martine knew that it was usual to take the birds almost everywhere one went; it accustomed them to the company of people. Still, she thought them a peculiar sight in church.

The entire household had turned out for the ceremony, even Geneva. She had a wan, irritated look about her, as if she had been bullied into participating. Of the women present, only she had taken no care with her appearance. Her hair was concealed in a muslin turban, and she wore a discolored white tunic. But she had left her chamber and shown up, and Ailith acted as if it were the most exciting event of her life. On the way to the river she danced and skipped around her mother, laughing and tugging at her, clearly thrilled to see her up and dressed. Geneva ignored her daughter until the child took up the long sleeves of her tunic and began flapping them back and forth, as she had Martine's the day before. Far from being charmed, Geneva wheeled around and yanked them from Ailith's grasp, hissing, "Stop that!"

The day was mild and clear. Puffball clouds made stately progress across the sky, propelled by a clover-scented breeze. The clover grew in sprawling blankets in the meadow east of Harford Castle, among myriad wildflowers and wind-borne grasses. This meadow was separated from the village and castle by the river, upon the rocky banks of which grew hawthorne in spiny bushes as tall as apple trees. Along the eastern bank Martine could see long trestle tables draped in white linen and shaded by a white silken canopy that flapped in the breeze.

In order to get to the eastern bank, one had to cross the river. It was spanned by a narrow wooden bridge, but Edmond chose not to use it. Instead, he trotted a few yards downstream to where an outcropping of boulders rose from the rushing waters, forming the apex of a craggy waterfall about twenty feet high. Lifting his ankle-length maroon tunic, he made powerful leaps from boulder to boulder, some of which were separated by a wide expanse of churning water. Oblivious to the risk, he sprang carelessly ahead, purple mantle and black hair flying, while Ailith clapped and cheered.

Downstream from the waterfall, a natural dam had formed from fallen logs and uprooted hawthorne bushes. As a result of this dam, the part of the river into which the waterfall emptied had widened into a kind of pond, so deep that it looked like a bottomless, boiling cauldron. Martine cringed to think of what would happen to Edmond should a slip of the foot pitch him into the murky, roiling depths of that pond. Several times Martine thought he couldn't possibly reach the next boulder, but he always landed with surefooted grace before springing quickly ahead.

He looked much less like an infidel today, Martine thought, watching him from the bridge. With his well-brushed hair and long, ceremonial tunic, he seemed quite civilized, and extremely handsome. Had he not fidgeted so during the betrothal ceremony, he might almost have appeared dignified. He had seemed to vibrate with suppressed energy; she could feel it when they held hands to pledge their intent. She had known other young men his age—students of Rainulf's—but none had seemed quite so jumpy. Then again, they were scholars immersed in academia. Edmond was unschooled, a creature of nature, hunter and animal both.

Bernard whooped his praise when Edmond reached the other side, and Edmond grinned back at his brother with pride, adoration in his eyes. He never once looked in her direction, yet Martine did feel someone's curious eyes upon her.

It was Thorne, standing some distance away, watching her from beneath the canopy as she gazed at Edmond. She realized Thorne might misinterpret her gaze as one of admiration or tenderness—or even blossoming love. Ridiculous, of course. Edmond was beautiful to look upon, but so were many things and creatures for which Martine would never feel love. When he had held her hand during the ceremony, she had felt not the slightest thrill, only a vague cramp in her wrist and a desire for the whole spectacle to be over with.

"Don't you care for venison, my dear?" Lord Godfrey asked.

Martine considered the untouched plateful of meat that Edmond had sliced for her. Whenever she looked at it, she saw the pain-crazed eyes of the stag that Bernard and his men had tormented for sport the day before. "I've lost my taste for it, Sire."

"The next course will suit you, I'm sure," he said, nodding toward the cooking pits that had been dug into the field several yards away. A team of young men turned a long spit impaled with the boar that Edmond

had killed for their betrothal dinner. Black, greasy
smoke rose from the pits to stain the blue sky.

Feeling the sting of bile in her throat, Martine quickly
turned away and took a sip from the goblet of Rhenish
wine that she shared with Edmond. She sat at the high
table between Lord Godfrey and her betrothed, who had
left her side some time ago to join some of his brother's
men for wrestling and foot-fighting in the meadow. Next
to Godfrey, in a grand, high-backed, chair, sat the earl,
Olivier. Martine was surprised to find him on such
friendly terms with Bernard, but Godfrey explained that
his elder son had been fostered out to the earl at an
early age for knightly training, and the two had therefore
grown quite close. Martine had never seen any man as
fat as Olivier, nor as red in the face. His wife, plump
and pink, was a female version of her husband. Several
of the neighboring barons—all vassals of Olivier's—sat
with their families at tables lined up perpendicular to
the high table.

Rainulf settled next to Martine, in the chair vacated
by Edmond. Pointing, he said, "Look at Ailith."

The child had climbed on top of an empty bench and
commenced to twirl around in circles, her arms out.
"Mama!" she squealed. "Look at me! I'm a dancing girl!
Mama!" Geneva disgustedly shook her head and looked
away.

"She's so desperate for her mother's attention," Rainulf said. " 'Tis sad to see her try so hard, for naught."

Thorne had been watching as well, and now he crossed
to Ailith, lifted her from the bench, and wrapped her in
his arms. She kicked and squirmed, and Martine heard
him say, "You might have fallen off the bench and
ended up looking like me." He lowered his head so that
she could get a better view of the wound on his forehead, an ugly cut amid blue-black swelling. "You
wouldn't want that, would you?" Ailith ceased her struggles while she examined the injury, wide-eyed.

Godfrey said, "She's like a wild animal, that child. In
a boy, one expects a bit of temper. 'Tis only natural. My
sons were always in one scrape or another. My Beatrix
was the only one who could handle them." He smiled
wistfully, his rheumy eyes focused far back in time, then
turned to face Martine, a sad and serious look on his

face. "You see you make me some grandsons, my lady. I've already told Edmond I expect a boy within the year."

Martine blinked, speechless. Thorne, having evidently heard the baron's statement, met her gaze briefly, his expression pensive.

"A boy, do you hear?" the baron continued. "Someone to carry on the title. For every grandson you give me, I'll deed you a choice piece of land. In a few years, you'll have doubled your bride price."

Hardly a compelling offer, thought Martine, since whatever lands she owned, including her bride price, would be Edmond's to dispose of as he pleased during his lifetime. Wives had no control over their property until their husbands died, and given Edmond's youth and obvious good health, she did not expect widowhood to be soon in coming.

Such considerations seemed to escape Estrude, however. Leaning forward on her elbows, she said, " 'Tis a handsome offer, my lord. Will I earn such bounty as well, if I produce a son?"

Bernard, next to her, growled, "You don't quite get the point, do you, my dear? You're never going to produce a son, and everybody knows it by now. 'Twas the only creative act you were ever called upon to perform—certainly the only thing I ever expected of you—and you just weren't up to it."

Crimson-faced, Estrude sat back in her chair.

Bernard absently twirled his jeweled eating knife between two long, slender fingers. "In desperation, my father is now using my own birthright to bribe the lady Martine into doing the job which I brought you all the way from Flanders fourteen years ago to do." He chuckled humorlessly. "If she proves exceedingly fertile, I just may end up with no barony to inherit."

Thorne had taken Ailith out into the meadow as soon as Bernard began speaking, apparently sensing that his words would be unsuitable for the child's ears. Eager to avert her gaze from Bernard's ugly sneer, Martine watched the child and the falconer, hand in hand, he pointing out blossoms and she picking them. His tenderness with Ailith surprised her, considering his commanding and self-contained nature. It seemed he only let down his guard with the young girl who reminded him of—what was his sister's name? Louise. Why had he been so reticent to talk about her?

The other guests pretended not to hear Bernard's public humiliation of his wife, although no one spoke. They all looked down at their meals except for Clare, who gazed at Bernard as if in a trance. When Estrude said, in a tremulous whisper, "I'm only thirty," Martine turned to look at her, as did everyone beneath the canopy.

Stabbing the knife into the table, Bernard bellowed, "You're only barren and useless! You should consider yourself lucky I've kept you on here out of pity instead of sending you back to Flanders. I've often been tempted, and may yet do so. Ask my sister how it feels to be sent packing. If bribery can produce a son, perhaps fear can, as well."

That he would stage such an outburst on such an occasion and in front of so many people shocked Martine, but seemed to surprise no one else. The rest of the company looked as if they had heard it all before, and no doubt they had.

Estrude, still blushing in shame and frustration, sat staring into the distance beyond the river. Suddenly she looked puzzled and, squinting, said, "Who invited Lord Neville?"

"Don't tell me . . ." the baron groaned, as all heads turned toward the river. Crossing the small bridge on horseback was a tall, angular, opulently dressed man accompanied by a small woman in shimmering silks and barbette. They dismounted and came to pay their respects, first to Olivier, then to Godfrey.

Neville's gaze took in the canopy, the richly dressed guests, the lavishly appointed tables, abundant food, and dozens of servants. He looked perhaps forty, with a blond beard trained into a long point. On his head he wore a snug purple coif.

With a slight nod toward Godfrey, he said, "Had I known you were entertaining, Sire, I'd have chosen another time to pay my call." Behind him, eyes rolled.

His wife was pale and jumpy. Her eyes darted back and forth between Godfrey and the earl, and her clasped hands were actually shaking. She wasn't just embarrassed at having arrived uninvited; she was frightened. Martine wondered why.

Godfrey mumbled something civil but meaningless and called for two fresh place settings. The cooks approached him, presenting for his approval the boar's head on a platter. He nodded and yawned. The pages served the boar, although many of the guests, having eaten their fill, had left their seats.

Thorne returned from the meadow and handed Rainulf a book. "Thank you for the loan. 'Tis more pleasant to wake a falcon when one has a book for company during the long night." He stood on the other side of the high table, directly opposite Martine, tall and elegant in a russet tunic bisected by a tooled black leather belt from which hung his sheathed sword, a symbol of his knighthood. As she appraised him discreetly, she saw him glance in her direction, then hurriedly look away.

Father Simon appeared behind Thorne. He stood on his toes to peer over the Saxon's big shoulder at the book. "Cicero's *De Amictia*," he announced with a smirk. "Greek philosophy. Tell me, Father Rainulf, don't they frown on pagan writings at the University of Paris?"

Rainulf sat back and crossed his legs. " 'Tis one of the reasons I've decided to teach at Oxford when I return from Jerusalem. And Cicero was Roman, not Greek."

Simon dismissed the distinction with a shrug. "We have a monk nearby who shares your unorthodox views, Father. Perhaps you know of him."

Rainulf nodded. "Brother Matthew, prior of St. Dunstan's. I knew him well in Paris. We studied together under Abelard."

Simon smiled knowingly. "I can't say I'm surprised."

"Brother Matthew has invited me to St. Dunstan's for a long visit," Rainulf said. "Thorne has agreed to accompany me."

Bernard leaned forward and frowned. "What of the lady Martine? Won't she be going with you as well?"

Rainulf shook his head. "We thought perhaps 'twould be best if she remained at Harford. She'll want to get to know Edmond, perhaps visit the house in which they'll live and oversee the furnishing—"

"Well, of course," Bernard interjected, "she's more

than welcome, if that's what she chooses. But I hardly think it's what she'd truly prefer. After all, you'll be leaving on pilgrimage shortly after the wedding, and she won't see you for years."

"Two at the most." Martine saw Rainulf direct an uncomfortable glance toward her. Bernard was right, of course. She would have preferred to accompany her brother to the monastery, but he had insisted that the separation would be good for her.

"Two years is a long time," Bernard persisted. "Surely she'd be happier with you than here among virtual strangers."

Why, Martine wondered, did Bernard insist so strenuously that she spend the next month away from Harford? It was almost as if there were something he wanted to keep from her. She looked toward the meadow, where Edmond and another man exchanged kicks and punches while a group of Harford's "dogs" cheered rowdily. Her betrothed had discarded his tunic, and fought in his shirt and chausses. His hair hung in his face as he circled and ducked and kicked, his expression one of savage and single-minded determination. Was it Edmond that Bernard wanted to keep her from? Perhaps he thought it best that she not get to know her betrothed too well before the wedding, lest she be tempted to break the marriage contract.

Even if that were so, it didn't matter. Martine already knew she could never care for Edmond, and that was as it should be. Were she to have feelings for him, he would someday use them against her, turning their marriage into a union of sorrow for her and power for him. Martine would marry, but she would marry on her own terms. Hers would not be the jongleur's bond of love, nor Thorne's of property. She married for duty. She married for Rainulf. Eight years ago, he had given her— a terrified and lonely child—her future. And now she would return the favor.

"When are you going to St. Dunstan's?" Olivier asked Rainulf.

'Tomorrow, Sire."

Lord Neville had joined the group at the high table, and now he said, "Tomorrow? St. Dunstan's is a day's ride, Father, most of it through dense woods. Are you sure it's wise to set out on a trip like that while the bandits who murdered Anseau and Aiglentine are still at large?"

After a moment of perplexed silence, Olivier said, "Haven't you heard? Those men were captured. My hangman's spent the last two days giving them a taste of what they'll find in hell once he's stretched their filthy necks."

As Martine watched, the color drained from Neville's face. His wife's hand immediately clutched his sleeve, but he shook her off testily and said, "Captured? Nay, no one told me. Someone might have sent a messenger." He paused dramatically, preparing his audience for his next statement: "After all, I *am* Anseau's only living relative."

There was complete silence beneath the canopy. Martine knew that Anseau was believed to have left no family at all—at least, none in England. Olivier and Godfrey, frowning, consulted with each other in a whisper. Finally Godfrey shrugged, and Olivier, looking a bit taken aback, said, "I am informed that there may be a distant connection."

"Distant, perhaps," Neville conceded. "Nevertheless, I am his heir. I thought that was widely known."

The silence gave way to excited murmuring. So this was Neville's purpose in arriving uninvited at Martine and Edmond's betrothal feast—to present himself as Anseau's heir and, presumably, set the stage for his inheritance of Anseau's barony.

After a thoughtful pause, Olivier said, "This is not the time or place in which to discuss these matters, Lord Neville. You may or may not be Anseau's legitimate heir." Neville made as if to speak, but Olivier silenced him with a sharply raised hand. "Understand that the barony in question is the largest and wealthiest within my fief. Its inheritance is not a matter to be decided lightly. Assuming you are, as you claim, Anseau's only survivor and heir, rest assured that what is yours will come to you in due course. For now, I will discuss the matter no further."

Again Neville tried to speak, but Olivier turned to Godfrey and said, "Are there not betrothal gifts to be exchanged? This would be a good time, since everyone is gathered about."

Eagerly taking the cue, Godfrey called for Edmond to be summoned from the meadow and the gifts to be presented. Edmond presented Martine with a great heap of ermine skins, white with black-tipped tails, all of superb quality—a generous gift, and much admired. Estrude seemed particularly impressed, and Martine consented to allow her to trim her wedding costume with them.

Martine's gift to her betrothed, in addition to the bloodhound pups, was a chess set that Rainulf had commissioned from a renowned Danish artisan. The white pieces had been carved of whalebone; the black of ebony. What made the set so distinctive was that the kings and queens, rather than being represented by tiny figures, were small sculpted heads—miniature busts on short pedestals. The black king wore a regal crown over his short hair, his queen a barbette and veil beneath an elaborate coronet. Olivier noted that they resembled Henry and Eleanor, and Rainulf acknowledged that the resemblance had been deliberate. The earl passed the pieces around, and there were many compliments on the cleverness of the idea and the skill of the artisan.

Boyce, one bandaged arm in a sling, the other hoisting the pitcher of ale from which he drank, said, "Young Edmond's going to have to learn how to play chess now! And he hasn't even mastered draughts!"

Bernard's men laughed uproariously. Edmond laughed, too, but Martine sensed his discomfort, as if he didn't know whether to shrug off Boyce's comment as good-natured teasing, or take offense.

So, thought Martine. *He can't even play chess. Can't read and can't play chess. No wonder all he does is hunt.*

Apparently unnoticed, except by Martine, Thorne lifted the white king and queen to examine more closely. The uncrowned king, young and long-haired, he inspected briefly and put down. Cradling the queen in the palm of his large hand, he gently rubbed his thumb over its small, smoothly sculpted features—the prominent cheekbones, wide mouth, and straight, aristocratic nose. The hair was hidden beneath a tucked and twisted veil, as Martine had worn it when she had posed for the sculptor. Thorne smiled with secret pleasure at his discovery, and Peter, next to him, said, "You seem quite taken with that piece."

Thorne's eyes met Martine's and held them for a brief moment. He seemed slightly embarrassed to find that she had been watching him. Handing the chess piece to the other knight, he said, "I *am* quite taken with the workmanship. Don't you recognize her?"

Frowning, Peter examined the piece and then passed it around. Several people ventured guesses as to the lady's identity. Most thought it to represent the Virgin Mary.

Thorne laughed. " 'Tis another lady of great beauty and virtue. Our Martine of Rouen!"

There were gasps of delight and many apologies to Martine for not having recognized her image. It was curious, Martine reflected, that only Thorne had seen her face in the whalebone.

As the afternoon wore on, the clouds began to darken and fill up the sky like smoke. Martine, strolling along the edge of the river, saw, far away, the tiny figure of a horseman on the road to the castle, but paid him little mind. Bending her head, she continued to search the wildflowers for blossoms to add to the half-finished chaplet in her hand, which she wanted to finish before it began to rain. She was making it for Ailith, who followed along behind, collecting a bouquet for her mother.

Martine heard Thorne's faraway voice and squinted to make him out from the group of men hawking some distance away, where the meadow met the woods. It wasn't hard; he was by far the tallest one. A spaniel scented quarry and danced excitedly around some low bushes. The master falconer had brought not Freya, who had yet to be taught to hunt, but an experienced peregrine. He unhooded the bird, rewarding the dog with words of praise.

All afternoon, in addition to picking flowers and weaving them together, Martine had watched Thorne and his companions fly their falcons, unnoticed from her discreet vantage point at the river's edge. She wanted to know something of hawking—it would be expected of her— and found that she had already learned a great deal from this covert observation.

After giving the unhooded peregrine a few moments to get her bearings on his gauntleted fist, Thorne cast her off with a twist of his arm. She circled above the dog in graceful, ascending spirals, attaining a remarkable altitude. When she had gotten almost out of sight, the well-trained spaniel rushed the bushes, flushing a covey of grouse into the air while Thorne alerted the peregrine by means of a loud, singsong cry.

Martine's eyes, like those of the men in the meadow, immediately sought out the peregrine. Her flight ceased, and in the brief moment that followed, Martine held her breath in anticipation of the kill. Like something dropped from a great height, the peregrine dove with blinding speed, talons outstretched, toward her prey. From the distance at which Martine watched, it looked as if the two birds—falcon and grouse—collided in mid-air, the grouse dropping to the ground and the falcon soaring sharply upward.

In reality, Martine knew that the event had been nothing as random as a collision. It had been a carefully planned, flawlessly executed attack by a creature born to the purpose and trained to perfection by southern England's greatest falconer. The men in the meadow cheered as much in appreciation of Sir Thorne's mastery over the falcon as for the falcon's mastery over the grouse.

The falcon turned over in the air and dropped onto the dead grouse, but her attention was soon stolen by Thorne's shrill whistle and the lure—something heavy on the end of a cord—that he swung in circles over his head. He let the lure drop, and the peregrine flew to it and began enthusiastically pecking at it. Then he knelt close by, whistled again, and held something toward her, which Martine assumed to be a bit of meat. She flew to his fist and ate the meat, then he slipped the little hood back over her head, leaning over and tightening the braces with his teeth.

The rumbling of wooden planks on the bridge made Martine turn with a gasp. It was the horseman, the one she had seen on the road—a young man on a dun stallion that had been ridden to the point of exhaustion, judging by the foam trailing from its mouth. Reining in his sorry mount, he called to Martine, who happened to be closest, "I've a message for my lord Olivier!" Martine pointed to the meadow, and the young man took off toward the hawking party.

Sudden movement from the direction of the canopy caught her eye, and she saw Lord Neville and his wife hurrying toward their horses, which they mounted hastily and kicked into a gallop. Several of the guests stood to watch their abrupt departure, although Bernard and his men, including Edmond, were too preoccupied with drinking and storytelling to notice much else. Rainulf, standing alone just outside the canopy, stared grimly at the baron and baroness as they rode away, then turned toward the meadow, as did Martine.

The messenger dismounted and bowed to Olivier, then stood at attention while he communicated his message. Although they were far away, Martine heard the earl exclaim, "Dear God!" After a brief and impassioned exchange, all the men began striding purposefully toward the canopy, Olivier bellowing, "Detain Neville! Don't let him get away!"

Martine ran to her brother, who was standing quietly with his arms crossed, his expression sad and detached. Looking down at her, he said, "We can't hope to overtake Neville at this point. All our horses are in the stables. I can't imagine the earl will be pleased about *that*."

"I don't understand," said Martine, grabbing his arm. "What is it? What's happened?"

Gazing calmly at the distant, retreating figures of the baron and baroness, he said, "Neville had Anseau and Aiglentine killed."

Martine gasped. *"What? How do you know?"*

"They bolted like rabbits as soon as that messenger arrived looking for Olivier. My guess—and Neville's, I'd wager—is that the bandits have confessed and named him as the man who paid them for their crimes."

Martine began to understand. "Neville wanted that barony."

Rainulf nodded. "Aiglentine was about to bear a child. If she had done so, and the child had lived, Neville could never have hoped to inherit that holding. But with Anseau and Aiglentine gone, and no heir—"

Ailith's voice, shrill and insistent, piped up from the direction of the river. "Mama! Mama! Look at me!"

As Martine turned to look, she caught sight of Geneva sitting on a bench nearby. The older woman glanced toward the river, her expression of weary disinterest giving way to shock and fear as she sprang to her feet. "Ailith!" she screamed.

Martine wheeled around. Ailith stood on one of the boulders at the top of the waterfall, her arms out to the side to balance herself. After a second of stunned disbelief, Martine dropped the chaplet and ran, along with Rainulf and Geneva, toward the river, screaming the child's name.

"I'm going to jump across like Uncle Edmond did!" Ailith called out. "Watch me, Mama!"

Ignoring the screams of warning, she turned, lifted her ivory kirtle, and leaped.

Chapter 9

The boulder at which the child aimed was fairly close, but her short little legs were barely adequate for the job. Her bare feet slid and she landed on her hands and knees.

"Ailith!" Geneva screamed. "Stop that! Come back!"

Rising unsteadily, Ailith yelled, "I'll do better next time!" The next boulder was much too far away for her to reach.

Martine, at the apex of the waterfall, tossed aside her mantle and kicked off her slippers. Gingerly she stepped onto the first boulder and then the next, her eyes on the child about two yards away. The stone beneath her stockinged feet felt cold and wet, and her heart hammered in her throat.

Rainulf grabbed one long sleeve of her silver tunic and tried to pull her back. "Martine! Let me—"

"Nay! I can swim, and you can't. Let go, or I'll lose my balance."

He did, and she reached a hand out to Ailith. "Ailith, please. Take my—"

"Nay! Go away! Mama's watching! I want Mama to see!" Ailith swatted angrily at Martine, nearly throwing herself off balance.

"*Ailith!* You can't make it!" Martine looked down at the jagged boulders over which the water fell, and the bottomless pool below, nearly opaque beneath rapidly graying skies. Memories, fierce and unbidden, rushed up at her from the water's smoky depths: the apple-green gown, the horrible thing hidden beneath the surface.

In a panic, she turned to Rainulf and Geneva, standing at the water's edge, the mother clutching for support from the priest, who murmured something and crossed himself. "*Say* something to her, Rainulf! You always know what to say! *Say* something to her!"

Beyond them, in the meadow, someone broke away from the group and raced toward them—Thorne.

Suddenly Rainulf and Geneva both stretched their arms out, screaming Ailith's name. She turned and saw the child suspended, arms outstretched, like an angel in her ivory kirtle, between the two boulders.

Time moved slowly. Martine heard the dull flap of the kirtle, the rumbling of the angry waters, the musical splash as first one little foot, then another, missing the boulder, disappeared into the churning water. A sound filled Martine's ears, and she realized it was her own scream as she watched the little girl, the angel, fly into the air, rotating slowly, flung up with eerie grace by the relentless force of the river.

For a split second, as Ailith hung above the waterfall, hair flying, kirtle billowing, Martine saw her face clearly, and thought she looked directly at her, beseechingly. Then she became, not an angel, but a rag doll, bouncing once, twice, against the waterfall's jagged boulders before the frothing waters consumed her, swallowing her whole.

"*Ailith!*" Martine didn't know whether it was her voice, or that of Rainulf or Geneva, or all of them, that screamed the child's name. With numb hands, she flung her circlet and veil aside, then grabbed her heavy tunic and tried to pull it up and off, but it had been too tightly laced. Poised at the edge of the boulder, looking down, she thought, in terror and panic, *I can't do this.* Then she closed her eyes and saw Ailith's eyes as she fell, pleading for help.

Blindly she sprang from the boulder, half expecting to hit the rocks beneath the waterfall on her way down, as Ailith had. But her spring had been powerful, and the first thing she hit was icy water, which bubbled around her, closing over her head and pummeling her, its force squeezing the breath out of her. Consumed with terror, she struggled to the surface. She heard her name, and Ailith's, yelled by people on the shore. *I must be calm,* she thought. *Ailith needs me.* She took a deep breath and dove, swimming underwater with all her strength away from the waterfall and toward the calmer waters downstream, where Ailith would have been carried.

Martine peered through the green-tinged, shadowy water, deep and wide as a lake. The layers of wool, silk, and fur in which she was laced felt leaden, weighing her down as she swam. She tried to ignore the wild drumming of her heart and the growing pressure within her lungs.

The sides and bottom of the pool were encrusted with boulders, rotten tree limbs, and bits of debris—wine jugs, crockery, a rusty scythe—all festooned with green algae. Up ahead, through the obscure waters, loomed the tangle of hawthorne bushes and fallen trees that formed the river's natural dam.

A shimmer of white caught her eye, and she made for it, her overtaxed arms and legs struggling against their confining garments to propel her, so slowly, forward. *Please, God,* she prayed, *let it be Ailith.*

It was. But at the sight of her, Martine's heart lurched.

Her little body—senseless at best, and possibly lifeless as well—hung suspended in the cold gloom, her arms posed gracefully above her head, as if stilled in the act of dancing. Her eyes were closed; her mouth hung slackly open. She had a raw scrape on her chin and an open cut on her forehead, from which blood seeped, forming a pink cloud in the greenish water.

The dam had stopped her progress downstream, which was fortunate, but in the process, the bottom half of her kirtle had become entangled in the hawthornes' spiky branches. With her lungs close to bursting, Martine grabbed the child under her arms and pulled, again and again, but she didn't budge. Looking more closely, she saw the hundreds of needle-sharp thorns embedded in the thin ivory wool.

Quickly she swam toward the sunlight above, gasping for air as she broke the surface. People were gathered on the riverbank, including Thorne, close by, whipping his brown undertunic over his head. Beneath it, he wore a white linen shirt and brown chausses.

"Sir Thorne!" she called hoarsely.

"My lady! Thank God you're all right! Did you find—"

She nodded impatiently. "Your sword! Bring it!"

As he slid the weapon from its scabbard, she filled her

lungs with air and dove toward Ailith. The child was as she had left her, and with dismay, Marine saw how deathly pale she was, how still, how like a shell without a soul. *Dear God, please don't let her be dead,* she begged, wrapping her arms around the little body and holding her tight.

The hand on her shoulder made her start, and she turned to find the Saxon, holding his sword. Martine pointed out the snagged kirtle and Thorne, with careful aim, swiftly cut the wool loose from the hawthornes' grip. Dropping the sword, which floated to the river bottom, he took the child in his arms and swam with her to the surface. Martine set out to follow him, but her ascent was stopped short before it even began.

She couldn't move! She pumped her arms and legs furiously, not comprehending, in her sudden alarm, what was wrong. When she looked down and saw her own garments held fast by the hawthornes' tiny claws, her alarm turned to terror. Up above, Thorne swam away from her with swift, sure strokes.

She tugged at her tunic, then reached down to try to pry the thorns loose, but they pierced her fingers, drawing blood, and for every one she loosened, two more took its place. Below, on the river bottom, Thorne's unreachable sword glowed dimly, tauntingly. Her lungs burned and her heart slammed painfully in her chest.

She knew. She had always known, always, that she would die by drowning—struggling in terror, waiting for the moment when her lungs would fill with water.

Trying to ignore the pain and pressure in her chest, she reached behind, groping for the knot that Estrude had tied. Useless. With both hands, she yanked at the neck of the tunic, but the heavy silver braid could not be torn. Mindlessly she thrashed, wrestling with her prison of silk and wool, as bubbles of air escaped from her nose and mouth. Her chest spasmed and her throat contracted as she resisted the instinct to inhale.

She closed her eyes. *Don't breathe don't breathe don't breathe don't breathe.* She let her body go limp . . . *don't breathe* . . . let the water embrace her, suspend her . . . *don't breathe* . . .

White light filled her vision. She lost all track of time, all sense of space, all fear . . . until a pair of large hands gripped her shoulders, breaking the spell, and she opened her eyes.

Thorne. His expression of dread gave way to relief as he took her face in his hands and, closing his eyes, pressed his forehead to hers. Then he released her, retrieved his sword, and swiftly set about cutting away the fur and braid-trimmed hems of her tunic and kirtle. The urge to breathe was all but irresistible, and Martine shook as she struggled for control.

Thorne freed her from the hawthornes' clutches, and with an arm around her waist, swam with her to the surface. Gulping great lungfuls of air, they struggled to the shore. There, Rainulf and Albin waited, the rest of the guests having regrouped near the canopy. From their direction came a dreadful wail, like that of an animal in pain.

"Martine!" Rainulf exclaimed, running toward her. "Thank God!"

Her legs were quaking so badly that they could barely support her, and she knew that she would collapse without Thorne to hold her up. "Ailith! Where is she?"

The knight and the priest exchanged a grim look. With a hand on Martine's arm, Rainulf said, "She's gone."

At first Martine's overwrought mind refused to accept her brother's meaning. "Gone where? Back to the castle?"

For a moment, neither man spoke. Then Thorne took her by the shoulders. "My lady ..." he began, but seemed unable to finish. He didn't have to. Martine could read the grief in his transparent eyes, and when he looked toward the group near the canopy, her gaze followed his.

They stood in a circle, gentlefolk and servants together, silent and still, their heads bowed. From within their midst came the wailing, as well as a man's steady, low murmuring. Someone moved, creating a gap in the circle. Through it, Martine saw one of the white linen tablecloths spread out on the grass, and atop that, the ivory skirt of Ailith's kirtle, sliced off raggedly at the hem, and, emerging from the kirtle, the two little bare feet, pale and still.

"No," she choked, half running on her quivering legs,

shaking off Thorne's attempt to hold her back. He released her, but followed close behind.

"Martine," Rainulf called, following as well, "you did everything you could. You risked your life for her. 'Twas God's will that she be taken—"

"To hell with God's will!" she spat out, as the circle parted to admit her, some of the servants crossing themselves at her heretical words.

Ailith lay on her back with her arms crossed over her chest as Father Simon administered last rites. At the sight of her—her blue-gray skin and violet lips, the ugly wounds on her face—a moan of disbelief arose within Martine. *She can't be dead.*

The wailing came from Geneva. She crouched over her daughter's inert form, her face buried in her hands, rocking back and forth as she sobbed and shrieked her grief. "My baby, my baby! Please, God, give me back my baby! I'm sorry, I'm so sorry! Just give me back my baby!" Martine had never witnessed such uncurbed despair. Rainulf, kneeling next to the distracted woman, put his arms around her and spoke soft, insistent words into her ear, but she seemed unaware of his presence.

Martine's legs gave out. Sinking to her knees next to the child, she laid a hand on her cold cheek. "Oh, God," she whispered. "This can't be." She uncrossed the limp little arms and rested the other hand on her chest to check for breathing, but felt no movement of any kind.

Father Simon scowled at her as he mumbled his prayers, and she heard whispered comments about her hands from the onlookers. They were both covered, front and back, with myriad tiny lacerations, the result of her struggles with the hawthornes. They bled badly, but oddly enough, Martine felt no pain.

Ailith's coloring clearly indicated that she had been starved for air. Her skin and lips looked like that of a baby boy Martine had helped deliver in Paris. He couldn't breathe, but the physician, having found a heartbeat, saved him by breathing into his mouth.

Martine leaned over and put an ear to Ailith's chest, but could hear nothing but her own ragged breathing and Geneva's lamentations. Pressing two fingers against the side of Ailith's throat, she closed her eyes and held her breath. Presently she felt a faint pressure beneath her fingertips, and then another. A pulse! Contrary to appearances, she wasn't dead yet.

What now? With the baby, the physician had covered both the baby's mouth and nose with his own mouth and blown into them. But Ailith's mouth and nose were too far apart for that, so she pinched the child's nose closed, covered the little open mouth with her own, and blew. Ailith's chest rose, and Martine felt encouraged. Her optimism waned, however, when she heard a faint gurgling sound, which suggested the presence of water in her lungs.

Father Simon ceased his praying. The whispered comments became a buzz of collective shock and bewilderment. Geneva began raining frenzied punches on Martine's shoulders and back, screaming *"Leaving my baby alone! What are you doing to my baby?"*

As Martine raised her head to take a breath, she saw Rainulf seize Geneva's fists and draw her into his arms. "It's all right," he assured her. "She just needs to feel she's done all she can." Geneva collapsed in his embrace, sobbing, and he held her tightly, stroking her and whispering comforting words.

Martine forced breath after breath into the child's lungs, commanding herself to think of nothing but the mechanics of what she did—not of what people might think of her for doing it, and not even whether she would succeed in making Ailith breathe again. Especially not that, because she couldn't bear to think that she would fail.

"My lady!" Father Simon exclaimed. "What are you doing? This is outrageous! Someone stop her!"

"Leave her alone," Thorne commanded, standing between Martine and the horrified priest.

"Nay!" Simon cried, reaching toward Martine. He probably meant to push her away, but before he could, Thorne yanked him abruptly to his feet.

"Get away from here," he ordered, roughly shoving the priest, who stumbled and fell. Raising her head to take a breath, Martine saw that Peter and Guy had emerged from the crowd, their swords drawn in automatic and unquestioning allegiance to Thorne.

"The child is dead!" Simon exclaimed, gaining his feet. He glanced toward Bernard as if for support, but the other man just looked on passively, smiling his humorless smile. "To attempt to bring her back is unholy. The devil's work."

"You're wrong," Thorne said. "If the devil is here today, 'tis you who act as his instrument, not the lady Martine." His right hand contracted into a fist. "Now, leave."

Simon's lip curled. "You wouldn't strike a man of the cloth."

From the corner of her eye, as she blew into Ailith's mouth, Martine saw the Saxon's big fist whip through the air toward the priest's astonished face. The punch connected with a dull crack, and suddenly Father Simon lay sprawled on his back, howling and shielding his face with his hands.

"Wrong again," Thorne said dryly, returning to tower protectively over Martine and Ailith. Bernard and his men laughed uproariously as Father Simon writhed, blood from his nostrils spattering the white tablecloth.

Pausing to take a breath, Martine heard a new sound, a kind of liquid rattling, coming from Ailith. It sounded like a death rattle, which she had heard more than once in Paris. Alarmed, she put an ear to the little chest. The sound came again, and again. It had a strained quality, as if the result of great effort.

Thorne crouched next to her. "What is it?"

"I think she's trying to breathe," Martine whispered.

The child's small body began to twitch convulsively. Vaguely aware of the onlookers' startled gasps, Martine took hold of Ailith and, with Thorne's help, turned her onto her side and held her there. Spasms shuddered through Ailith, and water poured from her mouth. Her indrawn breath grated raggedly, and then she coughed with a kind of hoarse croak, spewing water. Again she coughed, and again the water spilled from her mouth.

"Ailith!" Geneva cried. "Ailith! My baby! Ailith!" She strained toward her daughter, but Rainulf, his eyes wide with amazement, held her back. The gasps became a chorus of murmurs and exclamations.

Presently Ailith's eyelids fluttered open. She blinked, as if the light hurt her eyes, and coughed once more, weakly.

"Thank God," Rainulf said. He smiled at Martine,

and it warmed her heart to see the joy and pride in his eyes. Releasing Geneva, who gathered her daughter in her arms and covered her face with tears and kisses, he executed a solemn sign of the cross.

Many of those watching did the same, but in their eyes Martine saw not joy but bewilderment and even fear. She heard whispered comments about sorcery, but paid them little mind.

Let them wallow in their ignorance, she thought exhaustedly. *Ailith is alive, and that's all that matters.*

Thorne slammed the hawk house door behind him and stripped quickly, peeling off his sodden chausses and shirt and pulling on a pair of dark linen braies. The long trousers were threadbare, but they were loose and comfortable and, best of all, dry.

Shuttering the windows against the rain, he thought how late it seemed, although the sun had yet to set and supper was only now being served in the great hall—a supper that he had no appetite for. The rain clouds blocked the late afternoon sunlight, giving the illusion of a night sky. His overwhelming fatigue only fueled that sense of lateness. It had been an arduous day.

First, the betrothal ceremony. He recalled how his heart had twisted in his chest as he watched the lady Martine coolly accept the white glove from young Edmond, take his hand in hers, and speak the words that sealed their betrothal. He should have felt relief at being one step closer to earning his manor. Instead he felt only profound regret.

How, in the space of two days, had this woman so thoroughly stolen into his every waking thought? It was a bewildering dilemma, and a troubling one, not only because his ambitions depended on her marriage to Edmond, but because it would be foolish indeed to allow himself to start caring so much for anyone. Caring made one vulnerable. He had cared for little Louise, cared deeply, and it had all but stripped him of his sanity when she left the world. Her death taught him a painful but valuable lesson: Love had a price. If one did not want to pay it, it was best to school one's emotions, to keep strong feelings in check.

Yet he craved Martine, craved her as he had never

craved another woman. There was, of course, no question of his ever having her, even once. All he could do was pray, with all his heart, that his desire for her would diminish over time. Perhaps when Lord Godfrey deeded him his land and he reaped the benefits of her union with Edmond, he would be able to rein in his unruly feelings.

First the betrothal ceremony and then the sobering news from Olivier's messenger that Anseau and Aiglentine's killers had implicated Lord Neville in their crime. Upon their return to the castle that afternoon, the earl and his barons conferred and decided to allow the murderous Neville his freedom for the time being, deeming it unseemly to incarcerate one of noble blood without proof of guilt. Neville would have to be summoned to King Henry's royal council, and if his peers found him guilty, he would then be punished.

The best he could hope for would be a pilgrimage of penance to Jerusalem. His head would be shaved and he would be fitted with neck and wrist chains forged from his own armor, then forced to walk barefoot, alone, from one shrine to the next for years, possibly decades. The worst—if Henry felt not particularly disposed toward mercy—would be the same treatment accorded the bandits who had done his bidding: preparatory torture followed by a public hanging, a great disgrace both to himself and his family. The most likely sentence would be a swift beheading with an ax, a more humane and respectable form of execution than the noose.

Would Neville come willingly to Henry's tribunal? Knowing him as he did, Thorne thought it unlikely. Had it been up to him, he would have organized a party that very afternoon to seek out the cur and arrest him. Unfortunately, the decision had not been his, although the consequences might; as Godfrey's soldier, Thorne must needs also fight for his overlord, Olivier, and his king, Henry. Should Neville find some way to resist justice, Thorne would be among those called to enforce it, a prospect he did not fear, but also did not relish.

After tending to the needs of his falcons, he lay facedown on his narrow bed and closed his eyes.

Martine's face floated before him, pale and terrified in the dark waters. Groaning, he rolled onto his back and studied the thatched ceiling of his little hut, chilled by how close she had come to death. Her death would have meant Ailith's death as well, for only she had detected the flickering spark of life in the little body. Everyone else, Thorne included, had assumed the child was already gone.

Someone began knocking at the door. Let them knock. He needn't answer. He had no need of company and much need of sleep.

He covered his face with his hands. Could he have borne Ailith's death? Losing her would have been like losing his sister all over again. In a way, Louise lived for him through Ailith, softening the hurt that lingered in his heart, the hurt that would never leave, but could at least be made bearable. Ailith had done that for him.

The knocking ceased. Rising, Thorne dipped a rag in the washbowl and bathed his face, arms, and chest. Exhaustion had overcome him, and he wanted nothing more than to sink into a dreamless sleep.

Rain pattered softly on the thatch and rattled the window shutters. A gust of wind blew one open and he went to close it, noticing as he did the dark form walking away from the hawk house toward the keep—his unwelcome caller. He wore a long, hooded mantle and walked with his head down against the wind and rain. Who would have crossed the bailey in this weather to see him? Perhaps it had been important business. Feeling a small tug of remorse, he squinted into the rain. Was it Rainulf? No, he wasn't quite tall enough.

Another gust whipped the caller's hood back off his head—*her* head, Thorne now realized, in the brief moment before she replaced the hood. A very brief moment indeed, but he had seen the pale blond hair—that extraordinary hair.

He was out the door before he knew it, sprinting, half clothed, in the rain toward Martine.

Chapter 10

Thorne grabbed Martine's shoulder and she turned, startled, her hood flying off again. He pulled it back into place for her and, with a hand on her arm, guided her quickly back to the hawk house and through the door, shutting it firmly behind them.

For a moment they stared at each other in the dim room. The hesitance in her eyes surprised him; she had always seemed so sure of herself. Whatever the reason for her coming to him like this, she clearly found it difficult. Her smooth face, drained of color, looked eerily like the whalebone chess piece carved in her image. In the little sculpture, however, her hair was bound beneath a nunlike headdress. The Martine who stood before him wore hers loose, falling halfway to the floor in unkempt flaxen tendrils. She was beautiful, achingly beautiful. How could he ever have thought her plain?

Finally she spoke. "I had decided you weren't here."

"I was sleeping."

She frowned. "I'm sorry. I didn't meant to—"

"No, no, that's all right." Her mantle was soaked through; taking a step toward her, he reached for the gold brooch to unfasten it. She stiffened, and he drew back. "I just—I only meant—your mantle is wet, and I thought—" He stammered like some weak-minded boy. What must she think of him?

'Oh. Of course." She tried to undo the brooch herself, but her hands, heavily wound in strips of bleached linen, were unequal to the task.

"Allow me," he said, and with chivalrous reserve, waited for her nod before unpinning the mantle and hanging it on a hook. She had replaced her ruined betrothal costume with loose, dark garments.

From the corner of his eye, he saw her glance at his

bare torso and then look away, two bright spots of pink staining her pale cheeks. Thorne smiled inwardly. He had grown quite fond of her blushes, the only hint he ever had of her true feelings. Nevertheless, he took a shirt off its hook and pulled it over his head, then lit two candles.

She shivered. He motioned for her to sit in his large chair, then poured a stiff brandy and offered it to her. Holding the cup gingerly with both bandaged hands, she took a sip.

"I can fetch some coals for the brazier," he offered.

She shook her head. "Don't trouble yourself. I'll be fine."

Indicating her hands with a nod of his head, he said, "Do they hurt much?"

"A bit."

"Then you must finish that brandy quickly. 'Twill dull the pain."

She looked into the cup as if weighing a decision, then tilted it to her lips and swallowed its contents quickly. He took it from her and reached for the jug again.

"Nay," she said. "I'll fall asleep if I have more."

He conjured up an image of her asleep in bed, then remembered what Ailith had said about her sleeping in the nude, and cleared his throat. Sitting on the edge of his bed, he asked, "How was Ailith when you left her?"

Martine allowed herself a tired smile. "Still asleep in her mother's arms."

Thorne nodded slowly. "She'd be dead now if it weren't for you, my lady. I've rarely seen such courage as you displayed today. She means a great deal to me. I wanted to tell you ... I wanted to thank you."

She nodded, meeting his eye. "I want to say something. I know what you think of me. I know you think I'm ... spoiled and ... and willful and—"

"Nay, my lady."

"Please don't deny it. It's what everyone thinks, and I know you're no different." She looked into her lap, where her white-sheathed hands rested atop the dark wool of her tunic. "Perhaps I am that way. I know that some things are hard for me, hard to say. Especially to ..." She glanced uncomfortably at Thorne, then looked back at her hands.

Especially to me? wondered Thorne. *Especially to men?* But she never completed the thought.

Martine shook her head somberly. "I haven't been fair to you. In truth, I ... I didn't like you or trust you. But now ... now I feel differently. I hope very much that you can forgive my past rudeness and that we can be friends."

Thorne took a deep breath to ensure that his voice would be steady. "I'd like that very much."

She met his eyes and held them, her expression grave. "Thank you for saving my life."

"You're welcome."

He thought sadly that perhaps she would prepare to leave now, but she didn't. For a moment it seemed she might speak, but then she paused, biting her lip. He reflected on her hesitation, wondering what else she wanted to tell him, and why it should be difficult for her.

She struck him as the kind of person who said what she thought. If anything, she could be too outspoken at times, lacking in the diplomacy one expected from a wellborn lady. Some men might object to that—Bernard, certainly, and perhaps Edmond as well. But Thorne had little use for the smooth ways of wellborn ladies, and he found her frankness appealing.

After a period of silence, he said, "Where did you learn to swim?"

Staring at one of the candles, her voice distant, she said, "I grew up near a small lake."

"Near your father's castle? Or perhaps you meant near the convent."

She tensed, and Thorne instantly regretted the question. He had only meant to relax her with pleasant conversation, but she didn't know that. To her, it must have sounded as if he were still intent on interrogating her, unearthing her secrets.

"Neither," she answered.

He rose. "I didn't mean to—"

"There's something else I need to tell you."

"Nay." He closed the distance between them in one long stride and knelt at her feet. Covering her hands with both of his, he implored her with his eyes to look at him. She did. "There's nothing you need to tell me. You owe me nothing. I really didn't mean to—"

"I owe you nothing?" She shook her head, her brows drawn together. "You saved my life."

He lifted one hand to her hair, brushing it away from her face and tucking it behind her ears. It felt cool and smooth and heavy. "You have a right to choose what you reveal to others," he said quietly, stroking her cheek. "I never should have tried to pry information out of you. And it's quite true that you owe me nothing. What happened at the river has nothing to do with ... with what you want to tell me."

She looked away from him. "You don't know what I want to tell you."

Taking her by the chin, he turned her to face him. Softly he said, "You are not Lord Jourdain's legitimate child." The tension in her hands, and her indrawn breath, provided his confirmation.

"You knew?"

He rubbed his thumbs gently over the thick padding of linen strips that crisscrossed neatly over her hands. "Not for sure. But it did seem the most likely possibility. Is that what you wanted to tell me? Is that why you came here?"

She nodded. "That, and to thank you. I felt that you deserved to know. It was wrong to keep it from you, especially after what you did for me. If this were found out after the marriage, it would serve you badly, and that would ill repay you for having saved my life."

Mention of her upcoming marriage made Thorne acutely conscious of her indiscretion in coming here, and his equal indiscretion in sitting at her feet with his hands enclosing hers. Nevertheless, he made no move to release them. He couldn't let her go; he needed to touch her. And he told himself that she needed the comfort.

Earlier, at the river, as Thorne had been wrapping Ailith in his mantle and preparing to carry her back to the keep, Martine began to shiver most alarmingly. The magnitude of what she had been through, and the toll it had taken on her, suddenly became clear to him. It seemed that her facade of remote self-confidence might be thinner than he had imagined.

He'd seen her look toward Rainulf, but although her brother asked after her most solicitously, he'd been too preoccupied with Geneva to offer any real comfort to his sister. Thorne's instinct had been to rush to her and take her in his arms, to soothe her trembling with his warmth and strength—but it was an instinct he couldn't possibly have acted on. Even had he not had Ailith to take care of, such an embrace, however well intentioned, would have been scandalous.

Not half so scandalous, however, as this revelation of her illegitimacy, should it become public. That she had been willing to confide in him touched him deeply. "Does Rainulf know you're telling me all this?" he asked.

She nodded. "He never wanted to keep the truth a secret from you—although it never seemed to bother him to keep it from everyone else."

"How was that possible?"

" 'Twas easy while I was at the convent. Few people knew I existed. Then, when I joined him in Paris last summer, he introduced me as his half sister and left it at that."

"And they all assumed you were the child of your father's second marriage."

She nodded. "Just as Lady Estrude did. But that would have been impossible. Jourdain's widow—his second wife, the lady Blanche—is but one and twenty years of age."

"Three years older than you." Thorne shook his head and smiled ruefully, ashamed at having assumed so much and investigated so little, especially considering the importance of this marriage and his part in arranging it. "That *would* be a clever trick."

She looked down, her expression pained. "Rainulf is afraid you'll feel deceived. He's afraid you'll hate him."

He closed both hands over hers and squeezed gently. "I can't imagine his ever doing anything bad enough to make me hate him. And I don't feel deceived, not really. Misled, perhaps, but only because of his love for you. He's incapable of true deception."

She looked at him with wonder, her eyes brilliant in the candlelight. "You're quite as forgiving as he is!"

"Is that so surprising?"

"Everything about you is surprising," she answered quickly. Then, as if she had said too much, she looked down, and that hot, telling blush came again to her

cheeks. Her troubled gaze rested on his hands covering
hers. Reluctantly he withdrew them, reaching for the
brandy jug to defuse the awkwardness of the moment.

"Another cup? I won't let you fall asleep." She nodded and he poured one for each of them. "Your mother,
then, was . . ." He had hoped Martine would complete
the thought and elaborate to whatever degree she found
acceptable. Instead, she inspected the dancing flame of
the candle thoughtfully and at length. Very well. Although consumed with curiosity, he would not press her.
He swallowed his brandy in one gulp, and Martine
promptly did the same, then offered her cup for a refill.
He obliged her, and she gripped the full cup with both
hands and stared into it.

"My mother . . ." she began.

'You needn't—'

"My mother was Jourdain's mistress." This, of course,
hardly shocked him, given her illegitimacy, but to speak
of it appeared to distress her greatly. It suddenly dawned
on Thorne that this might be the first time she had said
those words, had ever admitted out loud that her mother
had not been a baroness, but the mistress of a baron.
Realizing this made him appreciate how hard this admis-
sion was for her, and why she had felt the need to steel
herself with strong drink in order to say the words.

"Her name was Adela," she said. "Her father was a
Paris wine merchant. He sold her to Jourdain for a handful of silver when she was very young." She swallowed
some brandy. "I know that now. I know everything, the
whole horrible . . . everything." She drained her cup. "I
look back on my childhood—the first ten years, anyway—
and wonder how I could have been so naive, so—" she
lifted her cup to her mouth, found it empty, and lowered
it, "happy. I *was* happy. Life was so simple . . . until I
discovered the truth. . . ."

In the summer of Martine's tenth year, she began to
notice the same name cropping up repeatedly in her
mother's prayers.

"Mama," the child finally asked, "who's Odelina?"

Adela knelt at their wooden chest, lighting the six
rows of foul-smelling tallow candles that she had arranged on top of it. She looked up, and in her high,

girlish voice, said, "Odelina is a lady who's been very ill for a very long time."

Even at five and twenty years, Adela still looked very much the child, with her slender arms, small breasts, and enormous eyes. Martine, although just as fair in coloring, had her sire's height and presence, and seemed older than her years.

"So you're praying that she'll get better?"

Grimly Adela shook her head. "I'm praying that she'll die."

Martine gasped. "Die! Why? Because she's in pain and you want to end her suffering?"

"Nay," Adela replied, returning to her candles. "I care naught for her suffering."

And then she said something that changed everything. She said, "I want her to die so I can marry her husband. The lady Odelina is your papa's wife."

Martine gaped at her mother. "But *you're* Papa's wife! Aren't you?"

Adela looked at Martine with disbelief in her eyes. "If I were his wife, would we be living here? Barons don't keep their wives in little clay huts in the middle of the woods. They keep them in their castles. Didn't you know that?"

Martine merely shook her head, dumbstruck. To Martine, her father was a glorious, golden-haired giant in furs and silks who came galloping through the woods on a white stallion when she least expected him.

She would shriek with delight as he dismounted and lifted her into the air, whirling her around and around before squeezing her in his massive arms and pressing a little trinket into her hands. For Jourdain of Rouen never arrived without gifts of some sort for his daughter and her young mother. Silken ribbons, tiny gold rings, vials of aromatic oils, polished steel looking glasses with ivory frames, silver combs, beaded slippers ... Their dark little wattle-and-daub cottage seemed to fill up with these dainty treasures as the years passed.

Martine adored him, heart and soul. He brought laughter and excitement into their dreary lives. He was magnificent. He was her papa.

What a change came over Mama when Papa came to visit! Her eyes lit up as she flew around the little cottage attending to his needs—hanging up his mantle, unlacing his boots, fetching him ale and bread and meat.

Once he was rested and his belly filled, there would be other needs of his to attend to, and Martine would be sent outside to forage in the woods or swim in the lake, or, if it was raining, upstairs to the little loft where she slept at night. From below, she would hear the crackle of straw in Adela's mattress, and other sounds—his groans, her breathless cries—sounds that frightened and confused her.

"No, no, Martine, your papa would never hurt me," Mama always assured her after he left. "He fills me. He makes me whole. Without him I'm an empty shell."

Martine watched her mother light the last candle, listened her incomprehensible murmurs. Every time she heard the name Odelina, she cringed inside. "It's wrong, Mama! It's wrong to wish for someone's death. It's almost like murder. God will punish you!"

Her mother rose to her feet, her blue eyes wide, their pupils tiny black pinpoints. "I'll gladly risk the flames of hell if only my prayers are answered." With a quivering arm she swept the candles onto the earthen floor, where they sputtered and died. "I would spend eternity writhing in agony in exchange for just one day as the rightful wife of my lord Jourdain!"

Martine ran from the cottage and swam in the lake until the sky grew black and the water cold.

It was shortly thereafter that Adela ordered the material for her wedding gown, yards of luxurious shot silk the crisp green of apples in late summer, before they ripen. It took her many days to sew the voluminous tunic with its long, flowing sleeves, weeks to complete the embroidery and beading. Martine had never seen a gown like it; it was dazzling, extraordinary.

The morning she finished it, one of Jourdain's men arrived with a load of firewood. The lady Odelina, he said, had ascended to heaven that very morning, God rest her weary soul.

"He arrived just as I was sewing on the last bead," Adela told her daughter as rode away. " 'Tis a good omen. A lucky sign for the marriage, don't you think?" Soon, she said, her lord Jourdain would come riding out of the woods and carry them back to his castle. Martine bathed and dressed and brushed her hair, dizzy with anticipation.

But that day passed, and the next, and yet more, and he didn't come. His servants no longer arrived at their door with deliveries of foodstuffs, firewood, cloth, and other household necessities. Weeks went by. Martine felt lost and confused. She adored her papa. It perplexed her that the hadn't come for them, or at least sent the provisions they'd always depended on.

Autumn came, and it was a wet, chilly autumn that year. They used up the wood and ran out of food. Martine collected roots and berries in the woods, but Adela spent all her waking hours in fevered, tearful prayer. The child knew without being told that she and her mother would not survive the winter.

One afternoon Adela came back from a trip to the village, sat at the window, and stared wordlessly into the woods.

"Talk to me," Martine begged. "What happened? Is it about Papa? Did someone tell you something? Is he sick? Is he—is he dead? *Please* talk to me!"

She still sat there when the child went up to her loft that night. But when Martine came down in the morning, her mother was gone. Her clothes still hung on their hooks, all except the new green tunic.

Martine looked everywhere for her. She even went to the village all by herself and asked if anyone had seen her since the day before, but no one had. While walking back, she passed the lake, and that's when she saw, floating on its breeze-rippled surface, the apple-green silk of her mother's wedding gown.

Why had Mama thrown it into the lake? It would be ruined, and it was so beautiful, and had taken so long to make. She waded into the water and tried to pull it out, but she'd been weakened by hunger, and it seemed to be caught on something. At the sound of whistling, she looked up. A farmer, a man known to her, led his ox along the path at the edge of the woods.

"Can you help me?" she called. "Mama's wedding gown is in the lake!"

"Her wedding gown?" he said. "Who's she going to marry, then?"

"My father. Baron Jourdain of Rouen."

The farmer laughed incredulously. "Child, His Lordship remarried last week. Her name is Blanche. Thirteen years old." He shrugged. "Some men like them young."

Martine stood in the icy water and watched him continue down the path, her emaciated body racked with shivers.

It would have been better, far better, had Papa been dead, as she had feared. That would have hurt, but it wouldn't have approached the pain of knowing that he had turned his back on them, abandoned them. They meant nothing to him, less than nothing, if he would so casually cast them aside for this Blanche. This was what Adela had found out in the village, this was the cause of her despair. This was why she had discarded her wedding dress.

She shouldn't have. It was exquisite, and she'd worked so hard on it. She deserved to keep it and wear it, even if Jourdain didn't want to marry her.

Filling her lungs with air, Martine dove fully clothed into the lake to retrieve the dress. The water was brutally cold. Green silk billowed beneath the surface, surrounding her and enclosing her. With flailing arms she pushed it aside.

What she saw then would haunt her and torment her for the rest of her days. It was the face of a monster, the face of death, the face of terror.

It was the face of her mother, bobbing in the hellish cold mere inches from her own, her clouded eyes staring sightlessly into the wide and horrified eyes of her daughter. She looked like a demon from hell, all swollen and purple, her mouth agape, revealing a distended black tongue.

Martine gagged and choked, a blinding shriek of disbelief filling her skull. She tried to surface, but the green silk enveloped her like a cocoon, and she clawed and struggled against it. She saw the rope around her mother's neck, and the sack of rocks it was tied to, and realized that she had died by her own hand, a grievous and unforgivable sin.

That revelation was her last coherent thought for some time. When her senses returned, she sat crouched in a corner of her cottage, her arms wrapped around her updrawn knees, listening to a man outside calling her name. Her clothes and hair were wet, and her throat felt painfully raw; she realized she must have been screaming. Her eyes, however, were dry, so she knew she hadn't cried. But then, she had never been much for tears.

The man walked in through the door and frowned at her. It was the local priest, fat little Father Tancred.

Without preface, he said, "We can't bury the body, I hope you realize that. Wouldn't be proper, seeing as how she took her own life. She's been dragged into the woods and left for the wolves. They'll make short work of her, don't you worry."

Martine just stared, her throat far too sore for speech.

Father Tancred pursed his lips. "Don't bother praying for her, it won't do no good. She's roasting in hell this very minute, and nothing you do can save her. If you must pray, pray for your own salvation, seeing as how you've got her wicked blood in your veins."

Raising his eyebrows at her lack of response, he continued. "It isn't safe for you to stay here all alone. Not all men are good and kind, like me. There's some that'd take advantage of a girl like you. You know what I mean, don't you?"

Martine didn't so much as blink.

Nodding, the priest said, "Aye, you know what I mean. And then, afterward, you'd be no better than your mother. You know she died a whore, don't you?"

He inspected her up and down with a look of disgust, and Martine considered how she must appear, skinny and hollow-eyed, her loose hair a damp, tangled mane. The priest lifted his black skullcap to smooth his own greasy yellow hair, then glanced out the window. Martine followed his line of sight to a curtained litter waiting in the harsh noon sun in front of the cottage. A woman's bejeweled hand parted the brocade drapery and then quickly let it fall closed.

Father Tancred cleared his throat. "All them things the baron's given you and your mum over the years, all them rings and bracelets and fancy baubles?" he glanced unerringly toward the trunk in the corner, its lid covered with half-melted candles. "You know there's brigands that'd slit your throat for just one of them little pretties, don't you? You're not safe here. You'd best be getting along."

He waited, but Martine made no move to rise.

"Get along," he repeated, waving his plum hand. "Scat! Go!"

Where am I supposed to go? Martine wondered. *This is my home. I have nowhere else to go.*

The priest looked back toward the litter and shrugged. The pale hand with its many rings beckoned him impatiently and then yanked the curtain closed.

Licking his lips nervously, he edged toward the door. "You mark my words," he said. "It's not safe here for you. You be gone by nightfall, or most likely by tomorrow you'll be burning in hell right alongside your mum."

Alone once more, Martine rested her head on her knees and closed her eyes. For a long time she thought about what it would feel like when she died. Having her throat slit would be quick, but it would hurt. Starvation took a long time, but as she well knew, it had its own kind of peculiar, grinding pain.

But drowning—struggling for air, waiting for your lungs to fill with water—was inconceivably horrible to her. How her mother must have suffered, even though she chose her own fate. Despite Father Tancred's command, she did try to pray for Adela's soul, but found that no words would come from her throat.

Thinking she could hear the wails of the damned as they agonized in hell, she clapped her hands tightly over her ears.

Slowly she uncovered them. It wasn't the damned, merely the whinny of horses. She opened her eyes. By the long shadows outside she could tell it was already late afternoon. She couldn't see the horses, but she could hear the footsteps of a man on the packed earth outside the cottage.

Quick as a squirrel, she darted to her feet. Grabbing the big meat knife from its hook, she scrambled up the ladder to her loft and half buried herself in straw in the far corner.

She heard him enter the cottage, and then came a thump as he laid something heavy on their little trestle table. She sensed his curiosity as he looked around. The ladder squeaked as he stepped on the first rung, and then the next. Martine braced herself, the knife handle gripped tightly in both sweaty fists.

A black skullcap appeared, half covering a head of pale blond hair. The child tensed, ready to spring. And then she saw his face.

Martine sucked in her breath. It wasn't Father Tancred at all. This priest was young, as young as her mother had been, and handsome.

He paused on the ladder, calmly inspecting first the knife and then her face. Finally he nodded. "My lady."

He mocked her. Martine's grip on the knife handle tightened.

As if he had read her mind, he said, "You're the daughter of a baron, are you not? I only meant to show respect."

He descended the ladder. "But if you'd prefer," he continued from below, "I'll call you Martine." She heard him unbuckle something—a leather satchel?—and then begin to empty things onto the table. "And you may call me Rainulf."

Not "Father Rainulf"? Thought Martine.

"Just Rainulf," the priest said, again suggesting that he had plucked her thoughts right out of her head. "There's no need for formality between brother and sister."

Between ... For a few dazed moments, Martine sat perfectly still in her cocoon of straw. *Between brother and sister?*

Finally she pushed the straw aside and, holding the knife at the ready, crept forward just far enough to peer over the edge of the loft.

Rainulf looked up at her. He was tall, and stood with the easy grace of the aristocrat. In one hand he held an apple. Behind him, on the table, were more apples, a loaf of white bread, a wedge of cheese, some pastries, some dried fruit, and a wineskin. Her mouth watered instantly at the sight of all that food, and she could do nothing to keep her eyes from widening in amazement.

"Will you join me for some supper?" Rainulf asked.

Biting her lip, she looked from the priest to the food and back again, then backed up, shaking her head.

After a thoughtful pause, he said, "My horse is very fond of apples. You don't mind if I step outside to give him one?" She didn't respond, and presently he turned and left.

Martine stared at the food for some time. Then, with her eye on the door and a tight grip on the knife, she climbed down the ladder and sidled up to the window. Outside, the priest stood with his back to her, feeding the apple to his chestnut stallion. Nearby had been tethered a petite gray mare and a packhorse to which had been harnessed a stretcher-litter. Bound to the litter was something wrapped up in bleached white linen ... a shrouded corpse. Her mother? But they had dragged her mother into the woods. He must have retrieved the body and brought it here. Why?

Although her mind reeled with questions, the ripe aroma of the cheese soon drew her to the table. With her eyes on the man in the front yard, and her hand still clutching the knife, she picked up the wedge and bit off a generous mouthful. Its taste flooded her senses, and she took another bite before swallowing the first. The pastries tempted her next, and she grabbed one and made short work of it, and then an apple. Dropping the knife, she ripped off a hunk of bread with trembling hands and ate it greedily, following that with a handful of chewy little figs. She uncorked the wineskin and squeezed it into her mouth, finding it filled with sweet apple cider. She gulped it down breathlessly, then reached once more for the cheese.

It was then that her stomach, empty for so long and now so swiftly engorged, began to heave in protest. Fingers of icy cold crawled up her back, and her head swam sickeningly. She staggered on quaking legs to her mother's narrow rope bed, dropped to her knees, and fumbled beneath it for the chamber pot. Hunching over the clay vessel, she whimpered as her stomach contracted.

Suddenly he was there, kneeling behind her, gathering her hair with one hand while the other firmly cradled her head. She groaned in despair, fighting the inevitable.

"Easy, now," he said soothingly. "Let it come."

It did, of course. Afterward, he sat her on the bed and patted her face with a damp cloth. "We must get you into some dry clothes, and then you can try eating again, slowly this time."

He took a fresh kirtle off its hook, brought it to her, and squatted down so that their heads were level. Softly he said, "I know you found your mother's body. 'Tis little wonder you've been struck dumb. It's all right with me if you don't talk. I'm a teacher, so I'm quite capable of carrying on a perfectly adequate conversation with no help from anyone."

He smiled and patted her arm, then stood and deliberately turned his back to her. As Martine undressed, he said, "Your arms are like sticks. When I first saw you up there in that loft, I was half tempted to give you last rites. But then I saw that knife, and the spark in your eyes. God might be ready for Martine, I thought, but Martine doesn't seem quite ready for Him."

Martine tossed her wet kirtle aside and shook out the dry one. Could this grown-up, this priest, really be her brother?

"You have two brothers," he said, and this time the child hardly even noticed his intrusion into her thoughts, so natural did it seem. "Half-brothers, of course. We're Jourdain's sons by his late wife, our lady mother Odelina." His back still turned, he made a solemn sign of the cross. "Etienne is the eldest, and our father's heir, naturally. I teach logic and theology at the University of Paris. I've been in Rouen for the past fortnight, to be with my mother."

As Martine contorted herself to lace up the back of her kirtle, a service her mother had always performed for her, Rainulf explained that he had known about her since she was a baby, but few others were privy to her existence. When word of Adela's death came to Jourdain's castle earlier that day, Rainulf had inquired of his father whether Martine would be provided for. The baron told him that he had been forced to abandon the child and her mother as a condition for marrying the lady Blanche, an orphaned heiress to vast holdings. His powerful overlord, Blanche's great-uncle, had refused to permit the union, which would double Jourdain's holdings, unless he severed all communication with his mistress and bastard daughter.

In her mind's eyes, Martine saw her father, larger than life and bright as the sun, thunder out of the woods and sweep her up, pressing her to his massive chest. *My little Martine,* he always said, *how Papa has missed you!*

Rainulf had turned and was watching her, his eyes sad. "I don't pretend to know why he went along with it, why he left you to . . ." He shook his head. "God knows the varieties of human weakness better than I."

Jourdain weak? thought Martine. *'Tis Mama and I who were weak. We let him use us. No one will ever use me again. No man will ever do to me what Papa did to Mama.*

Rainulf led her to the table, soaked a piece of bread with cider, and told her to eat it slowly.

"I understand Father Tancred paid you a visit earlier," he said. Martine glanced at him, and what he saw in her eyes made him nod in understanding. Quite soberly he said, "What you must try to understand about Father Tancred is that he's an ass."

Martine choked on her bread, and Rainulf patted her on the back, then tore off another piece and squeezed some more cider onto it. "I can imagine the things he told you, but you must put them all out of your mind. And you must never doubt that your mother is in heaven."

He held the bread out to her, but she just stared at him, consumed with doubt and confusion. He leaned closer. "She suffered, and now her suffering is over and she's with the angels. Because she took her own life, some would say she's damned. Others would disagree. I'm one of them."

Martine frowned. She found it incomprehensible that a priest would disagree with the established dogma of the Church.

"God gave us free will so that we might question what we're told," Rainulf said. "Reason, as well as faith, is the gift of God. I learned this from a great man named Peter Abelard. It's what I teach my students, and now I'm teaching you. Someday I'll lend you his *Discourse on the Trinity,* and you can study these ideas for yourself."

He took her hand, placed the bread in it, and guided it to her mouth. It occurred to her then that her half-brother might be mad. Priests could read—most of them, anyway. But ten-year-old girls?

"Oh, you'll learn to read," Rainulf said. "Where I'm taking you, everyone knows how to read. 'Tis a convent very far to the south, in Bordeaux. I know the abbess, and I believe you'll like her as much as I do. Girls from noble families are brought up there, and the nuns teach them many things, including reading and writing. Do you think you'd like that?"

Martine stared dumbly for a few moments and then nodded slowly. "Y-yes," she rasped. She coughed raggedly and nodded again, with enthusiasm. "Yes, I'd like that." Rainulf smiled at her, and she smiled back. "I'd like that very much."

"We set out for St. Teresa's that same afternoon," Martine said. "On the way, Rainulf buried my mother in consecrated ground, a beautiful little churchyard just south of Rouen." She gazed at the candle's flame with unseeing eyes, lost in the past.

Too much brandy, Thorne thought, *and too much sorrow. A heady mixture.* He watched her, transfixed, her eyes shimmering in the candlelight. "No one asked questions?" he said.

She answered him with a small shake of her head, and from each eye a single tear spilled slowly, like honey.

Once, in a chapel in Marseilles, he had seen a statue of the Virgin carved from some kind of smooth, pale stone, the eyes of which were said to produce tears from time to time. He had been young and full of faith, but although he knelt at the statue for days and prayed fervently for the honor of observing the miracle, the Weeping Virgin did not weep for him. Had she done so, the sight would have astounded him no more than the sight of these tears from the eyes of Martine of Rouen.

She stared at the candle as if in a trance, the tears unchecked. Tentatively Thorne reached out and wiped her cheeks with his fingers. Her skin felt cool, the tears surprisingly hot. His touch seemed to transport her back to the present. When her eyes met his and he saw the confusion and pain in them, he automatically rose to his knees, reached out, and took her in his arms.

She clutched his shirt in her fists, and he held her head to his chest while she sobbed. He rocked her gently and whispered soothing words to her, as he would with a child, or a falcon. Not until she finally quieted did he realize he'd spoken to her in the old Anglo-Saxon tongue.

"Foolish of me," he murmured. "You couldn't understand a word I said."

"I understood," she whispered, lifting her head from his chest to look at him. She was so close that he could feel her warm breath on his face. Her lips were but an inch from his. Were he to lean forward just that much . . .

She turned away. "Perhaps . . . perhaps I should go. It's gotten dark."

He followed her gaze to the open window, and saw that night had fallen and the rain had died to a light drizzle.

He sighed in resignation. She was right; it was unwise for them to be together like this. No, it was madness. He had almost kissed her, for God's sake. What had happened to his self-control, his resolve not to let himself care? He'd best remember what was at stake here and keep his distance.

Releasing her and rising, he said, "Aye. It's late. They might come looking for you."

He helped her to her feet and followed her to the hook from which her mantle hung. Taking it from her, he stepped behind her to drape it over her shoulders, and this time she didn't recoil from him.

He said, "Is it your wish that I keep the circumstances of your birth from Lord Godfrey? 'Tis your decision to make."

She took a moment answering; he couldn't see her face. "You're willing to keep my secret?"

He reached around her to pin the mantle closed; it was if he were embracing her from behind. *Keep your distance* . . . he silently reminded himself.

Quietly he said, " 'Twould serve us both, would it not?"

Slowly she nodded. "Then please do. This marriage means a great deal to Rainulf."

He felt her rapid heartbeat through his arm as it touched her chest, and knew she must be just as aware of his own racing pulse. "To you as well, I should think."

"Yes, of course," she said, her voice slightly unsteady. "But only inasmuch as it frees my brother to go on pilgrimage."

Thorne pulled her great sheaf of blond hair from beneath the mantle and smoothed it down her back.

She turned to face him, breaking the contact. Her eyes were huge. " 'Twould be disastrous if the baron found out after the wedding. You don't suppose Lady Estrude—"

"Don't worry about her. She presses you about your past because she's nosy, not because she seriously suspects anything. Even so, I advise you to spend as little time with her as possible, especially during the next month, while your brother and I are at the monastery. I'm surprised he's willing to leave you alone here, all things considered."

"He'd wanted to see how I got on without him, but he's changed his mind. A little while ago he told me he'd prefer it if I came along to St. Dunstan's. He says there are whispers about my having raised the dead, and that it might not be safe for me here alone. Ridiculous, of course."

"He's right," Thorne said. "People fear the unknown. They need time to accept the fact that it was your powers of healing, not sorcery, that saved Ailith. By the time you come back, they'll have settled down."

She shrugged. "I still think it's silly. But I'll go to make him happy."

"It makes me happy, too." He lifted her hood and adjusted it around her face. "To know that you'll be safe," he added quickly, opening the door. "I'll walk you to the keep."

"Don't trouble yourself. I'll be fine."

He tried to insist, but she refused. She was right, he realized; it wouldn't do for them to be seen together after dark.

Since he couldn't escort her, he watched her from the window as she crossed the bailey and disappeared into the looming blackness of the keep. He stared at a point high on the dark stone wall until a little golden square materialized there, and he knew she had lit a lamp in her chamber. Presently her silhouette appeared in the window and stood unmoving for a moment. Just as it occurred to him that she might see him looking up at her, the little patch of light blinked out; she had closed the shutters.

Thorne reached out and did the same, then took a deep, shuddering breath. His chest ached. He lifted his hand to rub it, and found his shirt moist with her tears. Without thinking, he gathered the damp linen in his fist, willing the tears not to dry, because they were all he'd ever have of her.

Christ, what manner of spell had been cast on him? It would take all of his strength to resist its power.

He sank to his knees and prayed for that strength.

Chapter 11

Rainulf felt the empty grind of hunger in his belly. Slowing his mount and the packhorse tethered to it, he looked up through the rustling leaves of the forest canopy and saw that the sun was almost directly overhead; it was nearly noon. They were making good time and would be at St. Dunstan's by late afternoon. He turned in his saddle to ask Martine and Thorne, riding some distance behind him, if they had given any thought to stopping for the midday meal.

He saw Thorne point to a flock of geese passing by overhead. The Saxon smiled, then leaned close to Martine to tell her something. She laughed in response, then noticed Rainulf watching them, and waved.

Rainulf had never seen his sister so happy and relaxed. Apparently Thorne's company suited her, now that they'd overcome their differences. It was a pity his old friend was unlanded, and therefore unmarriageable. Rainulf sensed he'd have made a good husband for Martine. Despite their dissimilar backgrounds, they were markedly alike in personality and intellect.

Not wanting to interrupt them, Rainulf turned back and continued along the little dirt track. He would wait for his meal. To see Martine and Thorne laughing like old friends after having been so quarrelsome pleased him greatly.

Presently he came upon a boulder as tall as a man, around which the path had been forced to curve. Growing out of it, anchored in a fissure, rose a crooked old tree of indeterminate species. Its roots grew over and around the boulder itself, enclosing it in a tangled web.

He waited there for his companions to join him. A stranger meeting these two for the first time would never guess at their true rank, so humbly were they attired.

Martine wore one of her nondescript tunics. Today, for some reason, she had chosen to leave her head uncovered and had plaited her hair in a single long braid which she wore draped over one shoulder. Thorne, in leathern leggings and a rough tunic, looked more like the woodsman his father had trained him to be than the knight he became.

Martine marveled at the boulder and the tree that sprang from it. The ingenuity of living things—their stubborn resilience—never ceased to amaze her. She slipped off a glove and laid her hand—unbandaged but still tender—on one of the gnarled roots. "How long do you suppose it's been growing here?"

Thorne reached out to touch the same root, his hand brushing hers—deliberately, she suspected. It was the first time he had touched her that day, and when she felt the heat and roughness of his skin, a ribbon of pleasure unfurled in her belly.

"This has been here as long as I can remember," he said, his expression thoughtful. He glanced at her, hesitated, and then added, " 'Twas my favorite thing to climb when I was a boy."

"You grew up in this area?" Martine asked.

Thorne nodded slowly. "Aye." He pointed north into the dark woods. "Our cottage was about five or six miles that way."

It dawned on Martine that she knew almost nothing about Thorne's life before the Crusade and his subsequent knighthood. That had been all right before, but now she ached with curiosity about his past. "Does your family still live there?"

"Nay. They ... they're gone. No one lives there, I'm sure. This land was taken by Forest Law about twelve years ago."

"Forest Law?" Martine said.

Rainulf caught her eye and shook his head almost imperceptibly, then said, a bit too brightly, "Shall we find a place to eat?"

"Shame on you, Rainulf," chided Martine. "I'm trying to learn something new, and all you can think about is your belly."

Her brother glared at her and began to say something, but Thorne interrupted him. "It's all right, Rainulf." To

Martine, he said, "Forest Law is an invention of the Normans, a way to steal the forests and pastures the Saxon people live off of so that the king and his barons can hunt for pleasure without competing with those who hunt to stay alive."

Martine looked around at the lush woods surrounding them. "This forest is just a hunting preserve?"

"All the land we've ridden through since midmorning has been a hunting preserve, my lady. Much of England is now under Forest Law, and more is claimed every year. No one who lives on such land may take deer or boar, or even rabbit. 'Tis all reserved exclusively for sport hunting by men like Bernard. Nor may the people chop down trees for wood or clear the land for crops, lest it reduce the game. So, you see, no one could possibly make a living in these woods. Even if you could find food without hunting or farming, there would be no way to make a fire and cook it."

"How dreadful," said Martine.

Rainulf said, "Am I the only one of us who's hungry? Let's eat."

Martine frowned. "Here?" brightening, she said, "Why don't we let Sir Thorne take us to his family's cottage? We can eat there."

Thorne said, "I haven't seen the cottage in ten years, my lady. It may no longer be standing."

Rainulf gave Martine a hard look. "Nay, sister. We'll find some clearing to eat in. Thorne has no desire to see—"

"Of course he does," Martine insisted, wondering why he forced her to bicker in front of Sir Thorne. "It's his childhood home."

"Martine, no! I'm sure Thorne doesn't want—"

Thorne raised a quieting hand. After a moment's thought, he said "Follow me," then turned and rode off the path into the woods to the north.

Martine threw a smug look of triumph her brother's way as she tugged her glove back on, but he just shook his head and nudged his horse into a walk.

She soon regretted having insisted on the trip. These old woods made for slow traveling. At first Thorne led them along a meandering creek, the banks of which were sparsely treed and easily ridden on. But when the creek

veered east and they continued north through the dense
woods themselves, the ride quickly became tiresome.
Certainly no one, not even hunters, had been in this part
of the forest for years.

Finally the woods opened up into an overgrown clearing. On the edge of it, shaded by an enormous old tree,
stood a thatched mud and stone dwelling almost completely covered with clinging vines. Martine looked
toward Thorne, whose neutral expression revealed nothing. He dismounted, as did Martine and Rainulf, then
removed the horses' bridles and hobbled them in a
grassy patch by a narrow little stream.

Rainulf partially unloaded the packhorse. He set the
two baskets housing Loki and Freya on the ground near
a chopping block, then unrolled a rug on the grass and
brought out their cheese, bread, and wine. Martine retrieved her cat, who instantly leaped from her arms and
darted straight for the cottage, disappearing into it.

"Loki!" She followed him to the door, pushing aside
the weathered bear pelt that covered it.

There were two rooms connected by a doorway from
which a deerskin curtain had fallen down. The back
room, essentially a straw-filled shed, had probably served
as a stable. From within it, Martine could hear the furious rustling of straw. Of course—what better attraction
to a cat than an abandoned stable. It must be teeming
with vermin.

She stepped into the front room and looked around.
There was plenty of light to see by, since the skins
tacked over the windows had mostly rotted away. Near
one wall stood a large board on stumps flanked by two
benches, furred with dust. Three straw pallets, draped
with wolf pelts, had been stacked in a corner.

Various implements and household items were scattered around the clay-lined cooking hole in the middle of
the earthen floor: an ax with a broken handle, a cracked
wooden trencher, an enormous iron kettle pitted with
rust . . .

Separated from this debris, alone in its own empty
corner, was something quite remarkable, and Martine
crossed the room to examine it more closely. It was a
cradle crafted of smooth, dark wood, the headboard
carved in an intricate geometric pattern surrounding a

central cross. Draped over it, as if to protect a baby from the dust, was a neatly hemmed square of coarse woolen cloth, its color obscured by age. Martine crouched and reached out to pull the cloth aside, then hesitated, contemplating what she might find beneath it. Curiosity won out, though, and she turned back the little blanket, gasping at what she found.

The face of an infant stared back at her with unblinking eyes. In shock, Martine stood and retreated a step before realizing that the baby's head, so perfect and round, was carved of pale, creamy wood, that the blue eyes and pink lips had been painted on. It was a doll.

Kneeling, she uncovered the wooden infant completely, shaking her head in wonder. About the size of a newborn, it was perfectly proportioned and carefully dressed. The little face looked startlingly lifelike, with full, dimpled cheeks and a well-fed double chin. Its head was covered with a neatly fitted white linen coif, from beneath which peeked strands of fine blond hair, apparently human. Its costume, although fashioned from humble brown homespun, had been styled like the tunic of a royal babe, with rich embroidery and long, fur-lined sleeves rolled back to expose the linen kirtle beneath. A little wooden cross hung on a leather cord around its neck. The plump little hands were bare, but each foot was encased in a slipper of soft deerskin.

Martine pulled off her gloves and pressed the cushion on which the doll lay. It was stuffed with feathers, not the coarse straw with which the family had made do. She stroked the smoothly polished cheeks, the fur that lined the sleeves, the tiny hands. As she began to lift it from its cradle, Thorne's voice broke the silence: *"Don't."*

She recoiled from the cradle and turned toward the voice. The Saxon stood in the doorway, ducking his head and holding the bearskin aside, his large form silhouetted against the light. Dust motes, stirred up by Martine's entrance, formed a glittering haze in the air between them.

He dropped the bearskin and slowly walked toward her, his eyes on the doll in its cradle. Squatting next to her, he said, in a gentler voice, "It's old. I wouldn't want it to be damaged." Carefully he rearranged the doll exactly as she had lain and centered the little cross on its chest.

He handled the doll as tenderly as it if were a human babe, and Martine yearned to know what lay hidden beneath his carefully governed features. "It's an extraordinary doll," she said. "Did it belong to your sister?"

Still staring at the round little face, he said, "It *was* my sister. I carved it in Louise's likeness, soon after she was born."

"*You* carved it?" He nodded. "And the cradle as well?"

"Aye." He rubbed the dusty wood with his thumb. " 'Twas Louise's cradle, and when she outgrew it, it became Bathilda's."

Martine smiled. "Bathilda. I'll never get used to your Saxon names. Did you ... you didn't sew her clothes, did you?"

He raised a bemused eyebrow. "Nay, my talent with needle and thread extends only as far as imping. My mother sewed the clothes. I asked her to dress her as she would a princess."

"She did a good job," Martine said. "When I was a child, I used to dream about gowns with long, fur-lined sleeves. You must have loved Louise very much to go to so much trouble for her."

He gazed at her for a long moment, his eyes luminous in the dim room, and then continued to study the doll. "I was ten years old when she was born. There had been other babies in between, but Louise was the only one who lived past the first year. She was different from the beginning, so healthy, fat, and happy. She was very spirited, like Ailith. My parents couldn't control her, but she listened to me. Wherever I went, she followed. She was my little shadow. Every night, in my prayers, I thanked God for not taking her from us, as He had the others. And I promised Him that if He let her continue to live, I would care for her and protect her and make certain no harm ever came to her."

Grimly he shook his head, and when he spoke again, his voice sounded strained. "But I broke my promise. And for that, Louise paid with her life, as did my parents."

Martine stared at Thorne, hunched over the little cradle, his transparent blue eyes filled with pain.

"I don't understand," she whispered.

He reached into the cradle to adjust Bathilda's coif. In a distant, almost hard tone, he said, "At seventeen, I took up the cross. I knew my family needed me, but I was very young and blinded by faith. Instead of staying home and helping my parents to make a living, instead of protecting Louise as I had promised God, I followed a foreign king on a doomed Crusade. I was a fool."

His sorrow overwhelmed Martine. "You were trying to serve Christ. You were—"

"A fool," he spat out. "When I returned two years later and came looking for my family, I found this cottage as you see it, and not a soul in sight. I was told that these woods had been taken by Forest Law not long after I had left and that my parents and Louise had moved to a village not far from here."

He clenched his jaw. "My parents hated towns. It must have been hell to have to live in one. If I had been here, I would have built them another home in another piece of forest, one where they'd be allowed to hunt and chop wood. But I wasn't here, and my father was too old to do it himself. I abandoned them, and in doing so, I condemned them to death."

"What . . . what happened?"

"There was a fire." He shook out the little blanket, and dust blossomed in the air like smoke. Martine covered her face with her hands. "One breezy night someone's candle got too close to his thatch, and within minutes the entire village was in flames. They began rebuilding the very next day. 'Twas the seventh time in ten years that particular village had burned to the ground."

Martine opened her eyes to find him replacing the blanket over the cradle.

He said, "They collected all the unclaimed bones and buried them in a mass grave." He smoothed the blanket carefully, as if it shielded not a wooden doll, but the precious, unclaimed body of his sister.

Martine wanted to comfort him, but what could she say? The depth of his grief shook her profoundly. He seemed so self-contained, from all appearances the absolute master of his feelings. Yet he hadn't mastered them at all, she now knew. He'd merely shielded them—shielded the raw hurt, the stinging self-reproach—behind the armor of his celebrated self-control.

"I found Bathilda here," he said, "just as you see her now, carefully dressed and arranged in her cradle, with this cloth to protect her."

"Why was she left behind?" Martine asked. "It looks as if they took everything else of value."

"I've wondered that myself," he said. "Perhaps Louise thought Bathilda would be happier here in her own home than in a town. She was trying to protect her from a fate that she couldn't avoid herself."

"And you left her here."

He shrugged. "Louise knew best. This is Bathilda's home. She belongs here."

He rose and reached for Martine's hand to help her up. Even after she had gained her feet, he didn't let go of it, but held it firmly in his. His warm, callused skin felt wonderful against her own.

"I never speak of these things," he said. "Not only because they're sad, but because they make me feel ashamed. I don't know why I told you . . . I hope you don't mind."

She saw into his eyes, saw his uncertainty, his grief. The worst grief, she knew, oftentimes stemmed from guilt. "Of course I don't mind. But you mustn't feel ashamed. You're not to blame."

"Yes, I am. Lying to myself would only compound my guilt."

"But—"

"I left my family at the mercy of the Normans because I was young and misguided. I'm older now, and much less naive. 'Tis the power of the Normans—the power of wealth and property, of land—that enables them to crush the Saxons beneath their heels. The only way I can fight that power is to claim some of it for my own. That's why I must become landed."

Perhaps that's why he'd told her about Louise, so that she'd understand the reasons for his ambition, understand his part in compelling her to marry Sir Edmond.

He looked tired, as if it had drained him to reveal this much of himself to her. "Your brother will be waiting for us. Let's eat so that we can get to St. Dunstan's before nightfall.''

He led her by the hand to the doorway, releasing her abruptly when he pushed aside the bearskin and saw Rainulf a few yards away, drinking from a wineskin. Was it wrong to let him touch her? She quickly surveyed her conscience and decided that it wasn't. He had never taken liberties with her. How would she react if he did? She pondered that for a moment, but this time there was no easy answer. This time her conscience and her heart were at odds. She hoped that she would never have to choose between them.

From the moment Martine rode out of the woods and saw St. Dunstan's nestled within the cool green valley below, she felt a sense of contentment such as she had not enjoyed since leaving St. Teresa's over a year before. Looking down upon the neat arrangement of long, narrow stone buildings, she marveled at how peaceful and orderly they looked—and how inviting, compared to tomblike Harford Castle.

The monastery was surrounded not by walls and ditches, as with a castle or a great town, but by orchards, pastures, and tidy cultivated fields. As Martine and her companions descended into the valley, she saw, here and there, the industrious figures of lay brothers and servants tending the ripening crops and herding flocks of sheep. A river meandered over the valley floor like a bright blue ribbon that had fluttered down from the heavens; St. Dunstan's had been built upon its bank. In the distance, on a hilltop beyond the valley, rose a strangely beautiful round castle, which Thorne explained was the partially built keep that young Lord Anseau had been constructing at the time of his murder; his domain, the barony of Blackburn, encompassed the monastery.

Religious convents tended to follow a predictable layout, so Martine had little trouble identifying St. Dunstan's various structures. To the east, surrounding the central cloister, were the monks' private buildings, all of which would be off limits to her during her visit. She would be expected to confine her movements to the prior's lodge, stable, guest house, kitchen, and other public buildings clustered around the courtyard to the west.

The church stood between this public area and the inner precincts, accessible to both from different entrances.

St. Dunstan's was not an abbey but a priory, the small satellite of a large Benedictine abbey to the south. At an abbey, Brother Matthew, the prior, would have been second-in-command. Here, he served as the highest administrator, although important decisions had to be approved by his superior abbot.

The priory's modest size and somewhat isolated location were to Martine's advantage. At a more important and visible monastery, she might not have been permitted to remain past sundown, despite her rank. But Matthew seemed to have no hesitation about bending the rules, having written to Rainulf that his sister was more than welcome, if he wanted to bring her.

As she rode through the main entrance and into the public courtyard, flanked by Rainulf and Thorne, a beautiful, hypnotic chanting arose from the direction of the church.

Rainulf smiled. " 'Tis later than I'd thought, if they're reciting vespers already."

Thorne said, "You two seem pleased. What's so special about vespers?"

The priest scowled at his friend in mock outrage. "All the offices of the Church are special, you heathen!"

Leaning conspiratorially toward Thorne, Martine whispered, loudly enough for her brother to hear, "But vespers is particularly special, because it means supper's not far behind!"

Rainulf groaned and Thorne chuckled. His smile was so generous, so open, and when he looked into her eyes, she felt that same odd sense that she had when she first saw him standing on the pier at Bulverhythe Harbor . . . that he looked not at her, but into her, into her very soul, her heart.

"You're *both* heathens!" Rainulf said. "One's worse than the other."

In truth, Martine had smiled not in anticipation of supper, but of an entire month in this wonderful place, so like St. Teresa's. For, although she shared none of the religious fervor of the nuns who had brought her up, she had found the structure and harmony of convent life much to her liking.

She took a deep breath, as if to absorb the ethereal chanting, with its stately, soothing cadence. Although the voices intoning in unison were male, not female, the sound was comfortingly familiar to her. She felt a sense of rightness, of belonging. She felt as if she were coming home.

"Was that *Prayers to the Virgin* I saw you reading this afternoon?" Martine asked, setting down her eating knife and lifting her goblet.

"Aye." Thorne grinned inwardly, knowing she was deliberately sowing the seeds of another supper-table argument. Her enthusiasm for *disputatio* amused him—and her skill at it impressed him greatly. A week had passed since their arrival at St. Dunstan's, and during that time she'd won more of their debates than she'd lost.

The Saxon was glad not to have to join the monks for their silent, meatless dinners in the refectory, as did Rainulf, who had chosen to completely immerse himself in monastery life. He and Lady Martine ate their daily meals in the main hall of the prior's lodge, sitting across from each other at the one small table. Their initial reticence with each other had quickly melted into the camaraderie of those who find themselves thrown together for a time in a strange place, with only each other for company.

During the day they explored the lush countryside surrounding the monastery. Their favorite place was a section of Blackburn River that twisted and turned deep in the woods to the north. The lively waters had carved through the underlying bedrock, creating moss-lined walls of stone pitted with caves, a secluded, otherworldly gorge. Here they took leisurely walks along the high, rocky bank, sometimes picking their way carefully down to the river itself, where they would sit and talk for hours. Sir Thorne always held her hand to guide her steps as they descended, but at no other time did he allow himself any physical contact with her. He took great pains to be a real friend to Martine—and no more than that. It was often difficult to keep from touching her, from saying things that were best left unsaid, but so far he had managed to do so.

It surprised both of them that they had so much in

common, not just intellectually, but temperamentally. They recognized in each other the pride and hardheadedness that defined their own characters, as well as something deeper and more difficult to voice . . . an emptiness, a need.

"I take it my choice of reading material surprises you," he said. They both took liberal advantage of the monastery's small library, often taking turns reading the same books—Greek and Roman classics so far—and then discussing them like learned clerics.

She lifted an eyebrow. "Considering you almost never attend mass? Yes!"

"Faith takes many forms, my lady."

She paused thoughtfully, her indigo eyes glittering in the warm, wavering candlelight. At times, Thorne mused, it was almost painful to look upon her beauty.

"Are you truly a man of faith, Sir Thorne?" she asked.

He shrugged. "I did take up the cross for Mother Church."

She smiled wryly, and now it was to her mouth that his gaze traveled, to those luxuriously full lips—berrystained red, with a perpetually swollen look about them, as if they'd just been roughly kissed. The thought stirred his loins, and he silently chastised himself for his undisciplined imagination.

"I'm afraid your going on Crusade proves nothing," she said. "Rainulf tells me that some of the vilest scum of Europe took up the cross, merely for the loot they were able to collect along the way. Others went in the hope of having their own sins forgiven, and hadn't the slightest interest in recovering Jerusalem."

Thorne nodded and leaned back in his chair while Cleva, Brother Matthew's cook, cleared their trenchers. "I regret to say I sought neither plunder nor absolution, my lady. I was one of the third type—God's poor, Louis called us, because we were full of faith and gullibility. I actually *wanted* to recapture the Holy Land, and I was willing to give my life for the cause."

He spoke calmly, but Martine noted an edge to his voice that betrayed deep bitterness, a despair that had healed with a thick scar.

He sighed and took a generous swallow of wine. "At least those who died did so thinking we would succeed—

that we would free Jerusalem and return to a hero's welcome. They never knew how badly we would fail, and how miserably most of us would be received when we finally did get home."

Cleva set a bowl of spicy-sweet star anise on the table. Martine took one of the little gray-brown kernels and chewed it pensively while she reflected upon Thorne's early years—his initial piety, his brutal imprisonment in the Levant, and finally the homecoming he'd so longed for, only to discover his family's cruel fate. " 'Tis a wonder you've any faith left at all," she said.

"Oh, I still believe," he said quietly, and met her eyes. "Not the same way I did when I was young, of course. As a boy, I was"—he smiled sadly—"very innocent. I believed in a merciful God, a God of love."

"And now?"

He rose and crossed to the chest in the corner where the chessboard and chess pieces were stored. "I know better now. I know that God—well, that God has something of a temper, and that it's best not to cross Him lest He decide to exact retribution."

"It sounds as if you define faith as fear."

He set the board on the table and dug into the two green sacks that housed the chess pieces, withdrawing one pawn of each color. "And I suppose you have a better definition."

"Peter Abelard did," she said. "He said faith was private judgment."

Thorne hid his hands behind his back for a moment, then presented both fists to Martine, each closed around a pawn. She reached out to his right fist, hesitated, then tapped his left. He opened it to reveal the white pawn, his mouth curved in a sardonic smile, which Martine understood perfectly; she almost always picked the white. She laughingly snatched up the pawn, then shook the rest of the white pieces onto the table.

"Abelard," Thorne said as he took his seat and poured out the black pieces, "wrote many clever and insightful things, but he did not write the gospel. I know that your personal theology is rather ... unformed, and I'm sure Abelard's teachings suit you perfectly, but they don't quite suit me."

Martine arranged her pieces on the board. "He was brilliant!"

"Aye, exceptionally brilliant, but he was just a man, and a flawed man at that."

She slapped her bishop down with a crack. "Abelard was no heretic. His supposed sins were forgiven by those who convicted him."

"I'm not speaking of his beliefs," Thorne said. He paused in setting out his own pieces and glanced at her, looking vaguely uncomfortable. "I'm speaking of Héloïse."

"Ah. Well, love is a powerful force"—she felt her cheeks grow warm—"or so they say. There are those who would argue that it can't always be resisted."

Thorne lined his pawns up with military precision. "It can if one is strong enough. As an officer of the Church, Abelard was expected to be celibate. But he was weak, and he suffered as a result. Loving Héloïse was a mistake, as he undoubtedly realized with startling clarity when her uncle's thugs broke into his room and—" he glanced up sharply at Martine and then placed the last piece on the board, "emasculated him."

"Castrated him," Martine corrected. "I prefer to call things by their honest names. You seem almost to approve of such a harsh punishment for simply falling in love."

Thorne sat back and studied Martine until she grew self-conscious and dropped her gaze to the chessboard, pretending to contemplate her first move. "Sometimes falling in love is not so simple," he said quietly. "There can be consequences. Abelard knew the consequences, but he lacked the self-control to keep from falling in love." He paused thoughtfully, then added, "I would not have made the same mistake."

Martine's face burned as she inspected her pieces. She took a deep breath, then raised her eyes to Thorne's. "Neither would I."

With all the composure she could summon, she slid her queen's pawn two spaces forward, then nodded coolly toward the chessboard. "Your move, Sir Thorne."

Chapter 12

Late one afternoon, as the sun slowly painted stripes of gold across the fields, Martine watched Freya make her first kill, a fat little partridge. Sir Thorne explained that he would let her eat her victim this one time, though in the future, of course, she would be trained to give it up.

"Watch," he said, as the falcon dropped down to claim her prize. "First she'll plume it and then she'll break in, starting with the left wing." At Martine's look of confusion, he said, "She'll pluck off the wings and eat the flesh."

When she did exactly that, Martine shook her head in wonder. "How did you know?"

Laughing easily, the falconer said, "There's little about birds of prey I don't know, Martine."

His use of her Christian name instead of "my lady" appeared to surprise him as much as it did her. He looked away, his jaw clenched. Martine thought he was being a bit hard on himself, especially considering his customary disregard for convention. It was a small oversight, and one that pleased her, in a way. He rarely said her name, and she liked the way it sounded, spoken in his earthy English accent.

He frowned as he watched Freya tearing at the little bird. Amused but touched by his embarrassment, Martine said, "Will she be fully trained by the time we go home?"

"Home?" Confusion flickered over his features. "Oh, you mean Harford. Aye, she should be, for the most part."

"Of course I meant Harford. 'Tis your home, is it not?"

" 'Tis Sir Godfrey's home."

He withdrew a silver-handled dagger. Kneeling over the partridge, and taking care to keep out of Freya's way, he split its skull, exposing the brains. Freya instantly began feasting on the soft white tissue. Although Martine appreciated that Thorne was merely rewarding his hunting bird with a treat, she found that she had to look away.

Thrusting the dagger's blade into the dirt, the Saxon said, "I've not had a home of my own since I was a child."

Martine pondered this for a moment. "Nor I."

He met her eyes briefly and then wiped his dagger on his leathern leggings and stood up. "You will in a few weeks. You'll have one as soon as you're married."

She nodded. "And you'll have yours soon after that."

A troubled expression passed across Sir Thorne's face before he marshaled his features and returned his attention to Freya. They both watched in heavy silence as the falcon feasted on her prey.

He was watching her.

Martine saw Thorne out of the corner of her eye, standing with her brother in the middle of a nearby meadow. Freya clung to his fist, and a couple of borrowed spaniels sat at his feet. He had hooded the white falcon, her training evidently concluded for the morning. Now he appeared deep in conversation with Rainulf, although his attention seemed focused on Martine as she explored the monastery herb garden.

She squatted next to a particularly homely little plant and considered its large, hairy leaves. Ass ear, some people called this one. Also comfrey. But the nuns had always referred to it as knitbone, and so that's how Martine thought of it. She had hoped to find some here. It was one of the most important of the healing herbs, but difficult to start from seed. Since she wanted to include it in the garden she planned for her new home, she decided to take a cutting from this one to bring back to Harford. Removing her sharp little eating knife from its pouch on her girdle, she chose a branch, quickly shaved off its lower leaves, then severed it at an angle.

Yes, he was watching her. And not for the first time. Whenever she felt his eyes upon her, she grew pleasantly warm from her scalp to the tips of her toes. A curious, delicate thrill consumed her. It felt very much like that time Felda had combed her hair as she drank the brandy ... a kind of shivery tickle that left her slightly off balance.

It was like a fever of the brain, these feelings she had for him. She didn't want these sensations of longing and adoration—and, yes, infatuation—yet, paradoxically, she craved them. Never had she felt so alive, so full of excitement and wonder, as if anything were possible.

But, of course, many things were impossible. For her to think of Sir Thorne in this way was not only unwise, but potentially disastrous. She had contracted to marry Edmond. Rainulf needed for her to marry him, and marry him she would. Allowing her infatuation with Sir Thorne to take root could only bring her pain.

Refocusing her mind through an effort of will, she carefully placed the little cutting in her shallow harvesting basket and looked around for other plants she might like to propagate.

St. Dunstan's herb garden, maintained by Brother Paul, the infirmarian, boasted a good variety of medicinals: chamomile, yarrow, feverfew, valerian, foxglove ... There was also angelica, known as the root of the Holy Ghost, and dill, and rue, all of which were said to guard against witchcraft. There was quite a lot of St. John's wort, which Brother Paul recommended not only for lung ailments, but for exorcising evil spirits. Martine had yet to be convinced that it benefited the lungs. And as for the other, perhaps when she began to believe in evil spirits, she would be able to believe in a cure for them. Until then, she would concentrate on those herbs whose value had been proven.

Thus she returned her attention to the knitbone. A warm poultice made from its pulp and applied to a fracture caused the broken bones to heal like new. She had seen this work like magic on a young girl in Paris whose leg had been crushed beneath the wheels of a cart. It was also said that the root, boiled in a pot with pieces of severed flesh, would join them as one. Resolving to try the experiment for herself, she dug in the black earth with her fingers until the thick, white root revealed itself, and began cutting away at it. Of course, she still needed the severed flesh. ... Perhaps Cleva would see fit to donate a hen for the sake of scientific inquiry. After all, if the experiment didn't work, it could always be used for chicken soup.

Martine scooped the black earth back over the knitbone's roots and patted it in place, then gathered up the pieces she had cut off and deposited them in her harvesting basket with the cutting.

Was he still watching her? As casually as she could, she turned and looked back over her shoulder toward the meadow.

Thorne saw her look directly at him. Unable to do otherwise, he met her gaze for a long moment—too long—before wrenching his eyes from hers and abruptly turning away.

He looked down at Rainulf, who was crouching over one of the spaniels and scratching its belly. "When did you find out about her?" His friend looked up, puzzled. "I mean when did you ... when did you find out you had a half-sister?"

"Ah." The priest stood, and now it was he who turned and stared in the distance toward the herb garden. They both watched as Martine, standing now, pinched a leaf off a plant, crushed it between her fingers, and brought it to her nose. She smiled as she inhaled its fragrance.

"I was sixteen," Rainulf began, "and home from Paris for the Christmas holidays. One afternoon I went for a long ride with my brother, Etienne. He was nineteen and, well, very sophisticated. Very worldly, compared to me. We went to a little village some distance from our home, on some errand. I can't remember what it was now. Etienne pointed and said, 'Look there.' It was a blond girl coming out of church with a baby in her arms."

Rainulf shrugged. "I asked him if he knew the girl. He said he'd never met her, but he'd heard whispers about her. She had a lover who was much older and lived far away. The babe in her arms was his bastard."

"Adela," Thorne murmured.

Rainulf nodded. "Only I didn't know about Adela then, and neither did my brother. She must have been fifteen at the time, but she looked much younger, much too young to be anyone's mistress, certainly too young to have a baby." He sighed. "Etienne told me it was time I had a woman. Our father had bought one for him when he was but fourteen, and now he intended to do the same for me. He thought this girl was a likely prospect. The man who kept her was gone most of the time, she would be lonely. . . . I did want a woman, it was something I thought about constantly. but a *woman*. Someone older and experienced, someone with flesh on her bones. Not a skinny little child."

Thorne saw the glint of Martine's little knife as she cut some spiky blue flowers off a plant. "So you refused."

"Aye, but it made no difference to Etienne. He'd made up his mind. He cornered her and offered her a handful of coins if she'd take me home with her. 'Twas horrible. Her baby was crying, and she looked terrified. Later I found out that she knew who we were. Can you imagine how she felt, being propositioned by the sons of the man who had fathered her child? She ran away, and I held my brother back so he couldn't follow her."

Martine sniffed the little bunch of flowers before adding them to the basket. He wondered what they smelled like. "I take it he was angry with you for spoiling his plans."

"Aye. He even complained to our father, told him all about it."

"Did your father tell him who the girl was?"

"Nay. But the next morning he ordered us to saddle up, and we followed him to a little wattle-and-daub cottage in the woods near that same village where we had seen her. He brought us inside, and there she was, standing in the corner with the baby on her shoulder. Etienne was delighted. He nudged me and whispered, 'You see? He's bought her for both of us!' My father said, 'It's time I made introductions.' He rested a hand on the girl's shoulder and said, 'This is Adela.' My brother was impatient. He tossed his mantle onto a chair and began unbuckling his belt."

"What did your father do?"

"He calmly took the baby from the girl's arms and brought it over to us. He said, 'And this is your sister. Her name is Martine.' "

Thorne said nothing as Rainulf gazed across the years with unfocused eyes.

"At first I didn't understand, and neither did Etienne. For a moment, no one spoke, and then, when comprehension hit, Etienne just ... he became furious. He was purple with rage. He screamed horrible things at my father, even accused him of giving our mother poison to make her sick. He called the girl a whore, and worse. He said the baby should have been left in the woods to die. He grabbed his belt and his mantle and jumped on his horse and left."

"And you? Did you leave?"

"God, no. I was ... mesmerized. I just kept staring at that baby in my father's arms. My sister. I had a sister! She was so pink, so impossibly small. Etienne's outburst had upset her, and now she was screaming. Father looked helplessly toward Adela. I had never seen him look helpless before. He held the baby out to her, but I came forward and took her instead. She was lighter than I thought she would be, and warm, and she smelled of milk. Without thinking about it, I began to rock her. I spoke to her very softly, saying, 'There, now, settle down. Settle down.' And she quieted. She fell asleep in my arms. It felt so ... It's hard to describe."

"I know the feeling," Thorne said, his throat tight. "I had a little sister, too."

Martine pinched a delicate pink flower off a plant, reached behind her to drape her single braid over her shoulder, and threaded the flower's stem through the ribbon that secured it. Thorne had never seen her adorn herself before, and for some reason it pleased him.

Rainulf nodded. After a pause, he said, "That was the last I saw of my sister for ten years. I had returned from the Crusade and was teaching at the university when a messenger came from Rouen. My mother was dying. I returned home, of course, and, well, you know the rest. My mother died, my father married the lady Blanche, and Adela—" he shook his head slowly, "Adela tied a sack of rocks around her neck and walked into the lake."

Thorne followed his line of sight to the distant form of Lady Martine, stooped over a low hedge.

"And Martine," Thorne supplied, "was left to starve to death."

Rainulf shook his head, his face drawn. "When I

found her, she was already half dead, just this wet, shivering little skeleton in a kirtle. Well, not little, precisely. For ten, she was actually rather large, with long, gangly arms and legs. I could tell she was going to be tall. I would have known her anywhere. She resembled my father to a remarkable degree. She wasn't what you'd call beautiful, and I suppose she still isn't, but there was something about her, something very compelling. A light behind her eyes, a spark. I suppose that sounds very fanciful."

"Nay," Thorne said softly. "I know exactly what you mean."

What he didn't say, though, was that Rainulf was quite wrong about her not being beautiful. He watched her as she waded toward them through the meadow, the basket dangling from one hand while the other lifted her skirts above the tall, waving grass. Tendrils of pale, silken hair, loosened from her braid, danced in the warm breeze that flowed through the valley. She smiled, and he desperately wanted to know why so that he could share her pleasure. Her cheeks were flushed from the sun and hard work, and her eyes glittered with a spark that was not only compelling, but irresistible.

She wasn't just beautiful, she was exquisite. She was complicated and unpredictable and unique. She was both soft and sharp, warm and cool . . . she was endlessly fascinating.

And she was Edmond's.

Thorne swam up through the blackness of sleep to the distant clanging of bells. He opened his eyes and lay still in the dark. It was midnight, and the sacristan was summoning the brothers to matins. He heard the whisper of a light rain in the courtyard outside.

From the little chamber next to his, he heard Rainulf stir, getting ready, as usual, to join the brothers for midnight prayer. Why he bothered with it, when he was merely a guest and not obligated to observe the holy offices, was beyond Thorne. He thought it particularly unwise the night before a long journey. Tomorrow they would return to Harford, and in Thorne's opinion, Rainulf would do well to rest up for the journey instead of standing half the night in church chanting streams of

Latin. Most likely he'd be up at first light for lauds,
as well.

From beyond his chamber's leather curtain he heard
Rainulf greet Brother Matthew, and then the two departed, and all was quiet once more. He rolled over and
closed his eyes, but, as was often the case in recent
nights, he found it impossible to get back to sleep. It
was a problem he had never encountered before, and it
displeased him greatly. For his body to refuse to sleep
when he commanded it made him feel weak.

He arose, lit a lantern, and pulled on some chausses.
In the downstairs kitchen he poured a goblet of wine
and brought it back up to the table in the main hall. A
volume of Euclid's *Elements,* which he had just finished,
lay on the table, and he sat down and picked it up.

The prior's lodge was a large house built around a central hall on the upper level. Four sleeping chambers
opened onto the hall, one of which was Brother Matthew's, the other three reserved for high-ranking guests.
The servants spent their nights elsewhere, so at present,
the house was empty save for Thorne—and, of course, the
lady Martine, asleep in her own little cell. No sound
came from there. The bells did not appear to have awakened her.

He opened the book and leafed through the yellowed
parchment pages, each one densely inked in minuscule,
carefully penned Latin, but his eyes did not see the
words nor note their meaning. He saw only her eyes, lit
from within with blue fire ... heard her liquid, musical
laughter ... felt her hand, so cool and small in his. He
could not will these images from his mind, could not
command himself to think of other things.

He had never felt so helpless.

By Christ, he would miss her when they left this place.
Never again would they be together as they had this past
month. Every morning when he rose to the bells for
prime, his mind was filled with her. As he dressed and
washed his face, he thought, *Soon I will see her.* All
through the day, he contrived to be with her, just for
the simple physical pleasure it gave him to be in her
company. When he was close to her, he reveled in her
scent, which was like a wild, untended meadow, earth
and grasses and sweet blossoms all warmed by the sun.

But when she wasn't there, as now, he ached with wanting to be near her. How he ached. He had never ached like this, never felt so needful.

It was a cunningly cruel joke of God's, and he had to admire it. For the first time in his nine and twenty years, he'd been shown how it felt to have his emptiness filled by a woman ... only she was a woman he could never have. He'd return to Harford all the more empty for this brief taste of the unattainable.

God must still be punishing him for having abandoned his family to their cruel fate. Hadn't he already paid for his mistake? Hadn't *they*? Hadn't little Louise? With an oath, he snapped the book shut and slammed it on the table. In the numbing silence that followed, he thought he heard something—a whimper. A child?

He waited, listening. Nay. He was imagining things. It was thinking about Louise that—

There it was again. A halting, fretful moan.

It had come from behind the leather curtain of Lady Martine's chamber.

After a moment's hesitation, he rose and carried his lantern to her doorway, listening. Presently the silence was broken by another muffled cry. Was she having a nightmare?

He cleared his throat. "My lady?" He heard an inarticulate murmur of distress. "My lady?" he repeated, a little louder. Then she spoke, and he strained to hear the mumbled words, but couldn't make them out.

He parted the curtain just far enough to see into the little room. Her narrow cot stood against the wall immediately to the right of the doorway; he could have reached down and touched her sleeping face, but he stilled his hand.

She lay on her stomach, her one long braid dangling off the side of the bed. The linen sheet was crumpled about her hips, revealing the bare expanse of her back— the fine bones, the elegantly subtle curves, the narrow waist. Her pale skin, illuminated by the meager light filtering through the horn panes of the lantern, took on a faintly golden glow. It looked as smooth as ivory, and the impulse to touch her, to caress that silken flesh, to toss aside that sheet and take her in his arms, nearly overwhelmed him.

He must leave.

But as he turned, she spoke again. This time he could make out the sleep-slurred words, edged with panic: "Mama's wedding gown is in the lake!" It was more the voice of a frightened little girl than that of the self-possessed woman he knew.

Her breathing quickened, and she tensed, her hands twitching convulsively. A moan of fear arose from her, and he saw that her face gleamed with perspiration, despite the coolness of the night.

He stepped into the room, letting the curtain close behind him, and set his lantern on the floor. Taking hold of the crumpled sheet, he pulled it up to her shoulders. Beneath it, her hands began to clench and unclench violently.

"My lady."

"M-Mama's . . . w-wedding gown—"

"Wake up, my lady." He sat on the edge of the bed and gently shook her shoulder. "Wake—"

Her eyes flew open and she jerked awake, crying, "Mama! Mama!"

Her face held a look of pure terror, and she shook uncontrollably. With no thought except the instinct to comfort, Thorne stretched out next to her on the little cot and gathered her in his arms.

Chapter 13

She shivered at his touch, like a hatchling just taken from the nest. But he did not release her. He held her tight, stroking her through her cocoon of linen sheeting and murmuring comforting words, as he had done so many times with agitated young falcons. "Shh, 'twas just a dream . . ."

"Th-Thorne? Sir Thorne?"

"Aye." He brushed a wisp of hair from her damp forehead. "You were having a nightmare."

She moaned despairingly and nodded against his chest. Without thinking, he brushed his lips to her hair, inhaling warm sunshine and sweet lavender. Her body felt invitingly warm and soft; he wanted to wrap himself around her, bury himself within her. With an effort, he reminded himself that he was here to lend solace.

He heard her soft intake of breath as the intimacy of their situation struck her. It was the middle of the night, and she lay enclosed in his arms, naked beneath her thin sheet.

Gathering his wits, he said, "I'll go fetch your brother from church."

She shook her head. "Nay. I—I can't bother him every time. It's just a dream. It's nothing."

He rubbed her back to soothe her. "You're *trembling* from nothing, my lady. Do you often have nightmares?"

"Just the one. Every night it's a little different, but it always ends the same way."

"Every night? This happens to you every night?"

"Lately. The closer I get to—to the wedding, the more it comes."

After a few moments of silence, Thorne said "Tell me," and tightened his arms around her. He could not be all that he wanted to be to Martine, but he could be a comfort. He could share her pain, perhaps even ease it, if only she would let him.

"It's about my mother, about finding her body in the lake. She was ... she'd been so beautiful, and suddenly she was just this *thing,* this grotesque thing."

"Oh, my lady," he whispered.

"If it weren't for Rainulf, I would have died, too. He saved my life. Not only that, he made it worthwhile. He educated me. Everything I am, I owe to him. I'd do anything in the world for him."

"Even marry Sir Edmond."

Her answer emerged as a whisper. "Aye."

"Even though the very thought of marriage terrifies you."

She nodded.

"Perhaps ... perhaps you'll like being married. Edmond's not such a bad sort, just a little young." The words sounded hollow even to his ears. "You could probably learn to love him."

"Dear God, I hope not!" Her vehemence both gratified and alarmed him.

"You'd prefer a loveless marriage?"

"I'd prefer no marriage at all. I dread the very idea. But since my preferences don't seem to matter, I'd much prefer a civilized, bloodless union to one of love. Men use the love that grows in women's hearts to control them, keep them in their place, or even to destroy them if that becomes convenient."

He hadn't realized the depth of her bitterness. "I'm surprised you agreed to this marriage even for Rainulf's sake."

"He gave of himself in my time of need, and now I'm going to do the same for him."

"Are you willing to forfeit the rest of your life for him?"

"I've made my decision. There is no 'rest of my life.' I've lived quite well up till now, thanks to Rainulf. Now it's his turn."

What could he tell her? That she should default on a betrothal contract that he himself had arranged, and upon which his future depended? Thorne was not a man accustomed to self-doubt, so it was with some degree of confusion that he now pondered his role in negotiating this union. For Rainulf to benefit from her marriage was one thing, since she felt she owed him his freedom. But she owed Thorne nothing, and he hadn't hesitated for a second to barter her hand in exchange for property.

And now . . . now that he couldn't stop thinking about her, couldn't stop wanting her, needing her . . .

Things that had been simple were now complicated. The control he maintained over every aspect of his life seemed to be slipping away. His feelings, his desires, always so carefully schooled, rioted within him. They put him in mind of a bear roaring in frustration at being baited, straining at tethers that threatened to snap at any moment.

Through the hush of rain outside the window came the distant chanting of the long midnight service, dreamy and hypnotic.

He looked down at the woman in his arms, so warm, so sweet. Against his bare chest, through the thin sheet, he felt the delicious roundness of her breasts, the thrumming of her heart. . . . She still quivered with anxiety.

To be here with her this way, in her chamber at midnight, sharing her bed, was insanity. He knew he should leave, but he couldn't, not while she was so overwrought.

He would try to ease her mind, to soothe her enough for her to get back to sleep, and then he would leave. He lifted her braid, which felt remarkably heavy, pulled off the ribbon that held it, and began unweaving the plaits. In a few moments she relaxed in his arms, and her breathing steadied.

She said, "Do you ever think about fate?"

"Fate?" He trailed his fingers through her loosened hair, a blanket of golden silk.

"I do," she murmured. "I think fate is like a ribbon, a long, golden ribbon. It trails through our lives, and at first we just notice it slipping around us every now and then. We don't give it much thought until one day we discover that we're completely bound by it, wrapped tightly within its power, incapable of breaking its bonds."

He smiled at such fanciful imagery from such a rational woman. "Hasn't Rainulf told you about free will? 'Twas my very first lecture from him."

She chuckled. "Mine, too. Free will exists, make no

mistake. That makes it all the more frustrating to find oneself a prisoner of fate."

He pulled his fingers lazily through her hair. "I like to think I have more command over my destiny than that."

"Everybody does. But haven't you ever felt as if you were being carried along by forces you couldn't control?"

He instantly pictured the raging, tormented bear within him. "Nay," he lied. Well, not entirely a lie. Yes, he was being carried along by unwanted feelings for Martine, but they were feelings he could control. The bear wouldn't break free if he had the strength to hold it back.

"My mother was a victim of fate," she said. "Her love for Jourdain kept her captive for years. 'Twas only at the very end that she was able to break free. Drowning herself was the first, and last, independent act she ever performed."

His hands stilled in her hair. "You praise her suicide as an act of free will?"

"I don't praise it, but I do understand it. In a way, I even admire it. 'Twas the only way out, and she made the decision and acted on it."

"There was nothing admirable about what she did, Mar ... my lady. I know she was miserably unhappy, but you're wrong to misinterpret her weakness as strength. She surrendered. And in doing so, she condemned her child to almost certain death."

"Then it wouldn't have been so bad if she hadn't been responsible for me? If she hadn't had a child?"

"This isn't some academic dispute, my lady. Don't set up hypotheticals. The fact is, she had a daughter for whom she spared not a single thought when she took her own life."

"I survived."

"Thanks to Rainulf. But you carry deep, unhealed scars, do you not? These nightmares of finding her body ... 'tis a wonder they haven't driven you mad by now."

After a moment, she said, "The worst part isn't the body. I usually don't even see that. It's the water itself. In the dream, it turns to blood. A lake of blood." She shivered and wrapped an arm around him. "I've been terrified of water ever since that day. As a child, I swam constantly, but I haven't in years."

"But you did," he pointed out. "When you saved Ailith."

"I had no choice."

"Ah, but you did have a choice. You could have given in to your terror and let her die, but you didn't. You exercised your free will and overcame your fear and saved her." She seemed to ponder that. His fingers entwined themselves in her hair once more, and she sighed.

"You should swim again," he said, "just for your own pleasure."

"I'm afraid," she whispered.

"Fear exists to be conquered." He stroked her scalp, massaging with his fingertips. "You should swim."

"Mmm."

"You should."

"Mmm-hmm." She grew heavy in his arms.

"Tell me you will."

"Hmm?"

"Tell me you'll swim again, soon. It's important. Once that fear is conquered, you can work on the rest. Promise me."

She mumbled something blurry that sounded like "I promise."

He smiled ruefully. "You're humoring me."

She didn't answer that, merely snuggled against him, warm and drowsy.

"You are," he said, "but that's all right. I'll take what I can get."

Men were laughing.

Martine opened her eyes. Someone was in bed with her, his arms enfolding her, one long leg thrown over hers. She breathed in his familiar, masculine scent.

Thorne.

From the other side of the curtain, she heard voices. More laughter, followed by muffled conversation.

"What—" she began.

Thorne clamped a hand over her mouth. Even in the half-light from the lantern, she could see his incandescent eyes, read the warning in them. She nodded, and he took his hand away.

Bringing his mouth to her ear, he whispered, "They came back while you were asleep, Rainulf and Matthew. They've been talking out there ever since. I can't very well let them see me leaving your chamber in the middle of the night."

Again she nodded. It was still dark outside, but raining harder, and she had the impression that she had slept for a while.

She lay nestled snugly within his embrace, her outside arm draped over his waist. Her hair was loose, and he had a length of it wrapped around one hand. He was bare from the waist up, and they were crushed together like lovers. She felt a surge of panic before recalling that nothing had happened between them, nothing like that.

He had listened to her, had soothed her fears, had held her until she fell asleep in his arms. He hadn't kissed her. No, she was sure he hadn't. She would remember that. And she would remember if he had taken advantage of her in any way, done anything he shouldn't have.

It would have been little trouble for him, had he wanted to. A simple matter to pull the sheet aside and do as he wished. He was not a saint, but a man, with a man's appetites. And he was strong. She could feel the long, hard muscles of his legs, the unyielding planes of his chest. He could easily have overpowered her, had his way with her.

Or perhaps he wouldn't have had to force her. A man like Thorne would know how to coax a woman into giving herself to him. He would know how to touch her, how to caress her secret places until she begged him to take her. She grew warm thinking of the things he might have done, the things she might have wanted him to do.

His breath ruffled her hair. He held her so tightly that she couldn't tell whether the racing heart that shook her chest was her own or his. When his breathing quickened, hers followed suit. Her skin had never felt so tender, so ultra-sensitive. Every part of her that he touched burned with a strange and thrilling pleasure.

She turned to look at him. When their eyes met, she saw in his a raw and desperate need that exactly mirrored her own. *He knows how I feel,* she thought with amazement. *He knows because he feels it, too.*

She felt his hand tighten its grip on her hair, and then something else, a movement against her belly, his body stirring, growing hard. Her own body throbbed in response, needing him there, between her legs, needing him to fill her, to possess her.

She tensed, her mind a pandemonium of confusion, as he abruptly drew back from her.

What she wanted, she mustn't want. If his restraint failed, would she have the will to resist him?

More laughter from the main hall. Thorne pulled his arm out from beneath her, propped himself up on an elbow, and reached toward the leather curtain. With deliberate care, he pulled aside an edge and looked out, then closed it.

He sat up and rubbed his arms, the muscles jumping in his back and shoulders. With a ragged sigh, he dragged his fingers through his long hair.

She reflected on his reputation for self-control. He exercised it this night, she knew, for both of them. Part of her felt disappointed, another part relieved.

He had been a friend to her. Not just tonight, but all during this past month while they had been guests at St. Dunstan's. Granted, it was not a simple friendship. In truth, it had become quite complicated, even dangerous. Nevertheless, they shared something remarkable and precious and thrilling, something they would have to give up when they returned to Harford tomorrow.

Already she mourned the loss of that intimacy, grieved for its passing. She needed to thank him for his friendship, to tell him how much she would miss their time together.

"Sir Thorne—" Even before he whipped around and pressed his fingers to her mouth, she realized she had spoken too loudly. She heard the conversation cease in the main hall, and then the scrape of chair legs on the floor.

Thorne lowered his mouth to her ear, his weight on his elbows, one to each side of her head. "For God's sake, keep him out!"

"R-Rainulf?" she called.

"Martine?" She could hear the worry in her brother's voice. "Are you all right? Is it the dream?" From the sound of it, he stood just outside the doorway.

She took a deep breath and answered with studied nonchalance. "Nay. Nay, I'm fine. Just talking to myself." Thorne nodded his approval, and she smiled.

There came a short pause. "I'm going to bed now. You get some sleep. We've got a long ride ahead of us."

"All right. Good night."

Thorne and Martine listened carefully as the men on the other side of the curtain retired to their chambers. When quiet descended once more, she looked up into the infinite blue of Thorne's eyes as he held himself over her. Her heart twisted to think that in two weeks she would be Sir Edmond's wife. Nothing could ever come of her feelings for Thorne. Nevertheless, she felt compelled to share with him, even if it was foolish, even if there were consequences.

"Thorne," she whispered.

Again he touched his fingertips to her lips, but this time his eyes were filled not with caution, but with regret. His gaze traveled from her eyes to her mouth as he stroked his callused thumb across her lower lip. She thought he was going to speak, but he seemed to think better of it. Instead, he bent to retrieve his lantern from the floor and rose to his feet.

At the doorway, he parted the curtain and stood for a long moment with his back to her. Finally he glanced quickly over his shoulder, said "Good night, my lady," and left.

Sleep eluded Martine, although she hovered for some time in a dreamy, half-wakeful haze. Long golden ribbons and yards of apple-green silk swirled around her while muted voices whispered of fate and free will, fear and courage.

She saw the lake in Normandy from the perspective of a child standing at its edge. The water was the fathomless blue of Thorne's eyes, and very still, reflecting the cloud-speckled sky like a giant looking glass. It beckoned her so invitingly, as it always had when she was a child. It had beckoned her mother, too, but with a darker invitation, the comforting seduction of eternity.

In her mind's eye, she stepped into the water. Cold fear clutched at her chest, but she gulped it down and took another step.

Her conversation with Thorne had enlightened her. She knew what she had to do. If she didn't, she would always regret her cowardice.

Having made her decision, she lay awake the rest of the night, eyes wide in the dark, waiting for dawn.

Stretched out naked on his little cot, his crossed feet hanging off the end, his hands clasped behind his head, Thorne watched the first pale hint of dawn wash the blackness from the sky outside his chamber window. He wondered if he would ever sleep again.

He frowned in puzzlement at the muffled sounds from the main hall. Someone had gotten up early. They hadn't even rung the bell for lauds yet. He reached over and pulled the curtain aside just in time to see a black-clad figure disappear down the stairwell.

Presently he heard footsteps in the courtyard. Rising, he looked out the window.

It was still dark, but no longer raining, and he could clearly see Martine, in her hooded mantle, entering the stable. He watched until she reappeared, leading her saddled dun mare. Where could she be going at this hour? She mounted, rode out through the main entrance, then headed north. There was nothing of interest north of the priory except the river. Is that where she went?

He pulled on his chausses, sat on the edge of the bed, and thoughtfully scratched his morning stubble. She had never gone to the river without him, not that he knew. Why had she decided to go now, when it was barely light out, and they had to prepare for the ride back to Harford?

She wouldn't be eager to return, with her wedding, which she dreaded, but a fortnight hence. It was curious that the married state Adela had so coveted should be viewed by Martine as such a curse. What the mother saw as heaven, the daughter saw as hell, a hell she voluntarily condemned herself to for the rest of her life.

There is no rest of my life, she had said. *I've made my decision.*

Decision. She had used that word in regard to her mother as well, Thorne recalled. *She made the decision and acted on it. In a way, I even admire it.*

A chill crawled up Thorne's back and clutched at his scalp. *'Twas the only way out,* she had said. *She made the decision and acted on it. . . .*

I've made my decision. . . . There is no rest of my life.

Thorne stood up.

I've made my decision. . . .

"Sweet Jesus," he muttered, grabbing his shirt off its hook and sprinting from the chamber.

Thorne slid off the bare back of his white stallion and left the animal untethered above the river while he made his way swiftly down to the water's edge. It was barely light out, and a thick mist filled the gorge, trapped within its mossy walls. He could see nothing but what was close enough to touch.

"My lady!" he yelled, and waited, hearing nothing. Was he too late? Had she already done it? His heart filled his chest, pounding like Spanish drums.

He whipped off his shirt and waded hip-deep into the river, looking wildly around. Even without the mist, he wouldn't have known which way to turn.

"My lady!" he shouted. "My lady!"

Dear God, please don't let this happen, he prayed. *You've punished me enough. Don't take Martine.*

He imagined finding her, cold and limp, and a scream tore from his lungs. *"Martine!"*

A soft ripple from behind. He wheeled around and saw a form in the mist, pale and luminous and very close.

Her eyes, like lakes, met his through the swirling fog. She stood waist-deep in the water, her arms crossed on her bare chest, clothed only in long wet ribbons of golden hair.

"Martine! Thank God." In a heartbeat he closed the distance between them and gathered her in his arms, relief overwhelming him. "I thought you were dead." He held her tight and kissed the top of her head.

"Dead!" She looked up at him, her eyes betraying confusion and then understanding. "You thought I—you thought . . ."

His face must have mirrored the torment in his heart, because she reached up to comfortingly stroke his cheek. He closed his eyes, straining for composure. Such fear, then such joy. It was more than he could bear.

"I swam," she said, and he opened his eyes. She stood so close, her face inches from his. "You said I should swim, that I should face my fear. I did. 'Twas wonderful. I felt so strong." Her arms encircled him.

He laughed in relief, pulling her close. *She had been swimming. Of course. She had just been swimming.*

He kissed her forehead, her temple. He laced the fingers of one hand through her hair while the other kneaded her back, smooth and wet, pressing her to him.

Her hair covered her like a mantle. Where its cool strands parted, he could feel her breasts, warm and soft, against his bare chest. A small, civilized voice told him to pull back. *I will,* he thought. *Just let me feel her, just for a moment.*

Cradling her head with both big hands, he tilted her face up and pressed his lips to her eyelids, then to the skin stretched taut over her high cheekbones. Her eyes were closed, her lips so ripe and inviting. No, he wouldn't kiss her mouth. Then he would truly be lost.

I won't kiss her, he thought, lowering his mouth to hers.

Just a touch . . . He brushed his lips against hers and heard her sigh unevenly.

These are Martine's lips touching mine, he thought dizzily. Again, slowly, warm flesh against flesh, a fleeting caress. Not a kiss, not really, just a caress of the lips, nothing more.

Through his ragged breathing he thought he could hear the drumming of his heart, feel its driving rhythm in his loins. He closed his mouth gently over hers . . . *not a kiss, not really.* His tongue parted her lips, seeking her heat, the sweet, intoxicating taste of her. She trembled ever so slightly, and he felt her nipples stiffen against his chest.

There was no sound in the gorge save their breathing. But deep inside, heard only by him, rose an untamed howl, the roar of the bear straining at his tethers.

He had to touch her. Without moving his mouth from hers, he bared her by gathering her hair to the back, then brought both palms to rest on her breasts, which made her gasp. He filled his hands with her, stroking, caressing, thrilling to the pulse of her heart through the warm flesh, thumbing the rigid nipples until she moaned.

His body responded, rising and straining against his wet woolen chausses. He knew she felt it, but she made no move to back away, so he reached down beneath the water, closed his hands over her cool bottom, and pressed her to him. She molded her body to his, her own hands gliding down to the small of his back to urge him against her.

With one hand tangled in her hair and the other wrapped around her, crushing her to him, he surrendered to his need to take her mouth in a deep, hungry kiss. She kissed him back. He felt her passion, her heat, and knew without a doubt that she felt just as helpless as he, just as lost, just as overcome by desire.

Inside, he felt the tethers snap and fall away, and then a fierce, raw surge of animal power. Without breaking the kiss, he scooped her up in his arms and waded purposefully to shore, his head filled with a savage roar that only he could hear.

The bear had broken free.

Chapter 14

'*T*is *a dream,* she thought as he lowered her onto the cool, spongy moss. He rose over her in the mist, yanking at the drawstring of his chausses.

She closed her eyes. '*Tis a dream. Soon I'll awaken.*

And then he covered her with his large body and took her in his arms, and she knew it was no dream. She was here, on this foggy riverbank, at dawn. She was here with Thorne. These were Throne's lips on hers, she thought with amazement, Thorne's rough, unshaven cheek grazing her own. The restless hands exploring her body were Thorne's, the rigid heat pressed against her thigh belonged to him.

He awakened her untouched places, drawing sighs of pleasure from her throat as his caresses grew bolder, more impassioned. He lowered his head to her breast, drawing first one nipple and then the other into the heat of his mouth, sucking hard, grazing her with his teeth. He followed that torment with little licks and kisses, continuing them in a warm path down her belly.

She shivered when she felt his breath between her legs, gasped at the warm pressure of his lips, the hot intimacy of his tongue. Closing one hand around her hip, he slid a long finger inside her, caressing her from within.

It was a strange, dark sorcery he worked with his hand and his mouth. It was like making fire by rubbing two sticks together, the friction coaxing a red-hot glow from what had always been cool, generating a spark of excruciating pleasure that flickered breathlessly on the edge of flame....

Delirious with need, deafened by the blood pounding in her ears, she clutched at his hair. "Please ..."

He withdrew his finger, gently kissed her aching sex, and eased his large body down onto hers. She opened herself to him, holding him close. Then he shifted and reached between them. She knew what was coming and welcomed it, yet when he pressed into her, stretching her open, she tensed, her heart racing in panic.

Now he would own her. Now he would consume her.

He took her face in his hands and she looked up into his eyes, so close, so endlessly blue. He whispered things she could barely hear over the roar in her ears ... endearments, promises ...

In the depths of his eyes she saw reassurance, as well as a deep and profound hunger. On their glassy surface she saw her own reflection, and her own hunger, as great as his. Their coming together had been inevitable. She had known it from the moment she first saw him on the dock at Bulverhythe Harbor.

She could just make out his words. "... but if you want me to stop—"

She chuckled and shook her head. How could he think she would want him to stop?

He took her mouth in a kiss of thanks and fierce longing. The kiss muffled her gasp as he moved within her again, pushing with slow, deliberate care. The muscles in his arms and shoulders were as tight as bowstrings, and Martine knew that he held back for her.

He paused. Half sheathed within her, he reached down to caress her again where their bodies joined. That wondrous spark ignited once more within her, and she lifted her hips, seeking his touch, pleading this time not with her voice, but with her body. *Please, please ... oh, please ...*

In the heart-stopping moment before the spark flamed, she gripped his shoulders, crying his name. White heat consumed her, a flash fire that crackled along her veins, rocking her with its force. Dimly she felt his hands lift her hips and heard his groan of effort as he drove in hard. In a single, rending stroke, he buried himself completely within her, then gathered her in his arms and held her tight and still as her quaking subsided.

"Are you all right?" he asked softly.

She took a deep breath and nodded. So great had been her pleasure that it had overwhelmed the pain. She had barely been aware of it. No doubt it was as he had intended. He trailed his fingers through her wet hair, and she closed her eyes.

He filled her, possessed her. She felt impossibly hot and stretched, and knew that he'd torn her inside. She wondered if she would be sore tomorrow, then remembered that tomorrow she would be back at Harford Castle, preparing to wed Sir Edmond.

She opened her eyes. "We must be mad."

He pressed a thoughtful kiss to her forehead. "I lived among madmen once, in a hole in the ground in the Levant. All but your brother and I eventually lost their senses. They were the lucky ones. They forgot about the chains that bound their feet and the prison walls that surrounded them. Some of them were even happy."

He trailed a finger down her forehead and along her nose. When he pressed it to her lips, she tasted it with the tip of her tongue.

"If we're mad," he murmured, his mouth descending toward hers, "so be it."

His lips barely grazed hers. The kiss—the kisses, for there were many—were soft and worshipful, as if bestowed upon a precious thing, a sacred object. He worshiped her mouth, her cheeks, her eyelids, ears, and throat.

She became aware of an almost imperceptible movement of his hips, the thrusts excruciatingly slow, achingly gentle.

"Does this hurt?" he whispered hoarsely.

She wrapped her arms around him. "Nay." Through her breast, she felt his heart pounding in his chest. *He has seen to my pleasure,* she thought. *Now he will see to his own.*

Her pleasure had been a surprise to her, and she hadn't thought it could be repeated. Yet, as he moved within her, his strokes exquisitely measured, she felt that hot little spark rekindle at the juncture of their bodies. Flames of desire licked and teased her; he stoked them with thrusts that grew ever faster, more urgent, more intense. She matched his rhythm, straining unthinkingly toward release, insensible to anything except the rising flood of heat that consumed her. When the firestorm swept through her, it tore sobs from her throat.

He arched over her, rigid and quivering, his hair hanging in sweat-dampened tendrils. When her climax subsided, he swiftly drew himself out and fell on her, crushing her hard into the blanket of moss, his trembling hands fisted in her hair. The gorge echoed with his low, shuddering groans as he pumped against her. She felt his seed pulse hotly over her belly, and then he collapsed, slick with sweat, riding out the tremors that coursed through him.

He breathed an Anglo-Saxon exclamation that she recognized as the English equivalent of "*Mon Dieu.*" She held him tight, stroking his head as it rested on her shoulder, savoring the feel of him on top of her—his size, his strength, his warmth. She knew enough of reproduction to understand why he had withdrawn, and to be grateful that he'd done so, but she couldn't help wishing he was still inside her, still connected in that amazingly intimate way.

Presently he brought his mouth to hers for a sweet, languid kiss, then shifted so he could kiss her breasts as well. "You're so beautiful," he murmured. "Perfect."

Kneeling over her, he carefully touched the stinging flesh of her sex. "You're bleeding," he said, and leaned down to soothe this place of pain and ecstasy with soft kisses and healing licks.

The mist had thinned, and soft dawn sunlight glittered through the trees. Taking her hand, Throne led her off the mossy bank and back into the river. There they remained for some time, holding each other in silence until long after the cold, clear water had washed away all of his seed and the last traces of her virgin's blood.

The ride back seemed interminable to Martine. She and Thorne exchanged nothing more than innocuous pleasantries, conscious always of Rainulf's presence. By the time they arrived at Harford that evening, she felt completely exhausted, not just physically, but emotionally.

What have I done? she thought over and over again as she washed and changed out of her dusty traveling clothes. *And where do I go from here?*

Thorne waited for her in the stairwell when she came down for supper. She gasped as he wrapped his big arms around her, pressing her back against the curved stone wall, his mouth seeking hers for a hard, urgent kiss.

"Come to me tonight," he rasped. His eyes pleaded with her, his hands hungrily exploring her hips, her waist, her breasts.

"Thorne . . ." She moaned as he found a taut nipple through two layers of wool and tugged. "We have to . . ." He crushed his hips to hers, and he was so hard, so ready. "Oh, God . . ."

He bit her earlobe. "Come to me."

"We have to talk," she managed, as her arms encircled him.

"God, I need you so much. We'll talk. Just come to—"

Footsteps. Thorne released her quickly as Bernard came into view from below.

"My lady," Bernard said silkily, nodding toward Martine. "Woodsman," he added, glancing back and forth between them. "Supper is on the table, if you two can be troubled to join us."

"Enough of that damned Neville," Godfrey bellowed, rising unsteadily at the head of the supper table. " 'Twould please me if I never heard the bastard's name again!"

'Twould please me, as well, thought Martine. All conversation that evening had centered around the murderous baron, who had disappeared from Sussex, along with most of his men, on the day of the betrothal ceremony. His wife had sought and received sanctuary at a small local nunnery, but Neville had not been heard from since. There were rumors that he had fled to the Continent, but several more reliable sources claimed he had journeyed north in order to amass an army of hired soldiers. Not knowing his intent, Olivier had instructed his barons to prepare for battle.

"Everybody shut up!" Godfrey commanded. "You— Thorne. Stand up!" The Saxon, looking slightly wary, rose to his feet. "I have something to say."

Dear God, thought Martine. *Bernard saw us. He told Lord Godfrey. Thorne is ruined. I'm ruined.*

Conversation ceased. Everyone lowered their tankards and knives except Edmond, who continued to eat. The only sound in the hall was the pop and hiss of logs as they settled in the fire pit.

The baron fixed his unfocused gaze on Thorne, standing across the table from Martine. "For ten years you've served me, Thorne Falconer, and served me well. You've been a valiant soldier, without equal, but everyone who knows me knows that it's your skill with the birds, even more than with the bow, that has made you so indispensable to me."

"Hear, hear!" chorused Peter and Guy.

"Too indispensable," admitted Godfrey, a little sadly. "Aye, I'll admit it. What I do tonight, I'd have done years ago, but for my greed. I wanted you here, at Harford Castle, training *my* birds, not miles away at your own manor, training yours."

He sighed. "But the time has come. In betrothing my boy Edmond to the lovely Martine of Rouen—" he nodded toward Martine, who nodded back, relieved at the turn things were taking, "you have united my family with that of Queen Eleanor. 'Tis a service I find I cannot let pass without reward."

He gestured to a waiting manservant, who handed Thorne something long wrapped in purple silk. "Unwrap it!" the baron urged. Thorne did so, revealing a sheathed sword. He withdrew the weapon, a shimmering broadsword with a jewel-encrusted hilt.

Over the excited murmurings of the diners, Godfrey said, "Sealed within that hilt is a shred of the swaddling clothes of our Lord Jesus Christ!" The murmurs became exclamations, then cheers. Through it all, Thorne's carefully schooled expression never wavered.

"And now for your land." Silence enveloped the hall. Everyone, Martine included, stared at Thorne, who patiently waited for the baron to get on with it. Were it not for the white-knuckled grip with which he held the sword, one might have thought him disinterested in the proceedings.

Come to me, he had begged, his body rigid with desire. She remembered the feel of him inside her, the ache, the heat, and felt warm all over. Despite the rawness between her legs, which had pained her considerably during the long ride back, she wanted more than anything to take him into her once again, to close around him, to be united with him. She remembered how he had looked, arching over her, trembling, shaking with his need, groaning as he drove into her ... Could this man who stood before her now, accepting his reward for betrothing her to another, be the same man?

"As soon as is practical after the wedding," Godfrey continued, " 'tis my intention to deed to you a manor to hold in fief of me, specifically those thirty-seven measures of land bounded on the south and west by Harford River, on the east by the stone wall enclosing the property of ..." Loud cheers and hurrahs from Thorne's men drowned out the rest of Godfrey's description, the holding in question obviously familiar to them.

Thorne, appearing stunned, glanced briefly in Martine's direction. " 'Tis exceptionally generous, my lord," he said quietly, taking his seat.

" 'Tis no more than you're due," said Godfrey. "And now, if my lady Estrude will stand ..."

A smiling Estrude rose and smoothed her gown.

"My second announcement is also happy, and I daresay long in coming. Fourteen years in coming, to be exact. Friends and family, it is my great pleasure to announce that Lady Estrude of Flanders, my daughter by marriage, is, at long last, with child."

A roar of approval filled the great hall. Estrude beamed. Bernard endured a volley of backslaps from his men. "A baby! A baby!" squealed Ailith from her mother's lap. Curiously, Clare did not appear to share in her mistress's joy. Red-faced, her chin trembling, she surreptitiously wiped the tears that welled in her eyes as she stole anguished glances at Bernard.

Rainulf, sitting beside Martine, gasped. *"Thorne!"*

All heads turned toward the Saxon. He sat perfectly still, the sword in his right hand, his left resting on the table next to his trencher, the palm sliced cleanly open. He cupped his hand as it filled with blood. "Clumsy of me," he said tightly.

"Oh!" Martine started to rise, but Felda, rushing toward Thorne as she swiftly untied her apron, motioned for her to sit.

"Hold still, Sir Thorne," Felda insisted as he rose to his feet, his face ashen.

"I'm fine," he ground out.

Martine tried to meet his eyes, but he looked away, quite deliberately, it seemed.

Felda wrapped the apron around his hand, then ran after him as he strode toward the stairwell. "Let me bandage—"

"I'll be fine. Let me be."

"Thorne, just let me—"

He whirled around. *"Let me be!"* His anger drew a sharp exclamation from Felda. He briefly closed his eyes, the muscles jumping in his jaw. Raising both hands in a placating gesture, he said quietly, "Just let me be. Please."

Everyone watched in silence as he ducked into the stairwell.

Come to me tonight, he had said. From her chamber window, Martine gazed at the candlelit windows of the hawk house. It was dark in the bailey, and she had seen no one move about for some time. Was it too soon to go to him? Would she be seen?

Behind her, Felda bustled about the chamber, prattling on about Lady Estrude's announcement. "She's lucky, that one is. After fourteen years, we all thought she was barren. I'd just about decided she was going through the change."

Thorne's shadow crossed one of the windows. He had a bird on his fist. "At her age?" Martine said. "She's only thirty."

"Aye, but her courses have been failing her of late."

"How do you know?"

"Everyone knows everyone else's business in a castle keep, milady." Martine hoped, for her sake and Thorne's, that this was not true. "She says she can feel the babe already."

"That's absurd," said Martine. "She claims she's but one month pregnant. Perhaps she's not really with child at all. In Paris I helped treat a woman who'd been so desperate for a baby that her body actually went through all the changes of pregnancy. Her courses ceased, and her belly grew ..."

Down in the bailey, a lone woman, clad in a deep purple cloak, ran from the keep to the hawk house, casting furtive glances over her shoulder.

It was Estrude.

Without knocking, she opened the door and darted

inside. Martine suddenly felt very cold in her thin silk chemise.

Felda, watching over her mistress's shoulder, hissed a sharp Anglo-Saxon curse. Martine turned to look at her and found her sadly shaking her head. "Thorne, you fool," Felda muttered.

Martine stared at her maid. "What do you mean? Tell me."

Felda shook her head. "I'm not sure, but I think Thorne may have gone and done something very foolish indeed."

"What are you saying?"

"I'm saying maybe Lady Estrude's not just lucky. Maybe she's clever. Maybe it's not her that's barren, maybe it's Bernard."

Martine pondered this for a moment. "You think ... you think Sir Thorne is the baby's father?" Felda shrugged, and Martine struggled to control her chaotic emotions. "Are he and Estrude ... Is he in love with her?"

Felda's eyes widened. "*Her?* God, no. Thorne don't have to be in love with a woman to bed her, milady. He don't even have to like her. If a woman's willing, that's good enough for him. He loves women, but he's never been in love. He told me himself he don't believe in it. He said it was something the jongleurs invented to keep themselves in business."

Martine began to shiver. "I see."

"Funny thing is, he don't much care for highborn ladies, though of course he'll be marrying one someday. He's far too land-hungry to settle for a girl without property. But who he chooses to marry is altogether different from who he chooses to tup. Says he prefers a good honest tumble with a simple wench who knows what's what, and he don't mind paying for it if that's what it takes. Says all a whore wants from him is silver, but them fine ladies want all them pretty lies. They're too much trouble, make him work too hard for it. But with an appetite like his, I don't guess he'd be that fussy if one of them was willing and no one else was available."

There were now two shadows in the window of the hawk house, so close together that they looked like one.

Martine wrapped her arms around herself to ease the tremors that shook her. "I see."

Thorne slid the long needle into the tethered hawk's nostril. He worked slowly and carefully, his bandaged left hand holding the bird still while his right manipulated the needle. Even when Estrude let herself in and came around behind him, he kept his eyes on his work and his movements steady, lest he do the suffering creature more harm than good.

Estrude rested a hand on his shoulder, jarring him slightly. "What are you doing?" she asked.

Slowly he said, "Trying to keep my hand still."

She let go and came around to face him, her attention riveted on the bird. "That's quite the most disgusting thing I've ever seen. Really, what in God's name are you—"

He sighed. "I'm draining this hawk of a bad humor."

She smiled. "Do you think you could do the same for Bernard?"

Clever bitch. " 'Twould take more than a needle. My new broadsword, perhaps."

She chuckled and watched in silence as he continued the treatment. Nodding toward his bandaged hand, she said, " 'Twas a nasty cut you gave yourself at supper."

" 'Twas a nasty surprise you gave *me*." Christ, but he hated surprises.

He slowly drew the needle out, then looked her in the eye. "I'm curious. How did you know 'twas Bernard who was barren, and not you?"

She turned away and began fussing with things on his worktable. Finally she said, "I suppose it's safe to tell *you*. When I was fifteen, there was this man. My father's overlord. I lived in his household, serving his wife."

Thorne dabbed a bit of soothing oil on the hawk's beak. "You became pregnant by him?"

"Aye." She lifted the little wooden falcon head that he was carving in Freya's image and on which he would keep her leather hood. "I was a fool. I adored him— much as that little idiot Clare adores Bernard," Thorne glanced sharply at her, and she chuckled. "I've known all along how she feels about him. Of course, nothing will ever come of it. She's much too plain for Bernard's taste. I, on the other hand, was comely and ... willing. My mistress's husband found me easy prey. When he discovered I was with child, he talked a midwife into giving me a tonic that expelled the babe from my womb."

"And then you married Bernard." He pulled on a gauntlet.

"And no one ever knew," she finished, turning around.

"Why did you pick me to father your child?"

"Simply put?"

"I'm a simple man."

"You seemed like good breeding stock."

"Christ," he muttered, untethering the hawk and taking her on his fist.

"Big and tall and healthy," she continued. "And, from what I'd heard, quite the eager stud bull. I must say, I was somewhat put out by the trouble I had to go through for a bit of Saxon seed."

"I'm simple, not stupid." Ignoring the anger that sparked in her eyes, he said, "There's another reason you chose me. You were fairly sure I'd keep quiet. I take it you came here tonight to make certain of it."

"Aye."

"I hardly have any choice, do I? If I talk, I'll be destroyed right along with you. You knew I'd be forced to keep silent. 'Twas all part of your plan. You're a cunning woman."

"Thank you."

"That wasn't a compliment."

"Nay? What choice do women have in life but to be cunning, to get their way by sly manipulation? If I'm good at it, I consider it a compliment."

She was exasperating. But she was right. Straightforward reason would never work on Bernard. Her only hope lay in deceiving him.

Thorne was still troubled. "One thing bothers me greatly, though. I can stomach keeping quiet, and I can even stomach having a child who doesn't know I'm his father. But the idea that my own flesh and blood will be brought up by Bernard, of all—"

"He won't!" Estrude shrieked fiercely. "Not while I'm alive to prevent it."

Her outburst caused the hawk to pump her wings and strain against the leash wrapped around Thorne's gauntlet. He placated her with some gentle strokes and a few soothing words. "You sound almost maternal," he observed wryly.

"I *feel* maternal. I'm a woman, after all." She pressed a hand to her belly, and Thorne saw how its roundness stretched the silk of her tightly laced kirtle even tighter. No, it was too soon for her to show. It was surely a hearty supper that distended her so, and not the babe.

She said, "The child will be fostered out to a noble family. A good family. Far away from here. Far away from Bernard."

"Do you swear it?"

Her eyes were grim. "My own father was much like Bernard. I'd not submit a child of mine to his rages."

The image of Estrude as a little girl, suffering abuse at the hands of her sire, filled Thorne with a swell of compassion that startled him. It must have shown on his face, because she said, "I don't want your pity. Just your silence."

Thorne nodded slowly. "You have it."

Alone now in her chamber, Martine continued to watch the hawk house. Presently Lady Estrude emerged, pulled her hood up, and sprinted back to the keep. Martine waited until she heard her enter her own chamber down the hall. Then, taking a deep breath, she pinned her mantle over her knee-length chemise and, on bare, silent feet, traced Estrude's path back to the hawk house.

Thorne opened the door on her first knock, scooped her inside, and pushed her back against the door. His mouth closed over hers, hot and demanding. With his bandaged hand he fumbled with the brooch that secured her mantle, while the other stole beneath it to glide over a silk-clad breast. He groaned and tore at the mantle; the brooch went flying, the mantle fell to the floor. Before she could stop him, he pulled her chemise up, lifted her by her hips, and wrapped her legs around him.

He kissed her throat, then raised her higher and suckled a tight nipple through the chemise. Arousal flashed through her like lightning. She arched back against the door as he thrust against her, hard as rock through his loose shirt and chausses.

Nay. Don't let him do this, her inner voice cried. She pushed against his shoulders, and he lowered her to the floor, but when she opened her mouth to speak, her words were silenced with another searing kiss. He untied the front of her chemise with impatient fingers, and then she felt his hands on her bare breasts, squeezing, caressing, the bandage rough against her soft skin.

She wrested her mouth from his. "Thorne—"

He recaptured her mouth, then took one of her hands and pressed it between his legs. She felt the tautly stretched wool of his chausses, and the rigid shaft beneath. It jumped at her touch, and a growl rose in his throat. Molding her fingers around it, he guided her hand up and down its length. It felt hot and alive, frightening and wonderful.

Again she tore her mouth away. "Thorne, please!"

"I know we need to talk," he murmured hoarsely. "But, God, I need you. All day I've needed you. I'm in pain."

From needing me, or just needing a woman? wondered Martine, all too certain she knew the answer. *With an appetite like his,* Felda had said, *I don't suppose he'd be that fussy if no one else was available.*

Those words gave her the strength to wrench her hand out of his grip. Instantly his long arms enclosed her in a shuddering embrace. "I know I'm going too fast," he breathed. "But I've got to have you." She felt him gather the skirt of her chemise in his fist. "I need you now. *Now.* We'll talk later."

Gripping his shoulders, Martine drew in a deep breath and closed her eyes. "Is it your baby Lady Estrude is carrying?"

The whole world seemed to whirl to a stop. Thorne didn't move at all except to tighten his fingers around the silk clutched in his fist. Beneath her hands, his big shoulders tensed.

Oh, God. Oh, God. She wrestled out of his grip and jerked away from him, clutching at her chemise to cover her chest. Thorne started to reach for her, but her expression stilled his arm. Closing his eyes, he clenched his jaw and dragged his hands through his unkempt hair.

Christ, why does he have to be so handsome?

She found her brooch in the straw, shook out her mantle, and wrapped it around herself with shaking hands. Did she have the right to be jealous of a woman he had lain with before her? Did it matter? The horrible truth was that he felt no more for her than for that awful Estrude, on whom he had carelessly sired a bastard. And he undoubtedly felt less for either one of them than he did for the whores and servings wenches he preferred. Thorne Falconer cared nothing for women, not in his heart. They existed in his world for one purpose only—to slake his lust.

No, that wasn't quite true, for Martine herself served a secondary purpose—to marry Edmond of Harford and thereby earn for Sir Thorne the land he coveted. It was humiliating enough to be used in this manner alone, but to have allowed him to seduce her as well ... Martine cringed to think of how he must have laughed at her gullibility, even as he took his pleasure with her.

He had used her, just as Jourdain had used her mother, and she, fool that she was, had let it happen, had invited it, had willingly walked into the trap she had spent her life avoiding. He'd been so earnest, so convincing ... so skilled. Just as Jourdain had undoubtedly been. The knowledge that he had manipulated her so easily was inexpressibly painful, and for the first time in her life she understood—really understood—the despair that drove her mother to take her life.

She could not undo what was done, could not erase the pain and humiliation. But perhaps she could mitigate it, could salvage a few shreds of dignity to walk away with.

Summoning a tone of weary disinterest, she said "Is there any woman in this castle you haven't slept with?" then turned and began to pull the door open.

It closed with an explosive slam that made her ears ring. She found herself pinned facing the door, his hands on either side of her head, his heaving chest pressed to her back.

"Martine." He spoke quietly, obviously straining for control. "About Lady Estrude and ... and the baby. Don't judge me without knowing how it happened."

"Oh, I think I know how it happened."

She grabbed the doorknob, but he took her by the shoulders and turned her to face him. Hugging her mantle closed, she looked away from his intense blue eyes. He shut them for a moment and took a deep breath. "Does anyone else know about this?"

She kept her gaze averted. "Felda suspects."

He nodded thoughtfully. "I'll talk to her. She mustn't reveal this. Nor must you. If Bernard finds out—"

"He'll kill you, I know."

"I can take care of myself. But Estrude is helpless against him. God knows I've no affection for the woman, but—"

"That's right," she said coldly, looking him in the eye. "I understand you never waste affection on your bed partners. You care more for those birds of yours than the women you use and then toss aside."

She turned her head again, but he took her by the chin and forced her to face him. He had the grace to look affronted. He was a good actor, but then he would have to be, to have the kind of success he had with women.

"Is that what you think I've done to you?" he asked, looking convincingly pained. "Used you and tossed you aside?"

"You deny it?" He opened his mouth to speak, but she cut him off with a more pointed question. "What did you think would happen between us after . . . after this morning?"

"I didn't think. It all happened so fast, and I felt so overwhelmed, so . . ." He dragged his hands through his hair. "When you went to the river and I thought you might kill yourself, I just panicked. Nothing mattered except finding you and—"

"And making sure I stayed alive long enough to marry Sir Edmond so that you could earn your precious—"

He seized her by the shoulders. "Martine, you can't think that's why I—"

"Enough of your lies!" she cried, shaking him off. "I'm sick to death of your lies. You needed me alive for your own purposes, and that's why you followed me."

"Then why did I make love to you?" he asked hoarsely.

"Because I was . . . convenient. You bed whomever is

handy and spare naught a care for the damage you do to their lives. You're no better than Jourdain."

Gravely he said, "Martine, it's not like you think. Your perceptions are tainted by memories of your father, but you mustn't assign his sins to me. I have enough of my own."

"God knows *that's* true."

He gently stroked her face, and she squeezed her eyes shut, reminding herself it was all an act, it meant nothing. "I know you feel used," he said softly. "I know you feel hurt—"

Her eyes flew open and she flinched from his touch. "Not at all," she lied. The less he knew of his power to hurt her, the better it would be for her. "You're wrong when you say I wasn't thinking when I . . . when we . . . I knew exactly what I was doing. I was using you the same as you were using me. I'd wanted to take a lover before my marriage, for the experience. You were available, and willing. That's all it meant to me."

He searched her eyes. She held his gaze for as long as possible before looking down.

"I don't believe it," he said quietly.

She raised her chin. "Believe what you like." She turned and reached again for the doorknob, but he closed his hand over hers. "Is there some point to detaining me?"

Long moments passed before he slowly withdrew his hand.

"I thought not," she said, and left.

Chapter 15

Thorne, on horseback, watched from far up the road as the wedding procession approached the barony chapel, cheered on by an enormous crowd of villeins. First came the hired musicians strumming their lutes and pounding their Spanish drums, their multicolored costumes exceptionally bright under the harsh noon sun. . . .

And then came Martine, seated sidesaddle on a gaily decorated mule led by her brother. At the church door, Rainulf lifted her down from her mount and presented her to Father Simon. Edmond, his family, and all of the knights and retainers of Harford followed and dismounted, but Thorne spared them not a glance; his gaze was riveted on the bride.

She looked like a goddess of the North in ermine-trimmed gold brocade, her hair plaited in two long braids interwoven with gold threads. A veil of tissue-thin sendal silk floated around her, secured by a jeweled coronet. She was regal, ethereal . . . and haunting.

It was her eyes that made her so, eyes glazed with a kind of dreamlike melancholy, as if she had been drained of all of life's pleasures and had resigned herself to its woes.

It wasn't until Edmond joined Martine on the church steps and took her hand in his that Thorne was able to wrest his gaze from her. With an angry yank on the reins, he swung his mount around and galloped full speed away from Harford.

He'd go to Hastings, that's what he'd do. He'd go to Hastings and make himself forget.

The whores all brightened when Thorne walked into the brothel. Those without customers, and even a few with, swarmed to him like bees to sweet balm, taking his mantle, bringing him mead, and vying noisily for his patronage.

Fat Nan soon took matters in hand, grabbing girls by their hair and yanking them aside to clear a path for her formidable girth. "Back off, you squawking hens!" she berated them in English. "He'll make his choice in due time. Let the man breathe!"

Smiling sweetly, she offered Thorne her plump hand, and he kissed it. "Haven't seen you in some time, Sir Falconer," she said. "And I must say I'm surprised you picked this afternoon to pay us a visit. Ain't there a wedding at Harford Castle today?"

He drained his cup. "Weddings bore me."

Nan locked her arm with his. "Well, *we* ain't boring. Are we, girls?"

"Nay! Nay!" they chorused, crowding around again to offer their services.

Freckle-faced Tilda, whom Thorne had tupped once last summer and avoided since, called to him from the lap of her customer. "What about me, Sir Falconer? I got rid of them bugs."

"I liked them bugs," said the customer, one of the regulars, a red-faced wool boiler. "They made you frisky! For once you didn't just lie there like a bag of turnips."

Tilda looked bored. "Did you ever stop to wonder why a girl's gotta have a crotchful of insects before you can get her to squirm?"

A black-haired girl trailed her fingers through Thorne's hair. "This one just *looks* at me and I squirm!"

Thorne saw that his cup had been refilled, and he quickly drank it down. "Where's Emeline?" he asked.

There was instant silence in the brothel. Someone whispered, "He don't know!"

"Nan?" said Thorne.

Nan crossed her massive arms. "Emeline got her neck broke."

"Sweet Jesus." Someone poured some more mead into his cup, and he swallowed it automatically. "What happened?"

More silence, uncomfortable silence, until Tilda spoke up. " 'Twas one of them Harford dogs."

"Tilda!" Nan hissed.

"I ain't telling him *who.*"

"Well, you better not," Nan warned. " 'Twould be worth your life, and ours, as well you know."

"You were threatened if you talked?" Thorne asked Tilda.

"Aye, we was told we'd get what Emeline got if we didn't keep mum. And we got sixpence apiece from the cheap bastard." She spat into the rushes.

It was Bernard himself, most likely. There were rumors that he'd killed a whore about twenty years ago, the crime having been hushed up through the influence of Lord Olivier, who had always been fond of his former squire. But although Bernard suffered no formal punishment for the murder, news of it gradually infiltrated every noble house in southern England. That was one of the reasons he'd had to go all the way to Flanders for a bride; there wasn't a baron or knight in all of Sussex who would betroth his daughter to him after that. Yes, it was most likely Bernard, but why, after all these years of keeping his nose clean, had he done it again? He was vicious, but he wasn't stupid.

Nan patted his hand. "I know you fancied Emeline. But I got a new girl to take her place, and you'll like her just as well, I wager." She turned and waved a girl over. "Wilona?"

A young woman in a pink wrapper stepped forward, grinning. She was fairly pretty, with all her front teeth, and pale blond hair pinned up in two coiled braids. It was the blond hair that clinched it. "She'll do," he said.

She led him upstairs to a curtained-off alcove he'd been in many times before, but always at night. It looked squalid in the muted daylight from the shuttered window, and smelled of sour rushes and quick sex.

Wilona shrugged her wrapper off and lay down unceremoniously on a straw pallet covered with a stained blanket.

"Take down your hair," he said.

After a moment's hesitation, she sat up and did as he said. Her hair fell only to the middle of her back, and was thin and lank. "Do you like it?" she asked. "Does it look like hers?" Thorne just stared at her. "I can always tell. You can call me by her name if you want. I don't mind."

Christ. He went to the window and opened the shutters. It was a cool day, and the air, although it reeked of sewage and ale, felt good on his face. Beyond this rank, narrow street, he could see Bulverhythe Harbor, crowded this afternoon with boats, its docks piled high with goods pouring in from northern France.

He remembered how she had looked, half hidden on the deck of the *Lady's Slipper,* smiling that shy, mysterious smile.

From behind him, Wilona said, "Come on, what's her name?"

Her name is Martine, he thought, gazing at the distant horizon. *Martine of Rouen. And her hair is nothing like yours, and she looks nothing like you. She's nothing like any other woman in the world.*

And I can't have her. I can never have her. She can never be mine.

God help me to get through this day, he prayed. *And then the next, and the next, and the next, without going mad from needing her, without dying a little inside every time I think about her, which is every moment of the day, or see her, which, God help me, makes me want to gather her up and ride off with her and . . .*

And what?

Leaning his elbows on the windowsill, he buried his face in his hands. And what, indeed? Martine had avoided him utterly since that painful night in the hawk house. She clearly felt hurt and angry, but in his heart he knew she cared for him, knew their lovemaking had been more than the coldhearted exercise she claimed it was. A thousand times this past fortnight he had challenged himself to find a way to be with her, to keep her . . . and a thousand times he had realized, in despair, that it was impossible.

It all came down to property, of course. Right now he had nothing: no home, no wealth, no land. Were he to marry Martine, Godfrey would dismiss him in disgrace, and he would have to abandon all that he had pursued with such single-minded determination for the past ten years—his falcons, his knighthood, and the holding Godfrey had promised him. Could he bring himself to give it up? That was a question he had trouble answering. For all that Martine meant to him, he couldn't just casually dismiss a decade's worth of struggle, sweat, and hope.

The question was academic, anyway. Even if he did make that sacrifice for her, then what? Where would they go? What would they do? They would be poor, bitterly poor, and homeless. Perhaps he could make a living as a woodsman, but there was no guarantee of that, given the rate at which land was being claimed under Forest Law. He could hire himself out as a mercenary soldier, but then he would have to leave her, and there was hardly any point to that. And what of Martine? It was bad enough to give up his own hopes and dreams. How could he subject her to a life of deprivation when she could live in luxury as Edmond's wife?

Wilona sighed impatiently. "Come on, sir, let's have us a bit of fun. Take off them things and come on over here."

Edmond's wife. He rubbed his fists on his forehead. By now, the ceremony would be over, the vows spoken, the rings exchanged, and there would be feasting and rejoicing in the great hall. After the celebration, there would be the ritual blessing of the marriage bed at Edmond's new home. And then Father Simon and the witnesses would leave, and Martine and Edmond would be alone. . . .

"God help me," he muttered.

"What's that, love?" Wilona said, yawning.

He shook his head. *Don't think about it, for God's sake. She's his wife by now. It's done. You'll get over it. You'll get over her. Little by little, the pain will go away. You'll care less and less as time goes on.*

He never should have let himself care at all, of course. He had forgotten himself, lost all self-control, and his foolish, unchecked feelings had led to the madness at the riverbank. Ah, what sweet madness, though. *I lived among madmen once,* he had told her. *Some of them were even happy.* He'd never known such abandon, such ecstasy, never known that in uniting his body with a woman's, he could join his very soul to hers. He'd been awestruck, rocked to the very core of his being. And yes, he'd been happy, For a brief time, in his sweet, unthinking madness, he'd even been happy.

But that happiness had, of course, come with a price. And now, in his anguish, he was paying it.

"Sir? It costs the same whether you do me or not, so you may as well do me. Your time will be up soon."

He turned around. She had her legs spread and her arms open. He went to her, reached into his tunic, and withdrew his purse. She sat up, the sting of rejection in her eyes. But when he shook out a far too generous handful of coins, the hurt turned to awe at the sight of all that silver.

Taking her hand in his, he filled it with the coins and closed her fingers around them. "You're very pretty," he said. "And you have beautiful hair. The problem is mine, not yours."

As he left, he heard her pouring the money from one hand to the other. "No wonder you're so popular with the girls!" she called out. "You can ask for me *any*time!"

Kneeling beside Edmond, Martine stared out the window of the bedchamber as Simon mumbled his Latin and swung his censer over the big rosemary-strewn bed, trailing streams of aromatic smoke.

Her new home was much like the prior's lodge at St. Dunstan's, a big stone house with a kitchen on the ground floor and living quarters above, although it had but one bedchamber; the rest was an open hall. It was a short ride from Harford Castle and surrounded on all sides by a flat lawn ringed with dense woods.

The unusually large window afforded her a good view of the yard on that side. She studied the moonlit grass below, contemplating the best spot for her herb garden, the one she would spend the winter planning and the spring sowing. It was all she had thought about all day, even during the wedding, especially then, when she couldn't bear to think about what she was doing, about the overwhelming, irrevocable step she was taking ... about Thorne.

She had pictured the garden in her mind—borage here, chamomile there, perhaps a border of silky wormwood—amending and rearranging the pattern over and over as she spoke her vows at the church door, scattered coins to the peasants, endured the wedding mass, and ducked beneath the shower of seeds that greeted her as she left the chapel hand in hand with Edmond: Edmond, in his long, elegant tunic with his dirty, ragged fingernails ... Edmond, with his feral good looks and his breath like rancid meat ... Edmond, now swaying drunkenly on his knees as this last tiresome rite of marriage concluded.

Rainulf kissed her cheek, whispered " 'Twill be all right, you'll see," and left with Father Simon and Lord Godfrey. Felda led her into the hall, dressed her in a silken shift and wrapper, brushed out her hair, and dabbed her with fragrant oils.

When Martine took a deep, shaky breath, Felda said, "You oughtn't to be nervous, milady. Not with a bridegroom who's as scared as that one out there."

"Scared?"

"Why do you think he's got himself so sotted? If you ask me, he's terrified of you. I can see it in his eyes every time he looks your way."

"*Why,* for God's sake?"

Felda shrugged. "I think it's because you belong to a different world from him. You can read and play chess and talk about something other than hunting and whor—" She bit her lip and glanced sheepishly at her mistress. "I'd best getting to bed, milady." She reached out with both fleshy hands and pinched Martine's cheeks until they burned, nodding approvingly at the results. "And so should you," she added with a wink as she turned and disappeared down the stairs.

It was some time before Martine could work up the courage to return to the bedchamber. When she did, she found Edmond facedown in the rushes, snoring. With a silent prayer of gratitude, she swept the rosemary sprigs off the bed, climbed under the covers, wrapper and all, and gave herself up to the blessed numbness of sleep.

"Do you suppose he's dead, milady?" Felda asked.

The two women stood on either side of Edmond, still prone in the rushes, unaware of the late morning sun streaming in through the bedchamber window.

Martine sighed. "Probably not."

Felda shot her a curious look, then leaned over her mistress's comatose husband. "Sir Edmond, wake up! We're due back at the castle for the noon meal. They're expecting us." Edmond didn't move. "Please, sir. Milady's brother leaves on pilgrimage today. She's wanting to say good-bye to him."

Shaking her head, Martine squatted next to him. "Give me a hand, Felda. Let's roll him over." With Martine pushing and Felda pulling, they managed to turn him faceup. He grunted but didn't open his eyes. His normally swarthy complexion looked gray, his mouth gaped open, and rushes clung to one side of his face. Martine peeled one off, which left a dark mark like a fresh scar.

"Let's go."

"But, milady, we can't go without—"

"Do you propose to drag him behind us on a litter?"

"Nay, milady, but—"

"Then let's go."

Why do I always end up sitting across from Thorne? Martine wondered as she inspected the whole glazed rabbit on her trencher. She'd never eaten rabbit before and didn't much feel like eating it now.

Godfrey, at the head of the table, frowned. "I wish Edmond were here. Doesn't seem right."

"She couldn't wake him up," Rainulf reminded him.

Bernard's men snickered, except for Boyce, who shook with laughter. "My lord, if I may say so, you're the one who wanted grandsons. Most likely the boy's exhausted himself from trying too hard to plant one."

Martine, her face scalding, saw Thorne suppress a scowl. So the Saxon didn't like the idea of her sharing with Edmond the pleasures that he had taught her at the riverbank. But what right had he to disapprove? Edmond was her husband and Thorne Falconer was merely a selfish rogue who had used and discarded her.

Still, she couldn't bear to be the subject of those crude whispers and giggles. Glaring at the red-haired giant, and ignoring Rainulf's look of warning, she said, " 'Twas trying too hard to empty the brandy jug that exhausted my husband, and nothing more."

Boyce laughed, of course, but the rest of the group exchanged the look of disapproval that had become so familiar to her. All except for Thorne, who looked directly at her for the first time since she'd sat down opposite him. Their eyes connected with stunning intimacy, and her heart betrayed her with a flutter of longing.

"Here he is!" thundered Godfrey, beckoning someone over to the table.

Everyone turned to see Edmond, uncombed and bedraggled, crossing the great hall.

Boyce guffawed. "Look at those marks on his face. Damned if the boy didn't spend the night in the rushes." His comrades laughed appreciatively, but Edmond, his jaw thrust out, his pallid face gone pink, clearly did not share in the mirth he'd spawned.

Oblivious to Edmond's distress, Boyce said, "Your bride's already told us you weren't up to doing your husbandly duty last night. She didn't tell us she made you sleep on the floor in punishment!"

Edmond stopped dead in the middle of the hall, his dark eyes filled with shame and confusion. Martine, regretting her part in the derision, felt a moment of pity. But the moment passed when he turned those eyes on her, for she saw something in them that chilled her. She'd seen that look once as a child, in the eyes of a wild dog that paced back and forth furiously in too small a cage. *Poor thing,* she had thought, but when she reached through the bars to pet it, it growled and bit her.

Glaring at Martine, Edmond turned and stalked away.

An uncomfortable silence followed before Thorne changed the subject by asking Rainulf about his pilgrimage, and a more relaxed conversation ensued. However, Martine noticed that Bernard did not join in. He sliced and ate his meat in grim silence, pausing every now and then to study Martine with his snakelike eyes.

"I can't bear it," Martine rasped against Rainulf's shoulder as they said good-bye on the outer drawbridge. She had promised herself she wouldn't cry, yet she couldn't stop her eyes from burning with tears. "I can't bear not seeing you for two years."

"You'll have—"

"Nay, please!" She looked up. "Don't tell me again that I'll have Edmond to take care of me. He can't even take care of himself."

He patted her hair. "I was going to say you'll have Thorne."

Momentarily speechless, Martine glanced toward the Saxon, who, having already bid Rainulf good-bye, now stood by the inner gatehouse watching them. "What do you mean?"

He hesitated. "Edmond is ... young. I'm confident that he'll mature in time, but while I'm gone, I'll feel better if there's someone more ... capable ... looking after you."

She stepped back and rubbed the tears from her eyes. "You asked Sir Thorne to look after me?"

"Aye. Your hasty temper worries me now more than ever. You've been married barely a day, and already you've publicly humiliated your hus—"

" 'Twas I who was humiliated," she spat out. "I had every right to—"

"I'm speaking of discretion, not rights. Bernard was also most displeased, in case it escaped your notice."

She shrugged. "I care naught what Bernard thinks of me."

"You care naught what anyone thinks of you," he said. "But people have ways of making one care. They have ways of punishing outspokenness such as yours. 'Tis why I made Thorne swear an oath on the relic in the hilt of his sword that he'd protect and defend you while I was gone, should you need it."

She laughed shortly. "He swore on that worthless scrap of linen? He doesn't believe any more than I do that it ever swaddled the baby Jesus. A lot of good that oath is worth."

Rainulf looked cross. "Thorne is a man of honor. He'll make sure no harm comes to you. But should you ever find yourself in need ..." He drew a purse from his robe and pressed it into Martine's hand. It was heavy, and when she pulled the drawstring and looked inside, she saw the glint of gold coins. "The Church has all my land," he said, "but I retained a certain amount of ... portable wealth."

She smiled knowingly. "Wealth you could hide, you mean."

He frowned. "Wealth I thought might someday be more useful to you than to the Church. But yes, it can and should be hidden." Martine slipped it into the pouch on her girdle. He beckoned to the boy waiting by the stables with his mount. "No one must know about it, not even Edmond."

Especially not Edmond, thought Martine. She was no fool. The property given her when she married him was his until his death. The gold in that pouch represented her only real wealth, and she had no intention of letting it fall into his hands.

Martine wept anew as her brother mounted up. It was so like that day eight years before, when he'd left her at St. Teresa's. Remembering the pain of that parting, and how dreadfully she had missed him afterward, only made this good-bye harder.

She took his hand as he leaned down in his saddle to kiss her wet cheek. "You're foolish and hardheaded, little sister, but I love you very much."

"I love you, too. Please, please be careful."

"I will." With a wave to her, and another to Thorne, he turned and rode away. She stood and watched him, tears streaming down her face, until he ceased to be even a speck on the landscape.

I'm really alone now, she thought. *Completely alone.*

Edmond did not come home until late that night, long after Martine had gone to bed, again wearing both her sleeping shift and wrapper, having abandoned her practice of sleeping in the nude. She awoke to the sound of him bumping into something, but lay still with her eyes closed, feigning sleep as he moved about the room. Her heart raced in panic as she waited for him to join her in bed, but the panic eased when she realized that, in his own clumsy way, he was endeavoring to be quiet.

He lifted the covers and crawled in next to her. Even though her back was turned, her nostrils were filled with his distinctive, sweetly sour smell, like wine that had gone bad. He fell asleep almost instantly and, with a sigh of relief, she did the same.

Martine stood at the bedchamber window, combing her hair and watching Edmond in the yard below as he tossed a stick to the litter of bloodhound pups she had given him. It was dusk, and she had already changed into her sleeping shift, having fallen into a pattern of retiring early, so that she was fully asleep—or could appear so—by the time her husband came to bed.

A week had passed since the wedding, but still Edmond had not, thank God, attempted to bed her. She would have to pretend to be a virgin, and she didn't know whether she was a good enough actress. Also, he grew more repulsive with each passing day. He looked worse, acted worse, and God knew, he smelled worse.

Martine suspected he didn't find her very attractive, either, but knew there was more to it than that. He seemed wary of her, perhaps even a little frightened, peculiar though that seemed given his brawn. Her outspokenness clearly intimidated him.

And of course, as far as he was concerned, she had called his manhood into question before the entire baronial household, with no provocation other than the desire to humiliate him. She did not disabuse him of that notion, partly because they hardly ever spoke, and partly because she felt that anything that kept him at a distance was good. In fact, since the wedding, she had tried to be as cool and remote as possible. Perhaps if she continued to intimidate him, he would continue to avoid her.

Edmond threw the stick across the yard and squeezed some more wine into his mouth from the skin hanging on a cord around his neck. The puppies scrambled after the stick, descending on it in a pile of squirming bodies. He whistled, and the victorious pup emerged from the pile with the stick in its mouth and dutifully returned it. Again and again, as darkness fell, he tossed the stick, took it back, and tossed it again. At one point the smallest pup claimed the stick but, instead of bringing it back, ran with it into the woods.

"Come back here," Edmond yelled. He whistled and slapped his thigh. "Here, pup!" Another whistle. Finally the puppy appeared, without the stick. "Where's the stick? Get the stick." The puppy just stood there, looking at him, its little head cocked.

Edmond squatted down and beckoned to it. "Come here, boy. Come on. That's right." The little creature ran to his arms, tail wagging. He picked it up, stood, and held it in front of his face. "What good are you if you can't even bring back a stick?"

As casually as he might break off a piece of bread, he

closed a hand around the animal's head and snapped its neck.

Martine gasped. Turning, he looked up at her, the dead puppy hanging limp from his hand. He looked surprised. Surprised that she'd been watching him? Or perhaps it was surprise at her shocked expression, her apprehension. He'd never seen her vulnerable before, and it seemed to amaze him. He inspected her with intense interest, looking her up and down as if this were the first time he'd ever laid eyes on her.

No, it was more than mere interest, she realized, feeling queasy. It was excitement, his dark eyes glinting as they took in her sleeveless linen shift, her loose hair, her fear. She backed slowly away from the window, watching him watching her.

He smiled. It was a lifeless smile like Bernard's, a smile not of pleasure, but of anticipation. He hurled the puppy's body into the woods, then turned and strode purposefully toward the house.

Martine dropped the comb and ran downstairs to the kitchen. With palsied fingers she unlocked her brass box, searching through its contents until she found the little blue vial.

"Milady?" Felda said from the stove. "What are you—"

"A jug of brandy and a goblet. Hurry!" While Felda fetched the brandy, Martine grabbed a mortar and quickly mixed a pinch of the hemlock with half a dozen other sedative herbs.

"What *is* that stuff?" Felda asked as her mistress funneled the powder into the brandy.

"Surgical sleeping draft." She recorked the jug and shook it, then grabbed the goblet from her wide-eyed maid and returned to the bedchamber.

Edmond stood at the window urinating in an arc onto the lawn below. Hearing the leather curtain part, he looked over his shoulder. Martine had returned with brandy. He saw the disgust on her face although she tried to disguise it. And he noticed her body, barely concealed through the thin shift she wore.

Martine's hands shook. He saw them, just before she set the jug and goblet down on the chest by the door and hid them behind her back. *What a dunce I've been*

to tremble before her like a whipped dog. She was the
one who trembled now.

"Take off your shift," he commanded, turning back
to the window.

She paused. "Don't you want some brandy first?"

"You know what I want." He shook himself off,
tucked himself in, and turned around. She tried to look
nonchalant, but he could see the panic in her eyes. He
drew strength from it.

She said, "I thought perhaps some brandy might
relax—"

"I'm relaxed enough," Any more "relaxed," and he'd
be in no condition to give her a proper tupping. Every
morning Boyce asked him if he'd broken that feisty new
mare to the saddle yet. He never answered, but they
always knew. And they always laughed. *She's put a spell
on him,* they said. In jest, but after a few days, he began
to wonder if they were right. After all, there'd been that
business at the river with Ailith.

Never mind. Tonight she'd cast no spells. Tonight he'd
ride the witch like she deserved to be ridden, and then
she'd not be so high and mighty. He'd make it hurt.
He'd make sure she knew it was he who held the reins,
he who wielded the whip.

"Take off your shift," he repeated. She just stood
there, but from the look in her eyes he could tell her
mind was racing—hatching some scheme to get away
from him, no doubt. He took a step forward, and she
took a step back.

She was his wife, by God! She had to do his bidding,
same as his dogs or his horses. But she treated *him* like
the dog, made him feel less than a man, same as Boyce
and the others did. Only he didn't have to take it from
her. Not from her. He wasn't some dumb creature. He
was her master, and she'd damn well learn it.

She turned toward the doorway, but he leaped across
the room, seizing her as she tried to run. Clutching her
shift by the neck, he ripped it open halfway to the waist,
then slammed her against the wall and held her there
by her shoulders. Looking down, he saw that he had
raked her upper chest with his nails. The sight of those
bloody scratches against her smooth white skin made
him hard as a club.

The bitch actually lifted her chin and looked him in the eye. And then she said the wrong thing. She said, "You're an animal."

He couldn't have stopped himself if he'd wanted to. Releasing her, he whipped his open hand across her face. He heard a crack as her head hit the wall, and then she slid down. He grabbed her and tossed her roughly onto the big four-poster bed. She looked dazed. A raw scrape marred her cheek, and blood ran from her nose.

He took off his belt and tunic and tossed them aside. "Pull up your shift."

After a moment's hesitation, she nodded meekly, reaching down to lift the ankle-length gown. *So,* he thought, removing his boots, *all she needed was the taste of my hand. I'll let her taste more than that before I'm done with her.* He stood up.

Then Martine kicked him, driving her foot with breathtaking force into his stomach. He grunted and toppled to the floor.

"Bitch!" he gasped, hauling himself to his feet. He grabbed her just as she reached the door, and flung her back toward the bed, taking no care with his aim. When she hit the bedpost, he felt the impact in his bones. For a moment she slumped against the thick column, as if embracing it. He saw the blood on the wood, and felt a carnal thrill.

I've killed her, he thought as she sank to the floor and collapsed on her side in the rushes. *I'm free of her now.*

He rolled her onto her back with his foot. Blood covered one side of her face. *She'll lie back and take it now, by God, just like she should have done in the first place. It's her own damn fault.* He kicked her legs apart and knelt between them. It was then that he realized she was still breathing. *Worse luck,* he thought.

It was at that moment he remembered Emeline—Emeline, the sauciest of Fat Nan's whores. Emeline . . .

His smile faded and his eyes narrowed as he gazed down upon the battered and senseless face of his wife. Emeline had laughed at him and called him a beast from the forest.

He reached down and softly stroked Martine's neck, feeling the life still pulsing stubbornly beneath the smooth skin. His fingers closed around her throat, and then the other hand joined the first, and he squeezed just as he'd done with Emeline. At first he hadn't meant to do it, but his hands had gone around her neck while he took his pleasure with her, and he found that her struggles excited him. He squeezed harder and harder as his pleasure increased. He came quickly, and then it was over. He realized he'd broken her neck.

He was terrified when he told Bernard what had happened, but Bernard told him not to worry. Bernard had taken care of everything, and it had cost but a few pennies. He'd fix it this time, too. For all her airs, this one was no different from the other. Women were all the same; Bernard had always told him so. *Don't let them laugh at you,* he always said. *If they get smart, teach them a lesson.*

The witch's face slowly turned blue, just like the little whore's. Soon . . . and then he'd be free of her.

"Sir Edmond?" The voice of Felda right outside the curtain interrupted his thoughts.

He released Martine and stood up. "What is it?"

"I . . . heard a sound before. Is everything—"

"Everything's fine. I slipped and fell is all. Go back downstairs."

After a few moments he heard her footsteps retreating. Wiping the sweat from his face with his shirt-sleeve, he grabbed the jug of brandy off the chest, uncorked it, and took a few gulps. He looked back down at his unconscious wife. He'd teach her a lesson, all right. He'd do her like he'd done Emeline, squeeze her throat while he took her. He grinned and swallowed down a good half of the jug, unconcerned about being too drunk to do her right. Just thinking about Emeline kept his weapon at the ready.

He corked the jug and went to set it back down on the chest, but it fell to the floor instead.

The damn brandy went to his head fast. He'd best make quick work of this. Kneeling again between her legs, he reached down and pulled at the waist cord of his chausses. His fingers were big and numb and clumsy, and it took a bit of doing to get himself untied. He raised Martine's shift and lowered himself onto her as the room began to slowly whirl. Closing his eyes for just a moment, he felt the numbness spread from his fingers to the rest of his body, and then he sank softly, softly into a dark and silent oblivion.

It hurt to open her eyes. When she did, it was so dark she didn't know where she was. Her ears rang; the sound filled her head. Something large and foul-smelling weighed her down, pressing her into the ground. Dried grasses prickled her back through her shift. It was night. Was she in the woods, trapped beneath a dead animal?

Presently her eyes grew accustomed to the moonlight. She saw the walls and ceiling of her bedchamber, and realized that it was rushes beneath her. She recognized the smell of her husband, heard his halting snore, and remembered everything.

Oh, God. Grunting with the effort, she pushed at the inert form pinning her to the floor, pushed and pushed until he flopped onto his back next to her. His chausses were down around his knees; her shift was bunched around her waist. *Oh, God, he did it after all,* she thought. She felt between her legs, expecting to feel raw and used—but there was nothing, no evidence that he had had his way with her. She saw the half-empty brandy jug in the rushes near the chest, and managed a smile. *It worked after all.*

When she sat up, pain seared through her skull, and she cradled her head in her hands. Her face felt sticky and swollen, one side of it, anyway. She patted it gently, wincing when her fingers brushed an open wound.

What happened? Where was she? Was she hurt? She looked around, her thoughts jumbled. She was in her bedchamber. Something about this realization seemed familiar. Looking down, she saw Edmond, his clothes in disarray, and it all came back. *I can't keep my thoughts straight,* she despaired. *I've lost my senses.*

With some effort she gained her feet. *I must leave here,* she thought. *I must get far away. I'll find Thorne. Thorne will protect me. He promised Rainulf he'd protect me.*

Feeling around in the dark, she made her way downstairs. The ringing became louder and louder, until she could barely think. *They're ringing the bells for matins,* she decided. Standing on the lawn, she looked back up at the prior's lodge, clearly visible by the light of the full moon, and then at the surrounding woods.

He'll come to me at the river, just as he did before. He'll come to me at the river where we made love. But which direction was the river? The ringing confused her, made her disoriented. Finally she blindly picked a direction and ran into the woods.

Something tickled her face. She opened her eyes and saw a shadowy form above her—licking her? She gasped, and the form turned and darted away through the crackling leaves.

It was dark. Where was she? In the woods? What was she doing in the woods in the middle of the night?

She stirred. Christ, her head was on fire. Was she hurt?

Slowly she sat up and struggled to her feet. *I must find Rainulf. Rainulf will help me. Rainulf will take care of me.* But where was Rainulf? At the university? No, it was the middle of the night. And ... and they didn't live in Paris anymore. He was at the castle, Harford Castle. She'd go there.

She turned around in a circle, peering into the black forest. Not knowing which way the castle lay, she eventually just picked a direction and walked.

The distant voice of a child woke her, and she squinted at the early morning sunlight. She lay on her stomach at the edge of the woods, where it opened into a field. Far away, a man and a woman were sowing grain from a sack held by a child.

She tried to move, but she ached all over. The light hurt her eyes, so she closed them. What was she doing out here? Mama would worry. Mama didn't like her to wander too far from home.

After a while she heard the child's voice again, but much louder, much closer. Opening her eyes, she saw a pair of bare, dirty feet right in front of her face. The child stood over her, yelling words that made no sense, words Martine had never heard before. It was a girl child, around nine or ten. Turning, she waved and gestured frantically, until the man and woman—coarsely dressed villeins—came running.

"Please tell my mama where I am," Martine managed to whisper, but they didn't hear her, so excitedly were they talking. The man said the name "Edmond" several times, but it meant nothing to her. The woman seemed to be arguing with him. Martine heard the words "Harford" and "Falconer." Finally the man walked with the girl to a dirt path and pointed, and the girl ran off.

Did he send her for Mama? Martine wondered as she drifted back into unconsciousness. *Please let her bring back Mama.*

Chapter 16

Thorne dipped the feather into the bowl and scooped up a bit of the egg white and oil mixture.

"Hold her still, Kipp," he reminded his assistant as he brushed the healing salve onto the eagle's wounded thigh. There came a knock at the hawk house door. "Come."

It was Peter, and next to him, a raggedy little girl with dark hair and enormous eyes.

"She showed up in the great hall while we were breakfasting," Peter said. "She keeps repeating your name." He ushered the girl inside and leaned against the worktable.

It didn't surprise Thorne that one of the villeins had sent his child looking for him. As the only English-speaking man of consequence in the area, they frequently summoned him to settle disputes or assist in emergencies.

He'd seen this girl a few times. "What's your name, child?" he asked in the old tongue.

"Hazel, sir." She was out of breath. That meant they'd told her to run; it was more likely an emergency than a dispute.

He dipped up some more salve and applied it with careful strokes of the feather. "Who sent you for me, Hazel?"

"Me mum, sir." She hesitated. "Well, me pa, but really me mum. Pa wanted to send for Sir Edmond, only Mum says he's most likely the one that done her like that, and to fetch you instead, and they fussed about it, but finally Pa—"

"Slow down, child, I can't follow you," Thorne said. "Is somebody hurt?"

"Dying, most like, Mum says. We found her at the

edge of the woods. Looks like a wolf's got at her, but Mum says 'twas probably just Sir Edmond."

Thorne dropped the feather into the bowl. For a moment he just stared at her.

"Thorne?" said Peter, who hadn't understood a word of the exchange. "What's the—"

The Saxon stood, his hands fisted at his sides. "Who is she? The woman who's hurt. Did your mother say?"

"She didn't have to. I knowed who she was. I was standing in the churchyard when they got married last week. She gave me a silver . . . *Sir?*"

He was out the door in two strides, moaning a Saxon oath.

Peter ran after him and grabbed his arm. "What's the—"

"It's Martine," he said. "Get the girl and come with me."

The girl, riding with Peter, led them to a tiny cottage within Edmond's manor. A man took the reins of Thorne's horse as he dismounted. "She's inside," he said. "I didn't want to bother you, Sir Falconer. I'd have sent for her husband, but—"

Thorne muscled past him and swept aside the skins that covered the door. It was a dismal, reeking little hovel. "Over there," a woman said, pointing. In a corner, on a straw pallet, lay Martine, as pale as death.

Christ, no. No! First little Louise and now Martine. And only because of his selfishness. . . . His trembling hand automatically drew the sign of the cross.

"She's still alive," the woman said.

With a groan, he crossed the room in two strides and knelt beside the pallet.

She lay on her back, her face turned toward the clay wall, dried leaves and twigs in her snarled hair, her complexion as white as her tattered shift. Not just tattered, but ripped apart, he saw. Gently pulling aside the torn, dirt-smudged linen, he inspected the scratches gouged into her chest, the purpling fingerprints on her throat. "Oh, Martine . . ." *God, what did he do to you?*

"I cleaned her wounds as best I could," the woman said. "Her feet are scratched up pretty good. We figure she spent the night in the woods. And there's her chest. But it's her face that took the worst of it."

Thorne brushed aside the tangled hair that clung to her face. Her cheek was abraded, her lip split, her forehead bruised; thank God it wasn't worse.

"The other side," the woman said, taking Martine's head in her hands and gently rolling it faceup.

Thorne sucked in a sharp breath. "Jesus!" The flesh, puffy and discolored, was further marred by angry bruises and two open wounds. Emotion swelled within him, squeezing his heart until he thought it would burst . . . rage, compassion, guilt. . . .

Edmond did this to her, of that he had no doubt. The man he had given her to had ravaged her like a wild animal. From the marks on her throat, he'd actually tried to kill her. Surely he was strong enough to break her neck.

Emeline got her neck broke, Nan had said. *'Twas one of them Harford dogs.* Thorne had thought it was Bernard, reverting to his old ways, but most likely it was Edmond, adopting them anew. He'd always revered Bernard, always tried to be like him. And Thorne, blinded by greed for his land, had paid no heed to the inherent danger of that. What happened to Martine was his fault, his responsibility; he should have known Edmond was capable of this, should have seen it coming. Had he ignored the warning signs because they interfered with his plans?

"Christ," he muttered, sinking his face in his hands. He had sworn an oath to Rainulf to protect this woman—this woman who had trusted him, had cared for him, had given herself to him. She haunted his dreams . . . she owned his heart. And he had failed her.

She moaned. He uncovered his face and took her hand. "Martine," he murmured, "I'm here."

Her eyelids fluttered open. "It *is* you," she whispered hoarsely. "You came."

"Aye. I'll take care of you. From now on."

She smiled weakly and then frowned. "My head hurts. What happened?"

She doesn't remember. He shook his head helplessly. What good would it do to tell her the truth—that her husband had savaged her, had taken her by brutal force, had very nearly killed her?

She said, "I must have fallen out of bed." He nodded, his throat tight. "Ask Mama to kiss it for me?"

He gazed for a long, painful moment at her wounded face, the childlike pleading in her eyes. His voice a ragged whisper, he said, "I'll kiss it for you."

Leaning close, he chose an uninjured spot on her forehead and gently pressed his lips to it.

She squeezed his hand. "I knew you'd come, Papa. I knew you'd come for us."

Papa. Thorne watched as she struggled to keep her eyes open. "Sleep," he softly urged. Nodding contentedly, she closed her eyes and went completely limp. If not for her quiet, steady breathing, he might have thought she had expired. Thankfully, her wounds, although cruel, were almost certainly not mortal. He opened her fingers, pressed her palm to his mouth, and kissed it.

Closing his eyes, he saw Edmond . . Edmond striking her . . . Edmond with his hands around her throat . . . Edmond on top of her.

He couldn't be allowed to get away with this—not this. By law and custom, she was under the rod of her husband. He was free to discipline her in whatever manner suited him, for any offense, with no threat of penalty. Such affairs were private. Any retribution must, likewise, be a private affair—Thorne's affair.

But right now Martine needed his help. He had to get her to a safe place and see to her injuries. He called Peter in from outside.

When his friend saw Martine, he blanched. Meeting Thorne's eyes, he said, "Edmond?"

Thorne nodded. "I'm sure of it."

"I'm at your disposal," Peter said, his right hand curled into a fist, which he cradled in his left. It was a seemingly casual gesture, but not one lost on Thorne. Peter's prowess with his fists was legendary.

He was a good friend, to be willing to exact Thorne's revenge for him—revenge on the son of his overlord, no less. It was a generous offer, but one Thorne couldn't accept. The revenge had to be his, otherwise he could never live with himself.

He stood. "I'll deal with Edmond. You go fetch Felda. Have her pack some of Lady Martine's clothes, then bring her back to Harford. If Edmond's at the house, stay out of his way. If he's not there, find out where he went."

"Are you taking Lady Martine back to Harford?" Peter asked.

"Aye."

"Do you think that's safe, what with Bernard and his men—"

"Not the castle. The hawk house, where I can keep an eye on her."

After Peter left, Thorne handed the woman some coins for her troubles, then wrapped Martine in his mantle and gently lifted her from the pallet. He gave her to the women's husband to hold while he mounted up, then took her back and cradled her in his arms, letting the reins hang loose.

She stirred, murmuring anxiously. "Everything's all right," he whispered. "Go back to sleep." She relaxed with a sigh. Using the pressure of his legs, he nudged his horse into a steady walk in the direction of Harford. First he would take care of Martine.

Then he would take care of Edmond.

Images drifted in and out of Martine's consciousness, like the shadows of passing clouds. The rhythm of a horse, strong arms, and warmth. She heard hoofbeats on the drawbridge, excited voices . . .

Then she was at a quiet place, a feather mattress beneath her. A woman's voice, familiar and reassuring, was saying, *Let's get you cleaned up, now, milady.* . . . A warm cloth on her face and chest and feet, a comb plucking at her hair, cool hands exchanging a fresh shift for the ruined one. *Sit up just for a moment, now . . . that's right . . . put your arm in the sleeve . . .*

Now sleep, milady. You need your sleep. Sir Thorne will take care of everything.

Martine moaned in her sleep, and Thorne instantly sat up in the chair he'd pushed next to her bed. Laying his sword down, he took the wet cloth from its bowl and wrung it out.

He'd spent the morning with her in the hawk house, watching her, praying, and making plans. For most of that time she'd slept fairly peacefully, although from time to time she'd seemed anxious, as now—a nightmare, perhaps.

When he pressed the cloth to her forehead, she started, whimpering in distress. He reached out to stroke her hair. "My lady—"

"No!" she gasped, lashing out with wild punches and kicks. "No!"

He rose and sat on the edge of her bed. "My lady ... Martine!"

Her fist caught him on the nose, the sudden pain blinding him for a moment. She bolted upright, arms flailing, crying, "No! Don't touch me!"

Seizing both of her wrists in one hand, he wrapped the other arm around her and held her tightly against him as she struggled. "*Martine.*" Her eyes were open but wide with terror. She moaned fearfully, clearly reliving Edmond's attack, thinking it was he who held her immobile.

"It's Thorne," he said. "*Thorne.*" Still she writhed and twisted in his arms. He kissed her hair, her temple. "It's me," he whispered in her ear, then kissed her cheek. "It's Thorne. I won't hurt you." He continued to kiss her, murmuring reassurances as he did so, until presently she calmed and slumped against him, her eyes closed.

"That's right," he said softly, laying her back down and smoothing her hair off her face. "Rest."

"Thorne," she breathed, her eyelids fluttering open.

He dipped the cloth in the water and wrung it out again, then gently stroked her face with it, avoiding the worst of the wounds. "I'm here to take care of you. No one will hurt you."

Her brow knit. "Edmond ... oh, God."

Thorne brought his face close to Martine's and looked deep into her eyes, filled with dread. "Edmond can't hurt you anymore. Not while I'm here." He touched his lips to her forehead, and then softly kissed each eyelid. "Rest easy."

She nodded and mumbled something he couldn't make out. He bathed her face and throat with the cool cloth and then untied her shift and opened it to examine the scratches on her chest. Claw marks; that's what they look like, he thought as he dabbed them gingerly with

the cloth. It was as if she'd been attacked by an animal.
She had, of course, for Edmond was but an untamed
creature, savage and unpredictable. He saw that clearly
now. But why had it taken *this* to make him see?

Because his greed had blinded him, that's why. It was
only fitting that his scheme to barter her hand for a
holding had crumbled to dust—for Lord Godfrey would
never reward him for arranging this ill-fated marriage.
If the truth be told, it was less punishment than he deserved for bringing this misery down on Martine. Filled
with shame and remorse, Thorne vowed to make amends.
He had promised Rainulf that he would protect and defend the lady Martine, and from now on, that's exactly
what he intended to do.

After the noon meal, Thorne, Peter, and Guy stood
in a tight cluster outside the hawk house while Felda
attended to her mistress. Each had his hand on the hilt
of his sword.

Peter said, "The stableboy told me Edmond saddled
up and headed for Hastings early this morning." Again
he fisted his right hand and cupped it with his left. "Let
me do it."

"Nay," Thorne said. " 'Tis my responsibility. You two
stay here and guard Lady Martine. She's not to be left
alone for a moment."

Both men nodded, but as he turned to leave, Peter
stopped him with a hand on his shoulder. "Don't kill
him."

"Why not?" Thorne said. "He—"

"He deserves to die, without question. But if you kill
him, Bernard will kill you."

"I can take—"

"Care of yourself, I know. But Lady Martine can't,
not in her present condition, anyway. You swore an oath
to protect her. If you intend to keep it, you must stay
alive, and to ensure that, Edmond must stay alive as
well."

It was brutally simple logic, and Thorne had to acknowledge the sense of it. Grimly he said, "Just make
sure no harm comes to Martine. And I'll make sure just
the right amount comes to Edmond."

*   *   *

Upon his arrival in Hastings early that afternoon, Thorne headed directly for Bulverhythe Harbor. In the fourth tavern he visited, he met someone—one of the harbor's omnipresent human water rats—who had shared a pint with Edmond around midday.

"Did he say where he was going when he left here?" Thorne asked, pressing some pennies into the knave's hand—his only hand, the other having been severed at the wrist some time ago, from the looks of it.

The man nodded, rubbing his thumb over the coins as if to shine them. "Says he needs a good tumble, but the harbor whores is all turning up their noses at him lately."

Word travels, thought Thorne.

His informant grinned, showing the blackened stubs of what used to be teeth. "Says there's a wench over to Fishmonger's Row he's been using. The eel man's daughter."

Fishmonger's Row was a dark, crooked lane no wider than a man was tall. Pedestrians pressing perfumed cloths to their noses peered into the open shopfronts to inspect the day's fly-studded catch, while fishwives shrieked their prices.

Thorne watched as a bald, thickset man hauled a keg out to the street. He paused to kick a foraging milch goat who stood in his way, then upended the keg over the central sewage channel. Glistening black serpents spilled out in a writhing mass, overflowing the channel and scattering across the mud.

He noticed Thorne. "Most of them's dead," he said in awkward French. "I got fresh ones. You want eels?"

"I want Edmond of Harford," Thorne replied in English.

The eel man paused just a bit too long before saying, also in English, "Never heard of him."

The Saxon knight strode past him, into his rank little shop.

"Hey!" The man dropped the keg and ran after him.

In the back of the shop stood a burly adolescent boy up to his elbows in a barrel of squirming merchandise.

"Where is Edmond of Harford?" Thorne asked.

The eel man looked pointedly at the boy. "I told him we ain't never heard of the gentleman."

The boy looked disgusted. "He's upstairs, with Udele," he said, cocking his head toward a narrow staircase.

Thorne leaped up the stairs, but the eel man clutched the sleeve of his tunic, holding him back. "Don't you go disturbing Sir Edmond. He pays good coin for her."

The boy seized him and pulled him off Thorne. "Leave off, Pa. You shouldn't be selling her like that."

Thorne took the last six steps in two strides and whipped aside the curtain at the top of the stairs. The second floor was all one dim, shabby room scattered with straw pallets and household items. On one of the pallets, on her hands and knees, was a plump girl with a tear-stained face and a bloody nose. Edmond knelt behind her, lifting her skirt.

"What—" Edmond managed as Thorne crossed the room, grabbed him by his tunic, and yanked him to his feet. "Hey!"

Thorne hurled him against the wall, and he crumpled like a rag doll, yelling, "Udele! Get help! Get your father!"

Udele leaped to her feet, screaming at Edmond in anglicized French, "I hope he kills you, you pig! I can't stand the sight of you anymore—you and your nasty ways! I hope you burn in hell!"

"I'll show you nasty!" Edmond growled, struggling to his feet. "You don't know what nasty is!" He lunged at the girl, but Thorne grabbed him and pinned him to the wall.

Emboldened by Thorne's presence, Udele came right up to Edmond and said, "Big talk from a *little* man."

"What's that supposed to—"

"A wee little tiny—"

Edmond took a swing at her, but she ducked and spat in his face. Then she hauled back and swung, but Thorne seized her fist just before it connected. He told her, in English, "If you finish him off, there'll be nothing left for me. Why don't you wait downstairs?"

"You promise to do a proper job of it?"

"I promise."

He saw her frank appraisal as she took in his height,

the width of his shoulders, the size of his fists. She nodded and turned away. "I'll be downstairs."

Thorne released Edmond and tossed aside his mantle, then unfastened his sword belt and threw it into the corner where Edmond's sword lay.

"This is about that witch you made me marry, isn't it?" Edmond asked.

"Witch?" Thorne tossed his dagger into the corner as well.

"She put a spell on me."

Just as it occurred to Thorne to wonder where Edmond's own dagger was, it appeared in his hand, a flash of silver streaking toward Thorne's eyes. He dodged the blade, grabbed Edmond's wrist, and slammed it against the wall. The dagger fell to the floor, and Thorne kicked it away.

From the edge of his vision, he saw Edmond's knee come up, and he moved aside just in time to take the blow in his thigh rather than its intended target. Thorne rammed his fist into Edmond's stomach, then backed off and rubbed his thigh as the younger man doubled over, groaning.

"I'm surprised at you, boy," Thorne said. "You're fighting like a wench. Is it true you have a wee little tiny—"

With an enraged bellow, Edmond rose and charged. Stepping aside, Thorne grabbed him and used his momentum to fling him across the room, into the opposite wall. He collapsed with a grunt, cupping his nose with both hands. Blood seeped from between his fingers.

"You broke my nose, you Saxon bastard!" he wailed nasally. "I did nothing to deserve this!"

"You brutalized an innocent woman."

"*Innocent?*" Edmond stood unsteadily, his eyes wild. "She put a spell on me. I *told* you! She unmanned me!"

"You were never a man to begin with. Don't blame it on her."

"She put a spell on me so I couldn't . . . couldn't service her as a husband ought. Couldn't bring myself to do it to her. Everyone laughed at me, but it wasn't my fault. It was the witch that done it."

Thorne envisioned Martine's face, torn and bruised, the scratches, the marks from where he had choked her.

Every muscle in his body tensed in fury. "So you forced yourself on her."

Edmond wiped his nose on his sleeve, staining it with blood. "I tried to," he said matter-of-factly, clearly seeing nothing wrong with that. " 'Twas about time, I reckoned. But she has her ways, that one does. Next thing I knew, it was morning, and she was gone."

"What are you saying? You never consummated the marriage?"

Edmond frowned. "If that means I never fucked the bitch, aye. But like I said, it's not my fault. I tried ... What's so funny?"

He never consummated the marriage. Thorne couldn't suppress a smile of relief at this revelation. She hadn't slept with him. In that way, she was still his and his alone.

Edmond slammed his fist into the wall. "What's so damn funny? I told you, she's a witch! She should hang for what she did to me! It's not my fault!"

He charged again, but this time Thorne met him with his fists, raining punches on his head and chest. Edmond stumbled back, then lurched forward, swinging. Thorne took a hit in the face, but blocked the rest, delivering blow after punishing blow. Edmond fought back, but he lacked focus, punching and kicking like a huge child having a tantrum. He had his bulk and strength, but Thorne was bigger and stronger ... and he knew how to use his fists to do the most damage.

In his mind's eye, Thorne saw Martine, battered and insensible, and sought to do to Edmond what Edmond had done to her. Something fierce and vengeful possessed him. Sport fighting was nothing like this, nor was hand-to-hand combat. This was revenge, this was justice, this was hate.

Don't kill him, Peter had said. Thorne closed his eyes for a moment and forced himself to remember why he shouldn't kill Edmond. It was for Martine's sake. He had to protect Martine.

Edmond crouched on the floor, heaving and gasping, his arms wrapped around his midsection. Thorne remembered having felt at least one rib crack, and he'd deliberately pummeled the kidneys. With any luck, the bastard would piss blood for a week. Every time he relieved himself, it would be a reminder of the lesson he'd learned this day.

The Saxon retrieved his sword and dagger, then grabbed a handful of Edmond's tangled hair and yanked his head up. His lips and nose were bloody and swollen; he had a cut above one eye, and by tomorrow his face would be mottled with bruises. Thorne saw fear in his eyes, but defiance as well. "My brother will make you pay for this, woodsman."

"Your brother will never find out. Because if he does, you'll die."

Edmond sneered. "Not if he kills you first."

"If he does, then one of my men will do away with you." With grave ceremony, Thorne wrapped his hand around the hilt of his sword and intoned, "I swear on the most holy relic encased herein that you will be punished with death should you tell anyone that I was in Hastings today."

Edmond's eyes grew wide; ignorance breeds superstition, and he was as superstitious as they come. He spread his hands helplessly. "But what am I to say happened? Look at me!"

"Say you were set upon by brigands who beat you and took all your money." He held his hand out. "Your purse."

"What? You don't expect me to give you my—"

Thorne yanked hard on Edmond's hair, and the boy yelped. "Your purse," he repeated.

"Thieving Saxon swine," Edmond muttered as he handed it over.

Thorne let go of Edmond and threw on his mantle. "One more thing, and listen well. You will also die—" again he rested his hand on the sword's jeweled hilt, "most slowly and painfully, should you ever touch the lady Martine again. Nor are you ever to speak to her. If she enters a room, you are to leave it. Am I understood?"

"But she's my wife! I've got to spend the rest of my damned life with her!"

"We'll see about that."

He turned and left, ignoring Edmond's "What's that supposed to mean?"

On his way out, he tossed Edmond's purse to the eel man. "I was never here."

Martine awoke in the hawk house, lying on her side in the narrow bed. Thorne sat slumped in his big chair pulled up close to the bed, his face turned toward the morning sun streaming in through the open window; he didn't notice her awaken. In contrast to his dark morning stubble, and the violet bruise that stained one cheekbone, his skin looked very pale. His eyes, transparent in the bright sunlight, were sad and distant.

She remembered now that he had returned around sundown, and sat up with her all night. From time to time she would awaken, always confused and disoriented, and he would soothe her, stroke her hair, and whisper soft reassurances to her. She noticed the sword lying across his lap and remembered his oath to Rainulf. He had promised to protect her, and now he kept that promise. He was a man of honor after all, at least in his dealings with other men.

Felda had spent the night here, as well, Martine remembered, changing her poultices, bringing her broth and wine to sip. Martine licked her cracked lips. "Where's Felda?" she asked, her voice raw.

Thorne rose and came to sit on the edge of the bed. "She'll be back," he said, laying a gentle hand on her uninjured cheek. "Do you know where you are?"

She nodded, wincing at a twinge of pain.

"Do you remember what happened?"

She closed her eyes. "Edmond," she whispered.

He took her hand. "Edmond won't bother you anymore."

After a moment she opened her eyes and looked up at him, her gaze lingering on his bruise. "What did you do to him?"

He smoothed her hair off her face. "Less than he deserved. I left him alive."

She looked into his eyes. "I suppose I should thank you."

He shook his head. "I don't deserve your thanks. If not for me, you wouldn't have married him in the first place. What I did to him was far too little, far too late." With a squeeze of her hand, he added, "But there is something more I can do. Or try to do. To protect you from him, to free you from him permanently."

Her heart beat wildly. "Is that possible?"

"I don't know. Perhaps. If it's true that ... that the marriage was never consummated."

She saw the hope in his eyes. "It's true."

He took a deep breath, his eyes lit up, he even smiled a little. "If I could arrange to have the marriage annulled, would you—"

"Annulled!" She tried to sit up, but pain speared her head, and she sank back onto the pillow.

"Easy." He leaned close, his hands cradling her head. "*If* I could arrange it, would you want that?"

"My God, do you have to ask?"

He chuckled. "I just had to be sure it was what you wanted before I start making inquiries. It ought to be a simple matter to annul an unconsummated marriage. Brother Matthew's an expert on canon law. We'll talk to him this evening."

She frowned. "This evening? Are we going to St. Dunstan's?"

He nodded. "It isn't safe for you here. Edmond is undoubtedly still in Hastings—he's in no condition to ride. But Bernard and his men are here. I've sent Felda and Peter to collect the rest of your clothes and belongings—"

"What about Loki? And my lockbox, with my herbs?"

"Them, too. And as soon as they're back, we'll leave."

"I'm sorry," Brother Matthew repeated. Martine admired his patience even as she lamented his words. "But you can't annul a marriage simply because it wasn't consummated. It won't work."

"That's outrageous," Thorne said, bolting to his feet.

"Outrageous or not, it's canon law," Matthew said. His fierce, dark eyes and great tonsured shock of hair, as black as his cowled robe, were a sharp contrast to his quiet intelligence.

"Damn!" Thorne strode to the one small window in the central hall of the prior's lodge. Martine and Matthew, sitting at the table, watched his back as he leaned on the windowsill, peering into the night sky and shaking his head.

Martine picked Loki up off the floor and hugged him. She had spoken barely a word since their arrival that afternoon at St. Dunstan's. Too weakened to ride, she'd had no choice but to make the trip in a curtained litter. Despite having slept most of the way, her head cradled in Felda's lap, she ached all over and felt incapable of speaking on her own behalf. Luckily, Thorne was willing to do that for her.

The Saxon slammed his fist down on the windowsill and wheeled around. " 'Tis an obscenity that she should be chained in marriage to this . . . *animal,* simply because of the Church's narrow-minded—"

"The Church has her ways," Matthew said quietly. "There are more grounds for annulment than laymen are generally aware of," Matthew said. He paused meaningfully. "Most notably, impotence."

Thorne stared at Matthew. "Impotence," he said, as if testing the sound of the word.

"It's used successfully all the time," Matthew said. "And in my judgment, I believe it to offer the lady her best chance for an official dissolution of the union. Actually, her only chance."

Matthew and Thorne regarded each other in silence for a moment, and then both turned and looked toward Martine as if to say, *Give us your permission and we'll proceed.*

Impotence. It was an ugly word, a shameful word, a word to spawn dark whispers and giggles. The thought of making a formal and public charge of it repelled her. She closed her eyes. She felt exhausted; her head throbbed. In her imagination, Edmond's face loomed close, his yellowed teeth bared by a feral sneer, his smell stinging her nostrils, his meaty arms grabbing her, hurling her toward the bed, toward pain and darkness.

Shuddering, she opened her eyes, met Thorne's, and nodded. "Do what you must," she said, then rose and went to her chamber.

Thorne, sitting next to Martine on a bench in the corner of Brother Matthew's office, watched in pensive silence as the prior handed the petition for annulment across the central table to Father Simon. The priest held the document close to his face and squinted as he read.

In the opposite corner sat Bernard and Edmond, deep in whispered conversation. Or, rather, Bernard whispered while his brother, his face still faintly bruised, stared sullenly at the floor. When Simon finished reading the petition, he joined the two men in their corner, leaning over and murmuring something in Bernard's ear.

"Impotence?" Bernard exclaimed.

"What's that?" Edmond muttered.

Father Simon mumbled something.

Edmond bolted to his feet. *"What?"*

Bernard rose and grabbed his brother's arm. "Edmond, I told you to keep your mouth—"

"You fucking witch!" Edmond screamed at Martine, stabbing the air with his fists as Bernard and Simon held him back. "This is your doing!"

"Shut up, Edmond!" Bernard hissed, shoving his brother back onto the bench. "Let me handle this. I told you." Holding Edmond down by his shoulders, he bent over and whispered into his ear for a few moments. "All right?" Thorne heard him say. Edmond hung his head, his hair obscuring his face. *"All right?"* Bernard repeated. Edmond nodded without looking up.

Bernard turned around and straightened his tunic. "We do not consent to an annulment. Edmond and the lady Martine must remain married."

Edmond buried his head in his hands.

"Oh, God," Martine whispered. Thorne patted her arm, wishing he could do more—take her hand, gather her in his arms—but knowing that any hint of impropriety at this stage of the negotiations would be ruinous for her. He hesitated to so much as look at her, lest his feelings for her show on his face.

Matthew stood and addressed Bernard. "If Edmond cooperates with the annulment, the matter will be handled as discreetly as possible. The charge of impotence need never become public knowledge. But should he object in any way, the lady will not hesitate to pursue her cause all the way to Pope Alexander—and then, I assure you, there will be no way to keep the circumstances confidential."

"Your threats change nothing, monk," Bernard said. "We refuse to cooperate in any way with a dissolution of this marriage."

Matthew said, "You do know that all of the holdings that were given up to Lady Martine upon her marriage will revert to Lord Godfrey upon annulment."

"Of course."

"Then why do you object?" the prior demanded.

Thorne stood and strode to the center of the room. "I'll tell you why. It's because that creature"—he pointed to Edmond, who looked up and glared at him—"will never be able to remarry after what he did to Lady Martine. Everyone at the castle saw her when I brought her back that morning. Christ, she looked as if she'd been attacked by a pack of wild dogs. All of Sussex must know about it by now."

Father Simon took a step forward. "How Sir Edmond chooses to discipline his wife is nobody's business but his. This marriage must not be dissolved for the simple reason that it was solemnized under the eyes of God, and can only be rescinded by God's will. 'Twill end when Sir Edmond or Lady Martine departs from this world, and not a moment before."

Thorne laughed humorlessly. "Since when did Edmond start caring about God's will?"

Bernard crossed his arms. "We are prepared to offer a compromise of sorts, if the lady is prepared to listen."

All eyes turned to Martine, who nodded hesitantly.

"Annulment, as I said, is out of the question," Bernard stated flatly. "Understand, my lady, that without our cooperation, the struggle to obtain such an annulment could take years. During this ordeal, perfect strangers will be prying into matters of an exceedingly intimate nature. It could prove quite unpleasant for you, and there is no guarantee that your cause will triumph."

"Your offer?" Thorne prodded impatiently.

"Providing you cease all efforts at annulment, my lady, you may remain here at St. Dunstan's and return in your own good time to Edmond, who is prepared to forgive your lack of wifely humility and take you back."

"Return!" She shook her head vehemently. "Never!"

"It's our only offer," Bernard said.

Martine rose. "I'll pursue the annulment."

Bernard shook his head. "I warn you, my lady, you'll find us formidable opponents. My brother will emphatically deny all charges of impotence."

"The lady states that the marriage was never consummated," Matthew pointed out.

"Edmond will testify that it was," Bernard said. Thorne saw Edmond glance uncomfortably at his brother and then nod, his gaze on the floor. "It's a simple matter of her word against his."

"Not necessarily," Matthew said. "It's perfectly within Lady Martine's power to prove that she has never engaged in the marital act. All that's required is that she submit to an examination by a physician." Matthew turned to Martine. "I trust you have no objection to such an examination, my lady?"

Martine looked helplessly toward Thorne, who shook his head fractionally. *Christ, what now?*

"My lady?" Matthew prompted.

"May I speak to you in private a moment, Brother?" she asked.

Matthew led Martine out of the room. When they returned a short while later, the prior pinned Thorne with a quick, knowing look. To Bernard he said, "As it happens, Lady Martine's tender sensibilities do, indeed, preclude such an examination. And as a lady of gentle breeding, it seems that she does not, after all, relish the loss of privacy required by a petition for annulment."

Thorne exhaled heavily and shook his head. Defeat ill suited him.

Bernard smiled his mirthless smile. "Can I take it that means she accepts our offer?"

"Aye," said Matthew, "as long as it's clearly understood that the lady may remain as a guest at St. Dunstan's for an indefinite period, and will not be abducted—"

"Certainly not," Bernard said.

"—or pressured in any way to return to her husband's home."

Bernard nodded. "You have my word. And," he added, seemingly as an afterthought, "my brother's as well, of course."

Martine waited gravely in the cool, dark stable as Thorne saddled up his white stallion in preparation for returning to Harford. It had been agreed that she would remain at St. Dunstan's for the next year or two, until Rainulf returned from pilgrimage and could take her to

Oxford with him. This went over poorly with Matthew's superior abbot, but his reservation about allowing a woman to live at the priory dissolved when Martine donated to his abbey a few of the gold coins that Rainulf had given her. Nevertheless, the abbot had commanded Brother Matthew to establish a strict code of behavior for Martine. She was to dress as modestly as a nun, attend mass every morning, avoid the brothers as much as possible, and conduct herself in general with the utmost decorum. Any violation of this code would result in immediate ouster from St. Dunstan's. As Matthew had explained it to her, a monastery was refuge for men who had given up all worldly temptations, including women, and it would therefore be cruel to expose them to what they couldn't have.

It was Thorne who negotiated for her, who made the arrangements, who took care of everything. Martine appreciated his efforts on her behalf, but knew that he went to the trouble primarily to fulfill his promise to Rainulf. It was hard to fathom how he really felt about her. If he did care for her, it was surely not as deeply as she cared for him. It shamed her to admit to herself how much she did care, despite how he had wronged her, and to acknowledge how very badly she would miss him when he was gone.

When the Saxon's preparations were finished, he came and took both of her hands in his. For a few long moments, he merely looked down at her, his eyes sad and iridescent in the semidarkness. Martine was afraid to speak, lest her voice betray the depth of her sorrow at his departure.

He turned her hands over and studied them as he rubbed her palms with his thumbs. "I'll come back for a visit in the spring."

Martine swallowed and nodded. *The spring?* It would be half a year before she saw him again!

"You'll be safe here," he said quietly. "Perhaps even happy. You'll have Felda with you, and you like St. Dunstan's."

"Yes," she whispered.

He released her left hand to gently stroke her bruised cheek and lower lip, barely mended from where it had been split. "Does it still hurt?" he asked.

She nodded. "A bit."

He trailed his fingers softly over her face, avoiding the worst of the wounds. "You'll be completely healed soon. And then you'll be even more beautiful than before." She must have looked skeptical, because he chuckled and added, "Suffering enriches the soul, and it's only those with the most complex souls who are *truly* beautiful."

He lifted her right hand to his lips and kissed it, then pressed her palm to his cheek and closed his eyes. "I don't want to leave," he whispered raggedly.

Without thinking, she reached up to stroke his lip as he had stroked hers. He captured her fingers with his free hand and kissed them, then leaned down and brought his face close to hers. She withdrew her hands from his to push against his chest, thinking of her sore lip.

"I'll be careful," he promised, his arms encircling her. She closed her eyes as his mouth descended on hers. He *was* careful. The kiss felt warm and soft and heart-breakingly gentle, like a bit of down brushing her lips. Another feathery brush, and another . . . and then he closed his mouth tenderly over her lower lip, and she felt the light, wet sweep of his tongue over her sensitized flesh . . . a little healing lick.

"Martine," he breathed, tightening his arms around her. Just as she moved to return the embrace, the stable door opened and they drew apart, breathless.

Brother Matthew paused in the shaft of sunlight from the open door. "I came to bid you farewell, Thorne. I didn't mean to interrupt—"

"Nay, Brother," Martine said, backing away from Thorne, whose gaze never left her. Matthew knew about them, of course—she had told him herself—but when he had outlined the rules she was to live by, he had explicitly asked her to remember that she was a married woman and must act the part. No sooner had she promised to do so than she had broken that promise! "I . . . we were just—"

"We were just saying good-bye," Thorne said quietly.

She nodded, feeling absurdly close to crying. "Yes. Well. I'll see you in the spring, then."

Thorne smiled a little sadly. "Yes."

Martine turned and walked away, tears spilling down her cheeks.

Chapter 17

Martine re-inked her goose quill pen and leaned over the small sheet of parchment on which he was recording a recipe for an elixir of rosemary extract. It was for her *Herbarium Medica,* a project she had begun upon taking up residence at St. Dunstan's and which, so far, had made the long winter months, if not less lonely, at least less tedious. Obligated to confine her movements to the monastery's public buildings, and discouraged from talking to any of the monks except for Brother Matthew and Brother Paul, the infirmarian, she had only Felda and the other servants for company, and little to do.

It was drafty in her chamber, with nothing to shield her from the icy January breezes but a piece of translucent oiled linen stretched across the window. Matthew had given her one of those cunning little desks that the brothers used in the scriptorium—a combination chair and writing surface—and despite the chill, she kept it next to the window, the better to see by. But, although her vision benefited from this, her penmanship suffered; her hands, stiff with cold despite the fingerless gloves she wore, struggled hard to reproduce a semblance of the graceful lettering that the nuns had drilled into her.

Nevertheless, she concentrated hard this afternoon on the task she had set herself, trying to occupy her mind with the various plants and their medical uses—of tonics and elixirs and potions and powders—and not with the distant and disconcerting sounds from beyond the valley, the sounds of battle from the direction of Blackburn Castle.

Setting down her pen, she pressed both hands to the container of hot coals that hung from her girdle, letting the warmth travel up her arms and into her uneasy chest. The delicious, spreading heat made her think of a different kind of heat that had blossomed within her once, on a riverbank not so very far away, a heat that had roiled within her, consuming her in a white-hot flash.

It made her think of Thorne. She'd not seen him for three months, and she found that his image—his voice, his sky-blue eyes, the dimpled smile that belied the ruggedness of his face—clung stubbornly to her thoughts.

She cupped her warm hands around her face, now healed of its wounds, and closed her eyes. Was Thorne among those laying siege to Blackburn Castle? Of course he was. When Neville thundered back into Sussex on All Hallows' Eve with his army of Welsh savages and seized Blackburn, claiming it for his own, Olivier summoned all of his vassals and every man who owed them fealty, to roust the cur. As Godfrey's most skilled soldier, Thorne would be at the forefront of the siege. According to Brother Matthew, he would most likely command the archers.

The siege had been going on for weeks. Knowing naught of warfare, Martine listened anxiously to the faraway sounds that carried so well in the cold, thin air— the whinny of warhorses, the blare of trumpets, voices raised to bellow orders . . . or to howl in pain. Once, a multitude of voices screamed simultaneously, and Martine shivered in dread. Shortly thereafter three cartloads of Olivier's men arrived at the monastery, groaning in pain from the burning pitch that Neville's Welshmen had dropped on them.

Brother Paul and his assistants had been tending the wounded in the infirmary. Martine, experienced in treating injuries and knowing that the infirmarian's expertise lay more in the arena of illness, frequently offered to help, but Paul always refused. She simply was not permitted in that part of the monastery, and so he asked her to serve them with her prayers instead.

The incessant tapestry of battle noise was punctuated by other, more mysterious sounds. The repetitive thudding, Matthew told her, was probably a battering ram being used to break down Castle Blackburn's curtain walls. The occasional loud crash might be a missile hurled from either side by a stone-throwing machine.

From Brother Paul, Martine learned that the men in the infirmary regarded this as an exceptionally challenging siege. The castle, although unfinished, was superbly built and seemingly impenetrable. Although they had succeeded in filling in several sections of the moat with stones and logs so that they could cross it, they found the curtain walls immensely thick and well constructed. And then there were Neville's Welshmen—a hundred or more ruthless brutes armed with crossbows for which they had a seemingly endless supply of bolts. They undoubtedly had provisions for a year or more, so it was quite possible they could hold out long enough against Olivier's forces, and inflict enough damage, than the king would ultimately be forced to concede the barony to Neville despite his dishonorable method of acquiring it.

Martine picked up her pen and wrote until vespers, broke briefly for her solitary supper, then lit an oil lamp against the dying light and continued to work until she heard the chanting of compline at nightfall.

It was while she was putting away her pen and ink and parchment that she smelled the smoke—not the odor of woodsmoke so much as the smell of scorched flesh and something else, something raw and noxious.

Grabbing her mantle, she left the prior's lodge and went to the front gate where Matthew and several lay brothers stood staring into the dark in the direction of Blackburn Castle. She saw no flames, just the pinpoints of torches on the battlements.

"What's happening? What's on fire?" she asked the prior.

"I'm not sure," he murmured, squinting into the distance. He put a hand on her arm. "Come, there's no point to standing out here in the cold. We'll find out what happened in the morning.'

Martine had barely gotten to sleep when Brother Matthew woke her. "Sir Peter is here, my lady," he said from beyond her chamber curtain. "He wants to see you."

She threw a tunic over her shift and found Peter awaiting her in the hall, in full chain mail, his helmet in his hand.

"Sir Peter?"

"It's about Thorne," he said grimly.

"Is he . . . he's not . . ."

"Nay, but he's . . ." His stricken expression said it all. "I thought perhaps you might have something to ease the pain."

Oh, God. "Where is he?"

"The infirmary."

"Brother Paul won't let me go there." She looked imploringly toward Matthew.

The prior's astute brown eyes seemed to pierce through to her very heart. "Brother Paul's asleep, and I see no need to wake him when you can tend to Sir Thorne yourself—that is, if you don't mind."

"Oh, thank you." Taking her lockbox, she followed the two men outside and through the moonless dark, past the cloister and chapter house to a dimly lit building at the easternmost end of the monastery. Inside, it was all one long room with dozens of beds lined up against the walls, occupied by injured men, most of them asleep. A skinny, very young-looking monk greeted Brother Matthew and Peter respectfully, but gaped incredulously at Martine, his gaze lingering on her unveiled braids.

"It's all right, Brother Luke," said Matthew. "We're here to see the knight who was just brought in."

Brother Luke pointed to a curtained-off area in the far corner, near a crackling fire pit. "We've got him back where it's warmest."

"Mother of God," Martine whispered when she pushed aside the curtains and looked down upon Thorne. Still in full armor, including a badly dented helmet, he was pale and sweaty, his breathing labored, his eyes glazed. Crossbow bolts protruded through the steel links of his mail hauberk from his right shoulder and forearm, and his leg on that side was twisted at an unnatural angle.

"Thorne," she said softly.

He focused his eyes on her and then, for just a moment, his face relaxed and he actually smiled. His mouth formed her name, although no sound came out, but when he reached toward her with his damaged arm, his smile became a grimace of agony and he groaned, squeezing his eyes tightly shut.

Brother Luke came up with a tray bearing a basin of water, a bar of soap, neatly folded linen bandages, a collection of surgical tools, and a jug of brandy, which he set down on a table next to the bed. Motioning Martine aside, he quickly unlaced Thorne's helmet from the hood of his hauberk, then went to work undoing the complicated system of straps and buckles that kept his mail hose, elbow pieces, knee guards, and greaves in place.

That brandy, Martine knew, was the only anesthetic the monks ever offered; it would be a far sight more effective with a little sleeping draft mixed in. Setting her lockbox down on the table, she withdrew a mortar and proceeded to grind the requisite ingredients into a powder.

"The siege was successful," Peter said quietly, his eyes on his friend, who seemed unaware of his presence. "We've retaken Blackburn Castle."

"How did you manage that?" asked Matthew. "I thought the castle was impenetrable."

"It is. When we realized we'd never get through those walls, Olivier started talking about a truce with Neville, but Thorne said compromise was an outrage after what that bastard did to Anseau and Aiglentine. So he came up with a plan, and Olivier agreed to it."

The monk wrestled the big Saxon out of his heavy steel and leather armor, tossing it piece by piece onto the floor. Every time his efforts jarred the two firmly embedded crossbow bolts, Thorne flinched.

Peter said, "The first part of his plan was classic siege strategy—mining beneath the curtain wall. We set up a big tent covered with hides next to the wall, and put a team of men to work underneath it, digging a tunnel. They shored it up with logs soaked in tallow, and when it was finished, we stuffed it with straw and dead pigs and torched it. I never saw such a fire in my life. You can't imagine the stink."

"We were downwind of you," Matthew muttered. "I don't have to imagine. The point of such a fire, I take it, is to collapse the tunnel and thence the wall?"

"Aye, but that's the thickest wall I ever saw. It never did fall. Of course, Thorne didn't think it would."

Matthew frowned. "He *knew* it wouldn't work?"

Peter said, "Aye, 'twas all a diversion. We waited till nightfall to set the fire, you see, so we could execute our real plan under cover of darkness. While the Welshmen were all congregated on the battlements above the tunnel, pouring buckets of water over the side, Thorne, Guy, and I took a scaling ladder around to the part of the wall they'd left unguarded."

Having divested Thorne of his mail, Brother Luke took a sharp little knife and proceeded to slice off his linen head-wrappings and blood-soaked quilted underclothes.

Peter shook his head, gazing sadly at the Saxon. "Thorne's reasoning was that the castle was simply too well built to destroy it. We had to find a weaker link in Neville's defenses, and that weak link was his Welshmen. For all their strength and skill, they were only hired soldiers. They worked for Neville not out of loyalty, but because he paid them. Take away their silver and you take away their reason to fight. The plan was for the three of us to infiltrate the keep, find Neville, and take him hostage."

"And be killed in the process," Matthew said. "How could you possibly think you could go unnoticed in a castle full of Welsh mercenaries? 'Twas suicide to even contemplate it. Didn't you realize that?"

"Of course. We all made confession and were absolved this afternoon. We assumed we'd never come out alive. Thorne hadn't intended for Guy and me to come along, but he couldn't talk us out of it. When he raised the scaling ladder, he insisted on going first, to make sure the coast was clear on the battlements. But when he got to the top, he pulled the ladder up after him so we couldn't follow." Peter shook his head, his eyes glimmering. "And then he grinned at us, as if he'd gotten the better of us in a game of darts and not just sentenced himself to death."

"And saved your lives," Matthew said softly.

Peter expelled a long, ragged breath. "He turned and ... was gone. The Welshmen put out the fire, and we waited. After a while we heard voices from the bailey and then a great commotion. Finally Neville's flag was lowered from the high tower, and the Welshmen called down that they were prepared to surrender, providing they wouldn't be hanged. Olivier agreed, and they raised the portcullis. We took their weapons and rounded them up into the tower. Neville was dead and Thorne was as you see him. Our chaplain gave him last rites immediately. The Welshman told us that he'd gotten into the keep, earning those two crossbow bolts in the process, and found Neville. Dragged him into the bailey at swordpoint and made him tell the Welshmen he hadn't enough silver to pay them."

"Was that true?" Matthew asked.

"I wouldn't think so. Neville wasn't stupid enough to surround himself with a hundred bloodthirsty barbarians unless he could afford their asking price."

"How did he die?"

"They set upon him and tore him into pieces. When we found him, he was ... he'd been ..." Peter glanced in Martine's direction as she stirred her powder into a cup of brandy. "I fear I'll never forget the sight. Thorne's leg got broken in the melee, but that was unintentional. If they'd meant to kill him, I assure you he'd be most unmistakably dead. My guess if they were too much in awe of him at that point to want to do away with him—or maybe they'd just given up trying. They couldn't believe he was still on his feet after taking two shots with a crossbow, or that he stood up to them the way he did. They invented a Welsh name for him that means something like 'English Giant Who Won't Die."

Thorne, lying half-dead and semiconscious in his linen drawers, hardly looked like a formidable English giant. Martine found his unaccustomed vulnerability heart-wrenching.

"What will become of Blackburn?" the prior asked Peter.

The knight shrugged. "No one knows, but this time Olivier's not taking any chances by leaving the castle empty again. He's moving his own household there until he figures out what to do with it."

Martine winced at the shudder that coursed through Thorne as Brother Luke gently touched his shin near the shaft of bone that protruded just below his knee.

"I think the leg might have to come off," he told the Saxon. Martine followed Thorne's gaze to the array of knives, probes, and bone saws on the table next to the bed. His expression never altered, but she saw him swallow hard.

Turning to Brother Matthew, the young monk whispered, "I'll go wake up Brother Paul. We'll also need at least four others to hold him down." With a glance at the big Saxon, he added, "Strong ones."

Before Matthew could answer, Martine said, "Let me try first. I can set the break and correct the dislocation, I'm sure of it."

"Have you done it before?" the prior asked.

"I've helped. More than once. Please. With a good strong splint and a poultice of knitbone, I'm sure we can save the leg."

"What if the wound festers?" Matthew asked. "Then he'll be worse off than if we had just amputated."

"There are ways of keeping that from happening," Martine said. "I can handle the crossbow bolts, too. Just let me try. Please."

Matthew said, "You'll need help setting the bone and pulling out those—"

"I'll help her," said Peter, unbuckling his hauberk.

Matthew leaned over Thorne. "Sir Thorne, will you allow the lady Martine to treat your injuries?"

Thorne looked toward Martine, and the trust in his eyes filled her with both pride and fear. *I mustn't let him down,* she thought.

He nodded. "Aye," he rasped. "She can treat me."

Brother Luke said, "We'll still need some of the stronger brothers to hold him down while she works."

Martine held the cup of doctored brandy near Thorne's mouth and slipped a hand around the back of his head to lift it, telling him, "Drink this and we won't need them."

He met her eyes. "What's in it?"

"Besides hemlock?"

The young monk gasped. Thorne chuckled, then quickly drank the contents of the cup. As Martine released him, he reached up with his left hand—or rather, his fist, for she now saw that he had it tightly clenched around something—and with transfixing gentleness, trailed his knuckles over her cheek, down along the curve of her jaw, and across to her chin, his eyes watching his progress as if memorizing the topography of her face. For a short while she forgot their differences, and the pain of having been used by him, and felt only a stunning wholeness, a rightness that took her breath away.

Matthew cleared his throat, and she took Thorne's hand and lowered it. Peter had thankfully been pulling his hauberk over his head and hadn't seen anything amiss. Brother Matthew already knew that her relations with Thorne Falconer hadn't always been entirely innocent. But the whole world needn't know it.

She laid a hand on Thorne's forehead, which was hot and damp. "Close your eyes," she whispered.

A small shake of his head. "Not yet." But his eyelids seemed heavy. "I want to look at you."

She smiled. "You're very stubborn."

He smiled, too, his eyes never leaving hers, although they were beginning to lose their focus. "Aye, I am that," he said, the words slightly slurred.

As he lost the battle to keep his eyes open, she murmured, "Sleep."

He silently mouthed the word *No,* and then his head fell to the side, his left arm slipped off the bed, and something fell out of his hand and rolled onto the floor.

Peter reached down and picked it up.

Ah, he thought, cradling the beautiful little object in his palm. *I might have known.*

He had wondered what it was that Thorne had taken to carrying around with him these past months. The Saxon refused to let him see it, but Peter frequently saw him reach inside his tunic to touch it, sometimes taking it out to run his fingers over it before hiding it away from prying eyes. And he had been holding it tightly in his fist ever since they found him upon retaking Blackburn Castle.

"What is that? What was he holding?" asked Lady Martine as she dipped her hands in the basin of water and soaped them up.

Peter hesitated. It was the white queen from the chess set that Lady Martine had given Edmond as a betrothal gift, the white queen carved in her own image—the piece that had turned up missing from the set shortly before the wedding. It was of little account, everyone agreed, since Edmond didn't even play chess. Indeed, no one even mentioned the theft to him and he did not seem to notice it.

It was the image of Martine of Rouen that Thorne carried with him and cherished, stared at longingly and held close to his heart. A poor substitute for the lady herself, but one with which he'd had to make do. Did she know of his feelings? Perhaps not. And if not, it wasn't Peter's place to inform her.

Drying her hands, Martine said, "What was it? A rock?"

"Aye," Peter said, secreting the white queen in the pocket of his undershirt. "Just a rock."

Nodding, she indicated the basin. "If I could just trouble you to wash your hands . . ." She brushed a lock of hair off Thorne's forehead, and then her gaze traveled down his long body, lingering on the bolt that pierced his shoulder and arm, the leg that had been all but destroyed. Taking a deep breath, and looking slightly overwhelmed, but very determined, she added, "Then we can get to work."

Chapter 18

Thorne opened his eyes. It was the middle of the night. From beyond the curtains enclosing his bed came the steady breathing of his fellow patients. The only light in the infirmary was the golden glow of the fire pit on the other side of the curtain to his right. No, not quite the only light; something glimmered to the left. Knowing better than to try to sit up without help—his right arm and leg being strapped into splints—he merely turned his head in that direction, hoping to see her there and praying that she hadn't stopped coming. . . .

She was there, curled up on the big chair they'd dragged in for her, fast asleep. The glimmer came from the oil lamp that shared the little bedside table with her puzzling collection of vials and jars, a stack of fresh bandages, a ewer, and a cup. She had sat up with him, tending his injuries and keeping him company, every day and every night for . . . how long had it been?

He had no recollection of being brought to St. Dunstan's, and only fitful, pain-blurred memories of the first day or two, but as near as he knew, this was his fifth night in this place. His fifth night, and she'd been here the whole time, only returning to the prior's lodge for brief naps or to wash up. Brother Matthew had tried to make her stop coming, maintaining that a monastery infirmary was no place for a woman, but she had argued ceaselessly, claiming Thorne needed her.

And, of course, he did. Needed her in ways too numerous to count.

Right now he needed simply to look at her. In obedience of the dress code enforced on her, she wore a plain dark tunic and a heavy white veil that completely covered her hair. Her face and hands glowed softly in the warm firelight filtering through the curtain, her eyebrows and lashes black as soot against her ivory skin. Those generous lips of hers were slightly parted, revealing the edges of her perfect white teeth.

One of her hands rested on an open book. When he tried to lift his head for a better view of it, pain lanced his right shoulder, and he sank to the bed, sucking in air. As the pain subsided, he reached out his uninjured left arm and carefully slid the book from beneath her hand.

The movement awakened her with a jolt, whereupon the little volume slipped out of his hand and tumbled to the floor.

"What . . ." she murmured, blinking in confusion. "Thorne, are you all right?" She noticed his arm hanging off the bed and carefully took hold of it, replacing it at his side, then retrieved the book.

"I didn't mean to wake you," he said, speaking in low tones so as not to disturb the sleeping men beyond the curtains. "I wanted to see what you were reading."

She showed him the cover. "Ovid's *Amores*."

"Would you read it to me?"

She glanced at the book, grinning self-consciously. "Are you sure you wouldn't prefer his *Heroides*? There's a copy in the library."

Thorne chuckled. "Nay, tonight I believe I'm in the mood for *Amores*."

Martine read page after page of the courtly poetry as Thorne watched her through half-closed lids, basking in her soft, melodious voice, her infinitely comforting presence. She finished reading, then poured herself a cup of water and drank it.

"Could I have some of that?" he asked.

"Of course." She poured another cup, then sat on the edge of his bed and carefully slid her arm beneath his back, avoiding his bandages. He gripped her shoulder with his good left hand and held his breath. "Easy, now," she coaxed as she urged him into a sitting position. He grimaced as pain coursed through him, realizing only after he'd sat up that his fingers had sunk deep into her shoulder.

"Sorry," he murmured, shaking out his left arm. "You'll be bruised tomorrow."

She smiled. "I'm covered with bruises. 'Tis one of the

drawbacks of tending the 'English Giant Who Won't Die.'"

"*One* of the drawbacks? Are there many others?"

He saw her glance at his bare chest, for he wore nothing beneath his sheet, and quickly look away. "Nay." She reached for the cup and brought it to his mouth. He steadied it by wrapping his big hand around her small one, wondering whether her slight trembling owed more to the late hour or his proximity. He'd noticed that she didn't seem to much care about his state of undress when she changed his dressings or spooned elixirs into his mouth, but at other times, such as now, she appeared uncomfortably aware of it. It was when she saw him as a man, rather than as a helpless patient, that she found him most disturbing. But then, how could it be otherwise, given what had occurred between them?

He drained that cup and another. "Thank you."

She set the cup down. He assumed that she would return to her chair then, but she surprised him pleasantly by bringing her hand to his face and stroking his five-day growth of beard. He closed his eyes, savoring the cool caress of her fingers. "You need to shave," she said.

"I can't do it with my left hand." A rather agreeable thought occurred to him. "Perhaps you could do it for me."

She dropped her hand to her lap and appeared to consider the possibility. With a small shrug, she said, "Very well. I'll do it in the morning." Thorne beamed in anticipation. For a few moments she stared at her hands, looking very prim indeed in her nunlike garb. He wished he could see more of her. That damn veil even hid her forehead. He smiled to himself, remembering the day they met. He'd been so sure that her headdress concealed pockmarks, patchy hair, and God knew what other defects. The next morning, when she glided across the bailey in her indigo gown, with her flawless face and her hair like spun gold, he'd felt as incredulously stunned as if the sun had just risen in the west.

"There's a question I'd like to ask you," she said. "I suppose it's actually a rather personal one."

He allowed himself a smile. "There's a favor I'd like to ask of *you*. I'll answer your question if you grant my favor."

Her brows drew together. "What's the favor?"

He shook his head, grinning. "You can't know beforehand. Where's the sport in that?"

She rolled her eyes. "All right. But first my question."

"Of course," he replied soberly.

She took a deep breath. "That night at Blackburn Castle, when you tricked Peter and Guy out of following you inside to find Lord Neville—" she shook her head, her expression troubled, "you knew you'd die. I mean, you *knew* it. It was a miracle you survived."

He closed his hand over hers, clutched together in her lap. " 'Tis your doing that I survived—in one piece, at any rate."

"Nevertheless," she continued gravely, "you shouldn't have lived. You knew you wouldn't."

He gently squeezed her hands. "What is your question, Martine?"

She shook her head in evident bewilderment. "Why? Why were you willing to do it? Why were you willing to die?"

"Someone had to—"

"Nay," she said firmly, and met his gaze almost fiercely. "Why you? Why you alone, when 'twould have been safer with Peter and Guy to help you? I think," she added, her voice quavering with emotion, "perhaps you wanted to die."

He let her statement hang heavily between them for a moment, and then said quietly, "There's a difference between wanting to die and"—he shrugged—"not particularly caring whether you live."

She frowned. "Everyone wants to live."

He looked down at his hand caressing hers. "Not if you have nothing to live for. Not if what you most desire in the whole world is forever denied you."

Their gazes locked in intimate communion for a wondrous moment. But the moment ended abruptly when Martine's eyes registered a sudden realization and she turned away. "Your land," she said.

Land? "Nay, I meant . . ." He meant what? What was he thinking, saying these things to her, preparing to deliver some sort of declaration of . . . of what? Love? Love was a liability he could ill afford.

That afternoon, when Peter had come to the infirmary

to say good-bye before returning to Harford, he'd handed him the little chess piece carved in Martine's image. "You dropped this."

Thorne had accepted it wordlessly, tucking it carefully beneath the straw mattress, where Martine wouldn't find it.

"Do you love her?" his friend had asked.

"Nay," Thorne had answered quickly. "I need her. It's not the same."

Peter had chuckled. "Isn't it?"

It wasn't, Thorne told himself, with more conviction than he felt.

"Don't worry, you'll earn a manor eventually," Martine said now, her tone that of polite conversation.

Thorne looked away from her and nodded. "Aye." Disengaging his hand from hers, he took her by the shoulder again. "Help me lie down?"

She wrapped her arms around him and eased him back onto the bed. He put the discomfort out of his mind, wanting to cherish the pleasure of her embrace, imagine it to be the embrace of a lover. His head sank into the feather pillow, and he closed his eyes, willing the last of the hurt to recede. When it did, and he opened his eyes, he found her looking down on him, her expression solemn, her sapphire eyes huge and glittering in the muted firelight.

"I owe you a favor," she said, so softly he almost didn't hear it.

Her innocent words shot a thrill of excitement through him. He could ask anything of her, anything at all, and she'd be honor-bound to comply. Swallowing hard, he reminded himself that she had spent the past four days and five nights nursing him back to health. It would ill repay her kindness to take advantage of her. He therefore resolved only to ask the favor he'd originally intended.

Raising his hand to her veil, he fingered the heavy linen. "Take this off."

If the command surprised her, she gave no hint of it. After a moment's hesitation, she reached up, unfastened the head covering, and pulled it off, tossing it onto the chair, then shook her head. His breath caught in his throat as her hair, freed form its confinement, spilled onto his bare chest, a cool, heavy mass of gleaming silk.

Her scent—sweet woodruff and lavender, warm skin and sunshine—blossomed into the air, enveloping him, overwhelming his senses. He brought a fistful of hair to his face and inhaled, breathing in her essence. She leaned over him, her hands braced on either side of his head, her face very close, her eyes fixed on his. Her hair enclosed them like a perfumed satin tent—a luxurious hiding place for just the two of them. It was intoxicating, this feeling of being completely surrounded by her, warm and golden, fragrant and mysterious. His mind reeled; his heart galloped in his chest until it pained him just to breathe.

Thorne couldn't keep from touching her, regardless of his good intentions. He brought his hand up and cupped her cheek. She squeezed her eyes closed, as if trying to resist him; but in the end, with a sigh of capitulation, she turned her head and pressed her warm lips to his palm. "Martine," he rasped, curving his hand around the back of her neck to urge her closer, closer ...

She paused briefly just before her lips touched his, and he saw the apprehension in her eyes. But then she closed them and kissed him, really kissed him, with a passion and intensity that drew an ecstatic moan from his throat. He threaded his fingers through her hair and gripped her head harder than he knew he should, deepening the kiss, reveling in her taste, her warmth.

Unable to stop himself, he trailed his hand down her throat and covered one soft breast through the wool of her tunic, thrilling at the little whimper of pleasure that escaped her. His body responded instantly. He'd never grown so hard so fast.

"Lie next to me," he whispered gruffly.

She kicked off her slippers and lay half on top of him, her mouth seeking his again, her hands in his hair, on his chest, stroking, caressing.... With a mindless urgency born of fierce arousal, he tugged at her skirt, yanking it up and gliding his hand between her soft thighs. He lightly stroked her with his fingertips, then found her tight entrance and probed deep.

She gasped. She was wet. She wanted him, was ready for him. He explored her with a sense of awe, enthralled by the narrowness of her passage, its slick, inviting heat. Withdrawing his finger, he slid it upward until it grazed her most sensitive flesh. She quivered. "Oh! Oh, God!"

She buried her face in the crook of his neck as he touched her; he kissed the top of her head, nuzzled her hair. "Yes," he whispered as her hips began to move to the rhythm of his caress. Her breath grew quick and shallow, her entire body tensed, and then she trembled all over, her fingers digging into his chest, her soft cries muffled by the pillow.

He held her until her breathing steadied, and then took her hand and guided it down over the sheet, shaping it to his aching need.

"Tell me what to do," she whispered.

"You'll have to be on top."

Martine's eyes widened, but then she nodded, seeming to comprehend. She shifted position, glanced around to make sure the curtains were drawn, and then lowered the sheet to expose him.

"I'll be quiet," he promised—a promise he broke almost instantly, crying out in agony when she tried to position herself astride him. Her knee barely nudged his splinted leg, but it was enough to send a bolt of fire along every nerve in his body.

"Oh, my God—Thorne!" Martine knelt beside him on the bed, cradling him helplessly as he panted like a wolf caught in a trap. "I'm sorry!"

"It's not your fault," he managed between clenched teeth.

She stroked his hair, leaned over to kiss his temple. " 'Twas foolish of us to try to . . . We can't do this. 'Twill hurt you."

He chuckled breathlessly. "Some things are worth a bit of pain. But perhaps . . . well, perhaps not quite that much pain." He listened carefully to the quiet, rhythmic breathing from beyond the curtain. "I didn't wake the others, but they won't be able to sleep through much more of that."

She glanced down at him. "Won't you be . . . frustrated?"

Thorne smiled. "I have no intention of being frustrated." He took her hand and closed it over his throbbing shaft. "There are other ways."

She watched for a few moments as he guided her fist up and down, and then he released his hand she continued the caress on her own. "Is this what you want?" she asked. "I mean, is this all, or is there—" her hand stilled and she glanced up at him a bit timidly, "something else?"

His gaze strayed to her mouth, to her lush lips the color of crushed berries. There *was* something else, of course, but he was loath to ask it of her. It was a service only whores had performed for him, and for extra payment, at that. Despite her intellectual sophistication, Martine was, he reminded himself, very much an innocent. Such an act might disgust her, make her feel defiled.

She had evidently noticed the direction of his gaze. Her tongue flicked out to moisten those tempting lips, a charmingly unconscious, but nonetheless provocative gesture; Thorne closed his eyes, praying for self-control.

"Last summer," she began, "at the river, when we ... when we were together, you ... kissed me." He knew without elaboration what kind of kiss she meant. "Is that something that a woman could do for a man?"

He swallowed. "Yes."

She glanced down at her hand resting on his erection, and then looked him in the eye. "Would you like me to do it for you?"

She seemed so sweetly sincere that he couldn't repress a smile. "Yes. I'd like that very much."

"Show me," she whispered. "Tell me what to do."

He trailed his fingertips down her face and tenderly brushed them across her lips. "Just ... I don't know. Do whatever you think I'd like. You could hardly go wrong."

Looking decidedly unsure of that, she lowered her head, her incredible sweep of hair blanketing him like a silken cape, obscuring his view of her—possibly, he thought, a deliberate ploy on her part to protect her modesty. He closed his eyes, and after what seemed an eternity, felt the first light touch of her mouth on his tormented, straining flesh.

Thorne bit his lip, struggling for composure. He felt the whisper-soft pressure of her lips, and presently the hot, wet tip of her tongue. The tentative nature of her efforts only intensified the stimulation. "Oh, God," he whispered shakily, his fist closing around a handful of her hair.

He'd told her she could hardly go wrong, and she didn't. The most practiced courtesan could have done no better. What she lacked in experience, she more than made up for in her touching desire to please him. Her generosity in doing this for him moved him profoundly, and he couldn't help thinking that perhaps, deep in her heart, she still harbored some real affection for him.

When she finally took him full in her mouth, he growled deep in his throat and shoved his hand through her hair. "Martine . . . oh, God. Yes!"

His climax approached swiftly. He released his grip on her head. "Martine, I'm . . . close." She didn't understand, and made no move to substitute her hand for her mouth. Given her inexperience, he thought it best if she did. "Martine," he gasped, taking her by her shoulder and pulling her up.

"Is something wrong?"

"Nay." He wrapped his arm around her, urging her to lie beside him. "Just touch me . . . like that. Yes . . . yes . . ." His heart seemed to swell in his chest until he couldn't bear it for another second. He clutched at her, his head back, groaning.

"Yes. Oh!" Spasms of pleasure rocked him. He erupted in her hand, losing all conscious thought, all sense of time and space. Nothing existed but this moment, this blinding burst of sensation.

Nothing existed but Martine and him.

Martine raced past the chapter house and refectory, around the cloister, and through the passageway to the outer courtyard. She held her skirts up off the snow with one hand and gripped her veil with the other, her hair fluttering wildly with every frigid gust of wind.

It was almost first light. The brothers would be up soon to file into church for lauds, and she had promised to avoid direct contact with them. Since the infirmary was in their private area of the monastery—an area normally off limits to her—this meant she had to time her comings and goings in keeping with their observation of the holy offices.

She saw not a soul as she entered the prior's lodge and sprinted up the stairs, but in the doorway of the central hall she stopped short, biting back the oath that rose to her lips.

Brother Matthew sat at the little table in the middle of the room, reading the Bible by candlelight. He looked up at her as she paused breathlessly in the doorway. His calmly assessing gaze took in the veil clutched in her fist, the loose hair that hung to her hips in a wind-whipped tangle, and, she had no doubt, the quick, scalding heat that stung her cheeks.

He nodded. "Good morning, my lady."

She cleared her throat. "Good morning, Brother."

She turned and swiftly ducked into her chamber, then collapsed on her bed, struggling to catch her breath and speculating miserably on how much Brother Matthew had surmised from her disheveled appearance—and her all-too-telling blush.

"Lady Martine," he said from the other side of the curtain. "May I have a word with you?"

Damn. She covered her face with her hands and sucked in a deep, pacifying breath, then sat up, swiftly tidying her hair and tunic. "Yes, Brother. Come in."

He crossed to her and squatted down next to the bed, taking her hands in his. For some reason—perhaps exhaustion, perhaps relief at his obvious intent to make this as easy on her as possible—her eyes began to burn with impending tears.

"Please don't misunderstand me, Martine," he said gently. "I have the greatest respect for Thorne—and for you, for that matter. I view you both as friends—very good friends."

She nodded, her throat too constricted to speak.

He drew a thoughtful breath. "And I'm not without compassion. Just because I renounced the pleasures of the flesh when I took my vows doesn't mean I don't understand them, even appreciate them. Such pleasures are a part of God's plan, after all."

He gave her hands a firm squeeze and released them. "It's not my place to pass judgment on your relations with Sir Thorne. But it is my place to govern what transpires in this monastery."

"None of the brothers saw me. I ran—"

"My concern is not for the brothers. My concern is for you."

"M-me?"

Furrows formed on his brow. "Your involvement with Thorne is far more dangerous for you than it is for him—you must realize that. You're a married woman, Martine, regardless of what you may or may not feel in your heart. When the abbot agreed to allow you to live here, it was with the understanding that you would behave with the greatest circumspection."

She nodded again, his image wavering through the hot tears that welled in her eyes.

"If he suspects, even for a moment, that you've violated that understanding, he'll order me to expel you from St. Dunstan's, and I'll have no choice but to obey. You'll be homeless then, and completely without protection. God knows how Bernard would choose to exploit such a situation."

She closed her eyes and tears trailed down her cheeks. *He's right,* she thought forlornly. *God, I wish he weren't, but he is.*

"Martine, are you in love with Thorne?"

Her eyes flew open. "I . . ." She shook her head. "No, I . . ." She choked back a helpless sob and dropped her gaze to her hands. "I don't know."

He closed his hand over her chin and tilted her head up, forcing her to look into his dark, perceptive eyes. "Has he told you he loves you?"

She shook her head. "He—he's incapable of love."

Matthew smiled and raised an eyebrow. "No one's incapable of love, my dear, even Thorne Falconer. But whatever his feelings may or may not be, he's done you a disservice by encouraging you to . . ." His gaze swept over her snarled hair.

She felt absurdly obliged to leap to his defense. " 'Twas as much my fault as his."

"Well . . ."

"It was. I'm weak. Just like my mother—" She broke down, sobbing uncontrollably. After a moment, Matthew awkwardly guided her head onto his shoulder and patted her back.

"There, there," he soothed. Martine reflected that he probably would have made a wonderful father. It was a pity monks couldn't marry. When she stopped crying, he dried her tears with her discarded veil. "You're not weak, you're just human. And Thorne is ... well, he's accustomed to having his way with women. Some men are remarkably skilled at bending women to their will, and Thorne Falconer is one of those men."

"Oh, God," she groaned. "I know. I'm so—"

"Nay. You mustn't judge yourself so harshly, my lady. But, for your own good, you also mustn't continue these sorts of relations with Thorne. In truth, it's dreadfully unfair of him to expect it of you. The risk to him is minimal, but to you—"

"I know," she said, her voice rusty from crying. She did know; Thorne had used her again, and again she had let him. "You're right. 'Twas foolish of me to have taken that risk. I won't take it again."

"Frankly, my lady, I don't intend to give you the chance." He stood and added quietly, "I'm afraid I'm going to have to forbid you to return to the infirmary."

Martine rose as well, her hands clasped demurely in front of her, summoning all the poise she could muster. "But Thorne needs my medicines. Perhaps just once a day, just to—"

"Nay, my lady. Brother Paul and Brother Luke will tend to him. You may send whatever medicines and instructions you wish, but you may not go back there."

She crossed her arms and stared at the floor. "Thorne will wonder why I don't come," she said, sounding a good deal more sullen than she would have liked.

"I'll explain things to him."

"He won't like it."

"He'll be furious," Matthew said easily. "He'll tell me the whole affair is none of my business and that he means you no harm. He doesn't, of course. But the harm will come just the same—to you, not to him." He shrugged. "In the end, he has no choice in the matter. He's confined to his bed, is he not?"

Martine nodded.

Matthew closed a hand on her arm. "My dear, surely you see this is for the best."

"I do, but ... it's hard."

He nodded sagely. "You must try to be strong and do

the right thing. You must put Thorne out of your mind. It's what Rainulf would want."

That was true enough. Rainulf, as always, would counsel discretion. Not for the first time since he'd left, she found herself missing him painfully. Again she felt the sting of tears in her eyes, but she blinked them back. Thinking of Rainulf always made her feel like crying, but she'd cried enough for one morning.

She raised her chin and looked Brother Matthew in the eye. "You're a wise man, Brother. "And I know you're right about this. I do. I'll try, I really will."

She filled her lungs with air and let it out slowly. "From now on, I'll put Thorne Falconer out of my mind."

"Thorne has made excellent progress," Brother Matthew told Martine as they walked to church. The first mass of the day was celebrated at prime, and it was this mass that Martine attended, along with the servants and lay brothers.

"Yes, I understand he's on his feet," she said, her chilly words hanging in the air between them as vaporous clouds. In the three weeks since she'd been forbidden to visit Thorne, she'd received only sporadic and cursory reports on his condition. Although she'd endeavored, as promised, to exile the Saxon from her thoughts, to hear so little of his recovery after having worked so hard to heal him galled her greatly.

Matthew nodded. "Yes, he's up and about. Brother Paul tells me he's never seen anyone so determined to walk again. Thorne insisted on getting out of bed long before they thought he should. At first all he did was fall down, but he kept at it. No one could believe he was willing to put up with that kind of pain." He shook his head. "Thorne can be very stubborn about things." He smiled. "Like you."

"Then he can walk now?"

"Short distances, with a crutch. Paul says he can make it from one end of the infirmary to the other, and back again. Not bad, considering he almost lost that leg."

She nodded. "Thank you for telling me this, Brother."

He smiled and patted her arm. "Let's not be late for mass."

She followed him into church, taking a seat between Felda and Cleva, Brother Matthew's cook. Although Martine found mass tiresome, she liked this particular church very much. Its whitewashed walls and pillars reflected what little light came in through the narrow windows above the altar, and the sanctuary was decorated, from ceiling beams to floor, with brightly painted frescoes depicting events in the life of Saint Dunstan.

"Good morning," came a familiar voice from behind her—Thorne's voice! She and her companions turned to find the Saxon edging awkwardly onto the bench behind them. He nodded toward the three women. "My lady. Felda . . . Cleva."

"Sir Thorne!" Felda exclaimed. "Is that you?"

He didn't look at all like himself, that was for certain. A dark beard concealed the lower half of his face, the features of which had been sharpened by weight loss. He wore a tunic of humble homespun, probably borrowed from one of the larger lay brothers. His right arm was immobilized in a sling, his left draped over the crutch on which he leaned. Speechless, Martine gaped down at his leg, still splinted and heavily bandaged. Leaning the crutch on the end of the bench, he sat slowly and carefully, his clenched jaw betraying the pain even this simple maneuver caused him.

"You walked all the way here from the infirmary?" Martine said. "Through the snow? With that leg? You're mad."

He smiled. Leaning toward her, he murmured, "If I'm mad, so be it. I understand some madmen are even happy."

The brothers began their chanting, and Martine turned back toward the altar, her face suffused with heat. His seemingly innocent words, meaningless to Felda and Cleva, were in fact words he had spoken to her on the mossy bank of River Blackburn, while he was buried deep inside her. They were clever, those words, conjuring up for her, as he surely knew they would, the heat and intimacy of their lovemaking, the ecstasy that they had known together.

Put him out of your mind, she commanded herself. *You* must *put him out of your mind. . . .* Why had he come here? she wondered. To see her? It was cruel, considering how hard it was for her to forget him, to forget the passion that sparked between them, the need . . .

All through the interminable mass, Martine felt his hot blue eyes burning into her. Dear God, would she ever be free of this longing, this empty place inside her with the shape of Thorne Falconer?

When the mass ended, Martine rose to leave with the others, but Thorne gripped her shoulder firmly and lowered her to her seat. He left his hand there until the church was empty save for the two of them and a young monk at the altar snuffing out candles. The Saxon removed his hand and they sat in silence, although the distance between them vibrated with unspoken words. Breathing in the pungent incense that lingered in the cold air, she watched the young monk, no more than a boy, move in and out of the hazy ribbons of sunlight that played over the altar. Without the press of surrounding bodies, she felt the full chill of the unheated winter air, even through her sable-lined winter cloak. Her gloves did little to keep her hands warm, so she tunneled them into the sleeves of her tunic.

Turning toward him, she said, "Don't you attend mass in the chapel off the infirmary?"

"Usually." He said no more until the boy finished his duties and left, and then he leaned toward her. "But I'd wanted to attend it here, so I've been working on being able to walk." He sighed heavily. "I had to see you. I haven't been able to think of anything else."

She turned her back to him again, struggling to maintain her distance, emotionally, from this man who wielded such irresistibly seductive power over her, holding her captive to the yearning that seemed to simmer beneath the surface of his words.

He reached out with one finger to touch the underside of her chin. A tingle of desire raced through her, and she sucked in her breath, awed at the capacity of one warm, caressing fingertip to heat the blood in her veins, to grab hold of her heart and squeeze it until it hurt to breathe.

She wanted him, nay, needed him, with a craving so instantaneous and so powerful that she had to close her eyes and breathe deeply of the cold, spicy air to regain her composure . . . to remember why she mustn't let him do this, mustn't let him make her want him. That he still had the power to do so, after all that had transpired between them, shamed her deeply, despite Brother Matthew's insistence that it shouldn't.

The struggle to resist him challenged her will. His touch, although surely calculated to serve his own purposes, felt so human, so warm, so redolent with promise. Were she to allow it, she had no doubt that, despite his injuries, he would take her hand and lead her to some dark and private corner and claim her body as fiercely and passionately as he had done at the riverbank. She could almost feel him inside her, and her body pulsed around the void within.

"Will you be here tomorrow?" he asked, stroking her throat ever so lightly with the tips of his fingers.

She bit her lip, arresting the words that leaped from her heart. . . . *Yes, I'll be here. I want to be with you, to talk to you, to see the hunger in your eyes as they look at me, to feel your hands on me. . . . Yes, I'll be here.*

She was susceptible to his skillful persuasions, and he knew it; how could he fail to, after having seduced her twice? Now he thought he could make her desire him again anytime he wanted. How close that was to the truth, and how she hated her weakness.

She might be weak, but she was also proud, and now she would use that pride to protect herself.

She met his eyes. "I won't be here, Thorne."

The light behind his eyes dimmed. He nodded, his mouth set.

She said, "I'm glad you're doing so well, but you've still got weeks—nay, months—of healing ahead of you. You should stay off your feet as much as possible. You certainly shouldn't be walking here all the way from the infirmary." This time he made no move to stop her when she stood and went to the aisle.

Her back to him, she said, "You're best off attending mass in the infirmary chapel." As she turned and made her way back through the nave to the rear door, she thought she heard him say her name, but she kept walking and didn't turn around.

Chapter 19

"Mayhap she's incubating a demon," suggested Father Simon, nodding toward Estrude's grotesquely swollen belly as she lay writhing and moaning in her bed.

Bernard glanced at the priest, thinking, *The little worm is serious.* Yet even Godfrey, nodding in slack-jawed amazement, seemed to believe it. Of course, he was pathetically gullible when he was drunk, which was all the time lately. With his mouth hanging open like that, and that dumbfounded stare of his, he looked for all the world like the village idiot. All Bernard could think was, *The day you start to drool, old man, is the day I smother you in your sleep.*

"Kill me," Estrude begged for the hundredth time that day.

Now, she's the one who needs a pillow over the face, thought her husband, not because a quick death would be a merciful end to her suffering, but rather because the sight of her disgusted him beyond measure. In recent months her skin, jaundiced and covered with mysterious sores, had shrunken down over her bones, the flesh beneath seeming almost to dissolve in the process. Her face, with its wild, terrified eyes and lips stretched back over too-large teeth, was the face of a living corpse. Her arms and legs were like twigs, a curious contrast to the enormous belly that grew and grew and grew, like an overripe fruit waiting to burst.

Would it indeed rupture if she waited too long to die? he wondered idly. And if so, what would come out? A horned minion of Satan, as Father Simon speculated? While his wife thrashed and clawed at her bedclothes, Bernard envisioned such a creature springing from her womb in an explosion of blood, and chuckled at the sheer primitive absurdity of it.

No, it was no demon growing within his wife's body, but neither was it a babe, of that he was fairly certain. Estrude's belly, but six months into her confinement, had swelled to outlandish proportions. The midwife assured him that twin babes at full term could not have distended it so. No, it was some malady or other that had done this to her, and not a pregnancy, normal or demonic. The bitch really was barren, after all, worse luck.

On the bright side, she'd be dead soon. He could start over with a new wife, someone young and healthy and capable of producing heirs. He'd keep this new one on a short leash and let her feel the sting of his belt right from the start, not give her time to grow insolent, as Estrude had. And it might serve him well to closet her in the bedchamber, where he'd always know where to find her. He'd have a door built, one that locked from the outside. This time he'd do it right.

Of course, in contemplating a second marriage, he was obliged to confront the same irksome problem that had forced him to go all the way to Flanders for a bride the first time. Although a full twenty years had passed, he knew it didn't matter how long ago it was, or that she was just a twopenny whore, or that she deserved what she got and more; the incident had plagued him ever since. It was his own damn fault for losing his head and doing her right there in the brothel, for making such a mess of it and leaving her on her pallet for them to find, knowing he'd been her last customer. His uncurbed rage had not only been unwise, it had been vulgar, uncivilized—and that shamed him, for he was, after all, a civilized man.

"Kill me," Estrude pleaded as she kicked and tore at her hair. "Kill me. Please!"

It was a tempting notion, that of pressing a pillow to her face in the dead of night, but an ill-advised one. A keep was a place with no secrets. Were it not, he would have eased her passage from the world—and his sire's as well—long before this. But the risk of being found out was too great, and, as far as Estrude was concerned, quite unnecessary, considering she'd be dead within days.

Edmond's voice rose from the courtyard below. Godfrey leaned out the window and called him inside.

How proud his little brother had been of himself after cutting his teeth with that little whore of Nan's, that Emeline. In truth, Bernard had found the incident somewhat flattering, for of course Edmond had only sought to emulate what he himself had done two decades before. But then the boy had tried the same business with the lady Martine, and that Bernard had found less than amusing. Edmond's childish enthusiasm was ever unfettered by discretion, and that could be a dangerous thing; it led to sloppiness, and, as Bernard well knew, sloppiness led to getting caught. Had he wanted to be rid of his own wife, Edmond should have had the patience to plan the act in advance, make it look like an accident.

"Kill me. Dear God, kill me. . . ."

He'd often been tempted to plan such an accident for Estrude, but fool that he was, he kept thinking his seed might eventually take root in the poor soil of her womb. He wouldn't make the same mistake next time. At six and thirty, it was high time he had sons. If his next wife didn't conceive within a year, he'd do what he should have done with Estrude long before this; he'd tell her to pack up a picnic hamper and take her on an outing to Weald Forest, just the two of them. Fingering his little jeweled eating knife through the pouch on his belt, he smiled as he imagined the exquisite punishments his imaginary bride's infertility would earn her. He wouldn't even have to bury her. He could, in fact, garner a certain measure of sympathy by claiming that she'd been tortured and raped by bandits before his very eyes.

"Ah, Edmond," Godfrey said.

Bernard turned to find his brother in the doorway, gawking at Estrude with an expression of repugnance. "I'm not going in there."

The baron followed his younger son into the hallway. Bernard could just make out his sire's words, thick with drink and muffled by the leather curtain that separated them. "She's dying, son."

"Well, I wish she'd hurry up about it. Jesus!"

"I've got a problem now, boy. No grandsons, and no good prospects for getting any. Geneva's been cast aside, and Bernard will be a widower soon. That leaves you."

A moment of silence. "Oh, no," Edmond moaned. "She's a witch, Pa! She's a fucking witch!"

"You'll ride to St. Dunstan's tomorrow and bring her back."

Father Simon looked toward Bernard and raised his eyebrows.

"I won't do it," Edmond said.

"You will! You're my vassal to command same as anyone else within my domain, and you'll do as I say or I'll put you in a monastery for the rest of your natural days. You hear me, boy?"

It was an unusually vehement speech from the old man, considering how weak and ineffectual he'd become. But then, he'd always been passionate on the subject of grandsons. Another long pause, and then Edmond mumbled assent.

"And you will live with her as man and wife until she bears a son. After that, you may do as you wish."

Christ, thought Bernard. *At this rate, Edmond will end up with heirs before I do.*

He'd thought he was well rid of her. He'd thought he'd never have to set eyes on the witch again, much less live with her.

Squeezing some more wine down his throat, Edmond kicked his bay stallion simply for the need to kick something. It lurched forward, throwing him back hard, feet in the air. Only by grabbing the saddle quickly did he manage to regain his seat. He pulled back sharply on the reins, and the bay snorted testily.

He'd not only have to live with her, he'd have to bed her—or try to. Who's to say she wouldn't use sorcery on him again, or sneak him another dose of poison? For all he knew, she had a spell to make his cock shrivel up and fall off! She might even kill him this time.

He looked around blearily in an effort to confirm that he was still headed west, toward St. Dunstan's. It was noon, so the sun was of no help. The snow-dusted terrain looked unfamiliar, and for the first time he noticed how steep it was. To his left, the rocky hillside dropped off precipitously, making his vision reel and his stomach turn over. The wineskin slipped out of his fingers and tumbled down the hill, bouncing over boulders for quite some time before disappearing in the woods below. No great loss, that. It was almost empty, and he had another.

Aye, but 'twould be better to be dead than to have to take that woman back, he thought, uncorking the second skin and filling his mouth. Everyone knew about her. Bernard even told him there was a rumor circulating in Hastings that she'd cast a spell on the pilot of the *Lady's Slipper* after summoning a storm on his boat!

He nudged his mount into a trot, drinking as he rode. He began to see double, but he didn't mind. Being drunk kept him from feeling the cold, not to mention taking the edge off this distasteful errand. But for the wine, he didn't think he could do it.

If his wife didn't kill him, more than likely the Saxon would. He'd sworn on the baby Jesus' saddling clothes that he'd kill him slowly and painfully if he laid a finger on the witch! But what right had that upstart woodsman's son to order him away from her? She was his wife, damn it. His lord and sire had commanded him to get her with child, and he would, by God, if he had to tie her to the bed to do it!

Again he kicked his mount, and again the stallion raced forward, its hooves skittering over the loose gravel that covered the narrow hillside track. Dropping the wineskin, he jerked back on the reins, whereupon the enraged bay bucked and squealed. In a panic over losing his seat, Edmond grabbed for the animal's mane, but it was too late. Off he flew, sailing over the side of the hill and rolling roughly over boulders and fallen trees until he finally landed with bone-crushing force on an outcropping of rock.

He looked up, squinting into the sun and listening to the receding hoofbeats of his mount. *Christ, my head's on backward,* he thought. And then a veil of red obscured his vision, and his mouth filled with blood, and he could no longer feel his body.

His last thoughts were, *She's a more powerful witch than I thought. She's killed me before I even got there.*

Standing at the window in the hall of the prior's lodge, Martine withdrew the sheet of parchment from her tunic and began to reread it.

5 March 1160

From Bernard of Harford to his sister by marriage, Martine of Rouen.

Know, my lady sister, that much has transpired recently of which I am obliged, with a great heaviness of heart, to inform you. It is with the utmost sorrow that I transmit herewith the news that your husband, my most beloved brother, Edmond, has passed from the world. Would that my melancholy account ended there, however, it appears that my dear wife, Estrude, gravely ill these many months, is destined to join him soon.

"Martine."

She turned toward the voice, Thorne's voice. He stood in the door of the stairway, dressed in homespun as he had been when she saw him in church a fortnight ago. This morning, however, he was again clean-shaven. He no longer wore the sling, but he had his crutch with him.

"Sir Thorne." She noticed in his eyes a flicker of disappointment at the formal address.

"Brother Matthew told me about Edmond."

She nodded and looked down at the letter.

He said, "I won't pretend I'm sorry."

"Then neither will I." They met each others eyes. *He always knows what's in my heart,* she thought. *That's the source of his power over me. That's why he can bend me to his will. I must try to be strong. I must close my heart to him and strip him of that power.*

Thorne frowned. "Matthew tells me you're riding back to Harford today for Edmond's funeral."

"Yes, I've just finished packing." She nodded toward the satchel in which she'd stowed a change of clothes and a jug of claret mixed with sleeping draft, which she hoped might soothe Estrude's torment. "I'll only be gone for a day or two. I'm leaving Loki here."

He closed in on her. "I don't think you should go."

She backed up. "Edmond is dead. I needn't hide behind St. Dunstan's walls anymore. Felda and I are riding back today."

"Without an escort?"

"No harm will come to us."

He sighed. 'If you insist on going, I'm going with you."

She straightened her back. "You're in no condition to ride. And there's certainly no need."

"It matters not what condition I'm in, and there certainly is a need."

She planted her fists on her hips. "You don't understand. I don't want you to come."

"But I do understand," he said soberly. "I know you'd rather I left you alone. I know you find my company . . . distressing, and that's Matthew's urged you to stay away from me. But the fact remains that the journey to Harford isn't safe for you, and neither, necessarily, is Harford Castle itself." He rested a hand on the hilt of his sword. "I swore an oath to your brother to take care of you, and whether you like it or not, that's exactly what I'm going to do."

He's a good actor, thought Thorne as Bernard, looking suitably grave, greeted him in the courtyard of Harford Castle. Martine dismissed Felda and asked to see Lady Estrude, whereupon Bernard turned and led his sister by marriage and the Saxon knight up the circular stairwell. Thorne, in agony from the long ride, immediately fell behind and was soon forced to stop and rest. Hunched over his crutch, he closed his eyes and tried to transcend the red-hot pain that coursed through his right leg.

In the privacy of the stairwell, the Saxon withdrew the chess piece and squeezed it, willing the hurt to disappear. As it receded, he ran his thumb over the little whalebone face, the high cheekbones, the full lips. He hadn't lain with another woman since that morning on the riverbank; it was the longest he'd gone without sex since the Crusade. It wasn't that his need was diminished. It was, in fact, more overwhelming than ever. But it was a need that his whores and serving girls could no longer hope to satisfy. It was a need with a name, and that name was Martine of Rouen.

God, give me the strength to keep my distance from her, he prayed. She wanted that distance, needed it— that was clear enough. She had her reasons, some of which were actually rather good ones, and he knew that nothing he could say or do at this point would change her mind. But the fact that she wanted nothing to do with him must not be allowed to interfere with his pledge to Rainulf to protect her; truly, he would do so even had he not sworn an oath. Now that she had abandoned the safety of St. Dunstan's, he must be her shadow, her personal soldier, but he must never presume to renew the intimacy they had once known. She felt threatened by his desire for her, and he wanted above all things for her to feel safe when she was with him, which now had to be constantly. And so he had resolved to be polite but cool toward her, a resolution that pained his soul as fiercely as his unhealed wounds pained his body.

When he finally entered Lady Estrude's chamber, Martine was readjusting her bedclothes and pulling up the blankets, having concluded her examination.

Martine—and Bernard, standing in the corner with his arms crossed—met Thorne's eyes and then lowered theirs to Estrude. Following their gaze, he automatically crossed himself. He hadn't seen the lady for four months, and although she'd looked sickly when he left Harford to lay siege to Blackburn, she hadn't looked anything like this. Never had he seen anyone so debilitated, so ravaged by disease. From her moans, and the way she clutched at her bedclothes, she was clearly in agony. Her distended belly added to his sense of horror. It was his babe in that enfeebled body, a babe that would die when Estrude succumbed.

Martine dipped a cloth in water, wrung it out, and bathed Estrude's face with it, then opened her satchel and withdrew a stoppered jug. The dying woman's eyes struggled to focus on her benefactress; she seemed unaware that Bernard and Thorne were in the room. "What is that?" she rasped.

"Some claret I brought back from St. Dunstan's, my lady," said Martine, pausing to sit on the edge of the narrow bed and take Estrude's clawlike hand in hers. " 'Twill help you to sleep." Martine's willingness to comfort a woman who had always treated her with contempt, to set aside whatever anger and jealousy she might feel and offer simple, unconditional solace, filled Thorne with awe.

With a seemingly great effort, Estrude shook her head. "I don't deserve it. God wants me to suffer. He's punishing me."

Leaning closer, Martine said, "That can't be true, my lady."

Estrude nodded. "Aye. 'Tis because I was too greedy for a baby. I sinned, and now He's punishing me."

Warning bells tolled in Thorne's brain. He glanced toward Bernard, who was frowning in the corner, and then at Martine, who met his eyes with a knowing look. "Sir Bernard," she said, "I wonder if you'd be so kind as to fetch Father Simon."

"She's already had last rites," he said.

"Ah. Well, then, perhaps you wouldn't mind bringing me a goblet for the wine."

Bernard, clearly unused to being asked to fetch anyone or anything, hesitated a moment. Then, as if deciding that his role of grieving husband might include a measure of compliance in such matters, he nodded and left the chamber. Thorne drew a steadying breath and directed a small smile of thanks toward Martine.

"God isn't punishing you," Martine told the suffering woman.

"He is," she insisted. "Because of what I did to get this babe. It . . . it's not Bernard's child. I sinned to get pregnant, so God gave me a babe who's sucking the life from my body. The babe grows huge while I waste away. Soon I'll be dead, and then I'll roast in hell for eternity. I'm doomed." The speech seemed to have exhausted her, for she closed her eyes and struggled to take in ragged lungfuls of air.

"God is merciful," Martine said. "He wouldn't punish you like this for adultery."

"Not just adultery," Estrude whispered, not having even the strength to open her eyes. "I used trickery. Sir Thorne didn't want me, so I tricked him."

Martine directed a puzzled look toward Thorne, who gave a small nod of his head.

"I wore your perfume. I went to him in the middle of the night and let him think I was you." Martine gaped at Thorne, wide-eyed. Estrude tossed her head, grimacing. "He was furious afterward. I forced myself on him. 'Twas wrong. 'Twas a very great sin. God let Sir Thorne's babe grow within me only in order to kill me with it, to send me to hell." Her weakened voice rendered the last few words almost unintelligible.

Martine placed her hands very gently on either side of Estrude's face and said, "My lady, open your eyes. Look at me. That's right. Listen carefully to me. You're not pregnant."

Estrude's eyes searched Martine's as if to divine the truth in her words. *Could it be possible?* Thorne wondered.

"But my belly," Estrude groaned, her words echoing Thorne's thoughts.

"I examined you," Martine reminded her. "And I assure you, you're not with child. You never have been. You suffer from an illness I've seen before, in Paris. 'Tis a ball of disease that grows and grows and never stops. You've probably been ill for a year or more, but didn't realize it."

"My courses . . . they had almost stopped, even before . . ."

"You see?" said Martine. "You're ill, that's all."

"Am I dying?"

Martine hesitated. Then, "Aye."

Estrude nodded. "Will it be soon?"

Another pause. "Aye."

"Thank God."

"And then you'll be with the angels," Martine assured her.

"With the angels," Estrude whispered, smiling. Thorne saw a sheen of tears in her half-closed eyes. "I'll be with the angels."

Bernard returned with the goblet, into which Martine poured the claret. She raised her sister-in-law's head so she could sip it, and then whispered, "Sleep if you can."

Within moments, Estrude's whole body seemed to relax. Her fingers uncurled; her limbs lost their rigidity, her face its rictus of agony. Her eyes closed and her breathing became calm and regular. An hour later, as the sun touched the horizon, the steady rise and fall of her chest quietly ceased. Death, which had waited so patiently for Estrude of Flanders, took her at last.

An hour after that, Bernard, Godfrey, and Father Simon sat huddled around a small table in the baron's chamber.

"But she's his sister by marriage," Godfrey pointed

out to the priest as Bernard refilled his tankard, thinking, *Just agree to it before you pass out, that's all I ask.*

Father Simon steepled his fingers and said, "Yes, well, that's not quite like being a blood relation. It's only affinity, not consanguinity. A small donation to Bishop Lambert"—he shrugged—"and there will be no objection from the Church, I assure you."

Bernard guided the tankard to his father's mouth. The old man drank for a while, then wiped his mouth on his sleeve and stared into the tankard, frowning his open-mouthed frown, as if trying to puzzle the whole business out.

Don't think, thought Bernard. *Drink.* Again he wrapped his hand around his sire's and aimed the tankard for his mouth. *He's usually more malleable than this when he's in his cups.*

But Godfrey stilled the tankard as it touched his lips. "Why tomorrow?" he asked. "Why first thing in the morning? Estrude's body is still warm, for God's sake!"

That woman's body was never warm, thought his son.

The baron shook his head in confusion. "I never knew a second wedding to take place the very day after the first wife—"

Oh, hell. "Look here," Bernard growled, his patience stretched about as thin as it could get. "Do you want grandsons?"

Slowly Godfrey lowered the tankard to the table, his eyes moist and reddened. "More than anything. You must remarry. I want you to. But why the lady Martine? There are dozens of suitable girls—"

"In Sussex," Bernard said tightly. "We'd have to go abroad, remember? Like we did the first time." He emptied the pitcher into the tankard, which overflowed a bit. "We'd have to go to Brittany, or Aquitaine, or Flanders again. Somewhere far away, where they don't know about . . . what happened. Remember?"

"Oh, yes," the baron mumbled. "The girl. That poor girl."

"Christ," Bernard grumbled. *'Tis a sin that a man that soft ever had control of a barony.* "I don't want to go abroad again," he explained slowly to the witless fool who had sired him. "It takes time. It's inconvenient. It's annoying. And besides, with Edmond dead, the lady

Martine now owns her bride price outright. Those lands have been in our family since the Conquest. Wouldn't you rather they remained under our control than under that of an eighteen-year-old girl we never even saw until last summer?"

"I don't care about that," Godfrey said. "I want grandsons."

Bernard leaned eagerly toward his father. "And I want to give them to you. The lady Martine is young and healthy. She could fill this keep with baby boys."

The baron's rheumy eyes glittered, and his mouth curved in a wistful smile. "Baby boys."

"Aye. Lots and lots of baby boys. Say the word and Father Simon will marry us in the morning."

"If it's by your command, no one can question it," the priest offered, cringing when Bernard shot him a look.

"Question it?" Godfrey muttered.

"No one will question it," said Bernard. "Not if it's by your order. And then will come the baby boys." *Christ, but this is a tiresome business.* "Lots of them."

Godfrey nodded slowly, smiling that pathetic smile.

"Do you order it?" Father Simon prompted.

The baron sighed. "Let it be so." Bernard sighed, too. *Finally.* But as he rose from the table, his sire said, "I must admit, though, I'm rather surprised you're agreeable to marrying *her,* even for the lands. You always say she's so willful and insolent. And I know you blame her for Edmond's death."

"I was distraught," Bernard said smoothly. "And as for her willfulness, all she really needs is a bit of discipline." He turned to leave. "Don't worry about all that. Just think about the baby boys."

"But what if she's barren, like Estrude?" Godfrey said to his back. "What if she can't bear sons?"

Bernard's hand unconsciously gravitated to the pouch on his belt, one finger slipping inside to stroke the knobby, jeweled handle of the little razor-sharp knife within. "Don't worry about that, either. I'll deal with that problem when it arises."

"I don't like that none of my men are here," Thorne said after the funeral that evening as he and Martine stood warming their hands over the fire pit in the great hall. "Godfrey sent Peter, Guy, and Albin to France. King Henry is still embroiled in those territorial skirmishes, and Godfrey supposedly felt he owed him some men. I wouldn't be suspicious, except that it was Bernard who put the idea in his head to send them."

He rarely even looked at her anymore when he spoke to her, Martine noticed. Unable to seduce her again, he'd become completely indifferent to her. No doubt he regretted the oath that made him feel obligated to keep to her side this way. "It doesn't necessarily mean anything," she said. "Perhaps, with you gone, your men simply had little to do."

"Perhaps," he murmured. And then he looked up, focusing on something over her shoulder, and his expression became grim. "Perhaps not."

When Martine turned, she saw Bernard and a contingent of his men advancing toward them. Bernard wore his humorless smile, but his men had the shuttered expressions of soldiers doing their duty. Geneva, who'd been playing draughts with Ailith in the corner, quickly hustled the child out of the hall.

Martine looked back toward Thorne. His hand rested on his sword, she noticed, but it was his right hand, and she knew that arm was still very weak.

Bernard paused before her, inspecting her with his hard little eyes. "My lady." He looked toward Thorne, his appraising gaze seeming to linger on his crutch. "Woodsman."

"What do you want, Bernard?" said Thorne.

"I want to remarry," he said. "As soon as possible."

"Then I suggest you start making travel arrangements," replied the Saxon. "Try Italy, or perhaps the Rhineland. They might not have heard about you there."

Bernard's eyes narrowed, and his hand closed over the hilt of his own sword. "It seems that won't be necessary," he said, turning again toward Martine and fixing her with a penetrating look that chilled her to the bone. "My sire has taken matters in hand, you see. He has already chosen a bride for me, and as it happens, she is conveniently close."

Martine stood utterly still, paralyzed with incomprehension. *Nay . . . he can't mean . . .*

She heard a metallic scrape as Thorne began to draw

his sword from its scabbard; in a flash of steel, four other swords were aimed at his throat.

It's true. Oh, God, Thorne was right. We walked right into a trap. Bernard lured me here so that he could . . . She couldn't even form the words in her mind, couldn't imagine the horror of being wed to this monster. If marriage to Edmond had been bad, marriage to Bernard would be a nightmare.

"Nay," she said. "I won't do it. I won't marry you."

"No one is asking for your permission," Bernard said coolly. "Our overlord gave you to me. There the matter comes to an end."

She swallowed down her outrage, her fear, and hid her hands in her skirts to conceal their trembling. From the corner of her eye she saw Thorne, still at swordpoint, frozen in watchful silence. "I'm going back to St. Dunstan's," she announced.

Bernard chuckled. "Aye, and if I gave you long enough to figure out a way to get back there, I'm sure that's exactly what you'd do. That's why I've arranged for the marriage to be solemnized in the morning."

"In the morning! Tomorrow morning?" Still the Saxon simply watched and listened. She wheeled on him. "Sir Thorne, please! Do something!"

He glanced at the gleaming blades of the swords and raised an eyebrow, as if to say, *What shall I do?*

"Say something!" she demanded. "Anything! You're supposed to protect me!"

"That's right," Bernard told Thorne. "I've heard about your oath to the good Father Rainulf. I daresay it must be a tedious business, following this viper-tongued wench about all day. I won't pretend to any great affection for you. Still it grieves me to see a knight of your caliber reduced to such lowly service. A galling assignment, is it not?"

Thorne just stared at him for a moment, expressionless. "What if it is? 'Tis no business of yours."

His words squeezed Martine's aching heart. She had known, of course, that he must begrudge his promise to Rainulf. Still, to hear the words from his own lips . . .

Bernard smiled. "Don't be so sure. Mayhap I could offer you an alternative to playing the vixen's faithful watchdog. Right now, you're a bug in my helmet, which

I must"—he gestured to his sword-wielding men—"eliminate, lest it drive me to distraction. However, I am always in need of good men. 'Tis a shame to destroy so much strength and skill when I can make use of it myself."

"What makes you think 'twill be easy?" Thorne asked.

"Let's not be coy. You want property. I"—he nodded toward Martine—"want my property back. If you renounce your oath to Father Rainulf and put in with me, I give you my word that I will deed you one of the holdings that comprised the lady Martine's bride price, in return for your faithful service to me."

To Martine's horror, Thorne took his time answering. Could he actually be weighing the offer? "Nay," he finally said. She breathed a sigh of relief. But then he added, "I want the land Lord Godfrey was going to grant me in the first place. 'Tis a far goodlier holding than those others."

No . . . Martine just stared at Thorne, who, unsurprisingly, refused to meet her eyes.

Bernard nodded slowly. "You're a greedy man. I admire that. Done, then. 'Twill be yours on the morrow." He nodded to his men, who lowered their swords. To Thorne he said, "And now, as a gesture of fealty, you will escort the lady upstairs to her chamber. Boyce will stand guard over her tonight, and in the morning,"—he took Martine's fingertips and lifted them—"we shall be joined in holy matrimony."

She yanked her hand out of his grasp. "I'll kill myself before I marry you."

"Thank you for the warning," Bernard drawled. He glanced at the pouch in which she carried her eating knife. With snakelike speed, he whipped his hand out, snatched it, and ripped it roughly from her girdle. "Boyce, search the chamber for anything she might use against herself . . . knives, rope—"

Thorne said, "Wouldn't it be safer just to lock her in the cell downstairs.?"

Rage struck Martine speechless. Bernard turned toward the Saxon, looking pleased, even impressed. "What an excellent idea. I had my doubts about you, woodsman. I'm glad to see you know where your interests lie."

Struggling to control her voice, Martine said, "Sir Thorne has never had any trouble discerning where his interests lie. Have you, Thorne?"

"Not generally, my lady." He took her arm, but she pulled away as he tried to lead her toward the stairwell, accompanied by Boyce. Quietly but firmly he said, "Don't make me hold a sword to you. I will if I have to." He closed a hand—the hand of his bad arm—around her wrist, but she punched it with her free hand. Wincing, he released her with a raw oath. He moved behind her and she heard his sword being withdrawn, then felt the pressure of its sharp tip through the back of her tunic. Urged forward by that pressure, she headed for the stairwell.

Chapter 20

For the first hour of her imprisonment, Martine stood in the middle of the tiny, fetid cell with her eyes closed, holding her skirts off the floor lest the vermin beneath the rotted straw crawl up them. At first she tried to pray, but she'd never been much good at that, and soon gave it up in favor of envisioning her imaginary herb garden, the one she'd planned in her head on her wedding day, and on parchment during her long winter's exile at St. Dunstan's.

Thinking of the herb garden calmed her, and presently she turned her mind toward her predicament. Once she thought about it, she realized that Thorne's cooperation with Bernard had been a foregone conclusion. He'd had but two choices: death if he defended her, or a valuable holding if he gave her up. What would Martine have done in his place? No, she mustn't make excuses for him. He'd sworn an oath to keep her from harm. He was supposed to be so resourceful, so brave. He might have thought of *something*. As it was, his betrayal was overwhelmingly painful, and coldly sobering. She was on her own now. If she was to be saved, she would have to save herself.

Outside, Boyce sat on a stool against the cellar wall, humming drinking songs. He was an odd sort, a fellow who, under different circumstances, she might almost have liked. She heard a creaking, accompanied by a kind of musical jangle, and knew the big man was shifting his weight on the stool, jarring the ring of keys on his belt— one of which would fit the lock on the cell's iron door.

After a few moments' thought, she approached the door and looked out through the peephole. "Sir Boyce?"

He stood, and suddenly his big face filled the little

square opening. "It's just Boyce, my lady. I'm not a knight, just a huntsman. But I must say it's rather nice to be called 'Sir.' I'm flattered."

As she'd thought he would be. "I'm terribly thirsty, Boyce. Do you suppose you could fetch me some wine?"

He frowned. "Nay, my lady, I can't leave my post."

She licked her lips and touched a hand to her throat, hoping she wasn't overdoing it.

He pulled at his beard. "But I could call for it to be sent down."

"Would you?"

"Aye, I'm a bit thirsty myself, if the truth be told."

She had, of course, counted on that, never having seen him without a cup in his hands. "I brought back a lovely claret from St. Dunstan's. Felda knows where it is."

And so the red-haired giant lumbered to the stairwell and called up for Felda to fetch down some of Lady Martine's claret.

"And two goblets," she prompted.

"And two goblets!" he roared.

Felda appeared with the claret, fussed and clucked over her mistress's captivity, exchanged a knowing look with her, then poured a small goblet for her and a rather larger one for her guard. Boyce drank his down quickly while Martine pretended to sip hers.

"Isn't that good?" Martine asked.

He looked a bit baffled. "It's ... different."

"That would be the spices," she quickly offered. "It's spiced claret, didn't I mention that?"

"Oh. Perhaps you did. But what kind of spices would make it taste so—"

"Take a guess," she said, indicating that Felda should give him a refill. "You tell me what you think they are."

Again he drained the goblet quickly. "Ain't cinnamon," he said, yawning. He took his seat on the stool again. "Ain't cloves." He inspected the empty vessel in his hand as he nodded sleepily, his expression of dazed puzzlement giving way to one of sudden illumination. He tired to focus on Martine's face through the peephole. "Wait a minute."

He stood, pawing at the wall for support, the goblet slipping from his fingers and rolling on the floor. "You're a crafty wench," he slurred, then lurched toward the door, shoving his face in the peephole; Martine jumped back. Presently he grinned, and then a deep, rumbly chuckle rose from him. "*Damn* crafty!" He laughed uproariously, his eyes watering. "That's a good joke on me," he choked out, pushing himself away from the door and stumbling toward Felda, who backed up swiftly. His roared with laughter. Tears streamed from his reddened face.

Suddenly he quieted, his eyes rolled up, and he toppled over like a felled tree, landing facedown with a *whump.*

The two women looked at each other in wonderment. Felda glanced toward the stairwell, then nudged the unconscious man with the toe of her slipper.

"The keys," Martine whispered. Her maid slipped the key ring off Boyce's belt. The third one she tried unlocked the door. Martine darted from the little cell and embraced her. "Oh, thank you, Felda. I knew I could count on you."

"What now, milady?"

"Ailith once told me there's a secret passageway down here."

Felda rolled her eyes, and Martine's heart sank. "It's hardly a secret, milady. Everyone knows about it—all the household staff, anyways."

Oh, thank God. "Where is it?"

It took longer than Martine would have liked to move aside the pyramid of barrels that concealed a small wooden door in the stone wall. " 'Tis a tunnel leading to the church," Felda explained, pulling open the door. "For use in the event of a siege. Lots of castles have them." She plucked a torch from its bracket on the wall, lifted her skirts, and ducked. "Follow me."

It was but a narrow passage burrowed into the earth and shored up with wooden posts. They had to hunch over as they made their way through it, and after a while Martine began to wonder if the church was, indeed, this far away. But presently the tunnel sloped upward, ending in a series of rough-hewn stones that served as a kind of stairway. Above the stairs, in a ceiling of oak planks, was a wooden panel. Felda forced open the panel's rusted latch and the two women pushed upward on it until it swung aside.

They found themselves behind the altar of the barony church. Once outside, Felda extinguished the torch in the snow. " 'Tis a good thing we're having a long winter," she said. "With all this snow, and that full moon, 'tis as bright as day."

It was true, Martine realized as she looked toward Harford Castle looming above the little village, its windows dark. She could see it as clearly as if it were late afternoon, and not the dead of night. It was so cold, though. She shivered, and wrapped her arms around herself. "I won't get far without a horse," she said. "And I could use a mantle."

Felda nodded. "Fitch Ironmonger's got a horse. And I'll wager his wife's got a mantle she could spare."

"His wife! Does she know about you?"

"Of course not," said Felda, leading the way. "And if Fitch don't want her finding out, he'll hand over the horse and the mantle."

Martine stood in the shadows while Felda hissed "Fitch!" through the back window of a little cottage. The ironmonger emerged, groggy with sleep, and they engaged in a brief and animated conversation, all in whispered English. Fitch growled and shook his head. He repeatedly called Felda a name that Martine knew meant a female dog. But finally, when Felda shrugged and made as if she were going to enter the cottage—undoubtedly to wake up the wife—he grudgingly saddled up his fat old palfrey and produced a threadbare woolen mantle lined with squirrel.

"Where will you go?" Felda asked as Martine mounted up. "The first place they'll look for you is St. Dunstan's."

"I know. I need to find someplace I can stay for a day or two, while I consider my options. There's an abandoned cottage I know of that's well hidden. Perhaps I'll go there."

"Can I do anything to help?"

"You've done quite enough. I don't want you getting into trouble on my account. When they question you, say that you brought the claret as Boyce asked, but you didn't know it was drugged. Say you came back upstairs before he drank it."

Felda sighed and took Martine's hand. "Be careful, milady."

"I will."

The reflected moonlight made it easy to find the tree growing from the boulder in the middle of the road. Then it was only a matter of following the meandering creek north, and then continuing in that direction when the creek headed east, until Martine at last came to the overgrown clearing and the snow-covered cottage within.

It was well past midnight, and it had been a long and fatiguing day. Martine kicked the pile of straw pallets in the corner, and two mice darted out. She kicked it again, but nothing else emerged. Wolf pelts were heaped on the pallets. She tossed aside the top one, which had been gathering dust for years, then curled up on the rest with her mantle wrapped around her, fur side down.

Even in her exhaustion, she found it difficult to get to sleep. Thorne's treachery felt more bitter than the frigid night air, and she found she could ease neither her body nor her mind. When she finally drifted off into a light, restless sleep, it was to a vision of her mother's apple-green wedding gown frozen in a lake turned to ice.

When she awoke later during the night, she realized that she was not alone. She sensed someone standing over her, felt his hands upon her. With a cry, she lashed out, but when she tried to swing her fists at the dark form above, her efforts were hampered by the mantle in which she was tangled.

"Easy." She knew that voice. It was Thorne. She relaxed . . . and then tensed. *Thorne!* He'd found her!

She sat up. "I won't let you take me back."

He paused in the act of covering her with something lined with fur—his own mantle, for he wore none—and sat on the edge of her makeshift bed. In the silvery light, his eyes looked enormous. "Take you back! My God, you're serious."

"You put in with Bernard! You betrayed me!" He reached for her, and she slapped his hand away. "Get away from me." She tried to rise, but he grabbed her by the shoulders and pushed her down into the wolf pelts. When she raised her fists to him, he captured one in each hand and pinned them next to her head.

"Listen to me," he growled.

"Nay!"

"You don't want to hear the truth, because then you'd have less reason to hate me."

She squeezed her eyes shut, but she couldn't close her ears.

He said, "The only way I could help you was by pretending to go along with Bernard so he wouldn't kill me straight off and I could figure out some way to get you out of there."

"Pretending? More lies."

"Martine, look at me." His hands tightened around hers, and he shook them. "*Look* at me, damn it!" She opened her eyes and looked into his as he hovered over her, pressing her down. "I can't wield sword or hold a bow. I can't even walk without that damn crutch. There was no way I could defend you physically. Bernard knew that. He was counting on it."

"You ... you told him it galled you to have to protect me."

"And you believed that?"

"You bargained with him over which piece of land he would give you!"

"He would have been suspicious if I'd thrown in with him too easily. It seems my strategy worked better than I realized. You believed it, too." She saw a flicker of something that might have been hurt in his eyes. "Did you really have so little faith in me?"

She looked away. "You locked me downstairs in that awful ... You wouldn't even let me spend the night in my chamber."

He released her hands to cup her face and turn it so she had to look him in the eye. "The tunnel leads from the cellar, Martine. If you'd been held on the third level, you never would have gotten out of that keep."

She considered that for a moment. "You locked me in that cell because you knew 'twould be easier for me to escape from down there?"

"Well, actually, I thought it would be easier for me to help you escape. I never expected you to be gone when I got down there." He chuckled. "I must admit, I was impressed. Boyce out cold on the floor with an empty goblet next to him, and the doors to the cell and the tunnel gaping open ... It didn't take me long to figure out what you'd done, or that you'd needed help to do it. Felda was the obvious candidate, so I woke her up and made her tell me where you went."

"But I didn't even tell her!"

"She said it was an abandoned cottage. This was the only likely choice." He stroked her cheek, and she breathed in his subtle, comforting scent. His fingers strayed to her lips, which he softly caressed. "Martine . . ."

Again she turned her head, deliberately breaking the contact. Presently he released her and stood, saying, "I'll get some wood and make a fire. Then perhaps we can both get a few good hours of sleep before dawn."

Taking up his crutch, he grabbed a broken-handled ax off the floor and went outside. She lay on her side facing the wall, listening to the repetitive *thwack* of wood being chopped and wondering how he managed it with his injuries. When he returned, he built a fire in the clay-lined cooking pit, which took him a while to light, and then he came and straightened the two mantles that covered her. Just as she thought to ask where he was going to sleep, she felt him behind her, fitting his big body to hers and tucking the mantles around both of them.

"What are you doing?" she asked.

"We can keep each other warm," he said, wrapping her in his arms and urging her against him.

"Thorne, I don't think—"

"Good night, my lady," he murmured.

He did feel warm, wonderfully warm. She felt enclosed and protected in his embrace—his innocent embrace, after all, for he made no move to render it otherwise. His breath on the back of her neck became steadily more regular, his body heavier, until presently she knew that he was fast asleep. Closing her eyes, she soon joined him.

When next she woke, it was still dark, and she felt chilled again. The fire had gone out, and Thorne was relighting it. When he returned to the stack of fur-covered pallets and settled in behind her, chafing her arm to warm her, she realized that the front of his tunic had become heated from the flames. She felt the delicious warmth even through her kirtle and tunic, and sighed in luxurious contentment, automatically snuggling back against him. She did it unthinkingly, unaware, even as his hand stilled on her arm and his breath caught in his throat, of the effect her actions might have on him. It wasn't until she felt the movement against her bottom—felt his manhood rise and press against her—that she realized what she had unconsciously wrought.

She lay perfectly still, thinking, *I should pull away from him,* but unable to will herself to do so. The rise and fall of his chest against her back accelerated in time to her thudding heart. For a few moments they lay together like two carved statues, and then slowly, very slowly, he drew his hand up her arm.

This time his touch was gentle, even tentative, as if he were waiting for her to object. She should object, she knew, but a longing deeper than her reservations had stricken her with a strange paralysis, and she found herself powerless to move. He stroked her through her wool sleeve, his hand traveling up to her shoulder and then down to her own hand. His fingertips skimmed gingerly over hers; he massaged her palm with his thumb, and the effect was so unexpectedly erotic that she gasped.

He caressed her rounded hip and the concave slope of her waist, then splayed his hand over her belly and let it rest there while he kissed, with aching softness, the back of her neck. Everything he did felt tentative, experimental, as if he were testing her acceptance of him. He trailed his hand upward, stopping just beneath her breasts. They tingled with anticipation. She felt her nipples harden; with every breath they seemed to scrape against the linen of her kirtle. Gradually his hand moved upward, molding itself lightly to flesh that seemed to swell beneath his touch, as if begging for a firmer caress. When his palm grazed the erect nipple, desire pulsed deep in her womb, and she felt his organ throb against her.

Again and again, with mesmerizing slowness, he traced paths of liquid fire over her body, although he made no move to disrobe her. His lingering exploration drove her to maddening heights of arousal. With a touch both cautious and intimate, he coaxed sensations in her that surpassed anything she ever thought herself capable of feeling. Her heart filled her throat; she was feverish with longing.

At last she felt him gather her skirts and pull them up, exposing her stockinged legs and bare hip to the silken caress of the fur-lined mantle that blanketed them. She felt darkly excited to be rendered naked only from waist to thigh. She felt the soft tickle of the fur on her sensitized skin.

His hand on her belly felt hot and rough. As he lowered it, she held her breath. When at last she felt his fingers softly brush the hair between her thighs, a whimper of desire rose from her throat. He explored her sex as patiently as he had the rest of her, investigating with a delicate and almost touching curiosity. She quivered and arched against him, thinking she would die if he didn't put an end to this exquisite torment. When he did—when he found and stroked the little knot where the torment was gathered—a sudden, convulsive pleasure shook her in its grip. Her own cries filled her ears, and for a few blinding moments, her senses fled.

When they returned, she lay still and sated in his arms. He rose on his elbow to rain warm kisses on her ear and cheek and lips, and then she felt him reach between them to untie his chausses. Thinking he'd want her supine, she tried to turn, but he stopped her. "Nay, stay as you are," he whispered hoarsely, urging her back as she had been, on her side facing away from him. She realized it would pain him less to lie on his left side, where there would be no pressure on his injured right arm and leg.

He shifted, and then came a hot, hard pressure as he guided himself into her from behind. Closing his hands around her hips, he filled her little by little, pausing between thrusts, letting her stretch to fit him. When he was at last completely sheathed within her, he slipped his arms around her to cup her breasts. Slowly he withdrew, and then pushed in, again and again. Through his heaving chest pressed to her back, she felt the wild beating of his heart; hers felt as if it would burst at any moment. Little by little, he increased the tempo and force of his thrusts until it seemed he had no conscious control over them at all—as if his body had disassociated itself from his mind. He drove into her with unthinking fervor, gripping her shoulders from in front to hold her still, forcing her to take all of him with each fierce thrust.

He overwhelmed her, possessed her. She craved this possession—wanted him to take her like this, to lose himself in her, wanted it desperately. Could something that felt so right really be so foolish? Was she a fool?

Thorne perceived her anxiety even through his sensual delirium; she stiffened, and he knew something was wrong. He was close, so close . . . too close to stop. She was exhausted, that was all; she'd had a long, harrowing day, and now she was suffering for it. "It's all right," he murmured, reaching between her legs to renew the intimate caress that had so transported her before. "Easy."

Slowing his thrusts to make himself last, for he had to be sure to pull out, he touched her with all the care and skill he could summon, determined to give her the pleasure that would ease her woes, erase her ugly memories. Presently her muscles relaxed and she moaned as if in surrender, clutching at the wolf pelts. *Hold off,* he commanded himself. *Hold off till she's done.* She writhed against him, and he strove for control. She was so tight, so hot, and as she teetered on the brink, so did he. . . .

He felt a shudder ripple through her, and then, deep within her, powerful spasms that squeezed him with stunning bursts of pleasure, wresting the seed from his body. With a strangled growl, he drove in hard, shaking with the force of his release. It was so right, so perfect, that for a few blissful moments, he allowed himself to forget that he should have pulled out, allowed himself to savor this primal ecstasy.

With a satisfied groan, he sank into the wolf pelts, drawing Martine's body tight to his. They were still connected; he wanted that to last forever. Breathlessly he kissed her neck. She was breathless, too.

"Martine, I . . . I didn't mean to finish inside you. I'm sorry." He reached up to stroke her cheek and found it wet. "Martine?" Levering himself up on an elbow, he pushed her hair aside, but she burrowed her face into the pelts. He felt her sobs. "Martine, it's all right. Don't cry."

Enclosing her in his arms, he held her tight and whispered against her neck. "It's over. Sleep now. Everything's all right."

She must have had blessed little energy left for her tears, because it wasn't long before she quieted.

"Martine," he whispered, but there was no response save her peaceful breathing. She had fallen asleep with him inside her. Carefully, so as not to wake her, he drew himself out, readjusted their clothes, gathered her in his arms, and closed his eyes.

It was midmorning when Martine awoke and found herself alone in bed. Sunlight flooded the little cottage, a lively fire burned in the pit, and from outside she heard Thorne at the chopping block. Arising, she tidied herself as best she could, then stole to the window to watch the Saxon.

He chopped with his back to her, wearing an unbleached linen shirt and coarse leggings, having removed his tunic; evidently his exertions kept him warm. He leaned on the crutch with his weak right arm and wielded the ax with his left, splitting chunk after chunk of wood and tossing the pieces onto a large pile next to him. He worked quickly, and with great power and accuracy, despite his injuries and the ax's broken handle. She gazed in rapt fascination at the bulge and flex of his muscles beneath his shirt, then shook her head and turned away, disgusted with herself.

Here she stood, just like her mother, staring out the window of a crude mud hut at the man who owned her soul. She was just as foolish as Adela, just as weak. Thorne wielded extraordinary power over her, power she conceded to him every time she yielded to his kisses, trembled at his touch. When would she learn? When would she finally find the strength to close her heart to him?

Embedding the ax in the chopping block, he grabbed a couple of pieces off the pile, came back inside, and added them to the fire.

"Do you intend us to stay here long?" Martine asked.

"Nay." He reached for his tunic and lowered it over his head. "We should leave this morning."

She glanced out the window. "There's enough firewood in that pile to last through spring."

He ran his fingers through his hair, which was damp with perspiration. "I got carried away. Chopping wood is so restful."

"Restful!"

"To the mind," he amended. "It helps me think. I was trying to figure something out."

"What?"

He looked away and took a deep breath, then met her eyes. "How to ask you to marry me."

Martine drew in an astonished breath and stared at him, wondering if she'd heard him right. He wanted to marry her! Thorne Falconer wanted to marry her!

He said, "I know I'm not landed, and I've not got the right. But I'm asking you anyway."

Martine felt the same peculiar buzz of anticipation that she had felt when she first set eyes on Thorne and mistook him for her betrothed. *It is this man,* she remembered thinking, *this regal man with eyes of sky, who will speak vows with me, who will take me to his bed and sire my babes. . . .*

But, of course, Thorne hadn't been that man at all. He was unlanded, and even if he weren't, he wouldn't have wanted to marry her. *He intends to marry a woman with property of her own,* Rainulf had explained. What was it Felda had said? *Funny thing is, he don't care much for highborn ladies, though of course, he'll be marrying one someday. He's far too land-hungry to settle for a girl without property.*

He was still unlanded, as he had just pointed out. Yet he had just proposed to her. What had changed to make him want to marry her?

She had become widowed, of course.

She had also become a woman of property. Edmond's death meant that she now controlled outright the lands that had comprised her bride-price.

"Why?" she asked him, dreading the answer but needing to know. "Why have you asked me to marry you?"

He hesitated. "Why does any man ask a woman to marry him?"

Evasion. What had she expected? "Some from love."

He hesitated, his gaze resting for some reason on Bathilda's little craddle in the corner. He hesitated too long.

Suddenly chilled, she continued, "But I don't pretend to think that's your reason. You're incapable of love." Her hands curled into fists at her side. "And, of course, you've never made any secret of the fact that you intend to marry for property. If we were to marry, my lands would, in effect, become yours."

His eyes flashed. "The *only* reason I want to marry you is to fulfill my promise to your brother to take care of you." He gestured helplessly with his big hands. "Christ, Martine, don't you realize how much danger you're in? Lord Godfrey ordered you—*ordered* you—to marry Bernard." He seized her by the shoulders. "Bernard is entirely as savage as his brother, but far more intelligent, and therefore far more dangerous. Do you *want* to be trapped in wedlock with that monster?"

"Of course not."

His grip tightened and his eyes drilled into hers. "Well, that is *exactly* what's going to happen if you're still unmarried when he finds you."

"Perhaps he won't find me," she said. "I'll go somewhere far away, where—"

"Martine, for God's sake!" He released her abruptly and wheeled around, raking his hands through his hair. "It doesn't matter how far away you go. Bernard is very cunning, very resourceful, and very determined. He will find you. He will find you, and he will force you to marry him." Facing her again, he added softly, "Unless you're already married. Think about it, Martine. The only way you can protect yourself from Bernard is to marry someone else. I'm offering myself. Not because I want your land. Because I want to keep you from harm."

"But the land doesn't hurt, does it?"

He shrugged his big shoulders in a gesture of weary frustration. "Would you have me say I'm displeased that we won't be poor and homeless? I won't lie to you, Martine. But if land was all I cared about, I would have taken Bernard up on his offer to join him in exchange for a holding."

"You had a more cunning plan—to get me away from Harford, manipulate me—"

"*Manipulate* you!"

"You took advantage of me last night when I was weak and tired and vulnerable. Now I realize why you did it, why you seduced me. You wanted me to think you cared for me, so that I'd agree to marry you. That way you'll have control over many estates, not just the one Bernard would have deeded you."

He took a step toward her. "You think me capable of such cold-blooded—"

"Absolutely."

He slumped down onto a bench, propped his elbows on his knees, and sank his head in his hands. Watching him, Martine felt a discomfiting stab of self-doubt. He'd argued with such disarming sincerity, maintained so convincingly that this marriage was for her benefit, that he didn't care about the land . . .

But that was absurd, of course. Land was all he cared about, all he desired. His hunger for property surpassed all other hungers. If she doubted his avaricious motives, it was only because he wanted her to doubt them and had manipulated her. *Some men,* Matthew had warned, *are remarkably skillful at bending women to their will.*

And Thorne Falconer is one of those men.

Nay. He wouldn't make a fool of her this time. She wouldn't let him exploit her, not again. It was her land he craved, no matter what smooth lies he fashioned. Her land, not her. He didn't even pretend to love her.

He dropped his hands from his face and looked at her; she saw the defeat in his eyes. "I take it you don't want to marry me."

She swiftly envisioned the alternative—fleeing to God knew where, hiding from Bernard. Thorne was right, of course; Bernard would find her. He would find her and marry her and make her suffer all the more for having tried to escape him.

It wasn't that she didn't want to marry Thorne; even knowing his selfish motives, she couldn't deny that the prospect intrigued her, even excited her. And, of course, she would be protected from Bernard. But she couldn't let Thorne think that she was the same pathetically trusting girl who'd let him use her so cavalierly in the past.

"I didn't say I wouldn't marry you," she said. Surprise, then relief, crossed his features. "I haven't particularly got anything against a cold-blooded marriage, as long as we're both honest about it . . . as long as we recognize that it's naught but a union of mutual convenience. You get your precious lands, and I get protection from Bernard. All I ask is that there are no lies between us . . . that you don't pretend to . . . to feelings that don't exist. That would make fools of us both."

His eyes were sad. "Martine—"

"Those are the only conditions under which I'll marry you."

He released a long, troubled sigh. "Very well, then. But we'd better do it soon, before Bernard finds us. We can go to St. Dunstan's. I think Brother Matthew is authorized to perform the sacraments." He hesitated, and it seemed as if he wanted to say something more, but then he just shook his head and turned toward the door. "I'll get the horses ready."

Martine watched through the window as Thorne saddled up their mounts. She would marry him, but she would close her heart to him. She would keep her distance, at least emotionally. She needn't be weak and foolish like Adela. Adela had lived for Jourdain.

From now on, Martine would live for Martine.

Chapter 21

"Do you have a ring?" Brother Matthew asked the couple kneeling before him in the dim, candlelit church, empty save for the two monks serving as witnesses.

This is really happening, Thorne thought with a sense of incredulous wonder. *I'm marrying Martine!* He pulled off his ruby ring and took Martine's left hand in his. It was ice-cold and trembled slightly. He gave it a gentle squeeze and tried to meet her eyes, but she wouldn't look at him.

Matthew cleared his throat. "In the name of the Father ..." The Saxon lowered the ring halfway down Martine's index finger. "And the Son ..." He did the same on her middle finger. "And the Holy Ghost ..." He slid it all the way down her ring finger, but of course it was far too big. She transferred it to her thumb, where it seemed to fit. "I now pronounce you man and wife."

"This chamber has the largest bed," Brother Matthew explained, pushing aside the leather curtain in the doorway of the prior lodge's best guest cell. Thorne noted that this bed was only very slightly wider than the others, but dismissed from his mind the notion of offering to sleep on the floor. When Martine agreed to marry him, she had implicitly agreed to sleep in the same bed.

"Thank you for letting us stay here," said Martine, cradling Loki in her arms. "We'll try to make other arrangements as soon as possible."

"You needn't be in any rush," Matthew graciously replied. "I'll enjoy your company."

Rainulf still protected her, even from afar, Thorne reflected. For it was surely Matthew's friendship with Martine's brother that made him so eager to extend his hospitality to her.

That evening, while Matthew ate with the brothers and attended to monastery business, Thorne and Martine endured their own carefully polite supper in the prior's lodge and took turns bathing in their chamber. Finally the servants left and they found themselves alone for the first time since they were wed that afternoon.

Thorne finally broke the silence. "Martine, there are things we should talk about."

"I know," she said. "We have to decide where we're going to live."

"Aye. And there are other things—"

She stood. "Not tonight. I'm too tired to think, much less decide anything. I'm going to bed now. I'll see you in the morning."

With that, she turned and disappeared into their chamber. Thorne sat for a while, nursing a brandy and contemplating the glowing coals in the brazier.

You're incapable of love, she had said. Was he? He'd long ago chosen not to expose himself to the torment that weaker men called love. In the process of refusing to give in to it, had he actually become incapable of it? Had he, in fact, become as cold and unscrupulous and grasping as Martine accused him of being?

For years he'd believed that marrying for love was a mistake. The wise man married for land. Love always died, whether quickly and cruelly, or slowly under the weight of its own lies. Land, on the other hand, lasted forever. Now he had what he'd always wanted—a marriage of property. He should be pleased. In a way, he was. Martine was his wife!

But she was a wife who mistrusted him and thought he'd used his lovemaking to manipulate her. Yet she had consented to marry him. Presumably that meant she consented to let him bed her. The prospect of having her whenever he wanted should have thrilled him. But could he make love to her now, knowing how powerless and exploited it made her feel? He recalled her tears last night in the cottage. Sex should be a simple act of joy, but to her, it would be an act of submission, a relinquishing of her will, and it would only drive her further from him.

He couldn't do it, not knowing that it would only deepen the rift between them. He needed to heal that rift, and the only way to do that was to make her trust him, make her accept the fact that he wasn't Jourdain. Jourdain had acted unconscionably—had used Adela and then abandoned her the moment she became inconvenient. His cruelty had wounded Martine deeply, had scarred her soul. To lie with her now would only scratch those scars open, make her feel used and manipulated. He must resist the temptation, at least for a while, gradually reintroducing her to his touch in small ways as he worked on regaining her trust.

Brother Matthew returned, and if he thought it odd that Martine had retired before her husband on their wedding night, he didn't say so. Instead, he challenged Thorne to a game of chess, which the Saxon accepted. Centering the board on the table, Matthew said, "I had an interesting message from Olivier this evening. Queen Eleanor is planning to join him at Blackburn Castle sometime soon."

"Really?" said Thorne, taking his seat opposite the prior. "I thought she was in France with King Henry." The two men began setting up their pieces.

"She was, but she returned to England without him shortly after Advent. Since then, she's been holding court at various royal seats throughout the realm, attending to the king's business."

"Isn't that Chancellor Becket's job?"

"Aye," said Matthew, "but the chancellor's abroad with Henry. According to Olivier, the queen's taken quite an interest in the siege of Blackburn. She wrote him that she wants to see for herself the impenetrable castle that withstood every weapon except Thorne Falconer. I didn't realize you knew her."

"Rainulf introduced us in Paris after the Crusade. She took a liking to me for some reason. We used to talk a great deal."

"They say she's a perfect combination of beauty and wit. Did she strike you so?"

"She's very beautiful," Thorne said. "And exceptionally intelligent. At the time I knew her, she was rather melancholy, though. She was with child but had already petitioned Louis for a dissolution of the marriage. She told me that she had thought to marry a king, but had married a monk instead. I liked her. I hope she's happier now than she was then."

"You'll have a chance to judge that for yourself," said Matthew, making his first move. "She's asked Olivier to arrange a supper in your honor."

Thorne stared at the grinning prior. "In my honor?"

"You're a hero. The savior of Blackburn."

"Good God," Thorne muttered.

Matthew chuckled and pointed to the board. "Your move."

Thorne couldn't concentrate on the game, and Matthew won easily. When the Saxon asked for a rematch, the prior begged off, wanting to get in some sleep before matins.

So as not to wake Martine, Thorne undressed down to his drawers in the hall before slipping quietly into their chamber. For a time he stood over the bed looking down on his sleeping wife with a sense of amazement. *We're wed!* he thought. *Martine and I are wed!*

She lay on her side, her arms and shoulders exposed by the sleeveless shift she wore, her palms together as if in prayer. Her breasts were soft and round beneath the thin linen. He recalled how they felt cupped in the palm of his hand, how they tasted when he took her firm pink nipples in his mouth. His pulse quickened and his loins tightened.

Aye, we're wed—in name only. For now. He slid quietly beneath the covers, summoning all the patience, all the self-control at his disposal.

It was chilly between the linen sheets, but Martine's body radiated warmth. She had her back to him, and he very softly touched the bare skin above the neckline of her shift, feeling her heat flow up his arm and spread within him. When it reached his throat, something caught inside, and he swallowed hard, astounded to feel himself suddenly on the verge of tears. Closing his eyes, he commanded himself not to cry. The last time he did so was when he found out about the fire that took Louise and his parents, and then he had been out of his mind with grief. The time before that was too long ago to remember, so it must have been when he was but a baby. Drawing in a deep, calming breath, he mentally chided himself for his weakness. This was what came of caring. His reactions were reduced to those of an infant.

Rolling away from Martine, he closed his eyes, but it took him a very long time to get to sleep.

Bernard of Harford quivered with frustration and rage as he stood at the window of his chamber, looking down upon his father emerging from the hawk house with Azura on his fist. *He could live for decades more. Decades. I'll be an old man before he's dead. At this rate, I might die before he does. Harford will never be mine.*

Who would ever have thought that damned woodsman, that upstart lowborn Saxon, would have the gall to marry Martine of Rouen—a cousin of the queen, for God's sake? Martine of Rouen, who'd been promised to him, who should have been his—warming his bed, bearing his sons. The falconer's audacity knew no bounds. He'd stolen her from him, pure and simple, and now he was laughing at him. They were both laughing at him, thinking they'd gotten the better of him.

Damn him! And damn the impudent, cold-eyed bitch he'd taken to wife! Damn them both to everlasting hell! She was to have been his—*his*—she and her lands, valuable lands that had once been part of Harford, that should have someday gone to Bernard. . . .

That still might, if he was clever. He had an idea, an exquisite idea, an idea of great beauty and promise, a way to avenge his humiliation at the hands of Martine and Thorne Falconer and recover his rightful property. But it was an idea that would have to wait until Queen Eleanor next left the country; not only was Eleanor Martine's cousin, but it was rumored that she knew and actually liked the woodsman. Should she choose to shield the couple with her royal protection, Bernard's plan would come to nothing. So he would wait until Henry summoned her to his side, as he frequently did. Once she took the royal smack across the Channel, he could make his move.

"Sir?" came a timid voice from beyond his chamber curtain. It was that hopeless little maid of Estrude's, Clare. Instead of returning to her own family after the death of her mistress, she'd stayed on at Harford Castle, mooning over him with her watery little eyes and generally getting in the way.

He sighed. "What is it?"

She parted the curtain and came to him, a cup in her outstretched hand. "I brought you a brandy."

With a lightning-quick backhand, he slapped the cup into the rushes, spattering its contents all over her satin tunic. "Did I ask for brandy? Did I tell you to come in?"

"N-nay," she mumbled, wringing her hands. "I'm sorry." She looked like a little white rabbit with a twitching pink nose. "I should have known not to disturb you, after everything you've been through. You must be sick with grief. First your brother, and then ... then my lady Estrude." She crossed herself with a shivering hand.

"Then why did you?" he ground out.

"I just wanted ... I don't know. To comfort you. To let you know you're not alone."

Christ. "Did it ever occur to you that I might *want* to be alone? That I might prefer it that way?"

"No, sir. I'm sorry." Her eyes were filling up with tears, her chin trembling. "I should have known better. I'm a fool. It's just ... oh, God!" She dropped to her knees and grabbed his hands. Appalled, he yanked them out of her grasp. "I know I shouldn't be here. I know it's too soon after ... after my lady's passing, but ... I can't help it. I had to come. I had to let you know how I feel about you."

"Dear God, get up. This is disgusting."

Sobbing, she seized the front of his tunic and pressed her face into it. "Please don't order me away. Please! I love you! I can't help it, I do! It nearly killed me when I found out you wanted to marry Lady Martine. She doesn't love you as I do. You wouldn't have been happy wit her. Marry me, *please*!"

Bernard laughed incredulously. Marry this homely, quivering little rodent? But then a thought occurred to him, and he asked, "Are you heir to any lands?"

She looked up at him, her face wet and red. "N-nay. M-my older sister—"

"Is she married?"

She hesitated, her eyes filled with hurt. "Nay, but ... but she's fat."

Bernard considered that and shrugged. "I'm tired of skinny women."

"And she has fits," Clare added hopefully.

"Fits," he hissed. He thought about it. Fat *and* fits. No, he wasn't that desperate. And who was to say her father would approve the union anyway, given Bernard's unfortunate reputation?

"You don't understand!" Clare wailed, shaking his tunic with her fists. "You mean everything to me! Everything! You're the sun and the moon and the stars to me. My heart weeps for love of you. I'd be whatever you wanted me to be. I'd be your slave if you'd only let me. I'd be good, I'd be obedient. I'd do anything for you!"

"Anything?" he asked, reflecting on the fascinating potential of such devotion as she crushed her tear-stained face against him.

"*Anything!*" She started to rise, but he clamped his hand over her head and pushed her back down to her knees.

"Nay," he said, reaching beneath his tunic to untie his chausses. "Don't get up."

On a frosty morning in mid-March, dozens of the queen's men and their horses descended upon St. Dunstan's to be billeted in monastery buildings and fed on monastery provisions. Many more traveled with Eleanor to Blackburn Castle itself, where Olivier would host them for perhaps a fortnight.

The servants and lay brothers regaled Thorne and Martine with breathless descriptions of the queen's arrival at the castle. First a procession of armed guards on horseback drew up, followed by a string of curtained litters bearing the queen, her ladies, the royal children, and their nurses. Mounted knights rode behind, accompanied by their falcons, hounds, squires, and packhorses, then a handful of plainly dressed clerks, and following them on foot, a rather curious contingent of animated folk in particolored costumes—most likely entertainers of some sort. Finally came a rumbling parade of hide-covered carts filled with beer, wine, and food, as well as open wagons loaded with kitchen utensils, linens, plate, and rugs. One seemed to contain a small altar, another an enormous, disassembled bed—undoubtedly Eleanor's own.

Later that day, one of the queen's clerks delivered a written message to Thorne, formally summoning him, his lady wife, and Prior Matthew to Blackburn Castle the following evening for the anticipated supper in his honor.

"But I have nothing suitable to wear," Martine fretted.

"Wear the blue tunic with the little pleats," said Thorne. "The one you wore your second day at Harford." He smiled. "The one that's the same color as your eyes."

The next afternoon, as she pulled the indigo gown down over her head and adjusted its long, fluttering sleeves, she reflected on the strangeness of her relationship with her husband. Not once since their marriage a week before had he attempted to bed her. This was uncomfortably reminiscent of Edmond's unwillingness to consummate their marriage, but she knew the reasons were different. Edmond's reaction to her—in the beginning, that is—had been fear. In Thorne's case, it was more likely indifference.

He treated her kindly enough. And from time to time he would look at her or touch her in a way that seemed to indicate he wanted her—but then he's turn away, seeming troubled and withdrawn. She supposed his disinclination to bed her had to do with her admonition that they were to be honest with each other and not pretend to feelings that didn't exist between them. He'd taken her at her word. Caring little for her, he would have no particular interest in bedding her, Norman gentlewomen not being particularly to his taste. No doubt he would soon enough resume his liaisons with his whores and kitchen wenches.

Her stomach burned with jealousy, and she mentally scolded herself. She ought not to care. This was a marriage of mutual convenience. He'd gotten all he wanted from her—her land—and now he would leave her alone. It was for the best. She knew that, yet had felt unaccountably sad when her courses came and she realized she didn't carry Thorne's babe in her belly, as she had half hoped ever since that night in the cottage. It wasn't that she particularly wanted a child. It was that, inexplicably, she wanted *Thorne's* child. She imagined telling him, pictured his rapturous response, his pride, the feelings that might grow in his heart for her if she were to give him an heir.

She sighed and proceeded with the tedious business of plaiting her hair with golden ribbons. Little good it did to wish that things were different. Fate held her tightly in its silken bonds. It was pointless to struggle against it.

Martine's mouth went dry as she rode across Blackburn Castle's long drawbridge and through its massive curtain walls, flanked by Thorne and Brother Matthew. Above them rose the remarkable keep which she had, until now, only viewed from a distance. Having been whitewashed in honor of the queen's visit, it glowed brilliantly against the dusky sky. It was really quite an extraordinary structure, perfectly round save for a rectangular forebuilding, two large turrets, and a tower, from which flew the royal flag. The tower had no roof and, here and there, a gap in the stonework reminded her that this extraordinary castle had been left unfinished when Neville had Baron Anseau and his pregnant wife killed.

They were greeted in the courtyard by a pinch-faced clerk who led them up a stairway in the forebuilding, which opened onto the great hall. Martine stifled a gasp as she entered the enormous, brightly lit room, festooned with colorful silks and Saracen carpets, and swarming with courtiers, jugglers, acrobats, harpists, drummers, servants, and several small, darting children. What the great hall at Harford lacked in majesty, its counterpart at Blackburn more than made up for. It was entirely round, with a carved balcony that spanned its circumference halfway between the high, vaulted ceiling and the rush-strewn floor. Directly ahead of her, on the far side of the room, a fire blazed in a massive fireplace built right into the thick stone wall, the only one of its kind Martine had ever seen. To one side of the hearth stood a huge, canopied chair, and sitting in that chair, laughing at the antics of the baby on her lap, was the Queen of England.

She looked different than Martine had expected, much younger than her eight and thirty years, and much prettier, with a round, soft face and glittering eyes. Her ivory damask tunic was sumptuous and fur-trimmed, and on her head she wore the expected barbette and veil. She locked eyes with Martine and smiled, then beckoned to Thorne, who, guiding his wife with a hand on her back, led her and Brother Matthew to the queen.

Numb with panic throughout the introductions, Martine could barely manage a curtsy, thinking, *I hope I'm doing this right.* Thorne sank to one knee with surprising grace, considering his recent injuries, and kissed Eleanor's offered hand. It occurred to Martine that her husband, despite his humble birth, was much more in his element here than she, as he had some experience of court life. He appeared properly respectful of the great lady, but not overwhelmed, and Martine could tell from Eleanor's warm greeting that she remembered him fondly.

He does remind one a bit of Charlemagne's elephant, Martine thought, comparing the Saxon knight to the dozens of other men in the room. In stature alone he was unique, a colossus among all those slender, soft-spoken young men with their highly polished manners. And unlike them, he was dressed simply, in a blue tunic with no ornamentation, and black chausses.

Eleanor handed her baby to a waiting nurse, then gave orders for the other children to be gathered and put to bed, the tables to be assembled, and dinner to be served. Rising, she reached a hand out to softly touch Martine's cheek. "So you're Jourdain's little girl." This open reference to her father startled Martine, considering her illegitimacy. But the queen, although she certainly knew the circumstances of her cousin's birth, apparently did not choose to pass judgment. "I'm delighted to meet you at last, my dear."

"And I you, my lady queen," Martine managed. Thorne patted her back, and she smiled at him, grateful for his support in spite of everything.

The food served that evening was surprisingly ordinary, but it was nevertheless a unique experience. Martine, Thorne, and Matthew sat before the hearth at the high table, along with Eleanor, Olivier, the earl's wife, and several of the more favored knights. The other tables were arranged not in rows, but around the edge of the hall, leaving a large central arena in which musicians, jongleurs, dancers, and mimes joined the jugglers and acrobats in providing suppertime entertainment.

When dessert was served, Eleanor dismissed the entertainers and nodded to Olivier, who rose and made a fulsome speech extolling Thorne's skill and bravery during the siege of Blackburn. Then the queen herself stood and led a toast in the Saxon's honor. She praised not only his character and military talents, but his reputation as a falconer and scholar. "Birds of prey and learning are both particular interests of the king's," she said. "Many times he has told me that the rest of a born nobleman is whether he can train his own mind as well as he can train that of his hawk."

Thinking on it later, Martine came to realize that the queen's purpose in repeating this statement of her husband's was not merely to compliment Thorne. In setting him up as the king's ideal of the true nobleman, she would forestall any objections, based on his humble origins, to the stunning announcement that followed.

Indicating for the Saxon to rise, she said, "I had another purpose in bringing you here than simply to honor you with this supper. I daresay you deserve more reward than a bit of food and song for having single-handedly recovered Blackburn. Your courage saved countless lives, and for that King Henry and Lord Olivier are eternally grateful. Blackburn is an immensely valuable barony, but it is a barony without an heir. Its disposition being a matter of great concern to the realm, Lord Olivier wisely sought the counsel of the king, who in turn put the matter into my hands. Having given it the gravest of consideration, it is my pleasure to award this fief, along with the title of baron, to the man who liberated Blackburn Castle ... Thorne Falconer."

A deafening roar filled the hall. Thorne looked toward Martine, who could merely gaze back in dumbfounded amazement. When the cheers died down, he simply said, "I'm most grateful, my liege."

She said, "My clerks have already drawn up the deed of conveyance. If you will return here on the morrow at midday"—she nodded toward Martine—"with my dear cousin, your lady wife, we will attend to the necessary ceremonial matters, and perhaps indulge in a celebratory feast."

Thorne bowed his head briefly. "Of course. Thank you, my lady." Meeting Martine's eyes, he smiled. She returned the smile, wondering at the strange and mysterious workings of fate.

"Lord, I become your man," Thorne said, kneeling in the tree-shaded courtyard of Blackburn Castle with his clasped hands between those of the earl. "I will be faithful to you and will maintain toward you my homage entirely against every man, saving the faith of my lord Henry, King of England, and his heirs."

The Saxon rose and, delivering the kiss of homage to Olivier, was transformed from Sir Thorne, a knight of the realm, to Lord Falconer, Baron of Blackburn.

Chapter 22

Queen Eleanor and her entourage vacated Blackburn Castle a week later, closely followed by Olivier and his men. When, on the morning after Easter, Martine and Thorne arrived to claim their new home, they found a dozen house servants lined up in the courtyard to greet them. They were male and female, young and old. The only thing they all had in common, Martine thought, was that they seemed nervous, though none of them could have been more nervous than she. Here she was, an eighteen-year-old girl with very little experience of castle life, suddenly the mistress of one of the greatest baronies in England. She felt like a little girl all dressed up in her mother's kirtle, playing princess.

One of the servants, a rather dignified-looking man of advanced years, stepped forward. "My lord, my lady," he said in English-accented French, "welcome to Castle Blackburn. My name is John Burgess. I was my lord Anseau's steward. If it please your lordship, I will be yours."

Thorne nodded, and responded to the steward in English. Martine saw a flicker of wonder in the old man's eyes, and most of the others exchanged looks. Surely someone had told them their new master was a Saxon, yet his use of their native tongue seemed to shock them. Doubtless they'd never thought to hear a man of his rank speak it.

The amiable exchange between the two men seemed to relax the others. When Thorne smiled and clapped Burgess on the back, they all broke into relieved grins and beckoned for their lord and lady to follow them into the keep and up the wide staircase in the forebuilding. Thorne took her arm in his and, apparently sensing her tension, patted it comfortingly.

He'd been increasingly affectionate of late, not in any overt way—he hadn't tried to make love to her—but in small, almost tender ways, and only when they were alone. In truth, she craved these little gestures, savored them, even while it shamed her that he still had the power to disarm her this way.

She couldn't help but wonder why, after his initial disinterest following their wedding, he seemed so intent on renewing their intimacy, albeit gradually. Perhaps it was merely that he was a man, with a man's appetites. Sometimes, late at night, as she lay in bed next to him, she sensed him watching her, felt his breath on her, felt his heat, his simmering need. Soon, she knew, he would tire of waiting. One of these nights, he would reach for her. By law, she couldn't refuse him her body. She had to acquiesce, but she didn't have to enjoy it. He liked to make her lose control, and three times he had succeeded. The memory of how she had writhed in his arms, had moaned and clutched at him in animal hunger, flooded her with shame. It would never happen again. Never. She would open her legs for him when he finally insisted, but she would feel no passion—nor would she feign it. He would know that she received him not because she wanted to, but because she had no choice.

Or perhaps his gentle affections promoted some hidden scheme that she had yet to fathom. Whatever cause they served, she would do well to remember that they didn't serve hers. She must close her heart to him. She must live for Martine, and only Martine.

When they entered the great hall, she felt like a mouse in a cathedral. Devoid of the people and furnishings that had filled it during Eleanor's stay, it seemed immense and hollow. Sunlight flooded the hall through the many large, arched windows, casting patches of gold onto the ornate Saracen carpets that still bedecked the walls.

"I thought those were the queen's carpets," said Martine as she released Loki. "Why are they still here?"

In French Burgess said, "Queen Eleanor left them here as a gift for the new Baron and Baroness of Blackburn, with her best wishes. Shall I leave them where they're hung, or would you like them moved?"

"Sweep the rushes up," said Thorne, "and lay the carpets on the floor."

Martine turned to him, openmouthed. "On the *floor*? Are you mad?"

Thorne smiled mischievously. "I've told you before— if I'm mad, so be it."

Her face grew warm at the memory of the two of them locked together on the mossy bank of River Blackburn. With a glance at Burgess, she said, "Really, Sir Th—"

"It's not 'Sir Thorne' anymore," he corrected. "So just call me Th—"

" 'My lord husband' is correct, is it not?"

He grimaced. "The carpets, *my lady wife,* will go on the floor. I grew quite fond of carpeted floors when I was in Spain and Portugal on my way to the Holy Land. We can get other hangings for the walls, if you're concerned about drafts."

Frowning, Burgess said, "Do the rushes go on top of the carpets?"

"There will be no rushes," said Thorne patiently. "Just the carpets."

The older man hesitated, as if weighing his new master's sanity, and then half bowed. "As you wish, my lord baron." He withdrew a sheaf of parchment. "I keep the barony accounts from Michaelmas to Michaelmas. I'm prepared to review them with you at your convenience."

"Thank you, Burgess, but for now I believe we'd prefer a tour of our new home."

"Of course, my lord. If you'll but follow me . . ."

Blackburn Castle, Martine soon discovered, was much larger and more complex than Harford, representing the latest in castle engineering. Running water was available on each level through a system of pipes that led from a cistern on the roof, and the architecture was wonderfully complex. Besides the great hall, the keep contained a dizzying network of large chambers connected by passages and stairwells. There was a two-story chapel in the forebuilding, with entrances both from the great hall and the huge master bedchamber off the balcony. It was actually more of an suite than a bedchamber, with three anterooms, one of which was tiled and contained a privy, a shallow trough with brass spigots and a drain, and a permanently affixed bathtub! Like almost every other chamber in the castle, it boasted its own fireplace and a heavy wooden door. There were many other bedchambers and storerooms, a lesser hall below the great hall, a guardroom, and various chambers for the servants' use. Martine was in awe of it all. The fact that she could actually get lost in a castle of which she was mistress both thrilled and unnerved her.

From the keep, Burgess led them on a survey of the grounds. The inner bailey had been walled off for gardens, which had never been planted. In the center of the outer bailey, surrounded by a cookhouse, granary, stable, kennels, and barracks, was a large and well-stocked fish pond. Crossing the outer drawbridge, Burgess pointed out St. Dunstan's, nestled in the valley below, as well as the vineyards, orchards, and grazing pastures that immediately surrounded the castle.

The manors and villages that comprised Lord Falconer's fief were numerous and vast, he explained, and yielded massive revenues. Since Lord Anseau's passing, he had continued without interruption to collect the taxes, fees, rents, and tolls that provided his lordship's baronial income, an income that normally amounted to thousands of pounds annually.

"Thousands?" Thorne asked.

Burgess withdrew a sheet of parchment, held it toward the young baron, and pointed. "This is the sum I've amassed since Lord Anseau's death, which I'm prepared to turn over to you immediately. And this is the sum I expect the barony to have earned by the end of September."

Martine watched as Thorne calmly inspected the numbers. "This money will come in handy. There's much work to be done on the castle and grounds." He handed the parchment back to his steward. "That's all for now, Burgess. Thank you."

Burgess recrossed the drawbridge, but when Martine made as if to follow, Thorne held her back. "Walk with me."

He took her hand and led her away from the castle and across a rolling pasture to a pear orchard planted in tidy rows. The orchard, like everything else at Blackburn, appeared to have been well tended despite the barony's recent upheaval.

"Are you very rich, then?" she asked as he guided her into the cool, green corridor between two rows of trees.

"Nay." He smiled and squeezed her hand. "*We're* very rich."

She couldn't help but return the smile. They strolled in silence down the shadowy lane, hand in hand, listening to the birds chatter in the trees, savoring the breeze that rattled the new spring leaves.

Gradually Martine began to relax, to actually feel comfortable walking with him like this. *'Tis as if we're lovers*, she thought. *Or truly man and wife, not two people bound in a travesty of a marriage.*

He was clever, she realized, to have maneuvered her into this situation—alone with him in a dark and private place, her hand in his. Their companionable silence began to strike her as insidious. Wanting to end it, she said, "Must you speak English to the servants? I can't understand a word of it."

He chuckled. "I can see I'm going to have to teach you the language of my fathers."

"Can't you just speak French instead? It's what everyone else speaks."

His features clouded momentarily. "It's what the nobility speaks. For now."

"For now?"

"The Normans persist in speaking it, but the people refuse to accept it. They're poor, they're landless, they're downtrodden, but they're wonderfully stubborn when it comes to their language. I think there's every possibility that the ruling class of England will one day have to give in and start speaking English."

Martine laughed. "You're m—" She bit off the rest, but it was too late.

Grinning, he seized her by the shoulders and backed her against a tree trunk, wagging a finger at her in mock reprimand. "You'll have to stop saying that—unless you want me to do this." He cupped her face, tilting her head back.

"Thorne—"

Her objections were abruptly silenced when he closed his mouth over hers. She stood stiff and unresponsive, her hands at her sides, as his lips shaped their warmth and softness to her own. It was the first she'd felt his

mouth on hers since the kiss of peace during the marriage sacraments. He kissed her with a firm but gentle
pressure, as if he knew she was determined to resist him
but had no choice in the matter. His tongue lightly
traced the shape of her lips, which she kept pressed
together.

He drew back fractionally. "Give in to it, Martine,"
he breathed unsteadily, his lips grazing hers. "Please—I
need this. Just this. I'll do nothing more." He implored
her with his translucent eyes as he moved his thumb to
the edge of her mouth and forced its roughened tip between her lips.

She gasped as her mouth parted, admitting a more
impassioned assault. Thorne intensified the kiss, his
hands wrapping around the back of her head to hold her
still, his lips and tongue caressing hers with a kind of
relentless ardor. Behind her she felt the hard, smooth
wood of the tree trunk. In front, pressing her into that
trunk, was the equally solid and unyielding form of her
husband.

The world around her receded into nothingness, and
then she felt only his mouth, hot and insistent. At what
point she began, with no conscious thought, to seek that
heat, to need it, to instinctively return the kiss, she knew
not. She only knew that, when it ended, she found her
arms wrapped tightly around him, holding him close. In
her chest she felt the frantic hammering of not one heart,
but two. . . . Over the roar in her ears, she heard not just
her panting breaths, but his as well.

He drew away slowly, and with a seemingly great reluctance, as if it took all of his strength to do so. She
withdrew her arms from around him, feeling a pang of
regret that the kiss was over, and that he'd managed to
uphold his promise to do nothing more. Of course, it
was the worst kind of idiocy to want more. She mustn't
hunger for his kisses, mustn't long for him to raise her
kirtle and lift her up against this tree and take her, right
here in this orchard beneath the overhanging pear
trees—yet she did.

"Can we go back now?" she asked quietly.

His gaze lowered to her mouth, his brow furrowing
slightly. He paused, then reached out and delicately

stroked first the top lip, and then the bottom; they felt swollen, and very tender to his callused touch.

Nodding, he murmured "As you wish," then took her hand in his once more and guided her slowly back through the darkness of the orchard toward the waiting sunshine.

"What think you, milady?" called the glazier from across the great hall, indicating the window that he had just finished working on. Martine stepped carefully through the mayhem that separated them, sidestepping the plasterers with their buckets and trowels, and the woodworkers with their stacks of wainscoting.

"I think my husband is mad," she murmured, reaching out to touch one of the tiny panes of bubbly, greenish glass. There were dozens of them set into lead, the whole shaped precisely to the dimensions of the tall, arched window. Thorne had ordered every window in the castle glazed; those in the chapel would be fitted with fragments of colored glass pieced together to form designs. It was a wonderment, a miracle. "Will this really keep out the cold in winter?"

"Aye, milady. But 'twill let in all the sun you want. And it opens"—he pulled a handle and demonstrated— "so that you can have fresh air on mild afternoons such as this."

During the month that they had been at Blackburn, winter had finally yielded to spring. From dawn till dusk, Martine planted gardens—herb gardens, kitchen gardens, even flower gardens—enlisting the aid of as many servants as could be spared from Thorne's never-ending tasks. There were so many things that needed doing, and although labor was plentiful, supervisors were scarce.

Peter, Guy, and Albin were in France, fighting for Henry. Two days ago Thorne sent them a message via Eleanor, who was due to set sail this day for Normandy to rejoin the king, informing them of recent developments and requesting their service when they returned. However, if they were in the field, it could be months before they even received the message.

And then there was Felda, whom Martine hadn't seen since escaping from that dreadful cell beneath Harford Castle. She wanted Felda with her, as did Thorne. Yes-

terday he sent two armed villeins, large men with sol-
diering experience, to Harford with instructions to fetch
her, as well as his precious Freya. They were to do it
quietly, avoiding Bernard if possible. If forced to confront him, they were to be diplomatic, using their weapons only as a last resort. They weren't back yet, but
according to Thorne, it was too soon to worry, so she
tried to put it out of her mind.

She leaned out the window to breathe in the blessed
warmth. On the far side of the inner bailey, beyond the
gardens, stonecutters measured and marked blocks of
granite for a hawk house; judging by the plans for it, it
would be as large as a manor house, and more elaborate.
Thorne said he wanted the birds to have enough room
to fly around inside it.

In the courtyard, Thorne stood with his back against
an oak tree and his arms crossed, observing Burgess as
he presided over a hallmoot. Twelve freemen listened in
silence as a large man made his case, railing furiously
in English.

"What's he saying?" Martine asked the glazier, a
Saxon. Since few people at Blackburn spoke French,
she'd had no choice but to put her mind to learning
English, and in fact, she could already understand quite
a bit if it was spoken clearly. But the man in the courtyard was sputtering and screaming, and she had no hope
of following along.

"He's a miller, milady," the glazier said. "He's de-
fending himself against charges of falsifying weights."
The miller finished his tirade, the jury voted, and Burgess rose and said something that made the miller bellow
in protest. "They found him guilty, milady, and now he's
to pay a fine to his lordship."

Thorne said something, and the jury and onlookers
cheered. Martine looked toward the glazier, who chuckled disbelievingly. "I do believe your husband *is* mad,
milady, no disrespect intended. He says the miller's got
to pay the fine to the people he cheated, and if he cheats
them again, he'll lose his mill."

It struck Martine that, whatever his faults, she had
married an extraordinary man. Just as she had that
thought, the object of her contemplation looked up and
smiled at her. Even at this distance, she could see the

sky in his eyes, the dimples carved into his cheeks. He had regained the weight shed during his convalescence at St. Dunstan's, and with it, the impression of strength and vigor that had always emanated from him. As lord of Blackburn, he was completely and perfectly in his element. He was a strong man, a man of honor and compassion ... but also ruthless ambition. If he had to choose between her and his beloved Blackburn, she had no doubt whatsoever how he would choose.

In truth, Martine loved Blackburn as much as he. For both of them, it was the first home they had known—the first real home of their own—since childhood. She felt more of a sense of belonging here than she had ever felt elsewhere, even at St. Teresa's and St. Dunstan's. Keeping her from complete contentment, of course, was her strained but studiously polite relationship with Thorne. If only she could cease this terrible longing she felt whenever she looked at him; if only she didn't secretly crave his company, his touch. It would be better by far if she didn't care at all about him. But to care like this, despite her better judgment, to care so much she could scarcely think of anything else, was a constant irritating distraction.

A movement in the distance caught her eye—two horsemen on the road leading to the castle. She squinted. "Oh, thank God," she breathed, making out Thorne's two villeins, one of whom had Felda riding pillion behind him. Behind the other was ... She frowned. *Clare?* What was Estrude's maid doing with them?

She negotiated her way through the mayhem of the great hall and met the party as they dismounted near the courtyard. Thorne left the hallmoot to join them. He thanked and dismissed his men, took Freya's basket from Felda, and greeted her, as did Martine, with a hug and a kiss.

"Lady Clare," Martine said, "why did you come here?"

Tears spilled from Clare's eyes, and she buried her face in her hands. "Oh, my lady! You have to help me! I had nowhere else to go!" She dropped to her knees. "I throw myself on your mercy!"

Martine bent to put her arms around the sobbing girl and urge her to her feet. "My lady, what's wrong?"

Clare collapsed against Martine, burying her wet face in the crook of her neck. "Oh, I'm such a fool! I brought it on myself. It's my fault. God forgive me!"

Taking the hysterical young woman by the shoulders, Martine held her at arm's length and demanded, "What happened, Clare? Tell me."

Clare's tear-stained face twisted in anguish. " 'Twas . . . 'twas Sir Bernard, m-my lady."

Martine and Thorne exchanged a look. Felda, her plump arms crossed over her chest, scowled at Clare.

"All right," Martine said quietly. "Tell me."

Clare's little eyes slid toward Thorne, then she looked at the ground. "I . . . I'm too ashamed."

Thorne cleared his throat. "I'd best be seeing to Freya. Perhaps a brandy would soothe the lady's nerves."

When they were settled at a table in the lesser hall and Clare was halfway through her second brandy, Martine again gently pressed her for an explanation.

Clare stared for some time into her cup, glassy-eyed. "I threw myself at him," she said hoarsely. "God, I'm such a fool. Everyone says it, and it's true."

"Nay," Martine insisted, knowing how it felt to be exploited by a man. " 'Twasn't your fault."

Shaking her head, Clare said, "I thought he was . . . different. But he was . . ." She bit her lip. "He defiled me. He . . ." She glanced nervously toward Martine and Felda, then whispered, "I'm not pure anymore."

"Oh, Clare," Martine said. "It's not your fault. Men have this way of making one lose one's senses. You're not to blame."

"My father won't think so," she rasped. "He'll . . . oh, my God, he'll kill me. He will, he really will, when he finds out."

"You're exaggerating."

"You don't know him, my lady." Her eyes refilled with tears. "I can't go home. Not now that I'm . . . that I've been . . . I can't!" Leaning over the table, she cradled her face in her arms and wailed.

Martine looked toward Felda, who frowned and shook her head. Felda had never liked Clare—for that matter, neither had Martine—but to let those base feelings stand in the way of simple human compassion would be unforgivable.

Martine stroked Clare's hair. "Would you like to stay here, my lady—"

Clare seized Martine's hands and squeezed them, looking into her eyes with teary gratitude. "Oh, my lady, thank you, thank you!"

"For a while, at least," Martine amended. "Until we can—"

"Anything!" Clare gasped. "Anything! Oh, my lady, I'll do anything you want! I'll be your slave."

Felda rolled her eyes.

"That won't be necessary," Martine said. "I'm just happy to be able to help."

"Do you know what day it is?" Thorne called out in English, sitting up in their enormous bed and pulling aside the curtains.

Martine, having already arisen, sat with her back to him in front of a window in the dressing alcove, brushing her hair. It shimmered like fire in the early morning sunlight that flooded the master suite—fire reflected in the gold silk of her dressing gown and the jeweled tones of the new tunics hanging on the alcove walls. Thorne smiled to himself, remembering how she had tried to dismiss the seamstresses he'd summoned ... *I don't have time for fittings. I have gardens to sow!* But he'd insisted, wanting not only to adorn her, but to give her something personal, something most women seemed to love. Her eventual concession had been less than gracious ... *All right, all right! But no tight laces, and none of those damned barbettes!*

Martine stopped brushing and sat still for a moment. He knew she was struggling to translate his question and compose an answer in English. Finally, "Is it ... May the first?" she asked without turning around.

Her accent was so charming that he laughed. "Aye, Mayday," he said, swinging his long legs over the side of the bed. "The first day of summer." He stood and stretched, rubbing the kinks out of his arms and raking his fingers through his hair. She looked over her shoulder at him, flushing when she saw that all he had on were the drawers he'd slept in. Turning back toward the window, she resumed her brushing.

He started to reach for his shirt off the carpeted floor, and then stopped. He'd been patient with her. They'd been married for nearly two months, and not once had he pressed for his husbandly rights. He'd hoped, of course, to ease her into acceptance of him, to regain her trust, perhaps even her affection, so that when he did come to her, she would want it as much as he ... and she would not, afterward, feel manipulated. But she revealed so little of her true feelings that he honestly didn't know how much progress he'd made toward mending the rift between them. Perhaps this morning would be a good time to find out.

"Do you know how the Saxon peasants celebrate Mayday?" he asked as he entered the alcove. Loki lay curled up on the cushioned bench next to his mistress. Thorne tossed him off, straddled the warm spot where he'd lain, and took the brush from his wife's hand.

"Wh-what?" Was it the question or his nearness that flustered her so? he wondered.

He ran the brush through her satiny hair. Quietly he said, in French, "Do you know how my people celebrate this day?"

"Nay," she murmured, her head falling back as he pulled the stiff boar bristles across her scalp. With his free hand he gently massaged her nape.

"They spend the night in the forest." Still brushing, he trailed his hand down her back and curled it around her waist. "Making love."

Her head came up. He put the brush down, encircled her waist with his other hand so that he held her in a loose embrace, and kissed the top of her head. She sat perfectly still, offering no encouragement, but no resistance. He kissed her temple, inhaling the scent of her hair and skin, his body responding with an urgency born of long abstinence. He tightened his left hand around her waist and glided his right up, between her breasts, to rest on her upper chest. Her heart tripped wildly against his palm; her breathing raced. Slowly lowering his hand beneath her dressing gown, but over her satin shift, he cupped a deliciously soft breast, lightly thumbing the nipple until it puckered.

"Martine . . ." he breathed into her ear.

She stood, turned, and walked toward the bedchamber. "I'd appreciate it if this didn't take too long," she said coolly, tossing aside her dressing gown and sitting in just her shift on the side of the bed. "I have a great deal to do this morning."

He just stared at her for a moment. What was she telling him? That she was willing, but only grudgingly so? That she had no choice but to do her wifely duty, but he'd best be quick about it? That stung. He'd been patient to a fault. He'd taken his time, hoping she'd come around—but it clearly hadn't worked. Perhaps he'd been too patient, too tentative. He couldn't take her by force—that was for animals like Edmond—but he could make her want him. She responded to his touch at hotly as he to hers.

Rising, he followed her into the bedchamber, noting how she glanced down at his erection, beneath his loose linen drawers, and then quickly looked away. She backed up and lay down on the bed, but as she began to gather her shift up, he reached out to close his hand over hers.

"Not yet," he said, joining her on the bed and stretching out on his side next to her. He smoothed her hair off her face, then trailed his fingers softly down her throat. "Let me look at you first."

He saw her swallow. "I really would appreciate it if you were—"

"If I were quick about it, but I have no intention of obliging you. I've waited too long for this, and now I'm going to take my time." He touched a fingertip to a pebbly nipple, and she drew in a breath. "I may keep you in this bed all day, and all night, and then all day tomorrow." He smiled, and smoothed his palm over her flat belly, bringing it to rest on the feminine swell between her legs. "It's Mayday, Martine, and I'm going to celebrate it by showing you how it can be between us. Let me show you. Tell me you want me to."

She closed her eyes and curled her hands into fists. "I don't want you to. All I want you to do is get it over with."

He rolled onto her, careful to rest his weight on his elbows so as not to burden her. "I'll get it over with in a day or two," he whispered. "And I promise you'll feel wonderful afterward. Happy and satisfied. And not in the least manipulated." He closed his mouth over hers and kissed her deeply, reveling in the warmth and softness of her lips. He touched the tip of his tongue to them, slipped it between them to taste her sweetness, and then withdrew, knowing he had to take his time, had to coax her slowly into responding in kind.

He kissed her throat, his hands tangled in her hair. Gradually he settled down onto her, molding himself to her curves and hollows. The feel of her breasts, warm beneath their satin covering, crushed to his bare chest, aroused him to the point of pain. Parting her legs with his knee, he pressed his swollen sex to her own, and felt her shiver. His muscles tightened of their own accord, crushing his hard male need against her, then released and contracted again and again, without his willing it. His big body ground sinuously against hers, driven by an age-old instinct he couldn't control.

He'd been too long without her. His mind told him to wait, but he was already on the verge of release. If he tried to hold off much longer, he'd spill his seed before he could even enter her—an ignoble way to initiate the promised marathon of passion. Claiming her mouth in another hungry kiss, he let his hands roam over her with abandon, caressing her through the liquid-smooth satin in all the ways and in all the places that he knew would most excite her—but she merely lay still beneath him, her face averted, a fistful of sheet in each hand.

"Relax," he softly urged. "Give it a chance."

"I feel trapped," she said tightly, her voice quavering. "I have no choice in this. I'm powerless."

"Powerless!" He took her right hand, opened her fingers, and pressed it to his throbbing shaft. Her touch almost sent him over the edge, but he gritted his teeth and strained for control. "You have the power to do this to me." She tried to wrest her hand from his, but he gripped it firmly, guiding her fingers up the length of him. "Feel me," he said raggedly. "Feel what you do to me. Feel how ready I am for you. It hurts, I want you so much. And I know you want me."

"I don't."

"I don't believe you." This time, when she pulled her

hand away, he let her. Whipping up the skirt of her shift, he reached between her legs. She flailed at him, but he seized both of her wrists in one iron fist and held them above her head while his other hand sought and found the damp heat that betrayed her own arousal. "You're body says you want me."

"That's my body, not my heart. You make me feel worse than manipulated. I feel violated."

"Violated?"

"Look at us!" she demanded, her voice cracking with emotion. "How can I feel otherwise?"

Christ, he thought, gazing down upon the trembling woman beneath him, her arms pinned above her head, struggling against the tears that filled her eyes. He had meant to be gentle, to ease her into his arms, to bring her closer to him. Instead, he had lost control—and driven her further away.

He released her, stood, and grabbed his shirt. "I didn't mean it to be this way, Martine. I meant to—"

"You meant to seduce me." She sat up, rubbing her wrists. "But you needn't have gone to the trouble, and I wish you wouldn't. By law I can't deny you. 'Twould be much simpler if you just tupped me quickly and got it over with."

"I didn't want a quick tupping. I wanted to make love to you."

"Why me? Why not one of the kitchen girls? That's the type you prefer, isn't it?"

"It had to be you, only you. Don't you understand?"

She met his gaze, her expression thoughtful, and he thought for a moment that perhaps she did, at last, understand ... but presently her eyes narrowed a bit, and then widened slightly, as if she had suddenly figured something out.

"You want to get me with child!" she said. "That's been the whole point all along. Your little attentions, your kisses ... 'twas all a kind of slow seduction. Just more manipulation."

"Martine, what are you—"

"You're a baron now, and a baron needs sons, legitimate sons. Any woman can give you pleasure, but only your wife can give you heirs."

"Heirs?" He shook out the chausses he'd worn the

day before. "Is that why you think I ..." Shaking his head, he tunneled his legs into the woolen hose and tied them. "God, Martine, I've been too busy to give any thought to heirs. 'Twas *you* I wanted." He pulled on his boots and yesterday's tunic.

Wrapping her arms around her updrawn legs, she said, "Nay, not me. If it's not heirs you seek, then it's simple sexual release. Any woman would have done."

"If any woman would have done, I'd have spared myself some bother and paid a visit to Fat Nan." She looked puzzled. "She runs a brothel in the harbor. No whore has ever accused me of manipulating her."

"Go, then," she said with a tone of studied indifference, rising and reaching for her dressing gown. "I know you have ... needs. If that's the only reason you came to me this morning, because you're frustrated, then by all means go to—"

"I didn't say that!" Christ, she was exasperating!

"I know perfectly well what—"

"You know nothing!" He took a step toward her and tried to pull her into his arms, but she flinched and shook him off. Something hot and unstoppable rose within him. Wheeling around, he sighted on the big, glazed window and, without thinking, hauled back and slammed his fist through one of the panes. The glass shattered. He heard her gasp as he withdrew his bloody hand. She ran to the dressing alcove and came back with the sleeve of one of her cotton chemises, which he took and wrapped around his throbbing fist. He felt suddenly light-headed and very weary, his mind as curiously numb as his lacerated hand.

For a few long moments they stood in silence, and then he said quietly, "Perhaps you're right. Perhaps I should go to Hastings. I'm not doing either of us any good here."

She opened her mouth to speak, and for a moment he thought, from the expression in her eyes, that she might beg him not to go. But she bit her lip and looked away, her arms wrapped tightly around her chest.

He grabbed his mantle and sword belt off their hooks. "I'll be back tomorrow evening." She nodded, facing away from him.

He swung the door open and collided with Clare, upsetting the tray of wine and bread in her hands.

"Oh, my lord, I'm sorry!" she squealed, kneeling to clean it up. She was always underfoot, that one. Always lurking about with food and drink no one had asked for. Not trusting himself to utter a civil response, he turned and stalked away.

Martine awoke that night to a furious knocking at her bedchamber door. She turned to the other side of the bed before remembering that Thorne wasn't there; he was in Hastings. It was surely well past midnight. Who would disturb her at such an hour?

"Milady! Milady!" The door banged open and Felda rushed into the room, dressed, like Martine, in nothing but her shift, and carrying a lantern. "Milady, it's Bernard! He's here!"

"Bernard?" Martine whipped aside the covers and leaped out of bed, following Felda to the window. She looked down and gasped. Dozens of mounted men in chain mail surrounded the keep, some leaping down from their horses and running inside with torches. She heard thunderous footsteps on the stairs, and a familiar voice shouting commands—Bernard.

She ran to the door and locked it, then remembered the door that led to the chapel and secured that as well.

"What's happening?" Felda cried as the footsteps neared. "What does he want?"

"Me, I think," said Martine in a shaky whisper.

"Sweet Mother of God," Felda muttered. "I wish Thorne was here."

Martine heard Bernard's voice on the other side of the door—"It's this one"—and then the doorknob turned. "Open the door, my lady," he bellowed.

Felda crossed herself. "Milady, what are we going to—"

"It's me they want," Martine said, feeling a cold calm descend upon her. "You can get away if you don't draw attention to your—"

"Nay!" Felda exclaimed as Bernard banged fiercely on the door. "I'll not run away. You need me with you."

"I need you to go to Hastings and find Thorne."

Bernard ceased his pounding, but the blessed silence

was short-lived, for presently there commenced a series
of deafening blows that rattled the door on its hinges.
He'd graduated from his fist to his foot, it seemed, and
from the sound of it, he'd enlisted a few of his men
to help.

Martine grabbed Felda by the shoulders. "Saddle up
and ride to Hastings as fast as you can," she yelled over
the explosive pounding. "Go to the harbor. There's a
person named . . . I think it's Nan . . ."

Felda's mouth flew open. "Fat Nan?" Martine nodded. "He left you alone here so he could run off to—"

Martine shook Felda hard as the wood of the door
began to splinter. "Just find him, Felda. *Find him!* Tell
him what happened."

Another deafening kick, and another, and finally the
door crashed open and dark forms swarmed into the
room.

Chapter 23

"Go!" Martine screamed to her maid as armored and helmeted men grabbed her and hurled her onto the bed. They flipped her facedown and held her there, kneeling on her back so hard she could barely breathe. Gloved hands yanked her arms behind her back while others encircled them with rope, pulling it so tightly that it bit into her skin. At the same time, someone else brought her ankles together, and they were similarly bound.

This isn't happening. Martine shivered violently, her eyes squeezed shut. *This can't be happening.* Her nostrils flared as she breathed in the odors of oiled steel, leather, and unwashed bodies. The feel of all those strange hands on her, of mail-clad knees and elbows digging into her, wrested a sob of helpless fury from her throat. *Nay, don't cry!* she commanded herself. *All you've got now is your dignity. Don't give them the pleasure of seeing you cry.*

Two men jerked her roughly to her feet, whipped her around, and held her there.

Bernard stood before her in the dim glow of the lantern, serene as usual amid the brutality he'd spawned. He alone wore no armor, but was clad instead in a tunic of black brocade embroidered in gold. He smiled that deathly smile that never reached his eyes, and then he said simply, "Lady Falconer."

"What do you want?" she asked, struggling to keep her voice from quivering.

"That should be fairly obvious, my lady. I want you."

"You're too late," she said. "I'm already married."

Bernard chuckled, and his men followed suit. "I'm hardly here to ask for your hand, my lady." He gestured, and a figure emerged into the light—Father Simon, a sheet of parchment in his hand.

"Read it," Bernard ordered.

The priest brought the document close to his face and intoned, "Unless proven otherwise, let it be known that the woman called Martine of Rouen, or Martine Falconer, Baroness of Blackburn, did, by charms, incantations, and potions, effect the acts of malefice which follow. Item: That she did breathe into the mouth of the deceased child Ailith of Kirkley, and by such means caused the corpse to regain its vitality and become reanimated."

"What?" Martine exclaimed.

"Item:" Simon continued, as if he hadn't heard her, "That she did render impotent both her first and second husbands by poisoning and other means. Item: That she did likewise poison Lady Estrude of Flanders and thereby took her life."

"This is preposterous," she said.

The priest glared at her and cleared his throat. "And let it be further known that said maleficia were performed at the behest of he who is known as Satan, and also by the names Lucifer and Beelzebub. And that the sorceress Martine Falconer has bound herself in service to this prince of devils, and in her allegiance to him, has renounced God, Jesus Christ, the saints, the Roman Church, and all the sacraments."

Martine stared in incredulous horror at Father Simon, Bernard, and the men surrounding her. They all wore expressions of the utmost gravity. She began to tremble uncontrollably. "I want my husband."

Bernard snickered. "As I understand it, your husband departed this morning for Hastings, and is therefore unavailable."

"Of course," she said, comprehension dawning. "You knew he wouldn't be here. You never would have tried this otherwise. How did you—"

"Oh, I've been kept exceedingly well informed of the Saxon's comings and goings. My good lady Clare has seen to that."

Martine sighed disgustedly. "Clare. I should have known." She nodded toward the sheet of parchment in

Father Simon's hand. "What does this mean? What will happen to me?"

Father Simon folded up the document and slid it beneath his robe. "You'll be encouraged to confess."

She swallowed hard. When she spoke, her voice was an unsteady rasp. "You mean tortured."

"Alas, no," responded the priest. "The more effective methods, the ones they use on the Continent, well, they're frowned on in England. But you will be interrogated. Questioned. And then you will be tried and found guilty."

Tried and found guilty. Just like that. "Wh-what is the punishment for sorcery?" she asked.

"Nothing much," Father Simon said lightly. "A fine, a few lashes, perhaps ... at the worst, banishment."

Relief overwhelmed her. "Thank God," she breathed.

"But of course," Simon continued, "it's not sorcery you've been accused of. It's *heretical* sorcery. Sorcery in the service of the Devil. And the punishment for heresy of this magnitude is death."

"Then I'm to be hung," she whispered.

Simon took a step toward her and smiled; so did Bernard. Both men seemed to be enjoying themselves immensely, like two cats toying with a trapped mouse.

"Not necessarily," said Bernard. "Oh, you might be lucky and get off with a hanging. But there are those in England, such as Father Simon here, who advocate that heretics be burned at the stake."

"As is the practice in the more civilized European realms," Simon elaborated.

Martine shook her head slowly. "No ..."

"Oh, yes," Bernard said, stepping close to Martine and gripping her chin to force her to look at him. "So you didn't much like the idea of marriage to me, did you? You thought you'd gotten the better of me, you and that damned woodsman. Well, now I'm in a position to return the favor, and I assure you I intend to take full advantage of it. I will petition Bishop Lambert to make an example of you. Make no mistake—you *will* be found guilty, and then you will die on the pyre, screaming and begging as the flames consume you. There's no agony that can compare to death by fire."

Martine wrested her head out of his grasp. "Except perhaps marriage to you."

Someone in back chuckled. Bernard, his jaw set in outrage, withdrew his sword from its scabbard and held its razor-sharp tip to her throat. "You seem to forget who has the upper hand here, Lady Woodsman. Perhaps you need reminding." To the men supporting her, he said, "Hold her head still."

A hand seized her braid and tugged her head back hard. She drew in a panicked breath as Bernard raised the sword high, its blade pointed upward. He paused briefly, a feral glint in his eye. She saw him aim the heavy, jeweled hilt toward her forehead—and then he grimaced and whipped it down with savage force.

Red-hot pain burst within her. Her legs collapsed, and she heard herself groan. Bernard's voice, strangely deep and muffled, said, "Let her go." The hands released her and she fell facedown onto the carpeted floor.

"Gag the bitch," Bernard said. The last thing she felt was gloved fingers prying her mouth open and stuffing a rag in . . . and then a cold, empty darkness engulfed her

"Wake up, milord." It was a woman's voice. She spoke the old tongue. Thorne felt himself being jiggled which precipitated a wave of nausea.

Groaning, he rolled over, squeezing his eyes against the pain that speared his head. He lay on a blanket covered straw pallet, and there was something hard under his chest—a jug. He was fully dressed, including even his sword belt. "Go 'way." His sticky mouth tasted like the muck on the bottom of a wine barrel.

He heard other women's whispers, and then a dozen hands took hold of him and turned him faceup. Hot breath near his ear: "Milord, wake up. It's Nan."

"Nan?" he moaned. Nan. Fat Nan. He must be at Fat Nan's. That realization only compounded his misery. "Leave me alone."

Nan said, "Leave *you* alone? After the way you pleasured me last night? The girls always said you was the best, a real stallion, but I never knew it till—"

"What?" he mumbled, squinting against the midday sun streaming in through the little window next to his pallet. He was in one of the brothel's seedy little upstairs alcoves. Fat Nan and an audience of scantily clad wenches were hovering over him.

Nan turned to her girls. "*That* woke him up!" They laughed appreciatively, and Thorne relaxed as it dawned on him that he hadn't, after all, shared a pallet with Fat Nan last night. He sat up slowly, wincing at his headache, and scanned the lineup of whores, struggling to remember which one . . .

Nan said, "You went through three of 'em, milord." The girls giggled at Thorne, who wasn't quite sure whether to feel proud or ashamed of this feat. " 'Just keep 'em coming,' you said. You tried for a fourth—" she kicked the almost full brandy jug next to him, which rolled off the pallet, "but one sip out of it and you were out cold."

The whores laughed uproariously, which made the Saxon's head pulsate with pain. "You mean all I did was—"

"You don't remember?" Nan said. "Small wonder. You showed up here yesterday, surly as a bear, ordering one jug of brandy after another. You drank yourself into a stupor, came to, drank some more, then passed out again. Over and over."

Befreckled Tilda curled up on the pallet and laid her head in his lap. "Just like a babe at his mum's teat," she said wistfully. " 'Twas quite sweet, really."

Another swell of sickness rose within him, and he swallowed it down, wondering how sweet Tilda would find it if he vomited up three jugs of brandy all over her.

"Took seven of us to haul you upstairs last night," Nan said. "I would have let you sleep it off a bit longer, only there's someone showed up just now, asking for you. A woman."

The girls whistled and cooed. "He's got them coming to whorehouses for him! Now, *that's* love."

Martine? Here? Christ, no. He struggled to his feet, shaking off Tilda's attempts to help, ran one hand over his needle-sharp morning beard, and tried to finger-comb his hair with the other, but it was still bandaged with Martine's chemise sleeve. The whores parted for him and he stumbled down the stairs, wondering what he would say to her . . . why she had come here, of all places . . . why she had to see him like this . . .

He stopped short when he saw the plump redhead in the doorway. "Felda!"

She closed in on him quickly and slapped his face hard. "You bastard!" There were tears in her eyes. "You left her, to come to this ... this ..."

"All he did was drink," said Nan from the stairs. "And now he's got the devil's own hangover, so why don't you show him a little—"

"Good!" Felda spat out. "I'm glad you're suffering. You left her. You left her!" She started beating on his chest with her fists, but he seized them and shook her.

"What happened?" She was sobbing too hard to talk. "Answer me! Did something happen to Martine?" Felda nodded. "What? *Tell me!*"

Nan squeezed his shoulder and handed Felda a cup of something, which she drank. Presently she calmed enough to talk. " 'Twas that Clare," she choked out. "That bitch, I knew there was something wrong about her. She was his creature all along, the lying trollop. Soon as you rode away yesterday, she vanished. I didn't think nothing about it at the time, but must be she run off to Harford and—"

"What are you talking about?" he demanded. "What happened?"

"Milady, she—she's gone. They come for her in the middle of the night, Bernard and his men. They carried her out in her sleeping shift and threw her in a covered cart. I saw her. There was blood on her face, and they had her tied up and gagged."

"What? Jesus!"

"She'd told me to find you, to look for you here."

"Oh, God," he groaned, sinking to his knees and holding his stomach. Someone thrust a bowl in front of him. He grabbed it with both hands and instantly emptied the contents of his stomach into it. Solicitous hands took away the bowl and wiped his mouth with a damp rag. Gaining his feet, he fumbled with his purse, emptied some coins into Nan's conveniently open palm, then lurched out of the brothel and into the harsh noon sunshine, with Felda close on his heels. "I've got to go to Harford. I've got to get some men and go to—"

She grabbed his arm. "Nay! She's not at Harford. I heard some of Bernard's men talking about it. They

were to take her here, to Hastings. She'll be held at
Battle Abbey until the trial."

"What trial?" he asked, knowing even as the words
left his mouth what the answer would be. Of course. It
all made sense. He should have known this would
happen.

"Heresy," said Felda. "Bernard denounced her. They
say the bishop's going to make an example of her. They
say . . . Oh, God, Thorne. They'd say she's going to be
tied to a stake and burned alive."

"I went to Battle Abbey to see her," Thorne told
Matthew that evening, "but they wouldn't let me in."

"Of course not," the prior said matter-of-factly. He
was seemingly unperturbable—like Rainulf, a creature
of the mind. "You won't be able to see her for weeks,
not until the trial. Please sit down," he urged for the
third time, indicating the seat opposite him at the little
table in the hall of the prior's lodge.

Thorne shook his head and continued pacing. He still
felt the poisonous aftereffects of all that brandy, and
moving seemed to help. "Can you imagine how she's
feeling right now? What she's thinking? They're threat-
ening to burn her, for God's sake. Can they do that?"

"They've been burning heretics in France and Italy for
more than a century. Not only that, but their property is
confiscated, often to the profit of their accusers. That's
what makes this concept of heretical sorcery so dangerous, so ripe for abuse. If men like Father Simon—
priestly lapdogs to greedy monsters like Bernard—are
given free reign to make such charges, who knows how
many innocent lives could eventually be destroyed."

Thorne stopped pacing and leaned on the table. "The
only innocent life I care about right now is Martine's.
We have to come up with a strategy for this trial. I have
no intention of letting them find her guilty."

"They're already found her guilty," the prior said
somberly. "We have to prove her innocent."

Thorne dragged out a chair and straddled it. "That's
not the way a trial works. At my hallmoots—"

"Your hallmoots," Matthew patiently explained, "are
conducted according to the old Anglo-Saxon tradition,
where the accused is assumed to be innocent until

proven guilty. That's not the way things work in an ecclesiastical court. They'll start out assuming she's a heretic, and go on from there."

Thorne sighed raggedly. "And the Normans think they brought civilization to England," he muttered.

Brother Matthew tapped the folded parchment on the table, his ebony eyes, usually so piercing, now focused on nothing. "The most serious accusation is that of ligature, the causing of impotence. And considering that she's supposed to have caused it in the service of Satan . . ." He shook his head. " 'Tis a relatively new concept, heretical sorcery. There have been few trials to use as models, and that means there are few rules."

"Is that good or bad?"

Matthew grimaced. "Probably bad. Bishop Lambert will be able to make the rules up as he goes along, so they'll be to his advantage, not ours."

Thorne felt as if the walls were closing in around him. "His advantage? What's his stake in this?"

"If Martine is . . . if she can't prove her innocence, and she's . . ."

"And she's burned," Thorne supplied shortly.

Matthew nodded. "Her estates will be confiscated. The bulk will be distributed by Olivier as he sees fit, and I have little doubt that he'll grant them to Bernard. They've always been close, and Bernard can argue that those lands have been in his family for nearly a century. He can be uncannily persuasive when there's something he really wants. A smaller part—one or two holdings, perhaps—will go to the bishop. From what I know of him, 'tis he who will benefit from their revenues, and not the Church. 'Tis therefore very much in his interest that Martine's guilt be maintained. Were it not for his avarice, I doubt she'd stand trial at all. Officially, canon law denies the existence of true heretical sorcery, although more and more those provisions are being overlooked."

"You're telling me it's hopeless," Thorne said tightly. "Is that what you're saying?"

Matthew didn't answer right away. Thorne felt as if he were suffocating. Rising, he went to the window and leaned on the sill, staring into the endless night sky. "I should never have gone to Hastings. I should have known he'd try something. This wouldn't have happened if I'd been there."

Matthew came up behind him and laid a hand on his shoulder. "Don't torment yourself," he said quietly. "'Twill only weaken you, and you'll need all your strength to get through this. Go home and pray. Prepare your soul for the worst."

"If Martine—" Despair squeezed Thorne's throat, and he choked on the words. "If Martine is taken from me," he managed hoarsely, "I'll have no soul. I'll be empty."

Matthew patted his back. "I know how much you love her."

Automatically Thorne shook his head. "Nay. I should have loved her. I didn't let myself. I didn't allow it."

"*Allow* it? Thorne, love doesn't give a damn whether you allow it or not. It's the one thing even you can't control. I knew from the moment I first met you and Martine last summer that you were hopelessly in love with each other. 'Twas in every word you spoke, every shy glance, every careful touch. There was a force, a power, that bound you together irrevocably."

Thorne closed his eyes and pictured the ribbon of fate, wound around them both, as they clung to each other in the cold, cleansing water of Blackburn River. He lifted his hand, still wrapped in the sleeve of her chemise, and breathed in the scent of her—the herbal oils in which she bathed, the honey of her skin, the sunshine of her hair ... "Sweet woodruff and lavender," he murmured.

From the direction of the church came chanting. "I must join the brothers," said Matthew. "Go home and pray."

Alone now, Thorne stared sightlessly into the dark, letting the tranquil tones of compline enter his soul and steady his thoughts. Yes, he would go home and pray. He would spend the entire night on his knees in the chapel, as he did during his preparations for knighthood. Only this time he would pray not for the strength to be a valiant soldier, but for guidance. He would beg and plead with the Lord to show him a way to save Martine. She couldn't die; he mustn't allow it. She was a part of him now, she was in his blood, their souls were connected. He loved her.

A gasp of astonished laughter escaped him. It was true! He loved her! He'd always loved her. He always would love her. God, what a fool he was to have fought it so, to have denied this irrefutable force, so terrifying, yet so liberating. He loved her!

The tightness rose in his throat, and his eyes stung with unshed tears. Drawing in a deep, steadying breath to hold them at bay, he whispered, "I will save her. God will show me a way."

At dawn, knowing what he needed to do, he rose painfully from the stone floor of the chapel, limped down the front steps to the bailey, and called to a stableboy. "Saddle up my mount, lad, and bring him here. And pack me something to eat and drink. I've a long ride today."

It was midafternoon when he dismounted in the courtyard of Harford Castle. Boyce greeted him with a drawn sword and a semi-apologetic shrug. Thorne handed over his sword belt and dagger without waiting for it to be ordered. "Take me to the son of a bitch," he said.

Boyce led him to the great hall and told him to wait while he fetched Bernard. "Thorne! Thorne!" squealed Ailith, clambering off Geneva's lap and running toward him. The Saxon lifted her high in the air, gave her a big hug, then allowed her to lead him by the hand to her mother and grandfather, who were sitting at a table by the fire pit.

"My lady." Geneva nodded. "Sire." Godfrey made no response. As Thorne came closer, he saw that the old man sat perfectly still, propped up in his big chair with the help of small pillows. He had his head thrown back, and at first Thorne wondered why he frowned so angrily, but in fact it was only half of his face that grimaced so, or rather, hung slackly. The other half appeared nearly normal. His eyes, glistening and blue, were the only live thing about him. They seemed alert but intensely sad.

"What ails him?" Thorne asked Geneva.

Shaking her head, she spooned up some porridge from a bowl on the table and carefully fed it into her father's mouth. "He's been this way for a week. They've bled him twice, but it hasn't helped."

"Poor Grandpapa," Ailith said, putting her little arms

around him protectively. "Please get better soon." Godfrey's eyes looked helplessly toward his granddaughter.

"Enough to turn your stomach, isn't it?" growled Bernard from behind them. Thorne wheeled around, his hand automatically reaching for the hilt of his sword, which, of course, he'd surrendered. Geneva ordered Ailith from the hall, and the child scampered away, unaware that anything was amiss.

Bernard had several men with him. "Search him," he told Boyce.

"He already gave me his—"

"Search him anyway. Check his boots. These Saxon bastards are sneaky."

Thorne allowed Boyce to pat him down, and then he removed his boots himself and shook them out to prove he'd secreted no dagger there. He had, in fact, briefly considered doing so. The notion of getting Bernard alone and opening his throat with a hidden blade had been tempting for an instant—before he realized it wouldn't help Martine. The charges of heresy were a matter of public record now, and Bernard's death wouldn't obliterate them. In fact, for Thorne to kill her accuser would surely only add fuel to the case against her.

Bernard took a seat at the table and bellowed, "Wench! Bring brandy!"

Lady Clare scurried out from a dark corner and set a pitcher and cup before her master, who then pulled her roughly onto his lap. She averted her gaze from Thorne's, but Bernard grabbed her by the chin and yanked her head around so that she had to face him. "She's not much for looks, but she does come in handy from time to time." He closed a hand over one of her small breasts and squeezed so hard that she winced. " 'Tis quite extraordinary, really. She'll do just about any damn thing you please. And there's no limit to what she'll put up with." He bit her earlobe, and tears of pain filled her eyes. "Is there, my unassuming little hare?"

"No, sir," she whispered, looking down.

Bernard turned his reptilian eyes on Thorne. "But then, you already know about her extraordinary devotion to me, don't you?"

"Quite well," he said tightly.

Bernard smiled coldly, then pushed Clare off his lap so abruptly that she stumbled and fell. As she scrambled back to her corner, he said, "She claims to be in love with me. Have you ever heard of anything so ridiculous?"

"I can't say as I have."

Bernard's smile faded as he reached for the pitcher. "Why did you come here, woodsman? Or should I say . . . *my lord* woodsman?"

As coolly as he could, Thorne said, "I want to give you Blackburn."

Geneva gasped. All eyes—even Godfrey's—turned toward the Saxon. Bernard inspected him through narrowed eyes over the rim of his cup, and then swiftly tossed its contents into his mouth. "In return for retracting my denunciation of your lady bitch, I assume . . . calling off the forces of Mother Church."

Thorne's hands contracted into fists. "Aye."

Bernard sat back and smirked. " 'Tis an empty offer, as you well know. You hold Blackburn in fief from Olivier. You can't just give it to whomever you please."

"But I can abandon it," Thorne said. "I can simply ride away and never come back. Since I have no heirs, 'twill be Olivier's again, to dispose of as he will. You should have no trouble convincing him to grant it to you. I understand he's the one person in England who actually likes you." Ignoring Bernard's sneer, he said, "I'm offering you a much greater reward than you stand to gain from Martine's execution for heresy. One of the most valuable baronies in Sussex, as opposed to a handful of scattered holdings."

Bernard said, "What if I want them both—Blackburn *and* those other holdings?"

"You'll have them," said Thorne. "You'll have it all. Just make them free Martine and I swear before God and all the saints that we'll walk away from what was ours and never try to take it back. We'll go to France. You'll never see us again."

"I'll have it all. . . ." Bernard said. "And what will you have? I don't see that this arrangement benefits you in the least. That makes me suspicious."

Geneva said quietly, "He'll have Martine." She smiled at Thorne. He had never seen her smile before, and was amazed at the way it transformed her face into that of the beautiful young woman she once was.

Bernard chuckled meanly. "Sister, you don't know Thorne Falconer as I do. Love has no place in his life." He spoke to Geneva as if the Saxon weren't even in the room. " 'Tis one of the few reasons to admire the man. Nay, he's got some mischief up his sleeve. As land-hungry as he's always been, there's not a chance in hell he'd give up Blackburn just to keep that troublesome wife of his from the stake. He'll lure me into releasing her and then double-cross me."

"There will be no double-cross," Thorne promised. "There are no cunning motives behind my offer. Your sister is right. What I do, I do so that Martine will live."

Bernard shook his head. "You've deceived me before, Saxon. 'Tis the way your kind operates. You've often said 'true love' is a trap for the weak, and the one thing you aren't is weak. 'Tis wretched creatures like that wench in the corner"—he nodded toward the cowering Clare—"who fall prey to the fiction of romantic love. She might be willing to give up everything for love, to become a slave, to humble herself, but not you. I know you too well."

"The love I feel for my wife," Thorne said slowly, "is nothing you've ever experienced or could hope to experience, nothing an animal like you could begin to comprehend. It *is* humbling, but in the same way that kneeling in a great cathedral is humbling. One feels like a small part of something vast and unfathomable. It's what separates men from beasts, which is why you're incapable of it. I thought *I* was incapable of it once, but I'm not, thank God."

"What a very pretty speech," drawled Bernard, sitting back lazily. "But why waste all those high-flown sentiments on me if I'm too base to understand them?"

Thorne crossed to the table and leaned on it, towering over Bernard and ignoring the tip of Boyce's sword, which rested just between his shoulder blades. "To convince you that I won't double-cross you and that my motives are simple and honest. I love Martine with all my heart, and that is the *only* reason I want you to free her. I give you my solemn oath. I'll swear on anything you want. Retract your denunciation, and everything that is mine will be yours."

"You love her that much?"

Thorne slowly straightened up, and Boyce withdrew the sword. "I do."

"I'd say she's put a spell on you."

"You'd say it if you believed it, but you no more think she's a sorceress than I do. You're not stupid enough to believe your own charges."

"That I'm not. But neither am I stupid enough to miss an opportunity to acquire Blackburn."

Thank God. "Then you accept my offer?"

Bernard smiled slowly. "Nay. 'Twas most entertaining to listen to you make it, though. Especially that charming bit about how you feel like a small part of something vast and—"

"But you said you wouldn't miss an opportunity to—"

"Woodsman," Bernard growled, sitting forward, "I don't need you or your pathetic deal to acquire Blackburn any more than I need your *permission* to take back lands that were rightfully mine to begin with. You *will* abandon Blackburn, but not in return for your wife's release. You'll abandon it because you have no choice. Because if you remain in England until the conclusion of the trial, I promise you that you, too, will be arrested for heresy—"

"Me! That's absurd."

"It's all absurd," Bernard countered, laughing. "Fantastically absurd, and ridiculously easy. If I denounce you, you'll stand trial and have to prove your innocence. It might be rather difficult. You criticize the Church, you rarely attend mass, you read pagan writings. . . . You will most certainly be branded a heretic, and then you'll be tied to a stake and roasted alive. Can you imagine the agony? You can't save your lady, but you can still save yourself."

"If I leave England immediately," Thorne said, and Bernard nodded. "That's clever, I have to admit. If I do leave, you won't have my meddlesome influence in the trial, and I'll be abandoning Blackburn, which you can talk Olivier into granting to you. If I stay to help Martine, you'll see that I burn, and you'll still end up with Blackburn."

"There *is* only one logical choice for you to make."

"Love has very little to do with logic," Thorne said. Bernard rolled his eyes.

"Why are you doing this?" Thorne asked. "Knowing that you can get Blackburn even if you release her, why go through with the trial? Why let her die?"

Bernard stood quickly, knocking his chair over. "For the simple, unadulterated pleasure of watching her writhe in torment as the flames peel the flesh from her bones!"

Thorne leaped on the table and lunged at Bernard, but Boyce and two others grabbed him and hauled him back.

Bernard laughed hysterically. "For the thrill of listening to her shriek and beg and moan. *That's* why I'm doing this, woodsman."

Thorne struggled against the three pairs of massive arms.

"She made a fool out of me!" Bernard screamed. More quietly he said, "So did you. But you'll see I'm not so easily bested. I hope you *don't* leave England. I want to see *you* burn, as well. There's no greater form of suffering known to man. Nor, I expect, any more enthralling form of entertainment." He turned toward the stairwell. "Get him out of here," he told Boyce. "And don't give him back his weapons until he's across the drawbridge."

Chapter 24

"It's time, milady," said the guard from the door of the windowless little chamber.

"Just a moment, please." Martine finished plaiting her single braid and secured it with a short bit of string, then slipped on the white linen coif they had given her, letting its ties hang loose. She smoothed down her sacklike gray kirtle, noting how it hung on her thin frame, evidence of the single daily serving of brown bread that had been her sustenance during the month of her imprisonment. She knew it had been a month, because the guards told her the date whenever she asked, and today, the first day of her trial, was June the second.

They'd dressed her almost exactly as the girls had dressed at St. Teresa's, in a severe uniform resembling that of a novice. That was good. It would enhance the impression of piety that she hoped to project, an impression that at one time would have been flagrant fiction, but now could almost pass for the truth. For she had learned something new over the course of this long and arduous month during which she had been questioned ceaselessly, deprived of food and sleep, and threatened not only with the flames of hell, but those of the pyre. She had learned to pray—not to pretend to pray because people were watching and it was what was expected, but to summon all the faith in her heart, inadequate though it might be, and beg God to show her the path that would save her.

"Is this necessary?" she asked as the guard tied her hands in front of her.

"Orders, milady," he replied, leading her out of the chamber for the first time since her captivity had begun. Three other guards surrounded her and together escorted her through the dark stone passages of Battle Abbey to the room in which her trial would take place.

It was a large room, with a dozen armed guards in attendance and scores of people seated on benches around the perimeter, every one of them looking at her. This was all she noticed before her eyes squeezed shut in response to the bright morning sunlight—sunlight she had long pined for but now couldn't bear to face—streaming in through the windows.

Is Thorne here? she wondered as her guards drew her forward, urging her down on a hard little stool in the middle of the room.

Her stool was situated in the midst of a beam of sunlight so blinding that for a moment she could see nothing else. Someone said her name. She raised her bound hands to shield her eyes, but someone else snapped "Lower your hands!" so she did. Voices buzzed, the charges—now all too familiar to her—were read, and other things were said, but she took little note of them, struggling as she was to accustom her eyes to this searing light.

When she finally got used to it and could take in her surroundings, she found that she sat facing Bishop Lambert, who occupied a high, canopied throne on a dais at the far end of the room; most of the onlookers were behind her. The throne, more majestic even than Queen Eleanor's, was upholstered in one shade of red silk, the obese bishop in another. As he spoke, he gestured with his fleshy, bejeweled hands, which glittered and twinkled with every move. Above him hung an ornate, gilded crucifix. To his right a clerk sharpened his quill at one of those little writing desks like the one she had used at St. Dunstan's. To his left, on a long bench, sat a row of black-clad priests, looking very much like crows on a tree branch.

One of them rose and approached her. It was Father Simon. "Lady Falconer . . ."

"Father Simon."

"My lady baroness," the bishop intoned, "you are not to speak unless asked a direct question, and then you are to answer in a simple and straightforward manner. Do you understand?"

"Yes, my lord bishop." If meekness was what was required to avoid the stake, she would swallow her pride and be meek. All of her senses were alert. She must do and say only the right things, the things that would convince the bishop of her innocence.

Bishop Lambert nodded to the clerk, who inked his quill, and then to the priest. "You may proceed, Father."

"My lady," said Father Simon, "when did you receive your demon companion, who most often takes the shape of a cat?" The onlookers murmured briefly before the bishop's upraised hand silenced them. The clerk hunched over his parchment, scratching away industriously.

Martine blinked. "My . . . my what?"

Simon pressed his lips together. "I believe you heard me. When did you receive the creature you call Loki?"

"I . . . three years ago."

"And what form did your master take when he gave you this companion?"

Martine took a deep breath and worded her answer carefully. "A man named Beal gave me Loki. He was a stable hand at St. Teresa's."

Simon turned to the clerk. "Note that this Loki is a minor shape-shifting demon." The clerk nodded as he wrote. "He was granted to her by her master in the form of a man three years ago at the Convent of St. Teresa in Bordeaux. 'Beal' is most likely a shortened form of 'Beelzebub.' "

Someone behind her said, "Oh, for God's sake!"

Thorne! She turned and saw him, on a bench against the wall to her right, sitting with Brother Matthew, Felda, and Geneva. He tried to rise, but Matthew held him down and whispered furiously into his ear as four guards closed in on them.

"Lady Falconer, turn around," the bishop demanded, but Thorne looked directly at her now, and said her name, and Martine couldn't wrest her eyes from his. "Lord Falconer, you will be ejected from this room if you interrupt again, do you understand?"

She saw her husband tense, his expression one of outrage, but then Matthew grabbed his arm and hissed something, and he marshaled his features. "Yes, my lord bishop," he said stiffly.

Bishop Lambert nodded to a guard behind her, who

took her by the shoulders and forced her to face the front once more. As her eyes swept the benches along the wall, she noticed Bernard, sitting back with his legs crossed, smiling, and next to him, Lady Clare.

The bishop nodded to Father Simon, who kept his back to her as he asked, "When your master copulates with you, does he continue to assume the form of his stable hand, or of some other being?"

"*Copulates* with me!"

"Answer!"

"How can I answer that? I don't know what you're talking about. I have no master!"

Simon swung on her. "Heretic! We all have a master, and His name is God Almighty! How dare you so boldly deny His authority!"

"I didn't!"

"You just did."

"Nay! You're confusing me!"

"Silence!" commanded Bishop Lambert. "Lady Falconer, you will cooperate with these proceedings or we'll take you to the pyre immediately, do you understand?"

Helpless and overwhelmed, Martine turned and glanced back toward Thorne. He looked furious, and very grim. Matthew met her eyes and nodded, as if encouraging her to answer the bishop.

"Y-yes, my lord biship," she murmured. "I understand."

Father Simon said, "Lady Falconer's rejection of God's sovereignty is a matter of public knowledge. Guards, bring in the first witness."

There followed a procession of house servants from Harford Castle who stood before the bishop and swore that Martine, refusing to accept Ailith's death, had been heard to say, *To hell with God's will.* They testified also that she had used sorcery to revive the dead child and that Thorne had attacked Father Simon when he tried to prevent it.

At midday the bishop suspended the trial for an hour, and Martine returned to her chamber for her bread and watered ale. When the proceedings resumed, a number of Bernard's men attested to the fact that Edmond seemed incapable of consummating his marriage to her. Bernard himself testified about the jug of adulterated

brandy found in his brother's bedchamber. Not only did
she poison Edmond, he claimed, but she forced his ailing
wife to drink from a jug of claret later found to contain
a suspicious sediment. He bowed his head and crossed
himself as he described how the lady Estrude had become insensible within moments of ingesting the potion,
and died shortly thereafter.

The last witness of the afternoon was Clare.

"My lady," Father Simon began, "the matters which
we must needs discuss at this inquiry are of a nature as
to bruise the sensibilities of an innocent such as yourself.
They are matters that pertain not only to marital affections, but to the marriage act itself. Much as it grieves
us to subject you to such questioning, we beg you to
understand that we do it to serve God's purposes."

"I understand, Father," Clare answered, her voice
soft.

Simon nodded. "Very well. During the time that you
served Lady Falconer at Castle Blackburn, did it ever
strike you that there was anything abnormal about her
marriage?"

An artful pause. "There were whispers. Among the
servants. 'Twas said there was no love lost between
them. And that even though they shared a bed, they
didn't ... that Lord Falconer didn't care to exercise his
marital rights."

"And why do you suppose that was?" the priest
asked.

"Well, I ... I knew she was a sorceress," Clare said.
"Everybody knew it. Everybody at Harford, anyway. I
just assumed she'd done something to keep him away
from her, the same as she did Sir Edmond, God rest his
soul." She solemnly crossed herself, and Father Simon
did the same.

"That would appear to be the case," said the priest.
"Thank you for your testimony, my lady."

That night, Martine dreamed that she was home again.
It was a remarkably vivid dream, and very colorful. She
saw the little panes of glass in her bedchamber windows,
glass the color of seawater with tiny bubbles trapped
inside. She saw beams of warm sunlight pour through
those panes, casting luminous squares onto the colorful

Saracen carpets. She saw her husband, asleep beneath the white down quilts that covered their bed. He woke up and looked at her. His eyes were so brilliantly blue, his gaze so intense, so full of yearning. She reached for him. He was gone.

Thorne! She awoke with a jolt, crying out his name.

She wasn't home. She was imprisoned in Battle Abbey, standing trial for heresy. She might never see Blackburn Castle again. She might never be close enough to Thorne to touch him, or even to talk to him. He had given her a home, had made it warm and beautiful, had protected her. It tormented her to think she would never have the chance to thank him for that, to tell him the things she should have told him long ago. It no longer mattered to her that his passion for land overrode all other passions, making it impossible for him to love her; she understood now that this was simply his nature and he wasn't to blame for it. What mattered was that he wasn't Jourdain, but had long been paying for Jourdain's sins.

She felt the same wrenching despair that had so overwhelmed her when, as a child, she watched Rainulf ride away from St. Teresa's, her heart swelling with words that she couldn't give voice to. But this new despair was even worse than that, flavored as it was with the guilt of having hidden behind her pain for so long, creating a fortress around her soul as thick as the walls around Blackburn Castle—a fortress Thorne had never had a hope of breaking down.

As soon as the guards led Martine into the big room for the second day of the trial, she looked for Thorne. He sat in the same place as the day before, and he smiled at her. Something lit his eyes. Hope? Encouragement? He tilted his head toward the front of the room. Following his gaze, she saw Brother Matthew, standing with a man she didn't know, arguing with Bishop Lambert.

"But what has my lord bishop to fear from the testimony of this man?" the prior asked as Martine took her seat on the little central stool.

The bishop gripped the arms of his throne, his rings

flashing. "Did I say I feared your witness? You are most presumptuous, Brother."

"Then you'll permit me to question him?"

"Nay!" exclaimed Father Simon, jumping up from his bench. " 'Tis most irregular! I'll not allow it!"

"I see," said Matthew. "Pardon me, my lord bishop. I didn't realize I should be making my case to Father Simon." Whispers and giggles broke out among the onlookers. "I'm just a simple monk, and I had no idea the authority to make this decision rested with—"

"It doesn't!" Lambert roared.

Simon bowed obsequiously. "My lord bishop, I only meant—"

"Take your seat, Father! And don't ever think to question my authority again. If I want to hear from this witness, I'll hear from him." He waved a plump hand toward Brother Matthew. "Go ahead. But make it brief."

"Thank you, my lord bishop." He turned to the man— tall, graying, and dressed in the dark robes of an academic—and said, "Are you not John Rankin of Oxford, doctor of medicine?"

"I am he."

Matthew turned to the clerk. "Please note that Dr. Rankin is a physician and a teacher of the healing arts, that he received his medical education at Salerno and Paris, and that he enjoys a sterling reputation among his colleagues at the *Studium Generale* of Oxford. He has treated King Louis of France and King Henry of England, as well as many members of their royal houses."

To Rankin he said, "My first question involves the herbal tonics that Lady Falconer gave to Edmond of Harford and Lady Estrude of Flanders. Father Simon claims they were provided to her by Satan for the purpose of causing impotence and death. The lady herself maintains that in both cases, 'twas naught but a surgical sleeping draft. Do you know of such a draft, and its properties?"

The physician nodded. "There are several recipes for such drafts. Basically, they're mixtures of various sedative herbs, and some are quite powerful. They can induce a very deep sleep with the right dose."

"Is there anything demonic about such drafts, anything supernatural?"

Rankin chuckled. "Nay, Brother. They're ordinary tonics, like any other. The medical community in Paris is well aware of them. I take it that's where Lady Martine learned of hers." Murmurs buzzed through the room; Father Simon scowled.

"One other matter, Master Rankin," Matthew continued. "Do you know of any way to revive a child who has drowned?"

"Nay," said Rankin, to Martine's dismay. "Not if the child is truly dead. But if there's a heartbeat, as I understand was the case with the child in question, and she isn't dead, but merely appears so, then one can try breathing into her mouth . . ." His voice faded beneath the swell of exclamations from the onlookers. The bishop roared for silence, dismissed the witness, and called upon Father Simon to answer the physician's statements.

"My lord bishop," said the priest, "Lady Falconer's knowledge of the healing arts and herbal potions in no way explains the charge of ligature, or impotence, against her present husband, Lord Falconer. For at no time have we claimed that she carried out such sorcery by means of a potion."

"Then how *did* she induce this impotence?" asked the bishop. Although worded as a challenge, his slightly bored tone gave Martine the distinct impression that he already knew the answer. He and Father Simon had undoubtedly discussed these matters at length some time ago.

Simon had his answer ready. "The clever witch can tie knots in a piece of string or leather and hide it, thus hindering the vital spirit from flowing to her victim's generative organs. In addition, 'tis well known that demons—even minor demons such as Lady Falconer's companion—can be employed to instill in a man an aversion for a woman so extreme as to impede carnal copulation. 'Twas undoubtedly this second method that Lady Falconer used on her lord husband."

Martine looked over her shoulder and saw Brother Matthew deep in whispered conversation with both Thorne and Geneva.

Bishop Lambert adopted an expression of curiosity. "Why is that?"

"Because by all accounts, the marriage in question is an unnatural union, devoid of affection of any kind—"

"By all accounts?" interrupted Brother Matthew, rising and pointing to Lady Clare. "By *one woman's* account! Let me ask Thorne Falconer himself whether he has any affection toward—"

"Nay, my lord bishop!" Simon interjected. "She could influence his testimony with her evil eye. It mustn't be permitted."

"Father Simon is right," the bishop decreed. "We couldn't credit his statement."

Brother Matthew strode to the front of the room. "Then let me question the Lady Geneva, Countess of Kirkley."

"Nay!" Father Simon exclaimed. "She knows nothing of these matters."

"Perhaps," Matthew smoothly suggested, "Bishop Lambert would prefer to be the judge of that."

The bishop speared the priest with a poisonous look. "Perhaps he would." Sighing heavily, he gestured toward the prior. "Make it quick."

Geneva came forward.

"My lady countess," Brother Matthew began, "were you present in the great hall of Harford Castle on an afternoon shortly after Lady Falconer's arrest, when Lord Falconer came to discuss certain matters with your brother, Bernard?"

"I was."

"Would you describe that conversation?"

"Lord Falconer offered my brother his barony in exchange for retracting his charges against Lady Falconer."

The room filled with excited conversation. Stunned, Martine wheeled around on her stool. Thorne met her gaze, and she saw in his eyes that it was true—he *had* been willing to give up Blackburn for her. Then he grinned, and she realized her awestruck expression amused him.

"Silence!" Bishop Lambert commanded, adding, this time with a touch of weariness, "Lady Falconer, turn around."

Brother Matthew glanced toward Martine, then asked

Geneva, "Did Lord Falconer say why he was willing to sacrifice so much so that his wife's life might be spared?"

Geneva nodded, her eyes shimmering. "He said he loved her." She met Martine's eyes. "With all his heart."

Again the room erupted in conversation, but Martine was oblivious to it. In a daze, she turned again, and found Thorne looking at her, his eyes filled with the same intensity, the same yearning, that they had held in the dream. The bishop bellowed something. Hands grabbed her and pulled her to her feet.

"Is it—is it over?" Martine asked the guard as he led her out of the room and down the hall.

"All but the formal verdict, milady. The bishop wants everybody back here tomorrow morning. He'll announce it then." He smiled. "Don't you worry none. From the looks of it, they ain't got much of a case against you. You'll be a free woman by noon tomorrow, mark my words."

No sooner had Martine taken her seat on the little stool the next morning than Bishop Lambert cocked a chubby finger at her. "Lady Falconer, rise and approach me." She walked on quaking legs to stand before the high throne.

The bishop looked displeased, and weary. She wondered whether this was good or bad. He cleared his throat; the clerk inked his pen. "As to the offenses of ligature, raising the dead, and murder by poison, I find evidence of demonic involvement to be inadequate, and I therefore declare you innocent of the charge of heresey."

Martine closed her eyes and breathed a silent prayer of thanks.

Many of the onlookers cheered. She turned and saw Thorne grin at her as Matthew slapped him on the back.

One voice rose above the others. "My lord bishop!" It was Father Simon coming through the doorway, his black robes flapping as he sprinted to the front of the chamber. Bernard followed at a more relaxed pace. He caught Martine's eye and nodded; a chill crept up her spine.

"If it please my lord bishop," Simon implored breathlessly, "we have another witness!"

The bishop scowled. " 'Tis a bit late for this, Father. I've just declared her ladyship innocent of all charges."

"But we have a new charge, and this witness—"

"This is outrageous!" Thorne declared.

"A *new* charge?" Matthew exclaimed, rising. "We had no notice that there would be—"

"*Silence!*" the bishop roared. "Monk, take your seat— and see that Lord Falconer keeps his counsel. Sir Bernard, Father Simon—you may approach me."

The three men spoke in hushed tones for some time. Finally the bishop waved them away and announced, "It appears that God's interests would be served by allowing this witness to speak."

Father Simon left the chamber and returned with three men, two of whom he directed to a bench; the third, he led to the front of the room. He was large and hulking, his face disfigured by boils, his gaping mouth revealing many absent teeth. Martine recognized him immediately.

"This man is named Gyrth, my lord bishop," said the priest. "He's the pilot of a merchant longship called the *Lady's Slipper.* 'Twas his craft that brought the Lady Falconer and her brother from Normandy last August."

The bishop nodded. "Proceed with your questioning."

"I'm afraid he can't answer my questions, my lord bishop, except by nodding or shaking his head."

"Very well. Get on with it."

Simon turned to the pilot. "You are mute, are you not?" Gyrth nodded. "Were you always so?" He shook his head. "Is it not a fact that you were struck dumb shortly after transporting Lady Falconer across the Channel last summer?" Another nod. "Is it not also true that, during the crossing, the lady hexed you when you objected to the tempest she had raised? That she claimed she would use her powers to silence your tongue forever?" Again the pilot nodded.

Simon summoned the two other men, one very large, the other very small. It took Martine a moment to recognize them as the two sailors who had been wide-eyed witnesses to her unfortunate outburst on the deck of the *Lady's Slipper.* The priest asked first one, and then the other, "Were you present when Lady Falconer cursed this man's tongue?" Both seemed hesitant, but finally said that they were.

The big one glanced toward Martine, exchanged a quick look with the other, and then said, "Father, if I may, there's something—"

"You may not!" shouted the bishop. "You may answer questions put to you, and that is all."

"But I just—"

"Disrespect for these proceedings carries punishments of its own. If you want to keep your tongue, I suggest you hold it."

The witness bowed his head and mumbled, "Yes, my lord bishop."

Matthew stood as Gyrth and the two sailors were led away. "My lord bishop, I'd like to ask them some—"

"I'm sure you would, brother Matthew, but this trial is now concluded."

"Concluded!"

"I've reached my decision. Take your seat. You, too, Father Simon." The two clerics sat down. "Lady Falconer ..." He gestured her to stand before him, and she obeyed.

The bishop sighed heavily and nodded to his clerk, who commenced to record his words. "It is my judgment that the man known as Gyrth was rendered mute through the workings of sorcery, that you are responsible for such sorcery, and furthermore that such sorcery savors of heresy. Inasmuch as it is written in Exodus, 'Thou shalt not suffer a witch to live,' and in Leviticus, 'A man or woman that hath a familiar spirit, or that is a wizard, shall surely be put to death,' and inasmuch as death by fire most suits the heretic, who will, after all, spend eternity in flames, I therefore sentence you to death by burning at dawn tomorrow, the fourth day of June, the year of our Lord ..."

The roar of blood in Martine's ears was echoed by a roar or disbelief and shock from the onlookers, who rose and began to press in on her. Guards surrounded her, turned her around, and swiftly guided her to the door. Dazed, she couldn't feel the floor beneath her feet or the guards' hands as they gripped her arms. Other guards cleared a path through the crowd for them. Matthew stood on a bench, shouting, "This is unconsciona-

ble! You can't do this! She must be allowed to appeal
to Pope Alexander!''

She heard her name being yelled. *Thorne!* She looked
and saw him being wrestled from the room, his long
arms reaching toward her through those of the guards
who had overpowered him. "Martine!" he screamed.
"Martine!"

Someone stepped in front of her, halting her progress
through the throng: Bernard stood perfectly still in the
midst of the mayhem surrounding them. He said, "They
built the pyre already, you know, outside the city near
the marshes. Our clever Father Simon made certain the
wood was green.'' His mouth smiled; his eyes remained
dead. "Green wood makes for a slow fire. It could take
all morning for you to die. Think on that tonight while
you're trying to sleep."

From inner reserves Martine had never known she
possessed came the strength to lift her chin, look Bernard in the eye, and say, "Whatever agony I may suffer
will last at most a few hours, and then I'll die and my
suffering will end. You'll die someday, too, but 'tis then
your suffering will truly begin, for you'll burn not for a
few hours, but for eternity." She even managed a smile,
to Bernard's evident amazement. "Think on that while
you're trying to sleep tonight."

She did not smile as she knelt on the straw pallet in
her little cell that evening, praying as best she could
while waiting for the priest she had summoned.

"Any priest in particular?" the guard had asked.

"Anyone but Father Simon," she had said.

She felt proud of her performance before Bernard that
afternoon, a performance that, quite satisfyingly, had left
the son of a bitch speechless. Of course, it had all been
false bravado. She felt far from calm and not remotely
brave. She was, in fact, terrified through and through.
The only way she'd been able to keep her senses was to
put her situation out of her mind, not to dwell on her
fate, as Bernard had hoped she would do, but to think
of other things ... of her beloved Rainulf, thousands of
miles away, seeking faith among the infidels. *God, don't
let him grieve too much when he discovers what became
of me,* she prayed. *Make him strong; temper his pain.*

She thought of her home, the first home she had ever truly considered her own, the home she had loved and would never see again. And she thought of Thorne, whose arms would never more embrace her, whose ears would never hear the words that she should have said long ago, and now would never have the chance to.

Finally she heard the key in the lock, and the door swung open. It was dark in her chamber, lit as it was by a single oil lamp, but the hall was bright with torchlight. Silhouetted against it were the stocky guard and a tall man in a cleric's robe, its cowl drooping down over his face. Curiously, the priest withdrew a purse and shook some coins into the guard's outstretched hand. She saw the glint of gold. A fortune had just changed hands!

"Remember," the guard hissed as he pocketed the coins. "One hour, that's all this buys you." The door slammed shut and she heard the snick of the key.

The priest lowered the cowl and she saw the face of her husband, his eyes incandescent in the dim room. She tried to say his name, but instead there rose from her an inarticulate cry of joy. Her hands abandoned their attitude of prayer and reached out to him as he crossed to her, knelt, and gathered her in his arms.

"Thorne! Thorne!" she gasped, her words muffled against his shoulder. He crushed her to him, kissing her hair, whispering her name. "Thorne ... thank God you're here. Thank God! I can tell you ... I needed to tell you...."

"Nay. I know what's in your heart. You needn't—"

"I do need to." She pulled her head back and looked him in the eye. "I need to tell you. This is my last chance to tell you, and I should have told you before, but ... I love you. I love you so much, and I've always loved you, but I've been such a fool. Please forgive me."

"I'm the one who needs forgiveness. I left you that morning. If I hadn't left you, they wouldn't have taken you."

"I drove you away. I was so cold, so ... I drove you to that ... that place."

He smiled slightly. "I slept with nothing warmer than a brandy jug that night. I haven't been with another woman since I was first with you. I never wanted anyone else after that. I never will."

He leaned down and kissed her. It was a kiss of great tenderness and passion, and Martine returned it spontaneously, her hands reaching up to pull his head closer. *I want to be a part of him,* she thought. *I am a part of him.* When they drew apart, they were breathless.

"I don't mind dying so much now," she said. "I can face it, knowing I've told you—"

"You're not going to die," he said huskily. "I won't let it happen. I can't lose you now. I love you too much to lose you."

Hope ignited in her breast. "Is there some way out of here? Have you come to help me get out?"

Grimly he shook his head. "The corridors are lined with armed guards. Bernard told them about your escape from Harford Castle, so they've made certain you can't get out of here."

"Then it's hopeless," she said. "Please thank Brother Matthew for helping me. If only he could have questioned those two sailors."

"They did seem rather reluctant witnesses."

"More than reluctant. There was something they wanted to say, but the bishop wouldn't allow it. They know something, something that would have pointed to my innocence. I'm certain of it."

"I sensed that, too," Thorne said thoughtfully. "But unfortunately, so did the bishop. You heard him—he threatened to have their tongues cut out if they talked."

"And their silence means that tomorrow I'll burn."

He gripped her shoulders hard. "Nay! You mustn't think that. I *will* save you."

"How?"

"Tomorrow at dawn, when they take you out of here, to transport you to . . ."

"To the pyre," she supplied.

He nodded. "Then you'll be in the open. Then 'twill be easier."

"But what will you do?"

"I don't know. I'll have to see what route they take you by, how many guards—"

"Nay," she said. "I'll be surrounded by guards, you know that. You can't save me, Thorne. Don't risk your life trying to. Get out of England now, tonight, before they arrest you, too—"

"You can't think I'd flee in the middle of the night and leave you to—"

"Go to the harbor. Get in a boat. There's no way to help me now. I can't be saved. But you can. Please—"

He stifled her objections with another kiss, this one harder, more desperate. "Nay!" he said when he broke away. "I'll not leave you." She opened her mouth to object, but he pressed his fingers to her lips. "Nay, love. I'll not leave you, and there's nothing more to be said." He kissed her forehead.

"Do something for me, then," she said quietly. "To-morrow, when they ... when they tie me to the stake and—" He started to speak, but she said, "Please, Thorne. Let me ask this of you." He nodded. "I'm a coward," she said. "I don't want to die ... that way. Not that way, not by fire."

He closed his eyes and clenched his jaw, and she knew he thought of Louise, his cherished little sister, lost to the flames.

"Don't let me burn, that's all I ask. You can make it quick." He looked puzzled. "With an arrow."

Comprehension dawned. "Oh, Martine ..." He shook his head.

"Please," she begged, holding his face in her hands. "Do for me what you did for the deer. That stag that Bernard and his men ran into the guardroom? Do for me what you did for it. Kill me quickly before I feel the flames. 'Twill be an act of mercy."

"It won't come to that."

"But if it does. Promise me, please."

"Martine, I love you! I can't—"

"If you love me, have mercy on me. Be strong, For me. Please! Promise me! Promise me you won't let me burn."

He lowered his head and closed his eyes. Presently he whispered, "I promise." Looking up, he added, "But I won't need to. I'll save you before it comes to that. I wish I could do it sooner. I wish I could take you away from here right now."

"You can," she murmured, then lifted her face to his and kissed him. "For a little while, anyway." She lay back on the pallet and drew him down on top of her, then kissed him again, lingeringly, ardently. He seemed momentarily stunned, but then he returned the kiss with a deep, almost anguished moan.

She arched against him, and he pulled away, rasping, "Are you sure?"

"Please. Make me forget where I am. Make me forget everything but us. Just for a little while."

He was gentle, very gentle. His hands moved slowly, deliberately, caressing her through her kirtle as he breathed words of love into her ear. He untied the string from her braid and pulled his fingers through her hair. They undressed each other in silence, then lay side by side, just touching, their eyes locked in wordless but intimate communication. His fingertips brushed her face, her throat, her breasts; hers traveled the width of his shoulders, grazed his chest. She felt his heart pulsing within him, felt the love flowing from him into her, coursing through them, uniting them.

When she reached down and cautiously closed her fingers around him, his breath caught. She lightly stroked him, awed at how he swelled in her hand. He touched her as well, smiling into her eyes when he felt how ready she was for him.

Still lying on his side, he slid his hand down her thigh, raised her knee, and guided her leg up, over his hip. His eyes never strayed from hers as he positioned himself, reached around her hips to hold her still, and entered her in one smooth, deep stroke. She moaned at the sweet invasion. He withdrew and reentered her, capturing her second moan—and third, and fourth, and all that followed—in his mouth. They moved together in perfect unity, intuitively matching each other's rhythm, like a single being.

He broke the kiss. "Look at me," he whispered hoarsely. "Please, love, look at me." She did. His eyes glittered like those of a man consumed by fever. *He's inside me,* she thought. *He's a part of me.*

She writhed on the edge of release until she thought she'd scream. As her pleasure crested, he rolled her onto her back, his large hands cupping her bottom, tilting her toward him. The thrusts that followed sank deep, filling not just her womb, it seemed, but her entire body, her very soul.

We are one now. On the verge of climax, she tightened

her arms around him, pulling him hard against her, her head thrown back. A desperate sob rose within her; hot tears spilled from her eyes.

He trembled. "I love you," he gasped as they both tumbled over the edge, their breathless, inarticulate cries mingling in the little chamber.

As their convulsive pleasure subsided, he sank on her, his face pressed into the crook of her neck. It was wet. His big shoulders shook, but not a sound came from him.

When he left Battle Abbey that night, Thorne headed directly for Bulverhythe Harbor, tossing his black cleric's robe in an abandoned well on the way. Beneath, he wore a plain dark tunic. That was good. Better to look like a common man tonight than a baron. If he was lucky, no one would know who he was.

Leaving Martine in her little chamber when the guard came for him was the hardest thing he'd ever had to do. But saving her would be even harder.

He tried the largest tavern first. Ordering a pint, he sat at a table in back and scanned the patrons—fishermen mostly, a few merchant sailors, and the standard assortment of cutpurses and knaves. Leaving his tankard full, he got up and went to the alehouse next door. The same sort of crowd, a little heavier on the criminal element perhaps. He counted three missing hands and as many absent eyes.

By the eighth tavern he grew impatient, and increasingly discouraged. This time he actually drank the ale he ordered, swallowing it all in one tilt and gesturing for another. There were only three or four more public houses in the harbor besides the ones he'd already been to. When he'd visited them all, should he start over at the first, or would he be wiser to move on to the brothels? . . . He emptied the second pint down his throat and slammed it on the table. . . . Or should he just get stinking drunk and tear this place apart—upturn the tables, kick over the benches, punch out the shutters, and perhaps one or two of the patrons?

It was then that he saw the two sailors, one enormous, the other short and thin, who walked in from the street and took a table near the door. *Thank you, God,* Thorne whispered under his breath as he slowly rose and walked over to them. They looked up as he approached, and he could see from their expressions that they didn't recognize him. He greeted them in the old tongue, and they responded in kind, a bit warily. Then he held up three fingers to the alewife, who poured three fresh pints and brought them over.

"Many thanks, friend," said the bigger man, hoisting his tankard. "But if there's something you want from us, you'd best come out with it now."

Thorne shrugged casually and took a seat. "I recognized you from Lady Falconer's heresy trial this afternoon."

The little one reached into his pocket and withdrew a mouse, which he held cupped in one hand while he petted it with the other. "You were there?"

He nodded. "Aye. Didn't think much of the way you were treated, though. Felt sorry for you."

The big one belched. "The one I feel sorry for is that young baroness they're going to burn tomorrow."

The other one grunted and nodded his head. He brought the mouse to his lips and gave it a kiss, then dipped his finger in his tankard and let the creature lick the ale from it.

"But . . . if she's a heretic . . ." Thorne began carefully.

The small man rubbed the mouse on his cheek. "She's no more a heretic than my little Rosamund. She never done what they say she done."

Thorne watched them drain their pints. *Careful, now,* he cautioned himself. *Don't act too eager, or they won't trust you. Trust will loosen their tongues. That, and enough ale.*

"Really?" he said, catching the alewife's eye and holding up two fingers. He took a deep breath and made his tone nonchalant. "And why do you say that?"

Chapter 25

"Are you ready, milady?" asked the guard, standing in the doorway of her chamber with a length of rope in his hand.

Ready? thought Martine as she adjusted the linen coif on her head. *How can anyone be "ready" to burn to death?* But she simply nodded and held out her trembling hands.

The guard looked sheepish. "Behind your back today, milady." He shrugged. "That's what they said."

Martine hesitated, then clasped her hands behind her and turned around. *I will be dignified,* she silently promised herself as the guard secured her wrists with the rope. *I will not cry or beg for mercy. I will not make a spectacle of myself.*

More guards converged on her as she left the chamber. By the time she stepped into the open air, she had quite an escort. It was barely light out, and many among the considerable crowd carried torches. The guards lifted her into a cart, and several of them got in with her. The sheriff and his men rode in front, with a dozen more armed men behind. A few priests, including Father Simon, brought up the rear. It was only the second time in her life she had ever ridden in a wheeled vehicle, the first being her abduction from Blackburn Castle. The cart rattled and bounced vigorously over mud that had dried in ruts on the roadbeds of Hastings. She couldn't have remained standing had the guards not held her up.

Despite the early hour, the streets were lined with people who'd awakened early to come out and watch her being transported to the pyre. Martine had expected this. Executions always drew a crowd. But in the past, whenever she'd seen people gathered for this purpose, they had been noisy, almost festive—taunting the condemned and even tossing garbage at him. Curiously, not a soul among the hundreds of people she passed spoke a word, except for one who shouted, "God be with you, Lady Falconer!" Instead, they silently crossed themselves; some were crying. Clearly the people of Hastings were unconvinced of her guilt, and most likely shocked at the form of execution. Hangings were common, as were beheadings for those of noble blood. But burning . . .

Don't think about it. Don't think about it, she repeated over and over to herself. Perhaps Thorne *would* save her, unlikely though that seemed. And if he couldn't, he had promised to end her life with a merciful arrow before she could feel the flames. She had to believe he would. It was the only way she could maintain her composure.

On the outskirts of the city, near the surrounding marshlands, the ground rose slightly. At the highest point, the stake had been driven and the pyre built. A large audience had gathered, but they were, like those who had watched her pass through the city, completely silent. The cart pulled up in back of the crowd, and Martine scanned the faces of those who turned to look up at her. With a sinking heart she noted that Thorne's was not among them.

Don't think about it. Don't think about it. But if he didn't come in time, if they tied her to the stake and lit the pyre . . . *Don't think about it!*

The guards lifted her down from the cart and led her through the throng, who parted for her, crossing themselves and murmuring blessings. Felda was there, sobbing. She reached toward her mistress, but a guard pushed her roughly back. Brother Matthew emerged from the crowd. When the guards went for him, he held up a little wooden crucifix, which stilled them. They even had the grace to back off for a moment while the prior tucked the crucifix into one of Martine's bound hands and kissed her on the cheek, whispering, "God is with you."

The sheriff stood before the pyre and read a document prepared by the bishop, which stated that the Church had condemned her to death for the crime of heresy and had given her into the hands of the secular authorities for execution. He glanced briefly at Martine, and she thought he looked sad, even remorseful. Nevertheless, he nodded to the burly hangman, who took her by the arms and led her to the place of execution, her hands still tied behind her. A barrel stood in the midst of the pile of green branches surrounding the stake, and this he lifted her onto. She smelled tar. Looking down, she saw it oozing from a crack in the barrel. To the side were two bushels of coal and several loads of peat. Clearly they expected to be feeding the slow-burning fire for a long time.

It could take all morning for you to die ... Bernard had said.

Chills coursed through her. A surge of nausea gripped her stomach, and she sucked in great lungfuls of air to dampen it. *Don't think about it, for God's sake!*

Someone threw the hangman a coil of rope. Reaching up, he looped it around Martine's neck and lashed it firmly to the stake. The pressure drew her head back; the rope tightened around her throat. Tremors seized her instantly. It hadn't occurred to her that they would tie her by her neck, and for some reason she found it inexpressibly terrifying. She couldn't move. She could barely swallow the sour bile in her mouth.

"N-not my neck. Please," she said hoarsely.

"I'm sorry, milady," the hangman whispered. "Truly I am. But I've no choice in the matter. These were Father Simon's instructions."

Her heart slammed painfully in her chest. Where was Thorne? Her eyes darted among the onlookers. *Thorne! Where are you? Please, Thorne, don't let them do this to me!*

Passing the rope around her chest and hips and legs, the hangman secured her entire body to the stake. Her breath raced and a whimper rose in her throat as she watched Father Simon approach with a torch in his hand, flanked by Bernard and Gyrth. She closed her eyes and tried to pray, but then she opened them and again searched for Thorne. *God, please! Send Thorne to me!*

The hangman tried to take the torch from Simon, but the priest held it aside, saying, " 'Tis the judgment of Bishop Lambert that the honor of lighting the pyre

should go to the victim of this heretic's evil sorcery."
He handed the torch to Gyrth.

The hangman looked to the sheriff, who said, " 'Tis *my* judgment that the Church would do well not to meddle so in secular affairs, Father. Lady Falconer is not the bishop's responsibility anymore, she's mine, and she'll be executed by the public hangman same as anyone else."

Father Simon glared at him. "The bishop's responsibility encompasses everyone's affairs. Most notably in the matter of excommunication—a punishment he rarely hesitates to pronounce when he is displeased."

The sheriff looked disgusted. Martine could tell he wanted to resist this seizure of his authority, but hesitated to risk the pain of excommunication. The hangman made it easy for him: "If I may, my lord sheriff, lighting this pyre is a task I'm not much looking forward to. Let the bastards do the job themselves, if that's what they want." He punctuated his words by spitting on the ground.

The sheriff sighed heavily, then stepped aside.

Bernard spoke: " 'Twould seem the time has come." He looked up and smiled maliciously toward Martine, then nodded to Gyrth. "Go ahead."

The big man shambled up to the pyre, holding the torch in his outstretched hand. Martine felt its heat as it neared, and flinched, imagining that heat consuming her, charring her flesh. Her eyes passed over the upturned faces one last time, searching wildly. A movement from behind the crowd caught her eye—someone leaped up onto the cart.

Thorne! He held a shortbow, and had a quiver of arrows slung on his back. Martine met his eyes and silently mouthed the word *Please.* He reached behind for an arrow and swiftly drew it, determination in his gaze. As he aimed, she closed her eyes. *'Twill be quick,* she thought. *Thanks to Thorne, 'twill be quick.*

The heat came closer. She heard the muffled *pfft* of the arrow as it flew, and braced herself.

Startled gasps erupted from the onlookers. It took her a moment to comprehend that she hadn't been shot, and then despair washed over her. He had missed! How could he have missed? At the sound of cheers, she opened her eyes. Gyrth, his hands empty, stared open-mouthed at something behind the pyre, toward which Bernard stalked angrily. When he came back into view, he held the still-flaming torch, impaled with Thorne's arrow.

"Gyrth!" yelled Thorne from the cart. "I demand that you speak!"

"This is absurd!" exclaimed Father Simon. "He can't speak. He's mute."

Thorne shook his head. "No, he's not. Speak, damn you!"

Gyrth raised his chin defiantly.

Thorne gestured to two men on the ground, who climbed up into the cart. It was the two sailors who had testified at the trial. "These are your men, are they not?"

"The trial is over!" said Father Simon. "Sentence has been pronounced. Sheriff, I command you to arrest Lord Falconer and those two—"

"I'm not yours to command, priest," the sheriff retorted, then turned to Gyrth. "Answer him. Are those your men?"

Gyrth nodded.

Thorne said, "These two tell me that you didn't stop speaking until right before you were called upon to testify. Did it take ten months for my wife's spell to take effect, or is it possible there was no spell to begin with? *Answer* me!"

Gyrth merely shook his head.

"What do you suppose the penalty is for false testimony in an ecclesiastical court?" Thorne challenged. "If I can prove you lied—and believe me, I can—what do you think they'll do to you? Cut your tongue out? Excommunicate you? Perhaps *you'll* be lashed to a stake and burned. There would be a certain amount of justice to that, I think."

Still Gyrth maintained his silence. It amazed Martine that he would continue so stubbornly to deny the truth, even when threatened with such cruel punishments. It occurred to her that, regardless of whatever other motive he had for lying about the spell, he must despise her intensely.

Steadying her voice, she said, "I—I want to say something, before you . . ." She glanced at the torch, and then met Gyrth's gaze. "I know—I *think* I know—why you hate me so much. In part I suppose it's simply because I'm a Norman. My—my husband is a Saxon, and he's told me things. He's told me what my people have done to yours, and I think I understand a little better why your people hate mine."

She glanced at Thorne, who nodded in encouragement. "But I also know that there's more to it than that. During the crossing, I was ... arrogant and thoughtless. The things I said, the way I treated you ... I ridiculed you in front of your men. 'Twas inexcusable. I thought your beliefs were ignorant, primitive. But my husband has taught me much about the ways of his people, and now I know that I was the ignorant one. That's all I wanted to say, just that I'm sorry, and that I understand ... why you're doing this. I forgive you. But I beg you, with all my heart, to forgive me as well."

No one spoke. Gyrth stood with his head bowed, his meaty hands fisted. When he looked back up at her there were tears in his eyes. "God forgive me for what I was about to do," he said. The onlookers murmured excitedly. Gyrth shook his head. " 'Twas ... 'twas wrong, very wrong." He pulled something out of his pocket, some silver coins. To Bernard he said, "I'm giving you back your six shillings. I don't want your money."

"He paid for your false testimony?" asked Thorne.

"Aye, milord." He shook his head and walked away mumbling, "God forgive me."

The sheriff said, "Bernard of Harford, I arrest you—"

"Not quite yet," Bernard growled, yanking the arrow from the torch. "I came here for entertainment, and will *not* be disappointed."

He turned to Martine, holding the torch not toward the pyre, but toward the skirt of her linen kirtle. It would ignite instantly, she knew. She would be mortally burned before they could find a way to put out the fire. Chuckling, he called to Thorne, "That was a pretty trick, woodsman, shooting a torch out of someone's hand. Think you can pull it off twice?"

Thorne whipped an arrow from his quiver, aimed, and shot, all in the time it took Martine to draw a breath. The crowd roared before she even realized what had happened ... before she looked down and saw Bernard sprawled faceup on the ground, twitching, the Saxon's arrow protruding from his chest.

"Probably not," said Thorne.

Bernard looked up, directly into Martine's eyes, his expression of surprise giving way to fury. But presently his spasms ceased, his eyelids closed halfway, and his lungs emptied in a final ragged sigh.

Martine felt a rush of cold as the blood drained from her head. The noise of the crowd blurred into a muffled din, and then everything went gray and she felt nothing. ...

Sensation returned in the form of a whisper. "Drink this. Come, now, love. ..."

She took a long swallow from the wineskin held to her mouth.

"That's right."

The wine was sweet. But the feel of Thorne's arms around her, the warmth of his chest against her back, his shoulder beneath her head, was infinitely sweeter. He held her curled in his embrace as he sat leaning against a tree. His touch was so warm, so comforting, so perfect ... She never wanted it to end.

She saw the pyre off in the distance. People still gathered about it, swarming busily, but she couldn't hear them. She could barely see them, although the sun had risen.

It's in the past, she thought dreamily, settling against her husband and breathing in his comforting scent. She pressed her ear to his chest, the better to hear his heartbeat. With every steady thump, the fear and pain that had long darkened her soul receded further and further into the past. Closing her eyes for a moment, she felt the whisper-soft tugs of an unseen ribbon as it twined lazily around them both, binding them together, always and forever.

Thorne kissed her hair, her temple, her cheek. He nuzzled her ear and murmured, "Do you think you can walk?"

Martine flexed her toes and grinned. "Probably not."

He scooped her up in his arms and rose gracefully to his feet. "I'll carry you all the way back to Blackburn if I have to. I can't wait any longer. We're going home.''

She wrapped her arms around his neck and gazed into his eyes, eyes as perfectly blue as the brightening morning sky overhead. "Home. Yes, I'd like that. Take me home.''

Dear Reader,

Thank you for sharing the excitement of *Falcon's Fire* with me! From the moment Martine of Rouen and Thorne Falconer first made themselves known to me, whispering their tale of forbidden love into my ear, I've been completely caught up in their world.

It is a world of superstition and salvation, betrayal and enlightenment ... a time of devastating ignorance and startling new ideas. In an era of arranged marriages and strict rules of behavior, there bubbles an irrepressible undercurrent of desire and intrigue, as natural human passions struggle to assert themselves.

One of this story's more enigmatic characters is Martine's brother, Rainulf, a freethinking teaching priest who epitomizes the intellectual awakening of the twelfth-century Renaissance. He is a man of great honor and virtue ... and grave self-doubt.

After Rainulf left for the Holy Land, I kept wondering what would happen to him. Would his pilgrimage cure him of his crisis of faith, or worsen it? Would it be possible for him to learn to live with his human frailties—even embrace them? Could a tormented and disillusioned medieval academic find redemption through the love of a woman? What kind of woman could crack his armor and teach him to love life and himself? And what of his vows?

The result of these musings is *Heaven's Fire,* in which Rainulf, during a visit to a humble village to administer last rites to a smallpox victim, comes upon a remarkable young woman digging her own grave. *Heaven's Fire,* a 1996 release from Topaz, will be a journey of suspense, rebirth, and liberating love, set in the medieval college town of Oxford. It's another journey I hope we'll make together.

I'd love to hear what you think of *Falcon's Fire*. p.ryan10@genie.geis.com is my electronic mail address. Or you can write me at the following post office box, including a self-addressed, stamped business-size envelope if you'd like to receive my newsletter: P.O. Box 26207, Rochester, NY 14626

Pat Ryan

Heaven's Fire
by Patricia Ryan

March 1161, Oxford

"Duck, Father!"

Rainulf of Rouen, also known as Rainulf Fairfax—Doctor of Logic and Theology, *Magister Scholarum* of Oxford, and ordained priest—lowered his head just in time to avoid being struck by a flying tankard of ale.

"What the—?"

"It's Victor, Father," said Thomas. The young, sandy-haired scholar pointed to the rear of the alehouse, where Victor of Asekirche was climbing on top of a table, cheered on by his rowdy friends. "He wasn't aiming for you," Thomas explained. "He's got a quarrel with Burnell."

Rainulf turned to see the tavern keeper—a huge, barrel-chested brute in a greasy apron—reach beneath the counter, from which he dispensed his ale and meat pies.

"Uh-oh . . ." Rainulf swiftly drained his tankard and stood as Burnell produced an oaken club studded with nails. He didn't particularly want to involve himself in this altercation, and he wouldn't, were it not for Burnell's reputation for viciousness. He'd savagely beaten more than one scholar since they began flocking to Oxford just a few short years ago. It was even rumored he'd been responsible for a young man found bludgeoned to death last August in an alley off Fish Street. Victor, despite his many faults, did not deserve such a fate.

"Put it down, Burnell," Rainulf said quietly.

"This is none of your affair, priest," Burnell growled in anglicized French. He hefted the club in a beefy hand as he muscled his way through the boisterous assemblage of half-drunk students. "I told that one not to come in here no more, but he don't listen too good." Gripping the spiked club with both hands, he swung it back and forth through the dark, stale air of the tavern, sending his young patrons scattering. "He'll mind me now, I wager."

"He's afraid to have me come in here!" Victor declared to the black-robed scholars crowded around the table on which he stood, hands on hips. "And do you know why?"

Rainulf ran a weary hand through his short hair. Young Victor, with his darkly striking looks and firebrand temperament, exercised tremendous influence over his fellow scholars. Were he of a mind to, he could use that influence to help dampen the spark of discord between the students of Oxford and the city's businessmen. Instead, he chose to fan it into flames of rage.

Burnell advanced a step, shaking his weapon in the air. "*I'll* tell you why I don't want you here! 'Cause you're a troublemaker, plain and simple. You don't know when to shut up."

Victor crossed his arms over his chest and adopted a careless, hip-shot stance. "Oh, I know when to shut up, all right, and I will. *After* I've told everybody about the sewage-tainted water you brew your ale with."

Burnell's face darkened with fury. "What? You've got no proof—"

"And God knows what's in those meat pies."

Burnell raised the club. "You little—"

"If you charged a fair price, I might not mind so much," Victor said. "But on top of it all, you're a thief!"

"That's it! Come down here and fight me like a man!" Victor withdrew something from beneath his black robe. Rainulf saw the flash of steel and cursed under his breath. The young man jumped down from the table and sliced the dagger through the air.

"Victor!" Rainulf stepped between the two men. "Both of you. Let's go outside and talk about—"

"No more talk, Father," Victor spat out. "It's time for action." He raised his voice and looked around at his inebriated audience. "It's time to let the brewers and innkeepers and landlords of Oxford know that those of

us who've come here to study will not lie down for this
kind of treatment anymore! It's time to demand decent
food and drink and clean, safe rooms for our money!"

Cries of "Hear, hear!" filled the tavern.

Rainulf gestured toward the blade in Victor's hand.
"And you think that's the way?"

"It's the only way his kind"—he nodded toward Burnell—"understands."

Burnell took a step toward Victor. "What's that supposed to mean?"

Victor stepped forward as well. "Let me state it simply, so you'll grasp my meaning. If I have a dog and it
does something wrong, do I try to reason with it? Nay,
twould be a waste of breath. I beat it, because that's all
it understands. 'Tis the same with those men who are
little more than beasts themselves—"

Burnell brandished the club. "Get out of my way,
Father."

"Nay." Rainulf reached for the club. "Hand it over."

Burnell yanked it away and stepped around him, raising the weapon high as Victor turned toward him. In
the space of a heartbeat Rainulf seized a small bench
off the floor and brought it swiftly upward. It shattered
on impact with the club, but succeeded in halting its
downward progress. The priest wrested the weapon from
Burnell and hurled it into the sawdust that covered the
floor.

Grabbing the plank that had formed the bench's seat,
Rainulf wheeled to face Victor as he thrust his dagger
toward the dazed tavern keeper. Throwing himself between the two, he slammed the plank into Victor's midsection. For a moment the hotheaded young scholar
froze, looking slightly confused. Then he sank to his
knees in the sawdust, the dagger slipping out of his fingers. Rainulf kicked it away and tossed aside the plank.

Raking both hands through his hair, Rainulf addressed
the wide-eyed onlookers. "It's over. Go back to your
ale." As the crowd dispersed, Burnell's wife guided her
husband into the back room. Rainulf hauled Victor to
his feet and aimed him toward the door. "I won't always
be around to protect you from your own foolishness,
Victor. Take my advice and keep clear of Burnell." He

gave a not-so-gentle shove, and the young man lurched out into the bright noon sunshine and stumbled away.

Thomas stared at him. "You handle yourself well, Father. Did you learn to fight like that in the Holy Land?"

"Nay—at the University of Paris. I didn't fight like that in the Holy Land."

Thomas frowned. "But surely, on crusade, you fought—"

"To kill," Rainulf finished shortly. "That's a different kind of fighting."

Thomas seemed to digest that for a moment, and then he nodded toward the front door. "Do you know that fellow?"

The man standing in the doorway had hair the color of polished copper and a milk white face showered with hundreds of freckles. He wore a plain, clean tunic and clutched a leather bag.

Rainulf shook his head. "I would have remembered those freckles."

The stranger scanned the room, stilling when his gaze lit on Rainulf. This interest surprised Rainulf not in the least. His height alone often drew attention. And in this dank little student tavern, he would seem sorely out of place, being the only master present and—and six and thirty years—by far the oldest man.

"Are you the one they call Rainulf Fairfax?" the stranger asked, his gaze resting on the priest's flaxen hair—the feature that had earned him the surname from his students.

"Aye."

He looked down at Rainulf's black robe—not a clerical robe, as would be expected, but the *cappa* of a secular master, the open front of which revealed an ordinary brown tunic and chausses beneath. "They told me you were a priest."

Someone cleared his throat; someone else chuckled.

"They were right—more or less," Rainulf answered. A few of the scholars laughed good-naturedly, but Rainulf maintained his neutral expression.

"Are you or aren't you?"

"Why is it so important?" Rainulf demanded.

"I need a priest who's had smallpox," said the red-haired man. "They told me you fit that description."

"They?"

The man shrugged. "A couple of the other masters. If they were mistaken, kindly advise me so and I'll trouble you no further."

"They weren't mistaken. But what's this about the pox?"

"There's been a lot of it in the village of Cuxham the past few weeks. I need you to perform last rites."

"I'm a teaching priest," Rainulf said. "I haven't performed the offices of the church in years. There must be a parish priest in Cuxham. Can't *he* do it?"

"He's *been* doing it," said the stranger. "Only now he's come down with it himself. A bad case, too, but hopefully one of the last ones—I think this outbreak has run its course. Anyway, Father Osred's dying, most likely, and I promised Sir Roger Foliot I'd bring back a priest to give him last rites. Only, I've got to find one who's already had the pox, so as not to spread the contagion."

He spoke like a man who knew something of disease. Rainulf glanced at the stranger's bag. "Are you a physician?"

"A traveling surgeon. My name's Will Geary. So, will you go?"

Rainulf spent a moment trying to summon up a good reason for refusing. Failing to do so, he sighed heavily and nodded. "I'll go."

Stopping briefly at his Saint John Street town house, Rainulf changed into sturdy traveling clothes and packed the things he'd need into his saddlebag. As an afterthought, he searched for and found a tiny silver reliquary containing a lock of hair of Saint Nicaise, and slipped it in among the vestments and vials.

It was unusually warm for March, and despite his grim mission, Rainulf found the journey to Cuxham a pleasant one. Keeping to the route suggested by Will Geary, he rode twelve miles to the southeast until he reached the mill that marked the northern boundary of Cuxham. From thence he followed the stream south through woods and farmland, until presently he came upon the small stone and thatch parish church. Behind it stood the rectory, as he had been told, and he would have ridden directly to it had his eye not been drawn to a figure in the churchyard, digging a grave. He drew up his mount and watched from a distance, strangely captivated by the sight.

It was a woman—her age indeterminate, for she faced away from him—dressed in a homespun kirtle, her black hair plaited in two long braids tied together in back. Next to her on the ground, shaded from the mid-afternoon sun by a yew tree, lay a corpse beneath a blanket.

Dismounting, Rainulf hobbled his bay stallion by the stream and approached the woman, who still seemed unaware of his presence. As he got closer, he saw not one but two empty graves dug into the earth. One appeared to be finished, given the sizable mound of dirt next to it. The other was still but a shallow trench. It was this second, just begun grave on which the woman labored so industriously, yet hampered by fatigue, if the slowness of her movements was any indication.

Rainulf looked around for a second corpse, but could see none. He did notice, scattered among the weathered headstones in the churchyard, several fresh graves—victims of the pox, no doubt.

He paused about ten feet from the woman and cleared his throat. She gasped and spun around, holding the shovel as if to swing it. Her face bore a bright red flush, and her hands shook. Rainulf saw fear in her wide brown eyes, then confusion. "You're not . . ." she began in the old Anglo-Saxon tongue. "I thought perhaps you were Sir . . ." She took a deep breath, as if relieved, and lowered the shovel. "Who are you?"

Rainulf took a step toward her, but she raised the shovel again, and he stopped in his tracks.

"Don't come any closer," she said. She had an odd, husky voice, unexpected in a woman of such slight build.

Rainulf held both hands up, palms out. "Easy," he said in English. "I'm Rainulf Fairfax. *Father* Rainulf Fairfax, from Oxford."

Her gaze took in his short, tousled hair, over which he wore no skullcap, and his rough traveling costume. "You don't look like much of a priest."

"I'm not," he dryly agreed.

A spark of amusement flashed in her eyes. Taking this

for encouragement, Rainulf stepped forward again, but she thrust the shovel at him. "Get back!"

"I won't hurt you," he said reassuringly.

She smiled somewhat wryly. "I didn't think you would. It's just that I've got the yellow plague, and I wouldn't want you to catch it."

Rainulf's gaze narrowed on her reddened face. What he'd thought at first to be a flush of fear had not subsided, nor had the trembling of her hands. He suspected that, were she to let him touch her, her skin would be burning hot. This was how this awful disease began, he knew—with fever and chills and that strange scarlet tinge to the face and body. The pox themselves would appear later.

"Rest your mind, then," he said. "I've had this affliction already. I can't catch it again."

Her eyes searched his face. "You've had this?"

"I had several interesting diseases while a guest of the Turks some years back. Smallpox—what you call the yellow plague—was one of them." He tilted his head, pointing at the two minuscule indentations on the side of his jaw.

Lowering the shovel, the woman approached him slowly, her gaze riveted on the scars. "That's all the pockmarks you've got?" she asked incredulously. "Just those?"

"I was lucky,"

"*I'll* say." She inclined her head toward the corpse under the yew. "Father Osred didn't get off so easily."

Rainulf walked over to the body and squatted down. He reached for the edge of the blanket to uncover the face but hesitated, smelling, in addition to the stench of death, the distinctive, sickening odor of the final stages of smallpox. It was an odor that conjured up vivid memories. Closing his eyes, he found himself transported back to the Levant, to that foul underground cell in which he and two dozen other young soldiers for Christ endured a year of hellish suffering. Their torment found new depths when the pox swept through their stinking hole, claiming one out of every four men and leaving most of the rest wishing they'd been taken.

Peeling back the blanket, Rainulf sucked in a breath and executed a hasty sign of the cross. The face on which he gazed was so densely covered with yellowish pustules as to completely mask its features. The poor creature's thin white hair was the only indication of age. Had Rainulf not known the body to be that of the rector, he might even have thought it to be female.

"It's best this way," the woman said. Rainulf turned to find her standing right behind him, leaning on the shovel and staring thoughtfully at the dead priest. "He went blind in the end. Some of them do, you know."

"I know." He swallowed hard. She looked at him inquiringly, and he met her eyes, drawn to something in them that surprised and touched him. Compassion. She felt compassion . . . for him! Here she was, suffering from this appalling malady that killed and blinded and disfigured; yet, sensing his own grief, his own nightmare, she had it within her to feel sympathy for him.

A most strange woman, he thought, holding her gaze. In their warm depths he saw curiosity and humor, and something else . . . wisdom. The wisdom of the ages.

"How old are you?" he asked.

She laughed, displaying teeth so straight and white as to be the envy of the noblest lady. Her smile was delightful, and infectious. Rainulf was actually tempted to laugh himself—odd, given that he hadn't laughed in a very long time, and somewhat inappropriate under the circumstances. Instead, he marshaled his expression and asked, "What's so funny?"

"You," she said. "You're rather an odd person, that's all."

"Me?" He pulled the blanket back over the body and stood. "What's odd about *me*?"

She shook her head, grinning. "Asking my age like that, out of the blue, and before you've even asked my name. That's the kind of thing *I* do."

"What?"

"Ask the wrong questions at the wrong time." He noticed a shiver course through her; she shook it off and smiled gamely. "Or so Father Osred used to say. He said I was like a little child, always asking questions."

"I'm very much the same, but then, I'm a teacher. It's in my nature to ask questions—and, of course, to question the answers."

She nodded knowingly. "*Disputatio.*"

Rainulf was taken by surprise that this obviously low-born woman knew the Latin term for academic debate.

She laughed again. "I know many things."

He bowed slightly. "Of that I have very little doubt." She was remarkably well spoken for a woman in her circumstances, in addition to being well informed about things no Oxfordshire peasant had any business knowing of. Rainulf wondered where she had learned so much.

She studied him for a moment. "I'm three and twenty years of age. And I know French as well as English and Latin, although I prefer speaking English. And my name, if it's of any interest to you, is Constance."

"Constance," he repeated. "A very pretty name. From the Latin. It means unchanging."

"I know."

Of course, thought Rainulf with amusement.

She screwed up her face. "I hate it. Why should one want to be *constant,* as if change were some great evil? If it weren't for change, everything would stagnate, would it not? And that which stagnates tends to putrefy, like a river that ceases to flow. What good can there be in that?"

Rainulf stared in awe at this fragile, exhausted young woman, her eyes glazed with fever, discoursing on the nature of change. She was right, of course; change was the very fabric of life itself. And death.

"My father wanted to name me Corliss," she continued, "but my mother wouldn't let him, worse luck."

"Corliss. Isn't that a man's name?"

She frowned indignantly, an expression that, on her, was unaccountably charming. "It's for a man *or* a woman! And it's much more suited to me than Constance!"

"Perhaps you're right," he conceded with a little bow. He nodded toward Father Osred's corpse. "I came to give him last rites."

"It's too late now," she said sadly as she rubbed her back.

"Too late for a proper job of it," he agreed, "but I can still perform the sacrament. There are those who believe it's useful, even when one has died unshriven."

She nodded. "Go ahead, then." Turning toward the half-dug grave, she added, "I'll finish here."

"Hold on there," he said. "You ought not to be digging

graves. You're ill, and ... well, isn't there someone ...
your husband, perhaps ..."

"I'm widowed."

"Ah. I'm sorry. Was it the pox?"

"Nay, it happened five years ago. There's no one but
me to bury him, Father. The men who haven't gotten
sick yet won't bury the dead for fear of catching what
killed them. And the ones who *have* gotten sick are still
too weak. I wouldn't want to trouble them."

"I'll bury Father Osred," Rainulf said. "And I'll finish
this second grave, if you'll tell me who it's for."

"I thought you knew," she said, grinning as if at a
slow-witted child. "It's for me."

The tall priest stared at Constance as if live eels had
just sprouted from her head. "You're digging your
own grave?"

"There's no one else to do it," she pointed out. "My
friend Ella Hest has promised to come by in the morning
and check on me. If I'm dead, she'll put me in the grave
and fill it in, but she's getting on in years, so I didn't
want her to have to actually dig it."

He frowned, clearly nonplussed. "You think you're
going to die between now and tomorrow morning?"

"I may. Others have died this early, before the pox
set in. The fever gets bad, and they lose their senses.
Sometimes they have fits ..."

"I know." He ran his long fingers distractedly through
his close-cropped hair. It was the pale, glossy blond of
a very young child. By contrast, his eyebrows and the
hint of beard that darkened his strong jaw were black.
His most distinctive feature, however, would be his
eyes—pale green lightly veiled with brown. Looking into
them was like peering into the water at the edge of a
lake where it meets the shore and mixes with the earth.
She saw kindness in his eyes, and intelligence, and now
she saw pain as well.

His jaw clenched. Was he remembering the time when
he himself had had the yellow plague? Judging from his
reaction, he knew more than he cared to of this particular pestilence.

She gestured with the shovel toward the grave. "So
you understand, then, why I need to finish this—"

"Nay!" He grabbed the shovel out of her hand. "I

have no intention of letting you do this kind of labor while you're so gravely ill. And you mustn't worry so about dying."

"I'm not worrying about it," she corrected, "I'm preparing for it—while I'm still able to." She reached for the shovel, but he jerked it away from her, and she lost her balance. Things began to spin, and she felt her legs crumbling beneath her.

"Constance?" His voice sounded as if he were speaking from a great distance. A fierce pain commenced behind her eyes, and she buried her head in her hands. She felt him grip her shoulders. "Constance?"

"I'm all right," she rasped, and struggled to rise. "I'll be fine."

Abruptly she felt weightless, and realized he'd lifted her in his arms. "Where do you live?" he asked.

"Nay," she protested, pushing against his broad shoulders. Quite useless, of course. She was weakened from illness, and he was clearly a strong man. He'd scooped her up as if she were but a child, and she could feel the solid muscles beneath the rough wool of his tunic.

"Where do you live?" he repeated patiently.

"Please ... my grave," she managed, as the pain in her head became blinding. "You don't understand. I promised Ella it would be ready."

"I'll dig it," he said.

"You will?"

"Of course, if it will ease your mind. Now, tell me where you live."

She pointed.

He frowned in evident puzzlement. "The rectory?"

Constance nodded. "I'm ... I *was* Father Osred's housekeeper."

She closed her eyes and felt the steady rhythm of his lengthy strides as he carried her across the churchyard and through the front door of the stone cottage.

"Where's your bed?"

"I sleep in there."

He brought her into the bedchamber and hesitated. She opened her eyes and saw him looking at the big feather bed, the vestments hanging on the hooks, the crucifix ... and then back at the bed. She saw compre-

hension dawn on him, but his expression betrayed no
outward sign of shock or disapproval.

He sat her on the edge of the bed and glanced down
at her kirtle, filthy from grave digging. "You'll want to
get out of that. Have you got a sleeping shift?"

She pointed to one hanging on the wall, and he
brought it to her.

"Can you manage by yourself?" he asked. "I mean,
if you need help, I can . . ." He shrugged self-consciously,
and Constance noted with amusement that his ears were
bright pink.

She smiled. "Nay, I can manage. Thank you."

He nodded and left. Constance exchanged her dirt-
smeared kirtle for the clean, long-sleeved linen shift and
lay down on the bed. Every time she blinked, the ceiling
beams appeared to shift and then slowly swim back into
place. She waited until this strange dance had ceased,
then sat up in bed and looked out through the little
window at the churchyard.

She saw Father Rainulf unbuckle his belt and toss it
aside, then whip his tunic off and throw it over a branch
of the yew tree. Beneath it he wore a white linen shirt
open at the neck; leathern leggings bound with crisscrossed cords encased his long legs. He rolled up his
shirtsleeves, revealing muscular forearms, then took up
the shovel and went to work on Constance's grave.

He worked quickly, digging with powerful, efficient
movements and making swift progress. Constance watched
with frank interest. Despite his intellectuality and aristocratic bearing, he struck her as remarkably virile—especially for a priest. She couldn't help wondering if he kept
to his vow of chastity or, like many men of the cloth,
had a mistress tucked conveniently away somewhere.

When the throbbing in her head and back became too
much to bear, Constance closed her eyes and lay back
down, hoping the pain would go away if she only kept
still. Upon awakening later in the afternoon, however,
she found it undiminished. Moreover, on sitting up, she
became aware of a vexatious burning sensation, as if her
entire body had been scalded in boiling water. It was
also clear that her fever had worsened considerably.
Wrapping a throw around herself, she got out of bed
and crossed unsteadily to the window.

Father Rainulf had climbed down into the grave, and only his head was visible as he dug. She watched him until, having completed his task, he set the shovel on the ground, braced his hands on the rim of the deep hole, and leapt out with one swift, agile motion.

He had removed his shirt; even from this distance she could see the sheen of perspiration on his chest and face. He was wide-shouldered and lean-hipped, and his gestures had an easy grace that made it hard for Constance to tear her eyes away. Lifting his shirt from the ground, he shook it out and scrubbed it over his damp skin. Then he put it back on, along with his tunic and belt, and strode out of sight.

When he came back into view a short time later, he had his saddlebag with him. Squatting on the ground and unlatching it, he withdrew another white garment. Constance thought perhaps it was a clean shirt, but when he unfolded it and donned it over his tunic, she discovered it to be a surplice. Next came a black skullcap, and then the stole, which he kissed and draped over his shoulders.

"So, Rainulf Fairfax," Constance whispered as he uncovered Father Osred's body and uncorked a small vial, "it would appear that you're a priest, after all."

She wished she'd had enough linen—and enough time—to sew the old rector into a suitable shroud. All in all, it hadn't been so bad living with Father Osred. In truth, he'd been good to her, even generous, and she'd actually grown to feel a certain grudging affection for him. It had pained her to see him die so horribly, and despite her fear of losing his protection from Roger Foliot, she had prayed ceaselessly that God would take him into His arms and bring him peace.

As Constance watched Father Rainulf kneeling in prayer, his image began to drift and fade. A chill swept through her, like the icy breeze from an open door in the dead of Winter. She held on tightly to the windowsill as the frigid pressure squeezed the thoughts from her mind and robbed her eyes of the power of sight.

God, please don't let me go blind, she begged silently as she felt her body hit the floor.